Mitzvot

and Selected Letters

Mitzvot

and Selected Letters

Post-Self book IV

Madison Scott-Clary

Also by Madison Scott-Clary

Arcana — A Tarot Anthology, ed.

Rum and Coke — Three Short Stories from a Furry Convention

Eigengrau — Poems 2015-2020

ally

Post-Self
Qoheleth
Toledot
Nevi'im
Mitzvot

Sawtooth
Restless Town
A Wildness of the Heart

Learn more at *makyo.ink/publications*

ISBN: 978-1-948743-27-3

Mitzvot

Cover and illustrations © Iris Jay, 2020 — irisjay.net

First Edition, 2023. All rights reserved.

This book uses the fonts Gentium Book Basic, Gotu and Linux Biolinum O and was typeset with X$\exists$L^{A}T$_E$X.

Whatever it is in your power to do, do with all your might. For there is no action, no reasoning, no learning, no wisdom in Sheol, where you are going.

— Ecclesiastes 9:10

Part I

Conversation

What lives we lead we lead in memory.

The grandest contribution offered by newborn immortality is the ever-living memories of the dead. Our lives become a ceaseless eulogy.

From *Ode* by Sasha

Ioan Bălan — 2349

How has this become my life? Ioan thought—as ey always did—when stepping away from home to the now familiar café.

May had—as she always did—dotted her nose against eir cheek, licked over eir nose a little too wetly, and said, "Good luck, have fun, and do not die," and then ey stepped from home to arrive in front of the squat wood paneled coffee shop. The same sign proclaiming "Open 24 hours" fading in the sun. The same chipper baristas. The same sparklingly clean espresso machine. The same couch in the corner.

The same thing, month after month: step into the coffee shop to order the same coffee—delicious as always—and wait for the same True Name to arrive.

Their standard greeting would be for Ioan to stand and bow—ey was always there too early—set up a cone of silence and share a bit of chit-chat, however many little nothings felt appropriate for the day, for the month since they'd last seen each other, before settling back down on the L-shaped couch, each to work on their own projects.

Then, as ever, one or the other of them would call an end to the meeting, if meeting it was, and they'd stand once more, bow, and each would step back home.

Or, at least, ey would always step back home, where May would—as she always did—congratulate em on not dying. Ey didn't know where True Name left to.

5

The only thing that seemed to change was the topics they talked about—the this-or-thats of life—and True Name herself.

She was always smartly dressed, she always smiled brightly to em, always ordered the same mocha with extra whipped cream, and would always seem to get dabs of it on her nose-tip; but over time, the skunk had slowly picked up some ineffable quality about her that Ioan could only ever describe as 'harried'. It wasn't in her grooming, for her whiskers were always neat and orderly, the longer fur atop her head well brushed, and her claws neatly trimmed. It wasn't in the things she talked about, for she always had some interesting bit of news about any of the three— four, if one counted Artemis—Systems out there.

It was, ey decided, something to do with her eyes, her cheeks, the way her hands moved. It was in her voice, in her mien, in her bearing.

Once a month, ey'd meet True Name for coffee, and each time, she seemed that much more worn down, carrying that much more tension in her features, looking just that much older.

When ey first described this to May, the skunk had spent a silent minute staring out into the yard—or at least the corner visible from her beanbag—then stretched out on her belly, drap-ing over the outsized cushion. "Have you asked her, my dear?"

Ioan had shaken eir head. "It never felt polite to."

"Some day you should," she had said. "Though it is my suspi-cion that she is, as you have said, losing her easy confidence. She is struggling with the fact that she must constantly dump energy into keeping up the appearance of always being so in control."

Ioan had leaned back in eir chair and stared up at the ceiling. "That certainly tallies with what she's said in the past."

"She is the type of person who will always take more upon herself, more and more and more until she cracks," May had murmured, quiet enough that Ioan had to strain to hear. "That she has been at this for more than two and a quarter centuries and the strain is only now showing is, if anything, a testament to her perseverance. Or obstinance, perhaps."

Ever since that day, that conversation would rise to the fore of eir memory whenever ey met up with True Name for coffee. They would have their conversation, sip their drinks, and then get to whatever projects they were working on—but there would always be a small portion of eir mind dedicated to squaring what ey knew of her with just how old she was.

What ey'd strategically left out of that conversation with May, however, was that eir fascination seemed to be driven by an almost pathological need to help. Somehow. Ey wanted to find what it was that was wearing so much on True Name and find a way to ease it. There was a problem there, and problems were made for solving, yes?

It was something about em that May knew, ey was sure, but which ey'd never shared with her, as ey knew that her response would either be the gentle teasing that she was so good at heaping on em or the gentle inquisition that she was equally adept at conducting. She'd ask em where the feeling stemmed from: was it from within eir mind, or within eir heart? Was it related to *all* problems? Was it because True Name looked so much like her, eir partner? When had it started? Launch? Convergence? Never mind if it were a problem that ey could not solve, as was almost certainly the case, what would ey do if it was a problem she did not *want* solved?

Ey knew she'd ask em those questions because whenever ey asked them of emself, ey heard them in her voice. Even when ey'd asked Sarah, eir therapist (or, well, all three of their therapists), there was some subconscious overlay of the skunk's lilting voice floating above the question, and ey'd find emself dropping contractions and leaning on the anaphora that all Odists seemed stuck with.

"You seem particularly lost in thought today, Ioan."

Ey jolted at the sudden intrusion of a voice on eir thoughts, then smiled sheepishly at True Name. "Sorry about that. I hope I wasn't mumbling to myself."

She grinned. "Not this time, no, though your lips were moving, so I suspect you were not far off."

Shaking eir head, ey capped eir pen, tucking it into a pocket and closing eir notebook on one of the place-marker ribbons. "I don't doubt it."

"What was on your mind, if I may ask?"

Ey hesitated, considering eir options. The desire to fix, to help, to aid and assist, still hung around em, but it'd be impertinent for em to just offer that out of nowhere. Instead, ey said, "Something May said. About you, I mean. Hopefully that's not weird."

The skunk laughed. "It depends on what she said, does it not? Though I am flattered to have been in your thoughts. What did she have to say?"

"That you're the type of person to take on whatever's in front of you, even if your docket's already full. I was trying to piece together how much of that applies to the rest of the clade, too." After a moment, ey shrugged and added, "And myself, for that matter."

True Name looked up to the ceiling, head tilted thoughtfully. "I do not think there is any disputing that I will load myself up with responsibilities, often to the point of overloading. I remember some of that from before I was forked, though I do not think Michelle was of quite the same temperament. She took on more than she could handle more out of a sense of social obligation than...whatever it is that drives me."

"Determination? Persistence?"

She shrugged. "Perhaps. What is it that Dear says so often? 'I do not make art because I know why; if I knew why, I would not need to make art'? It is like that for me. I do not strive because I know what drives me. If I knew what that was, who knows if I would continue to strive?"

Ey marveled, as ey so often did, at just how many of the Odists seem to speak in well structured paragraphs. Thesis, hypothesis, synthesis.

"It seems like it's wearing on you," ey said. Realizing that it had been nearly five minutes of em trying to psych emself up to say so, ey added, "All that you've got going on, I mean."

She frowned, leaned forward to pick up her coffee, and took a lapping sip. "Does it? I am feeling increasingly overloaded, yes, but that is not new. How is it visible?"

"You just seem more tired every time I see you."

She nodded. "I am, yes."

"Is there—" Ey caught emself up short, forcibly tamped down the urge to offer to help, and instead said, "I mean, what all are you working on? I can never tell with you and May. It just looks like thinking."

"It is perhaps a problem with doing all of one's work in one's head." she said. "We are not blessed with your affinity for paper."

"Or cursed."

She chuckled. "Your words, not mine. But, well...with the understanding that I cannot tell you everything that I am working on, I will say that there is much to be done when it comes to shaping sys-side sentiment around all of the various new tech."

"Oh?"

"The expanded ACLs on cones of silence, for example. It is nice to be able to obscure the occupants, yes? No more hiding one's mouth or expression. Limiting sensorium messages into or out of them by individual or clade is also quite nice for guaranteeing information security. Your interlocutor cannot be used to spy on you, yes? Ditto the refinements on sweeping unwanted occupants. We may shape our interactions more exactly with this tech. But how does one pass on the knowledge of the upgrades to the System? There are various feeds, yes, but even something as small as that requires some thought put into how to announce it. Do we hail it as a technological advancement, or do we put a tone of resignation on it, as though we have been given something no one wanted? Perhaps we announce it with a resounding chorus of 'fucking *finally*'."

"It seems to have gone over well, at least."

"It did, yes." Then, with a tilt of her head, ey felt the ACL-scape of the cone they were within shift, and there was a subtle blurring to the world around them as she opaqued the cone from the outside. "Now consider the effects of audio/visual transmission between sys- and phys-side."

Ey blinked and sat up straighter. "Wait, what?"

"You see? Much thought must be put into managing expectations."

"Back up a moment. Are we going to actually get that?"

"It is already enabled in a select few locked-down sims, yes. AVEC, we are calling it. Audio/Visual Extrasystem Communication. A faint hope to foster a sense of connection between our two worlds with a pithy name."

"Holy shit."

She laughed. "Holy shit, indeed. I have no clue as to the tech that goes into it, which is made all the more complicated from it being inspired by our dear Artemisian friends, but what I do know is that this will shift many of the plans in place around stability. When I sit here in silence, drinking my coffee and looking deep in thought, I am working on that. I write my speeches or talk with my cocladists or other versions of myself, and fill out the exo I have dedicated to the topic."

"And that wears you out?" Ey hastened to add, "Not to say that it isn't work, of course."

The skunk gave a hint of a bow in acknowledgement. "It is part of a larger work landscape in progress, yes. So much to keep in my head, so many conversations to be had, so many tiny social interactions to monitor, both in person and over the text of the perisystem feeds."

Ey nodded. There was so much to process in just the new tech, not to mention the reminder that, even if ey'd long since started thinking of True Name as a complete and complex person and not some shady, two-dimensional villain, she still had her fingers in just about every political pie that could possibly exist on the three incarnations of the System.

"Does writing not wear you out, Ioan?"

"Well, sometimes," ey hedged. "I guess it depends on what all is going into whatever it is that I'm writing. The *History* wore me out at some points, particularly during research, but for the most part, writing was just...what I did. It didn't wear me out any more than breathing might."

"And theatre?"

"Oh, that definitely wears me out."

"I remember that, yes. Even just standing backstage, waiting for one's moment to enter felt exhausting sometimes. I would get all worn out and want nothing more than to go home and fall over, afterwards."

"Didn't you go get shitty diner food or whatever?"

"Oh, nearly every time," she said, grinning. "I would never let so sacred a ritual be spoiled by something as silly as sleep."

Ey nodded. "A Finger Pointing certainly holds to it like a ritual, yeah. It's a toss up whether or not she drinks us all under the table."

"Of course." The skunk grinned and finished her coffee, setting the mug down on the table. "We studied long and hard to build up such a tolerance."

"Doesn't sound super healthy."

"I suppose not. At least, not back phys-side."

"I noticed that seems to be unevenly distributed," ey observed. "May and I rarely drink unless it's with someone else, but Dear and its partners seem to drink quite a bit."

"So I have heard. There are a few aspects of our past life that were only picked up by a few of us, beyond the obvious interests. Drinking, theatre and art, furry, that sort of thing. I have never figured out whether there is any rhyme or reason to it."

Ey nodded. "Makes me wonder if I might've done the same if I were more of a dispersionista."

"Perhaps," she said, shrugging. "Codrin has diverged quite a bit from you. They both have. You can put at least some of that on us, though. May Then My Name and Dear, I mean."

"Right," ey said, laughing. "May's fond of saying that it's the Odists' job to fuck with us until we loosen up."

True Name folded her paws in her lap primly, grinning to em.

This is it, ey thought. *This is why I keep coming back. Even if she is consciously turning up the friendliness to maintain some weird status quo, or even if she's naturally like that, she's still nice to be around.*

Ey considered letting the topic continue, but the thought was intriguing enough to voice out loud. "Why do you do this, True Name? Get coffee with me, I mean."

"There is nothing nefarious about it, if that is what you are asking," she said, pausing briefly. "In confidence?"

"Of course. I imagine most of what you say is in confidence."

"Indeed. I trust that you will not share the news about AVEC yet."

Ey nodded.

"Right. Then I suppose it is just nice to have a friend, for lack of a better term."

A conversation from years back wafted up through eir memory. "You said back during convergence, 'We will never be close, you and I.' Has that changed?"

"I do not know. Has it?"

Ey frowned.

"That is why I say 'for lack of a better term'. We are on good terms, are we not? We are able to co-exist, to talk about news and nonsense, yes? To chat?" She shrugged, smiled to em. "That is perilously close to friendship, I think. If you do not feel that the label fits, I understand, but I stand by what I said: it is nice to have a friend. Someone who is not another me."

"Aren't you friends with Jonas?"

The hesitation was brief, but still notable for just how tense it was. "We make pretty good colleagues, and we have a mode of interaction that is comfortable for us, but the dynamic that you and I have is far closer to friendship than that of mine and his."

Ey tilted eir head, asking, "Was that always the case?"

The skunk's expression never changed, but her tone grew far more careful as she bowed her head politely and said, "I am not comfortable with this topic, my dear."

"Of course. Sorry, True Name."

She nodded once more, the relief in her expression as plain as the exhaustion that came with it. "Thank you for being understanding. All of that to say that I enjoy our coffee and co-working sessions because there is a sense of friendship to them, and even I need that sometimes."

"Well, I'm happy to provide," ey said. The Bălan clade seemed to have undergone a collective reevaluation of True Name over the last few years, but even so, the plain earnestness led to a moment of tamping down suspicion that ey was simply being played. "And for what it's worth, that lines up with my thoughts. Glad we have the chance to do so."

She raised her cup in acknowledgment. "Thank you, Ioan. That is perhaps a good note to end on, as I would like to reconcile memories across my instances."

Ey nodded. "Sure. Until next time?"

The skunk stood and bowed. "Yes. Until next time. Enjoy the rest of your day, my dear."

The cone of silence dropped, letting in a jolt of noise, and the skunk stepped from the sim. Ey finished eir coffee, then stepped back home.

"I am pleased to see that you did not die," May said, looking up from her notebook.

Ey kicked off eir shoes and set down eir own notebook on eir desk before walking over to give the skunk a kiss between the ears. "Nope, not this time. Stuck with me for a while yet."

She set her pen down and stretched before leaning up to dot her nose against eirs, arms draped up around eir shoulders. "Good, I am not finished wringing all I can out of you. One day, you will be left a broken husk of a Bălan and I will move on to my next victim."

Shaking eir head, ey returned that nose-press before

straightening up. "You're doing a crap job of it, May. You keep adding to my life rather than taking away from it."

She laughed. "Even when you are joking, you are adorable. Love you too, my dear. How was True Name?"

"Oh, fine. Much the same, I guess. We just worked and chatted and drank coffee. Nothing unusual."

"Well, that can be good, right?"

"Yeah, comfort in familiarity. She did at least confirm your hypothesis that she's just been overloading herself."

May nodded, stood, padded to her beanbag, flopped down. "Of all of us, she is most prone to that, I suspect."

"I don't think the Artemis dump is helping out, there. They're pulling all sorts of stuff from it."

"You are as well, are you not?"

Ey laughed. "I suppose I am, at that."

She reached out and snagged one of eir hands, pulling em down onto the beanbag beside her. Ey lay back and let her rest her head against eir shoulder before settling eir arm around her. Comfortable, familiar.

"She said something else that was interesting I'd like to discuss, but I don't want to keep talking about her if you're uncomfortable with it. It can be later."

She shrugged, doodling a dull claw lazily over eir stomach through eir shirt and vest, sitting just shy of ticklish. "I do not mind. You know that I have been working on it."

"Sure, I just didn't want to—"

"I will tell you if I would like to drop the topic, I promise," she said, then laughed. "Sorry, Ioan. I did not mean to interrupt."

"No, it's okay. She actually did that quite well today." Ey leaned eir head back on the beanbag. "I asked why she kept up with me with the coffee meetings, and she said that it's just nice to have a friend."

May tilted her head up, enough to bump her nose against the underside of eir chin. "Are you? Friends, I mean."

"That's what we talked about. Neither of us could really de-

cide on anything beyond 'friends for lack of a better term'."
Ey hesitated, feeling incredibly conscious of eir partner resting
against em, her stated resentment of her down-tree instance,
how that had veered for so long into hatred over all that she had
done. Ey continued, speaking carefully, "I like having interesting people to talk to and she's been pretty good company. She
likes having someone to just be around and talk with that isn't
herself or Jonas."

"Are they still not getting along?"

"Worse, maybe. That's where she requested that I drop the
topic. She said that they made good coworkers, but not necessarily friends, and I asked if that was always the case, and she
said she wasn't comfortable having that conversation. Very politely, of course, but it looked like it took a lot of effort."

"Mm." The skunk lowered her muzzle, letting em peek down
at her again. "I have been working on how I define myself in relation to True Name. I do not like that I spent so long hating
her. I do not want that to be a part of who I am. I am May, who
loves, yes? I hold no such compunctions about Jonas, though,
and I am sorry that she still feels she must engage with him. He
was a piece of shit then and I imagine that he is far worse now."

"Huh?" Ey shook eir head as ey pieced together what she
meant. "Oh right, sorry. I guess you were forked off after he and
True Name started working together."

"Yes. I remember that from when I was her. We were not
friends then, and I am glad that she is not his friend now."

"I only met him those few times years back, and yeah, I'm
glad she isn't, either. He was definitely a piece of shit."

She laughed and poked em in the belly. "Mx. Ioan Bălan, you
watch your language."

"Hey, I curse!"

"Not well, Ionuț."

"Yeah, well, fuck you too," ey said, smirking at the teasingly
diminutive form of eir name.

The skunk sat up and gave em an exaggerated frown. "I am warning you, young man."

Ey rolled eir eyes. " 'Young man'?"

"Little miss?"

Ey grinned, shook eir head. "Try again."

"Young gentlethem."

Ey laughed. "I don't know what your hang-up is, you nut. I learned it from you."

"What, 'fuck you too'?" May shook her head. "It just sounds so strange coming from your mouth."

"I'm not as good at the well placed profanity as all of you."

"It is an art we have perfected. It increases the impact when they do show up. Even True Name does it, I am sure."

"She has once or twice, yeah. You two still sound similar enough in terms of your voices, so I feel like I'm used to it."

May nodded, leaned down, and licked em squarely across the nose before settling down against eir front again. "Yes, I suppose we do. Here is where we drop the topic, however."

"Alright," ey said, wiping eir face. "What should we do for dinner?"

"To be built to love is to be built to dissolve. It is to be built to unbecome. It is to have the sole purpose in life of falling apart all in the name of someone else.

"We all have a bit of that in us, do we not? You find yourself at a bar or maybe in some class somewhere, you look over, and there they are, right? You look over and you maybe catch their eye and you come undone at the seams. You fall into those big, beautiful eyes—for when you are built to love, every eye that catches yours is the most beautiful thing of all time—and you begin to flake away at the edges.

"And to be built to love is to be all edges. They catch on your clothes, they brush against walls and furniture. You are all edges so that love can fill the cracks and soften those jagged corners.

"You are spiked and barbed. It is as if you are built that way on purpose, so that the slightest breeze can blow you about and catch you up on some future love."

The skunk had been sitting on a barstool, hunched over a pint and slurring half to the glass, half to some absent bartender. She slid to her feet, wobbled for a moment, then righted herself.

"Actually, you know what? I have heard it said so many times that to hate—truly hate, burn up inside with that passion—is to actually be in love with the object of your hatred, but I think there is a little bit of hatred in love, too. You fall so completely for someone that you just cannot help but resent them. It is a mirror of that hatred for yourself, for all your jagged edges and prickly burrs, a reflection of the resentment that you feel towards yourself for having been built to love. And look at me!" She gestured down at herself, a grand sweep of the paw outsized in her intoxication. "I fuckin' loathe myself! Can you imagine how deeply I must love others, then?"

After a moment's wild laughter, she stumbled back until her tail crumpled against the edge of the stool. "Ow! Fuck. Yeah, I deserved that one, I think."

She moved to finish her pint, frowned on finding it empty, and shuffled away from the bar.

"So yeah, you hate yourself, and it actually feels kind of good, does it not? Hatred can fill in those cracks as easily as love. Sure, it may not leave so pretty a pattern as the...whatsit...the patina that stains a tea cup with crackled glaze, but maybe the edges of you do not catch on so many things anymore. Maybe those prickles are dulled and you bounce off everyone around you. You can ping-pong through life, then, loving everyone and loathing yourself."

The skunk stood up straight again, brushed her shirt out, and brought her tail around to rub at where she'd bumped it against the stool.

"Good Lord, May," Ioan said, laughing.

She grinned widely, all that feigned drunkenness suddenly gone from her expression. "How was it, my dear?"

Ey slouched back against the front row seat ey'd claimed, tapping the end of eir pen against eir lower lip. "Really, really good," ey said. "Was the stumble intentional?"

"The movement itself was," she said. "Though hitting my tail was not."

"So no 'I deserved that one'?"

She sat down on the edge of the stage, kicking her feet idly. "It was not in there, no, but I think I will keep it."

Ey grinned and closed eir notebook around eir pen, setting it aside to stand. "Yeah, it's good in there," ey said, leaning forward to give the bridge of her snout a kiss. She squinted her eyes shut and then scrubbed a paw over her muzzle. "I mean, the whole thing's good. Only note I really had is that you say 'hate' four times in a pretty short span right after you stood up. 'That to hate', then 'truly hate', then 'object of your hatred', and then 'little bit of hatred'."

"Should I make them all different?"

"I'd keep the first two because it works as an echo, so maybe just change the fourth? 'Loathing'?"

"Excellent, O great wordsmith."

Ey laughed and tweaked her ear before hoisting emself up onto the edge of the stage next to her. Predictably, she scooted closer so that she could lean against eir side. "Who would've thought, hmm? You getting me into theatre and me getting you into writing."

"This is still theatre! Just earlier on in the process," she said, indignant. "But yes, it is proof that the Bălans can shove us around instead of only the other way around."

Ey gave her a playful shove with eir shoulder, at which she let out an outsized yelp followed by a whimper. "So mean!"

"Yeah, that's me. Meanest person you know."

She rolled her eyes.

Ey let a long silence play then, looking out into the cool darkness of the theater while May summoned up her notebook and scribbled down eir tip from earlier.

"Do you really feel that way?"

"Mm?"

"The jagged edges and self-loathing."

She shrugged. "There is some of me in there, yes, but it is still theatre. It is about taking the particular and making it universal, if only for a little while, yes?"

Ey nodded.

When ey didn't reply otherwise, she shrugged and continued, "I would not say that I agree with that 'I loathe myself, so imagine how much I love others' bit. I do not loathe myself, and yet I still love others. Have loved and will love in the future, even, and I see no change in my rare moments of self-loathing."

Ey laughed. " 'Will love in the future'? You leaving me for some handsome guy you met in a bar, then?"

"A bar? Ugh. I am apparently more of a 'hunt nerds in the library' type." She poked em in the belly. "But I love *you*, Ioan, and will continue to do so."

Rubbing at the spot where she'd poked with her dull claw, ey nodded. "Love you too, May."

She beamed happily and settled back in against eir side, head resting on eir shoulder. "I am glad, my dear. I know we agreed early on that this—us being together, I mean—does not need to be permanent, but that does not change the fact that I will continue loving you. Even if we should split, I will not stop."

Ey nodded slowly.

"I have no plans for such," she added quickly. "You are stuck with me for a good while yet."

"What? Oh, no," ey said, shaking eir head to clear a few too many thoughts. "I trust you on that. Just got me thinking. Do you still love all the others you've been with?"

She laughed. "What I said does not apply just to you. Of course I still love them. Some long-diverged forks of me are even still in relationships with their partners."

"So you've said. You still love them as the root instance, though?"

She nodded. "I do not begin relationships as anything other than my root instance. I do not know why, but it does not feel fair of me to do anything but."

"Oh, so none of your forks went on to fork for other relationships?"

"Not that I know of, no. It is a firm conviction, so I would imagine that they hold to it, but perhaps some older ones have diverged. We do not speak much."

"How many are there, anyway?"

She lifted her head to dot her nose against eir cheek. "Are you jealous, my dear?" Her voice was calm and curious. Calm enough and curious enough, some distant part of em noted, that it kept em from falling immediately into defensiveness.

"I get the occasional pangs, more so early on," ey said after a long moment's thought. "When ey was first getting settled in eir relationship, Codrin told me about something that Dear had told em shortly after ey'd been forked, 'jealousy is a sign of needs not met'. Whenever I start feeling jealous, that's usually a sign for me to take a step back and think about what need that might be."

"See, this is what I like about you, Ioan. You feel a thing and then think about it until you understand it. Sometimes a little too much, but it has served you well."

Ey tilted eir cheek to rest it atop her head, a bit of closeness that also served the purpose of stopping her ear-tip from tickling eir neck.

"I feel a thing and am helpless before it. I cannot but wrap myself up in...it..." she said, pulling out her notebook again to jot down the words as they came. "Love, hatred, hunger, exhaustion. I am built for them all, and I cannot do a thing about them..."

Ey shared a secret smile with emself as the skunk trailed off, continuing to write, tongue-tip peeking out from her muzzle.

"Also," she said once she'd finished. "The answer is that I do not know how many of me are still in relationships. There are at least three, and I know of at least five that have quit, though I declined the merges out of privacy. I never made it a requirement that they keep in touch. Beyond that, I think there are...mm, seven, perhaps?"

"So that makes me your sixteenth relationship?"

"Something like that, yes. Sixteenth truly serious one." She slid over and swung her legs up onto the stage so that she could rest her head in eir lap. "Did my monologue really get you thinking about all this?"

"It's a good monologue," ey said, petting over her ears. "Or start, at least. You said it should be five minutes, right?"

She nodded. "Around that, yes. I am still working on it."

"Mmhm. It's good so far, though. It got me thinking, but I'm also just fascinated by you, which helps."

"Why, because I am weird? I think that is an Odist thing," she said, laughing.

"What, am I not allowed to be fascinated by my partner?"

"Absolutely not, no."

Ey tugged on her ear. "Fascinated and annoyed."

"Yes, well, too bad. You remain stuck with me, Mx. Bălan." She continued more seriously, "I did not expect this to be fascinating to you. I try to be careful talking about my other relationships."

"I don't really mind," ey said after giving it due thought. "That was past May, right? It'd be like getting upset over someone else having exes. If it were multiple partners at the same time, that'd probably be a separate conversation."

She shook her head. "I could not do that. I am not built the same as Dear. I am only in multiple relationships in the sense that there are multiple mes, but there is only ever one me involved with one other. It is parallel monogamy."

"Why?"

"Because," she said, rolling onto her back so that she could smile up to em. "I am also helpless before devotion, and that takes the whole of me."

"What about Douglas or A Finger Pointing?"

"I hold no romantic feelings for A Finger Pointing." She laughed. "She is nice, but in a boss-you-drink-with-on-Fridays-and-I-guess-occasionally-have-a-fling-with sort of way."

"And Douglas?"

Her answer was a while in coming. "Were our friendship to head in that direction, I would fork, but I do not foresee that being the case."

"Really?" Ey frowned. "Wouldn't that be awkward? Us going over there to see him and the other you together?"

"Oh, incredibly awkward," she said, rolling her eyes. "I have done similar in the past, and it would take a year or two to shake out. It is uncomfortable for me, as well, as I am left with the same desire even as my down-tree instance gets fulfillment and they are left with love for you."

"I can imagine."

"No, Ioan, I do not think you can," she said primly. "You actually think about the way you feel as you are feeling it like a normal person rather than just crashing headlong into overwhelming emotions like a fucking Odist."

"Well, fair."

"I do not think we need to worry about that, though. I am comfortable with my friendship with him just as I am comfortable loving you, and should someone catch my eye–"

"You'd need to start going to more libraries, I think."

She laughed and shook her head, continuing, "–should someone catch my eye—or yours, for that matter—we will tackle it then with plenty of talking."

"Oh, I believe you on that. Skunks never shut up."

She made as if to bite em on the belly and, when ey flinched away, grinned up to em. "Mx. Ioan Bălan, you are the one asking all the questions with long, involved answers. Do not pin this on me."

"Yeah, yeah. You just got me thinking is all. I think you're giving me too much credit saying someone might catch my eye, though."

"Why?"

Ey shrugged. "I'm not exactly that observant."

"You worked as a professional observer for, what, a century?"

"Not *that* kind of observation."

She laughed. "Well, okay, yes. I will not discount the possibility, though. If we are in this life for yet more centuries, there is no harm in being deliberate. Plus, I will get an inordinate amount of satisfaction out of seeing you fall for someone. It was so wholesome the first time! I see no reason why it should not be the same subsequent times."

"I guess. I don't know if there's anyone who–"

She waved a paw dismissively. "If there is not, there is not. We can speak in hypotheticals like fucking grown-ups."

"Fine, fine."

When the silence drew out, May grabbed one of eir hands and started mouthing on eir fingers, sharp skunk teeth just pricking skin.

"Ow!" Ey laughed and tapped a finger on her nose lightly. "Pest."

She licked at eir fingertip, saying, "Thank you, my dear, in all earnestness. It makes me happy to be able to have a conversation about this."

"Of course, May. I figure it ought to be an open topic for us."

She nodded and stretched out on the stage. "Agreed. We can come back to it later, though. I would like to run this through once more," she said, waggling the notebook at em. "And then head home to get ready for dinner. Debarre is coming over and I plan on flirting with him outrageously in front of you all night long to see if I can make you jealous."

Ey laughed and pushed at her until she sat up before sliding off the stage and walking back to eir seat. "Alright. Once more, from the top."

Ioan pulled together a stack of eir notes and, with a little concentration and a gesture, moved them over to a once-blank notebook, the pages now filled with eir scratchy shorthand. To this was added one of eir nicer pens, clipped to the cover, and a few slips of foolscap besides.

Tucking those under eir arm, ey walked over to May's desk and bent down to give the skunk a kiss atop her head, right between her ears. "I'm heading out. No messing with my pens, okay?"

Rather than the usual 'do not die' joke, she turned on her stool, looped her arms up around eir shoulders, and pressed her nose to eirs. "You will be okay, yes?"

Ey hesitated. Something about her tone pointed more towards anxiety than simple seriousness. Ey leaned forward to set eir notebook down, tugged up on eir slacks, and settled to eir knees in front of her. "Of course, May. Will you?"

"I will be fine," she said, smiling. "I am just a little worried today, is all."

"Any particular reason why?"

"I just am. I am trying to build trust, but..." She shrugged.

"Want me to leave a fork behind?"

"Will they be intolerable and antsy?"

Ey laughed. "Depends on how much pestering you do."

She lifted her snout enough to lick eir nose-tip, then shoved at em playfully. "I am busy, my dear."

"You fork more than anyone I know, you could just–"

"I am trying to tell you to get out of here, Ioan," she said, grinning in earnest. "Do not mind a little bit of anxiety. I am sorry that that spilled over. I will think on it and we will talk later. Good luck, have fun, and do not die, okay?"

Ey shook eir head and stood again, grabbing eir notebook. "Skunks. I swear..."

Ey stepped out of the sim before she could kick eir shin.

Ey ordered eir usual coffee and staked out eir usual spot on the couch. Rather than getting to work while ey waited for True Name, ey simply sat and enjoyed eir coffee as best ey could, staring off into nothing while mulling over May's words.

You will be okay, yes?

Ey frowned and shifted eir gaze down to eir coffee, half gone by now. There were relatively few things that would bring about such anxiety in May, and ey knew the majority of them stemmed from within herself.

She had occasionally gotten upset at em, usually when ey'd not picked up on some cue that she'd given for some emotional need ey wasn't meeting. In each case, she would express as best she could after the initial burst of anxiety. Her down-tree instance was another source, though that hatred she'd borne for so long had softened to something more like distaste of late.

All of the other times, though, had come from within. Whatever dire emotions that dwelt beneath the chipper, goofy, sarcastic, and delightfully earnest layer that made up the most of her would peek through and a little spark of something more profound and inexplicable would come over her.

Ey frowned down to eir coffee and considered whether ey should start laying in supplies in case she asked em to leave should waves of uncontrollable emotion take her, that 'overflowing' that seemed to affect most—if not all—of the clade. If this was the first sign, though, ey at least had some time yet.

"Mx. Bălan?"

Ey jolted and sat upright. True Name stood on the other side of the low table from em, not yet having made the move to sit. "Sorry, True Name."

She smiled kindly and bowed. "May I join you? You looked quite deep in thought, and I am happy to meet up at another time."

Returning the bow apologetically, ey gestured toward her usual spot on the couch. "No, no. Sorry, I was a bit stuck up in my head. Could probably do with getting out more often."

The skunk nodded and sat, blinking a cone of silence into being. She lapped at a bit of the whipped cream atop her mocha to get down to the drink. "I quite understand. Bit too cooped up of late?"

"A little, I guess. Heads down, maybe. End of the year performances, helping May write a monologue, working on my own next project."

She grinned. "Plenty on your plate, then. May I ask how May Then My Name is doing?"

"Oh, she's alright."

Ey must have hesitated before responding or not kept eir own anxiety out of eir voice, as True Name's expression fell. "Say hi for me?"

Ey nodded. "Of course."

"I am also curious to hear about her monologue. It is something I remember thinking about occasionally and yet never got around to doing. I am pleased that one of us is."

That also felt like a closed topic given its context of being purpose-built, so ey shook eir head. "I'm not comfortable talking about that without her permission. Sorry, True Name."

She smiled disarmingly and held up her free paw. "Of course, Ioan, no trouble. Can you tell me about your own project, perhaps?"

Ey opened eir mouth, closed it again, then laughed. "I feel like I laid a bunch of conversational landmines around me. Hopefully it's not uncomfortable, but with all that went down on Castor, I've been toying with rewriting *On the Perils of Memory* as a play."

The skunk got a strange look on her face, then laughed. "Oh really? Cheeky! I do not know if I will be able to make it to a performance, but I will be delighted to read the script, if you wind up publishing it."

Ey laughed as well, more relieved than anything. "I'll make sure you get a copy, then. Was worried you'd be upset by it."

She waved her paw dismissively. "Of course not, my dear. That whole kerfuffle was, what, forty years ago? Forty-five? It has been comfortably relegated to memory and is thus fair game for artists."

Nodding, ey finished eir coffee and set the cup down on the table so ey could pull out eir notebook and get to writing.

Ey worked for a few minutes. They both did, if True Name's thoughtful gaze up into nothing was anything to go by. Ey'd wound eir way past all those conversational mines—May, her monologue, the play about Qoheleth—and now felt free to relax into the afternoon.

"You know," the skunk said thoughtfully, bringing em out of eir writing. "I was quite pleased when that book came out."

"What, *Perils*?"

She nodded. "It was something of a relief in a strange, round-about way. While I would have preferred that it had not ended the way it did, it wound up being a pretty efficient way to bring all of that to the surface. A lot of very smart people have been thinking about it over the last few decades, and I am pleased to see some progress being made, especially on the therapeutic side."

Ioan tilted eir head thoughtfully. "Sounds like, yeah. At least, from what I hear from May and Codrin. A Finger Pointing has been pretty tight-lipped about her own therapy and I don't think End Waking went along with it."

"He does not seem the type, no."

"Is it working out well for you, too?"

"Well enough," she said. "Though I am not comfortable discussing beyond that."

Ey nodded. "Right, sorry."

"It is alright. Thank you for understanding." She raised her cup towards em in a small toast. "As to your book, however, I found it most interesting in that I was able to learn much about the assessment and impact of the events on the...ah, liberal side of the clade."

Ioan had to focus on keeping eir expression neutral. True Name hadn't always had the kindest of words for the self-proclaimed liberal Odists. "I'll admit, I was worried as to how the book would go over with the conservatives."

"There were no assassins in the night, I trust?" she asked, grinning.

"Uh...well, no," ey stammered, caught off guard by the humor. "Actually, no contact at all. I don't think I've even talked about what happened with the other side of the clade until now."

" 'The other side of the clade' is a more appropriate phrase, is it not? We are spread along a spectrum. Those like Dear, May Then My Name, and Hammered Silver at one end, those such as Praiseworthy, Those Who Forge, and Teeth Of Death somewhere in the middle, and then me and my ilk on the other. Death Itself and her stanza, out of all of us, seemed to have escaped that spectrum." The skunk finished her drink sitting in a silence for a minute, an acknowledgement of the losses from that stanza, then leaned forward to set her cup down before continuing. "To soothe any fears you may have, it was not me who hired Guōwei, nor am I pleased with what happened and how."

"Who did? Do you know?"

She smiled pityingly at em. "Ioan, please."

"Right, of course you do. I don't imagine you feel comfortable telling me who, though."

"It is not a matter of comfort, my dear, it is one of information hygiene. The fewer people who know, the less of a chance there is of plans going awry. Besides," she nodded toward em. "We considered the impact that *Perils* would have on the System, and leaving that element of mystery in it accomplished our goals."

"Goals?" Ey shook eir head. "How do you mean?"

The skunk folded her paws in her lap, leaning back against the couch. "What would you say the current public opinion is of the book?"

"I...well, hmm. If you'd asked me that a few weeks ago, I wouldn't have been able to say, but I've been digging back into it for this project. I guess most seem to see it as a sort of cautionary tale. I didn't publish the internal report, so I think the fact that it read like investigative journalism made people treat it almost like a work of fiction."

"Yes, and mystery plays a role in that. This is why we suggested you not publish the clade-side report. There is an appropriate level of mystery in what you did publish that aligned with our goals."

"So, similar to what you and Jonas did with the *History*."

There was the briefest flicker of a wince on the skunk's face at the mention of Jonas, quickly mastered. She replaced it with a smile and gave a hint of a bow. "Yes. In a relatively short time, both have started to fade into a near mythical status. A credit to your skills as a writer, Mx. Bălan."

Ey smiled warily. "Thanks. Why, though?"

"Why are they becoming myths?" She shrugged. "Life on the System is shaped by the modes of our existence. Creativity has assumed a level of primacy that was not feasible phys-side, and so successful creative works accelerate more quickly toward myth, here."

Ey nodded. "And you? What do you think of it?"

"Of *Perils*?"

"That, the possible play, the events as a whole."

There was a moment of quiet as the skunk thought, brushing a paw over one of her knees to smooth out her slacks. "With the understanding that there is much that I cannot tell you about my feelings on the proceedings, I found it all frustrating and unnerving. I worked with Qoheleth on several occasions throughout the years, and watching his...I will not say decline, as I think the analogy does not hold, but his metamorphosis from Odist to Qoheleth touched on some primal distress. As I have said, I am not pleased with what happened or how. I liked him quite a bit."

This seemed to deserve another moment of silence, one of acknowledgement rather than thoughtfulness, and so ey let it play out, the muffled clatter of the rest of the cafe coming through the cone of silence suddenly much more present.

"What news from Castor had you thinking about *Perils*?"

"I'm sorry?"

"Well, I do not associate aliens or time modification or the...ah, struggles that Answers Will Not Help experienced with what happened with Qoheleth."

Eir mind raced. How could ey possibly bring up the Name? That Codrin now knew it and that knowledge—at least at one layer of remove—had propagated through the clade? Surely she knew that, at least, but how could ey say that out loud to her?

"Mx. Bălan?" True Name was frowning, whether at eir silence or expression ey couldn't guess. "I am guessing that the answer is complicated."

"It...uh, yeah. What Codrin heard on Artemis...I mean..."

The skunk tilted her head, gestured for em to continue.

Doesn't she know? ey thought. *She has to. Is she faking it?*

"Well," ey stammered, hastily backtracking through eir train of thought. Perhaps ey should feign ignorance as well if that was indeed what she was doing. "All that about getting lost, and how fourthrace experienced similar and also dealt with long-term effects."

Still frowning, she nodded.

"It was all bound up in some clade-eyes-only thoughts," ey hastened to add, hoping that the slight untruth would be enough. "Eir worries about Dear, Death Itself...but I don't want to say any more."

That seemed to have been enough, as the tenseness that had been building in her shoulders relaxed, though her frown remained. "Of course, yes, I did not mean to press. My apologies."

Ey shook eir head and waved a hand. "It's okay, I just had to disentangle all those thoughts really quickly."

"You are a very thoughtful person," she said, a hint of a smile creeping back onto her muzzle. "In the common sense as well as in the sense that you seem to be at all times full of thoughts."

"I lost track of the number of times May's accused me of living up in my head a long time ago, yeah."

"There is no harm in it, my dear. It serves you well." She settled back against the couch once more and sighed. "Pleasant as it has been, I have spent more time talking than intended. I would like to get a bit of work done before I lose track of the threads, if that is alright."

Ey smiled and nodded. "Of course, True Name."

As the skunk's focus drifted away, ey opened eir notebook again and stared at what ey'd written already. The words were marks on the page, ey could tell, but eir mind was so wrapped up in the conversation that ey wasn't able to make sense of them. Too much had gone on in too short a timespan. All that talk of Qoheleth, of the conservatives' opinions of the events, or at least of True Name's.

She'd been so candid about it all, just as she'd been growing more candid with em in general over the last few years. She had all the reason in the world to use her centuries of skills intentionally, though. Ey'd never met anyone so tightly in control of themself as her. Perhaps even now, dozens, hundreds of sensorium messages were flying across her stanza preparing a soft landing for eir play in light of the fact that others now knew the Name.

And yet...

And yet ey couldn't stop emself from thinking, *Holy shit, I don't think she knows.*

Ioan half lay, half slouched against the headboard with May draped bonelessly up along eir front. She'd gotten up to make them both coffee to drink in bed, then proceeded to doze off again, using eir chest as a pillow and the rest of em as a mattress.

Ey, meanwhile, had made it through most of eir coffee, resting the cup between the skunk's shoulder blades between sips. It was technically Christmas, though neither of them cared much for the holiday. Michelle Hadje had been raised vaguely Jewish and Ioan the particular blend of spiritual humanism that pervaded Eastern Europe at the time, but both had been well-steeped in the broader secular Christian culture of the West. That meant it was the day for the *tocană* and *mămăligă* that had become tradition for them. Ey hadn't learned to cook much prior to uploading—just a few simple dishes for a poor student—and it wasn't until ey had wound up on the System in eir current sim that ey'd gone back to teach emself all the things ey'd loved growing up.

It promised to be a lazy sort of day otherwise, which felt necessary. May's spike of anxiety when ey'd gone out for eir meeting with True Name a few days prior had quickly tapered off, but it had not simply gone away. The days that followed had included a lot of asking em if ey was okay and taking breaks to sit and look out the picture windows, lost in thought.

Still, last night had been delightful, with the skunk far more relaxed while they cooked—or tried to cook—shitty fast food for each other. After dinner, they moved to the couch with Ioan resting eir head in May's lap so that she could tease her fingers through eir thick hair while they hummed silly little songs to each other.

Today promised to be equally comfortable.

Ey frowned when ey lifted eir mug, only to find it empty. Equally comfortable but for that, ey supposed.

"I'm going to drink your coffee, May."

"If you do, I will pin you down and pluck your eyebrows bald," she mumbled, slowly lifting her head and reaching out toward her mug on the nightstand.

"That's a new one. Sounds painful."

"Add it to the list," she said after she was able to get at least a few sips in.

"One day, they're going to find my body, clearly smothered to death, my eyebrows fully plucked, sand in my shoes, cracker crumbs in my bed, all of my pens un-capped, all of my book pages dog-eared, with skunk fur in all the food," ey said, laughing. "I'm pretty sure they'll know it was you."

She lifted her chin to park it on eir shoulder. "Mm, well, it is a risk I am willing to take."

Ey tilted eir head to give the top of her own a kiss. An awkward affair, but worth it. "You stay up too late again?"

She shrugged.

"Well, you're a pretty cozy blanket, if a little too warm, so I guess I'll allow it."

Lifting her snout, she licked at eir shoulder, getting a laugh out of em. "Whereas you, my dear, are not a very good pillow. Just chock full of bones."

"I need those to live."

"Lame," she drawled. After a moment, she added thoughtfully, "I am glad that you have skin, though. It would be quite disgusting without."

"Eugh. As am I." Ey leaned over to grab her coffee cup and steal a sip, threats be damned. "I'm still surprised you didn't wind up with another furry, though. Figured that would be more your style."

"I wind up with people that I like, whether they have fur or not." She shrugged. "Which is not to say that I have not wound up with other furries."

"I'm not complaining. You're soft."

"To be fair, that is what I like about you having skin. Skin is soft as well. Were you a furry, though, what species would you be?"

Ey pet along her back, thinking. "I don't know. I've only really had extensive interactions with skunks, foxes, and weasels. Maybe a squirrel?"

She rolled off eir front and sat up eagerly. "A squirrel? Really? Would you be one of those fancy red ones with the ear tufts and outrageous tails or one of the gray ones that were all over where I grew up?"

A quick query of the perisystem archive gave em a good idea of what each might look like. "The red ones sound really ostentatious. I don't know if I could pull that off."

She retrieved her coffee mug from em and settled in beside em instead. "Yes, but the *tail*," she whined. "Come on, my dear. You would simply *have* to be a red squirrel. You dress all fancy, even!"

"Are they bigger than skunk tails?"

She looked thoughtful for a moment, then shrugged. "Solid competition."

"I can't picture anything having a bigger tail than you, May. Definitely outrageous."

"I thought you liked my tail."

"I do!"

"Excellent, I shall allow you to live another day." She laughed and dotted her nose against eir cheek. "I had considered becoming a panther for some time, but I am too attached to my tail."

"Or you it is to you."

She laughed.

"You know, I've always wondered," ey said, getting an arm around her. "Why did the most political stanza of the clade stay skunks? Wouldn't it be more effective to be humans? It's not like the majority of folks on the Systems are furries."

"Only three of the ten are skunks anymore, and you have met all three. Besides, I think End Waking is the only one of the three of us who has not spent time in human form. Some of me in other relationships were—or perhaps are—humans. I spent six months with you in that form, even, remember?"

Ey nodded. "It was pretty weird."

"For both of us, yes. I like being what I am. Short, soft, furry, chubby," she said, poking at her belly. "It is just that these are all things that are disarming to a great many people. Even skunks, despite their reputation for smelling bad, are often seen as bumbling, stupid creatures."

"I wouldn't call you stupid, May. Bumbling, though..."

She rolled her eyes. "Thank you, I think? But yes, even bumbling is a calculated gesture to be inoffensive."

"End Waking said similar." Ey dug through eir exocortices until ey came up with the memory of the conversation, "He said it was a matter of intent."

"It is, yes. I am sure that some of the wider clade who remain skunks do so without a second thought, but that is not how True Name worked, and so it is not how we work."

"And she did that for the same reasons? To be inoffensive?"

She nodded. "In a way. At first, she could not be anything but, as that is how she was forked, but she kept it because of the way the Council worked. She was a skunk, Debarre was a weasel, Ezekiel spent half the time looking like a shambling pile of dirty rags and the other half like an unhoused man, and user11824 looked like the least remarkable person possible, as though your eyes simply slid right off of him. The ethos of the Council was to be just ordinary people who were weird before uploading and remained weird after."

"Jonas wasn't that weird when I met him."

She made a sour face. "But everything that he did was intentional. Every aspect of his appearance and personality."

Ey nodded.

"But I think True Name kept it after the Council disbanded for much the same reasons. She is a furry because there are plenty of furries on the System. She remains in her early thirties because that is what one expects out of those on the System. She is not unattractive among furries, maintaining that soft figure and well kept appearance without heading towards sex-symbol because that is what many on the System wind up doing. She is professional, I am cute, End Waking is the sad and introspective one, and so on."

"Right, that makes sense." Ey hesitated, composing eir next words carefully. "You talk about her quite a bit. I know that–"

"You asked, Ioan," she interrupted, frowning.

"I know, May, I just mean in general. I know you're consciously working on how you feel about her and I keep bringing her up besides. Just an observation."

The moment of tenseness lingered, then passed as she wilted against em, sighing. "I know. I did not mean to get short with you. You are right, and I am not sure how I feel about that fact, that she is so often on my mind. My feelings remain complex."

"Oh, I definitely get that."

"You seem to enjoy her company more."

Ey shrugged. "I guess. It started out as a way to keep things smooth between our clades during the convergence, but now it's just a thing to do outside the house."

"Coffee dates are good," she said, nodding.

"I don't know if I'd call them dates. No romance, there."

The skunk laughed and shook her head. "Just an expression."

"Oh, right." Ey shrugged. "She's just like…a coworker one is friends with. There are contexts that I enjoy her company in, but it's not like I'm inviting her over for the holidays."

"Which is good," she said, grinning. "I am sure that I will get to the point where she and I can coexist in the same space without either of us pulling each other's fur out, but sharing Christmas dinner with her would be far too much."

Ey nodded and tightened eir arm around her, kissing between her ears. "Same, I think. Thanks for reminding me, though. I should probably get up and get that started."

They both slid out of the bed to complete their morning tasks: Ioan to make another pot of coffee and prepare breakfast while May went through her grooming routine, eating, then a shower for em while she worked on her monologue.

The dinner itself wasn't exactly onerous. A stew of beef—ey'd been raised on a version with lamb, which May hadn't liked—tomatoes, and mushrooms in a garlicky, paprika-filled gravy served with polenta. Still, it benefited from a longer cooking time, so ey began that after eir shower and set it to simmering.

After that, they set some music to playing—the overlap of what they both enjoyed wasn't large, given the more than a century's age difference, but piano jazz seemed to work for both of them—and set to work on whatever it was that was occupying their minds.

Or tried to, at least.

Their conversation this morning as well as eir meeting with True Name a few days prior left Ioan in mind of skunks and the Ode clade, and even though those both featured quite heavily in the stage adaptation of *On the Perils of Memory*, nothing ey tried seemed quite in the right vein.

Ey flipped to a blank sheet of paper and began a letter, instead.

> True Name,
>
> I hope all is well.
>
> After our conversation a few days ago, as well as another that I had with May this morning, I got to thinking about a pattern I've noticed, and wanted to ask you about it. I hope it's not too impertinent of me. If it's too sensitive a topic, I understand.
>
> I've noticed that you and May have a tendency to talk about each other quite a bit. I know that there are a lot of factors that go into this such as my relationships with each of you, your shared history, and the fact that I have a habit of asking each of you about the other in turn.
>
> All the same, I was wondering if you had any thoughts on the matter. I don't want to sound meddlesome (indeed, I don't think I'd even be capable of meddling with either of you), I just want to better understand each of you in turn, given the dynamics between us.

I know it's not a huge deal for either of our clades,
but all the same, Merry Christmas.

Best,

Ioan

Ey read through the letter top to bottom three times, then,
with a brush of the hand and a bit of intent, sent it on its way.

Doing eir best to forget about it until the other skunk re-
sponded, ey puttered around the house, checking on the stew,
trying out a new ink in one of eir pens, and rehearsing some
lines in a cone of silence.

A bit more than two hours after ey'd sent the message, a reply spooled itself out of eir desk and into eir field of view.

IOAN BĂLAN INDIVIDUAL-EYES-ONLY MATERIAL

Mx. Bălan,

Thank you for your letter. Had we discussed this in
person or over sensorium messages, I think that my
responses would be quite different, but the inten-
tionality that is required when engaging with writing forced me to think this through more clearly.

You are correct in assuming that it is you being our
shared connection rather than any direct link between the two of us that leads to each of us discussing the other with you frequently. I do not think
that this is worth discounting, however, as many
know of each other only through one mutual acquaintance and yet do not talk constantly of each
other to that one one person between them. It is still
notable that we discuss one another as much as we
do.

I have spent the last hour in discussion with myself
while writing this, and would like this reply kept in
confidence.

Years ago, when the Artemisians first arrived, May Then My Name mentioned a letter that I had sent her regarding you. I am not normally in the habit of sharing the tools of my trade, such as they are, and sharing this with you in particular is uncomfortable. However you of all people—a friend and someone deeply entangled with the clade—deserve to have the chance to read it, and it may do well to explain where we have found ourselves. Here is that letter in full:

May Then My Name Die With Me,

I hope that you are doing well. I understand that there remains some concern about the outcome of your previous relationship, and I would like you to know that I am not so far diverged from our common ancestor that I do not share in some of those feelings. I remember how often I would come crying into the Crown, leaning on this shoulder or that as I tried to deal with yet another break-up. I know that I have not always been the kindest or most empathetic down-tree instance, for which I truly am sorry. You are, in many ways, a better version of me, and the completeness that you bring to our stanza ensures that, even if I am not a fully realized person as you have suggested in the past, we—whether that is you and I, our stanza, or the Odists as a whole—still do add up to something that is greater than the sum of its parts. You may not believe me, and for that I do not blame you, but I really do love you in my own way, May Then My Name.

I do not know if you have been keeping up with many other stanzas after Qoheleth quit, but it appears that Dear, Also, The Tree That Was Felled has welcomed a new member to its relationship structure, one Codrin Bălan. I am sure that you recognize the clade name from *On The Perils of Memory*. Codrin's down-tree instance, Ioan Bălan, was the amanuensis that Dear had chosen during that spate of trouble, and the series of events that followed led to a process of individuation. It is always exciting to see that happen, is it not?

The reason that I bring this up is that Ioan has picked up as eir next project an investigative piece surrounding the launch project. Given your role as sysside launch director, I thought that I would put you two in touch. Eir project would benefit greatly from your position as well as your history, both with the project and with our time on the System. I have had the chance to interact with both Ioan and Codrin in the past, and they are some of the most delightful, insightful people that I have met. Please look them up when you get a chance.

All my best,

The Only Time I Know My True Name Is When I Dream of the Ode clade

systime 197+3

That night, when she brought up this message, she

mentioned that she believed me when I said that I love her in my own way.

I understand the root of her feelings towards me and, as I also mentioned on that night, I do not begrudge her that. I will ever be what I am, and what that is does not mesh well with her view of the world, even as it is integral to my existence.

Just as she said that she still believes me, it is also true that I still love her. Codrin reported that Why Ask Questions said, "I have yet to meet a single person who has not fallen at least a little in love with May." There is perhaps a little bit of that involved in my own inescapably me way, but beyond that I love her as the version of me that I did not become.

Were you to ask me at the time, or even just a year ago, I do not think that I would have admitted such aloud, but even as I suspect that she is working on her thoughts about me with Ms. Genet, I have been working with Ms. Genet on my ability to be truly earnest with those I respect, which includes you.

I do not hold regrets for the path that has led us to this point. I have accomplished much that I set out to do, and, while the cost has been great when it comes to my interpersonal relationships (and, as you mentioned, my stress levels), it all very much still feels worth it.

Consciously or not, I make it a point to ask you how she is doing and to engage with her at one degree of remove because this is still a way to maintain that level of connection with someone I could have been after so long a time of disconnect.

Writing this has been both stressful and cathartic, so I appreciate having the chance to do so. While communications with my counterparts on Castor and Pollux have been somewhat scant of late, both of them have mentioned that they are striving to find situations in which they can be vulnerable and earnest. As I am sure you understand, this is still quite difficult for us.

Let us meet up on Secession Day for our next coffee date. Is 11:00 amenable? It can be a small celebration of our own.

I wish you and her both a delightful holiday. If you are comfortable bringing up the topic of me with her today and would like to get a laugh out of her, please say simply, "Jingle Bells stage blocking."

Sincerely,

The Only Time I Know My True Name Is When I Dream of the Ode clade

systime 225+359

END IOAN BĂLAN INDIVIDUAL-EYES-ONLY MATERIAL

Ey read the letter through a few more times, trying to digest all that it contained, trying to square this with what May had said of True Name steering her subtly into eir life, trying once again not to read too deep and guess that True Name#Castor simply hadn't told her about Codrin learning the Name.

Finally, acknowledging that ey wouldn't be able to digest it all in one go, ey dashed off a quick reply thanking True Name for the letter and confirming the time of the next meeting. Then, ey committed the letter to a new exo ey tagged "True Name–May 225" and destroyed the physical copy.

"May?" ey said, dropping eir cone of silence.

"Mm?"

"I was confirming a date with True Name and she said I should ask you about something called 'Jingle Bells stage blocking'. Do you know–"

The skunk let out a melodramatic groan and slid off her stool to the floor, landing on her hands and knees before flopping onto her side, laughing. "What a fucking brat."

Ey stared at her, nonplussed.

"Oh God, Ioan, you do not know pain until you work with choir kids."

Ey laughed and shook eir head, leaning forward to ruffle over her ears. It was a much more pleasant response to a note from True Name than ey'd expected. "You're right, I don't. I'll just have to trust you on that. Skunks are so weird."

Debarre — 2350

Debarre and Do I Know God After The End Waking stood, naked and frowning, on the granite that hung cantilevered above the pond that had dug itself into the forest floor beneath the falls. It wasn't a high drop, not enough to turn the stomach, but enough to keep them from simply jumping in.

"And you're sure it's deep enough?"

"I am not, no," End Waking said, then let out a shout and leapt off the overhang out over the water.

The weasel's frown deepened. No sounds of screaming below, at least.

"Fuck it," he muttered, and stepped off the edge of the rock, arms folded over his chest, and plunged, feet first, into the water.

The cold was enough to drive his breath from him. Even though there wasn't any snow this low down on the hillside, it was still cold out and even colder up-slope from whence the snow-melt came. He realized, too late, that another possibility for there not being any screaming from his boyfriend below was due to the frigid water.

All the same, there was nothing beneath his feet for at least another meter as he sank below the surface.

Thankful for small victories, he swam shakily for the surface, breaching the water with a shallow gasp and teeth already chattering.

End Waking floated closer, treading water. The skunk's smile was wide, but his teeth were clenched shut in a clear attempt to slow the shivering. "Pleasant day out, is it not?"

"F-fuck you," Debarre said, laughing breathlessly. "I'm getting up to the fire ASAP."

The skunk laughed, shoved at him weakly, and then swam for the shore, weasel in tow.

They slicked the water off themselves as best they could while walking. Fluffy as he was, End Waking had the larger job of it, spending most of the rest of the short trek back up the hill to the fire he'd built squeezing water out of his tail fur.

Once there, they parked a meter or so before the fire and huddled beneath his woolen cloak, held open toward the flames, soaking up as much warmth as they could.

"That was fucking cold," Debarre said once he was able to speak without stammering. "You're such an asshole, I can't believe I ever listen to you. Fine fucking way to ring in the new year."

"Yes, well, I love you too," End Waking said, grinning. "Thank you for joining me, and for your help today."

They'd spent the afternoon building up a rammed earth wall for the skunk's new house, pulling sandy clay from the pile they'd brought up from the pond's shore the previous day, mixing in deer's blood as a binder before stacking it in a frame, and pounding it with logs sanded smooth and cut down to a diameter that fit comfortably in their paws.

Part of the ramming process had involved carefully setting the chimney pipe for the wood stove between the layers of earth as they built up. This had seemed an unnecessarily fiddly process despite the admonitions that, if the pipe crumpled beneath the sand, clay, and blood while they pounded it, the wall wouldn't be sturdy and there might be gaps. As it was, after they built up the rest of the tent, they'd have to seal that spot with more bloody earth and a layer of pitch.

It had left them both feeling worn out and dirty, and when

Debarre said he was going to wash the sticky earth from his paws and fur, End Waking had suggested turning that into the icy plunge.

The skunk had then built up the fire higher than usual, told Debarre that they'd need to do so nude as he shed his clothes by the fire so they'd stay dry, and then pulled him along to the rock overhang.

Once their fronts were mostly dry, they turned out to face the waterfall and ravine, draping the cloak over their shoulders with their backs exposed to the fire, sitting in silence and leaning against each other, sharing warmth.

"Why don't you build your camp here?"

"The river may overflow, and come spring, the fall will be quite loud."

Debarre grinned, "Don't need the white noise?"

"Not particularly, though I am more concerned about flooding. I already had a tree fall on me while I slept, you will surely remember, and I do not feel the need to be carried away on dirty waters so soon after."

"Thanks for letting me back after that happened," he said, more quietly. "And thanks for forking to fix your leg."

"Of course, my dear. I do not know who else I would have called. And thank you for your patience during my solitude."

Debarre nodded and slid an arm around the skunk's waist. "I'm used to it by now. Besides, #Tracker had a larger merge than usual to deal with."

"That is what happens when I steal a version of you away and then aliens visit one of the LVs. I will accept half of the blame." He smiled, adding, "Perhaps less than half. You had your own stuff going on."

"Well, #Tracker did." He snorted, shook his head. "It's what I get for only part of me hanging around interesting people."

"Am I so boring, my dear?"

He shook his head. "No, just plain. Your life is pretty simple out here. #Tracker is still all caught up on all the political stuff with user11824 and Yared."

End Waking made a face. "Gross."

"They aren't *that* bad," he said, laughing.

"They are fine, I am sure," the skunk said. "You may keep the political stuff, though."

"I mean, that's why I'm out here. It's good to get away from all that bullshit."

"Oh, so you are using me for a vacation, then?"

Debarre laughed and poked at End Waking's thigh. "Where'd this sense of humor come from?"

"The audacity of weasels never ceases to amaze," he said. "I have a sense of humor. The squirrels and I share our private jokes. I practice them before the fire."

"Fucking weirdo," Debarre said, rolling his eyes. He tucked closer to the skunk all the same.

That End Waking was so open to touch over the last few weeks was something he was keen to take advantage of. Neither of them were necessarily the cuddly type, and most of the time, he was happy with the level of physical contact he got from the skunk, just as he was with the partners his other forks had settled down with. Still, it was nice every once and a while. A bit of touch to keep him grounded. It tended to happen when their relationship picked up again, after both of them had spent months or years apart, each living their separate, more cerebral lives.

Before long, however, they set the cloak aside to get dressed, and Debarre watched as End Waking prepped a sizeable hare and pushed it onto a cast-iron spit and set it over the fire, a tilted pan beneath it catching the drippings.

They dined on the hare and squash roasted in the fat, both pungent with thyme. They stayed up until it was well and truly dark, chatting.

Worn out as they were, though, they didn't last much longer, eventually retreating to the makeshift tent that End Waking had set up using the patched fabric that had been his previous shelter strung over a rope and draped over his recovered cot. Narrow as it was, they had to huddle close—the only time the skunk was consistently okay with close physical contact and intimacy—sharing each others' warmth beneath the cloak and a few blankets besides.

"E.W.?"

"I like it when you call me that."

"I'm a sucker for nicknames," he said, tucking himself back against him.

"That you are." He rested his snout over Debarre's shoulder. "What were you going to say, my love?"

"I...well, all these little changes are coming to the System. The ACL changes, the cones of silence..."

"I do not use those."

"Well, but you never leave here and you gave up on all the politics."

"This is by design."

Debarre laughed, shaking his head. "I'm just worried about so many changes in so short a time."

"How so?"

"I dunno," Debarre mumbled. "I just think there's a lot of subtle things—more like the little stuff May Then My Name talks about—and I'm worried those will break or disappear."

End Waking hummed thoughtfully. "They have survived Secession and Launch."

"Yeah, but those were political things, right? Not technological things."

"You are worried external engineers will tamper?"

He nodded.

"I do not know that they have a good enough understanding of the subtleties to do so. The System is greater than the sum of its component parts."

"Well, maybe not intentionally changing things. Just knock on effects, maybe." *Or maybe internal politics encouraging changes,* he added mentally.

"I imagine they will be careful, even around the subtle things."

They lay silent for a while, Debarre thinking and, if the slow slackening of his arm around his chest was any indication, End Waking slowly falling asleep.

"E.W.?" he whispered.

"Mm?" A sleepy reply.

"Do you still feel em? Like, at night sometimes. Like a dream or something."

There was a long, long silence before the skunk replied. "Sleep, my love. There is work to do in the morning. Sleep, and dream beautiful dreams."

As usual, Debarre woke alone. End Waking would doubtless be somewhere in the woods, checking snare traps or walking or simply sitting on a rock thinking, having slipped away at first light, quietly and carefully enough not to wake him. Still, they'd gone to bed early enough that the horizon down the hill had only just let go of the sun.

He slipped out of bed and into his pants—black denim traded in for a dirty green canvas—splashed some water on his face from the barrel nearby, and started the trek back out to the rock where they'd set the fire, figuring that'd be the most likely place to find his boyfriend.

End Waking was indeed there, crouching before a low fire with a pot for coffee already set above it, but another skunk knelt across from him as well, chatting quietly.

"Hey May Then My Name," he said, settling down beside her. "Whatcha doing here?"

The skunk started, grinned wide, and leaned in to hug around his shoulders. "Jesus, Debarre, you taking lessons from End Waking? Scared the hell out of me, sneaking up like that."

He laughed and returned the hug before reaching for the coffee pot. "Maybe it's contagious."

"Can you imagine a disease so miserable?" the other skunk said, waving the weasel back from the coffee pot. "Our guest here finished what was left. You will have to wait, my dear."

"Sorry," she said, holding her battered enamel mug out to Debarre. "You can have the other half."

"Nah, go ahead. I'll wait. You never told me what you're doing here, though."

She stuck her tongue out at him. "Am I not allowed to be a pest? That is my role in life."

"'Course you are, just that usually you're a pest with news."

"Fine, fine, yes," she said. "It can wait until after coffee, though. How are you, Debarre? I was not expecting you to be back just yet."

"It is my fault," her cocladist said. "A tree fell on me back around–"

"*What?!*"

He shrugged. "There was a wind storm late last year and a tree fell across my tent. It crushed the frame and floor, knocked over the back wall, and impaled my thigh on a splintered board."

She brought her paws up to cover her muzzle, eyes wide.

"I am okay," he said, smiling disarmingly. "But I asked Debarre to return to help me rebuild."

"He didn't want to fork to fix his leg," the weasel said, rolling his eyes.

"I do not fork often, you know that."

"There was a plank through your leg, E.W.," he retorted. "That wasn't just going to heal okay on its own."

It was the skunk's turn to roll his eyes. "You are no fun."

May Then My Name, having finally regained her composure, said, "Well, thank you, Debarre."

Debarre nodded.

She sighed, smiling weakly at End Waking. "I am glad you are okay, skunk. I would be lost without you.

"The trees do not know how to kill me, May Then My Name," End Waking said, frowning. "There is no virus within them. Debarre was right to get me to fork to fix, I will admit, but I would have done so anyway had it landed more fully on me."

When all that greeted this was silence, he sighed and let his shoulders slump. "I am sorry. I have set up the new camp in a location with sturdier trees. I will endeavor to remain cautious."

May Then My Name crawled around the fire to dot her nose against the skunk's cheek. He looked uncomfortable, but tolerated the touch.

"Thank you, my dear," she said. "I do not mean to lecture. I am just...well, if the coffee is ready, please pour yourself a cup, Debarre, and we will talk."

Once they'd settled back down and the kettle was replaced with a pot to cook oatmeal, she began, "To preface, this is nothing serious, I just need to talk with someone who is not Ioan."

"Why?" End Waking asked.

"You will see. That is also part of it."

He nodded.

"I am not even sure that it is actionable." She sighed, shrugged. "I have just been thinking about True Name a lot of late."

End Waking sat, conspicuously impassive, while Debarre shook his head. "Why? I thought you'd basically agreed to never talk again."

"We have not spoken; at least, not more than a few cordial words in passing. However, Ioan has been meeting up with her for coffee once a month since the first news of the Artemisians."

He and End Waking both tilted their heads.

"Ey has been ensuring that things remain polite and smooth between us." She held up a paw to forestall any comments, adding quickly, "I trust em in this. Ey is simply meeting her at a coffee shop where they each work on their own projects. They chat a little, and then do their own things. Ey describes it as 'friendly coworkers' more than anything, which I believe."

"Is that a thing that even needs to be done?" Debarre said. "Wasn't she just leaving you alone before?"

"Yes, thankfully. It is just..." She frowned, poking at the packed earth with a claw. "That has been necessary to prevent anger, but it has still not been comfortable. There are plenty of people who I no longer see and do not miss, or do miss and think about with some frequency. It was such an uneasy silence."

"And you think Ioan's doing the right thing?"

"Ey is," End Waking said. "Ey is ensuring that there remains a distance between you two without it being an unbridged distance. That would just leave you to stew, knowing how you work. You would never let it go and spin yourself into a whirlwind of emotion. The Bălans are perhaps a little awkward at times, but they do not lack all social graces."

May Then My Name rubbed her paws over her face. "I knooow," she whined. "And I love em for thinking of that."

"You just still resent her," the other skunk said.

"Yes."

"I know you said it probably isn't actionable," Debarre said, poking at the fire with a stick. "But what would you change about the situation?"

"As in 'in a perfect world'?"

"Right, yeah. Perfect world, what would you like?"

She frowned, watching End Waking dote over the oatmeal, dumping a pawful of dried fruit into it. Eventually, she said, "I do not know. She has apologized and done what I have requested. She has changed, too, from what Ioan has said. She is trying to be more earnest and willing to engage emotionally. She has been seeing Sarah as well."

Debarre nodded. "But it sounds like that's not it."

"No. I think what is missing is contrition. She has apologized for what she has done to me and Ioan and has maybe even begun to make changes. I do not know how to put it, but it feels like she is being earnest without being sincere. She is sorry, but not contrite. She does not feel bad for what she has done. Her apologies are not backed by understanding."

"There is no penance," End Waking said plainly, dishing out

the oatmeal into the mugs they'd been using for coffee. "True penance is borne out of feeling bad about what one has done and wanting to change, to make up for it, not merely about responding to how others are reacting."

May Then My Name toyed with her oatmeal. "Yes. Maybe she does and just does not know how to show it. I just do not know how to truly believe that."

"Worried she's just acting?" Debarred said, blowing on a still vigorously steaming spoonful of oats.

"Perhaps. That was ever the dilemma of us going into theatre. Did we love it or did we merely want to become someone else? To hide from who we were?"

"Be wary of your pessimism," End Waking said. "It takes attention and effort, May Then My Name, at least when one has intentionally tamped down emotions to the point that she has. If I could teach her, if either of us could teach her, I think we would, but I do not know that one can learn penance from anyone but oneself."

She nodded, looking distracted and thoughtful. "If it were as simple as merging down..."

End Waking stiffened, frowned around his bite of breakfast.

She smiled to him apologetically. "Sorry, I will stop for now. Thank you both for listening to me bitch."

"It's fine, skunk," Debarre said. "I think E.W. is right that Ioan's doing the right thing. It takes some pressure off of you and lets it...I dunno, be a process or something. You don't have to do anything now 'cause you've got an opening to deal with it."

"Yes, well put. Thank you, my dear," she said. "I will process as best I can. I do not suppose either of you have talked to her recently?"

They both shook their heads.

"Right, I thought not. That's enough of the topic for now, anyway." She waved a paw and took a bite of oatmeal, then pulled a face. "We need to get you some sugar or something."

Debarre laughed. "She's right, E.W. I've gotten used to it, but only just barely."

"Fucking lame," he drawled. "My sim, my rules. You must suffer without."

May Then My Name flicked some oatmeal from her spoon at him. "Call me lame, will you."

He grinned toothily, picking the bit of oatmeal off his shirt sleeve and adding it to his mug.

"Either way, my root instance is back at home, so I can stay as long as I like. Would you like some help, at least?"

"If you can swing a hammer, then yes, that would be wonderful."

Ioan Bălan — 2350

Through some stroke of luck or perhaps some forgetful nature, it was perpetually early summer at Arrowhead Lake, that abandoned mountain sim Ioan and May had long ago adopted. Whether or not winter had socked them in at home, they could at least take a summer walk somewhere.

"Winter has its place," ey'd explained to May when she'd gotten particularly whiny about the snow. "I like the snow so long as I'm inside."

"Did you ever even see snow, my dear?"

Ey'd shrugged. "Sure. We'd get dumped on once or twice a year."

"And was that pleasant?"

"Well, no, but—"

She'd laughed at em, then, shaking her head. "I miss our porch swing. I miss our lilacs and dandelions. Sometimes, I just want to lay in the grass and overheat. I have been betrayed by our weather."

So it was a good escape when it got cold. They could duck off—alone or together—to the lake and head for a walk.

May had chosen the name Arrowhead Lake over Ioan's protests that it looked nothing like an arrowhead, being more kidney shaped. The sim itself was tagged Peak Lake#587a9383. Maybe it was just Peak Lake? This seemed only to have emboldened her when ey brought it up, and ey was firmly overruled.

Whenever ey walked out there without her, as ey did today, ey'd think on this. Maybe it had little to do with the lake itself. Maybe it had to do with the silhouettes of the pines? Or something to do with way the snow lingered on pointed peaks?

"Or maybe she's just a brat," ey mumbled, smiling to emself as ey walked slowly along the deer trail. "No reasoning with an Odist."

Ey'd long wrestled with whether or not they were just normal people. Perhaps Michelle had been—ey'd not spent enough time around her to know, and what time ey had managed had been mostly silence. Toward the end, her conversations were more interruptions than not, although the impression ey'd gotten was that she'd been kind and gentle, while still being the type to care passionately about things or, more often, people. The impression just hadn't been a strong one. Not enough time for it to solidify.

Ey'd eventually come to the conclusion, confirmed through discussions with several of the clade, that each of them had begun more as a distillation of a singular aspect of Michelle than the whole of her. That wasn't to say that they weren't complete in their own right, simply that each was singularly focused on their interests and skills, a perpetual hyperfixation. What was it Codrin and Dear had said? Even True Name was a fully realized person.

Normal, though? Could one be both a singular facet and normal?

And maybe it went beyond them. Maybe it was a dispersionista thing. Ey could see such a habit building even without Michelle's unique experiences.

When the trail dipped down out of the trees toward the shore, ey stooped to pick up a handful of pebbles, enough to toss into the water once ey reached the boulder at the lake's outlet. Codrin had eir cairns, ey supposed, and ey had a heap of pebbles at the bottom of the lake, tossed in one by one over the decades.

I still don't know what I'm supposed to be doing, ey thought, rattling the rocks around in eir hand as ey continued walking. *I don't know if I'm supposed to help either of them, bring them together again, or what.*

It was still a week out from eir next meeting with True Name, from Secession Day, and while May's anxiety hadn't ticked back up, eir own had lingered. There was an unsettled feeling within em that made itself known whenever ey thought about heading to the coffee shop.

"Maybe I'm not supposed to do anything," ey muttered, climbing up the boulder. "Maybe I'm just supposed to be a friend, like she says."

Ey tossed a stone into the water with a small plunk and splash.

That gulf remained between the two skunks, and no one seemed happy with it.

Plunk, splash.

"I don't know why it feels like I'm supposed to be the one to do something about it. Friends are supposed to help, right?"

Plunk, splash.

"There's nothing for me to fix, really. They've each made their own decisions, and seem at peace with those, even if they're not happy with whatever's left between them."

Plunk, splash.

"And they'd probably both resent me if I *were* to do anything." Ey tossed a few pebbles in at once, splashing in a brief, watery static. "Whatever that'd even be."

Ey stood at the peak of that boulder, tossing pebbles into water and thinking, mumbling to emself about May and True Name. When ey ran out of pebbles, ey sat cross-legged and looked out over the lake, unseeing.

"I should just pinch myself whenever I start thinking that there's something I need to do," ey said to the water. "Pretty sure May doesn't want it, she's happy working on her emotions without me meddling, and I'm pretty sure True Name doesn't want it, since she seems content...what was it, maintaining that level of connection after so long a time of disconnect?"

The lake didn't answer, not in anything other than the water lapping at the shore and the chatter of the creek.

"This is stupid."

Ey sat for another hour, just watching the lake, the clouds, the trees, trying not to think about how complicated it was for one person to be so split among so many instances.

The walk back was spent unwinding the thought processes that led em here in the first place. Unwinding and re-coiling into a careful skein, now with fewer knots than it had had in it before, though it still remained tangled.

"Good walk, my dear?" May said when ey returned and plopped down onto the couch.

"Very. It's nice out there."

"It always is," the skunk said, walking over from where she'd been poking around in the kitchen to dot her nose atop eir head. "It could be here too, you know."

Ey laughed and waved a hand toward the picture windows facing out the balcony, out to the drifting snow. "It's pretty, May. It makes being all warm inside nicer."

She leaned down to rest her elbows on the back of the couch beside em. "I am not immune to the beauty, I am just a wuss when it comes to the cold."

"Well, if you ever wore shoes..."

She swatted at the back of eir head and laughed. "Jerk."

"Ow! Domestic abuse!" Ey laughed as well, rubbing at eir head. "Want to go out for dinner?"

At that, May perked up, grinning. "I take back the slap. Yes please! Can we get sushi?"

"Sure, J2?"

She bounced on the balls of her feet and nodded. "Yes! You, my dear, know just how to treat a girl."

"Skunk girl."

"Well, yes, but still." Still bouncing, she twirled around behind the couch, tail trailing along behind her. "I will get ready. I am hungry now, so too bad if you are not."

One of the things that Ioan appreciated most about J2 over all of the other sushi places May had dragged em to is that it was the most amenable to em eating with eir hands. May was quite nimble with chopsticks—no mean feat with paws and claws—but ey'd never quite picked it up, so being able to eat those little bullets of rice and fish with eir hands suited em quite well.

It had a channel of water floating along between the booths, small dishes drifting by lazily for the diners to pluck from the water. This obviated the need for any staff, real or simulated, as each dish would be replaced from behind a bend in the river. With no need to pay beyond a token amount of reputation, it simply became a pleasant evening out, plates stacking up at the edge of their table a tacit contest with other diners.

"Did you get what you needed out of your walk earlier?" May asked before popping a bit of fish into her muzzle.

Ey shrugged, finished chewing, and said, "I guess. Was doing some thinking into that feeling that I have to fix every problem in front of me when it comes to relationships."

"I have noticed that in you, yes," she said. "Beyond when we specifically talk about it, I mean."

"You have?"

"You are not a sneaky person, Ioan. When it comes up, it is there for me to see."

"Oh, uh," ey stammered, setting eir plate on top of the stack. "Sorry, May."

"No, no, you are fine! I accept it in the spirit in which it is given. You want to do right by me and your friends, even when 'doing right' is not your responsibility. So long as you do not overstep boundaries, I can at least understand it."

"Well, all the same, it's not like it's comfortable. I don't think anyone likes feeling helpless, but I just wish I didn't get hung up on finding solutions to everything."

"You know, it is weird," she said, gesturing vaguely with a

shrimp. "For someone who spent so long purely observing, a busybody tendency feels out of place."

Ey shook eir head. "Observing is situational. If there's something happening that has a start and end, or which I can come home from, then I can just observe it. If it's something that's ongoing or integral to a person, especially a meaningful person, then I feel like I really want to help."

She had taken the opportunity of em talking to eat the bit of shrimp she'd used as a pointer, and when she finished, she asked, "Is this a new thing?"

"How do you mean?"

"Were you always like this? Did you always want to help when it was something integral to people you care about?"

Ey frowned.

"Do not get me wrong, I am not suggesting one way or another. We have only known each other for a small portion of our lives. It is just that Codrin and Sorina both decided to specifically focus on that only recently."

Ey nodded thoughtfully. "Right. I don't know, honestly. Maybe? Maybe it's you, and–"

She rolled her eyes.

"No, I mean, maybe it's you in that you're the first person I've gotten close enough to to wind up feeling like that, at least since I uploaded."

The skunk paused in the act of picking another plate from the river, letting it drift on. "Did you feel that way about your brother? Was you uploading your fix?"

Ey felt eir muscles go rigid, eir jaw clench, eir hands start to tremble. "Uh...well, huh."

Ears splayed and eyes wide with alarm, the skunk reached out to take one of eir hands in her own. "I am sorry, Ioan. If I overstepped, I apologize."

Letting the skunk lace her fingers with eirs, ey shook eir head to dislodge the slight dizziness that had come with the realization and concomitant panic. "Maybe?" Ey forced a smile. "I mean, maybe uploading was my fix for that situation? I don't know."

She nodded, gave eir hand a gentle squeeze.

"I think you're the only person I've really loved other than Rareş," ey said, nudging the conversation back on track to avoid settling into that particular rumination. "That's what I meant. I want to make things good for you, whether it's you overflowing, stuff with True Name, or any other number of things that aren't my responsibility or even under my control."

May smiled, the expression veering perilously close to a smirk. "You have said that you want to fix things for True Name at times, too. Are you sure that you are not in love?"

"I've also talked about how often I'll wind up getting caught off guard by how much you two still look and sound alike," ey said, smirking right back. "She's nice and I do want to help her, but I think I'm a ways off from that."

She laughed. "I know, I know. You just leave yourself so open, sometimes, a girl cannot help herself. You are also allowed to want to help friends and acquaintances as well as me."

"Skunks, I swear..." Ey laughed when she pinched at eir fingers, tugging eir hand free so ey could grab another plate of sushi. "That's kind of what I was thinking about on the walk, though. I feel weirdly obligated to fix things. It's not my place to, I don't think either of you would be comfortable with that, and that's not even counting whether or not it's something either of you *want*."

"I do not know," she said, shrugging. "I spoke about that with End Waking and Debarre recently, and am no closer to an answer. We did all agree, however, that you doing what you are is a good thing, in that it at least sets up an avenue for change, even if neither True Name nor I decide to take that step."

Ey nodded. "I just want things to remain smooth between everyone, is all. Maybe it's a little...I don't know, overly conciliatory of me?"

"Perhaps, but that does not mean it does not have its own utility."

They ate in silence for a moment, Ioan eventually giving up after finishing eir plate. It was no less easy to eat too much, even in an embedded world.

"Are you okay with it?"

"Hmm?"

"Being between us. Interacting with the both of us even though I still resent her and she is still pleased with the work that she does. Are you okay being in the middle of that?"

Ey slouched back against the booth and watched the plates drift lazily by on the current, thinking. "I don't know."

"That is a perfectly valid answer, my dear."

"I don't really like the feeling. I feel weird about it every time it comes up, much as we need to talk about it." Ey smiled, taking one of her paws in eir hand again. "I agree that it has its uses. It's uncomfortable at times, but I don't think I'd be any more comfortable dropping out of the role."

The skunk brushed her thumb over eir fingers, saying, "I understand, Ioan. It is complex. If it needs to change, it can, and until then, even if I still harbor equally complex thoughts on True Name, I appreciate your position in our dynamic."

The conversation drifted away from the subject after that, and the two wound up back at home to poke through their own projects even as the night fell early.

It wasn't until they'd made it back to bed and curled up together that ey was finally able to truly let go of the topic, though; even throughout eir writing, a small portion of eir mind had been dedicated to the question of what eir role was between the two skunks and why it both rankled and felt necessary.

Ioan was surprised by just how wrung out True Name looked during their Secession Day coffee date. The skunk's blouse was wrinkled, her normally orderly fur mussed atop her head, and her whiskers all abristle. She looked as though she'd not slept for days and certainly not changed outfits in at least as long.

All the same, her arrival was much the same as all the others had been, with her smiling to em, ordering her coffee, and joining em on the couch in order to set up a cone of silence.

"Good morning, Mx. Bălan. I trust you are well?"

"Uh, I'm fine, I guess." Ey frowned, continuing carefully, "What about you, though? You look...well, terrible."

The skunk's smile faltered, betraying the exhaustion that plainly lay beneath. With another blink, the cone's ACLs changed to opaque it from the outside. She sagged against the couch. "I came in a rush, my dear, I apologize for my appearance."

"You don't need to apologize, True Name. I'm just worried. Lots of Secession Day preparations?"

"Of a sort, yes. Things have been rather stressful the last few days." She laughed, shook her head, and added, "Well, more than a little. I have been stretched very thin and am...struggling."

"Struggling?"

The skunk's eyes darted around the coffee shop, scanning each face within at least twice. "I am not comfortable expanding on that at the moment."

Ey held up eir hands disarmingly. "Of course. Are you at least excited about the day?"

"When I have the chance to slow down, I can feel some of that excitement. This provides me a good chance to do so. Twenty-five years since Launch and both LVs are continuing on in their journey with very few problems. Two and a quarter centuries since Secession and life continues smoothly here."

"That seems to fit with your goals pretty well."

She gave a slight nod of acknowledgement, though she remained distracted. "That it does, my dear."

"You and Jonas planning anything for yourselves, at least?"

"There will be a gathering, yes," she said. "Today at noon."

" 'A gathering'? Not a party?"

She shrugged. "His words, not mine. I do not know what he is planning."

"Well, hopefully a good one."

"Agreed. This will limit my time here, of course, I hope that you understand, and I may be distracted as several of my forks merge down to reduce conflicts while there."

Ey nodded. "That's alright. I've got stuff to work on, too."

Lapping at the whipped cream atop her drink, she once again scanned the crowd, which, as far as ey could tell, had not changed since she'd arrived. Something about her posture suggested that the topic of what was happening was closed, however, so ey made note to ask about it later instead.

They fell into work after that. True Name focused on her messages or dealt with merges while ey dedicated a token amount of effort to eir writing. The rest of em observed the skunk out of the corner of eir eye and thought about just how much must be happening for her to admit that she was struggling. 225 years since the System seceded from the rest of Earth's governments doubtless came with a lot of celebrations and announcements to make, speeches to write, hands to shake, or whatever it was that the non-leaders of Lagrange did in such an event.

Add in the twenty-fifth anniversary since Launch and certainly there would be an added note of joy for many across all three Systems. Ioan was particularly looking forward to the letters from Castor and Pollux in a month and change to hear how things had gone on each of the LVs. Perhaps ey'd even hear from Sorina from Artemis.

Still, True Name's mussed appearance and anxious expression seemed to go beyond that. Ey couldn't think of a reason related to the day that would have her in such a state. Things would be intense, but not so much so as to force her to drop her carefully constructed veneer of confidence.

Ah well, at least she got some time off, ey thought. This was followed by a gentle chiding which ey heard in May's voice. *And you are not supposed to be fixing things, remember?*

Right.

Forcing emself to concentrate on eir writing at least bought em ten minutes of work.

"Huh," True Name mumbled, frowning.

"Hmm?"

She shook her head. "Nothing, I suppose. Just got a merge from an instance, and it sounds like Jonas is looking for me. He knows that I am–"

Ey jolted back as the skunk leapt to her feet, gaze whipping about the room, then out through the windows to the street. Her tail was bristled out, ears pinned flat, and paws clenched tight, something ey'd only seen in May, and then only a handful of times.

"True Name?"

She held up a paw, beckoning em to silence, and, despite the way she kept searching face after face, ey could picture dozens of sensorium messages flying back and forth from her. Her frown only deepened.

Ey closed eir notebook, figuring ey was pretty well ruined for work at this point, and watched her carefully.

When nothing of interest appeared on the street, the skunk turned slowly to scan the room. Her eyes shot wide open, and ey followed her gaze out into the scant crowd of patrons. Everything was much as it had been: folks sitting and chatting, drinking their coffee, reading or doing work. She, however, seemed to be focused in particular on a middle-aged man walking from the back of the shop where a door opened onto patio seating.

"Fuck," she said, then shouted, "*Fuck!*"

She darted around the coffee table, knocking against it hard enough to send both of their drinks spilling across its surface, and grabbed eir hand. "Go, Ioan! Go, *go!*"

"What?!" Ey scrambled to eir feet, eyes darting between True Name and that oddly familiar man walking towards them. "Where?"

"Home! Anywhere!"

It didn't seem open to discussion, and enough of her panic had built up in em by now that ey quickly stepped from the sim to home, yanking True Name along with.

To home and chaos.

There was a flurry of activity down the short hall from the entryway, several instances of May blinking into and out of existence, along with several more of the same man they'd seen at the shop. She was forking close enough to each instance of him to exercise the collision algorithms of the sim, knocking him this way and that to keep him away from her. She was screaming, "Get the fuck out! I am not her! Get *out!*"

"May!"

A few of the skunks looked over to the door, and then suddenly another was beside em, grabbing eir free hand. With a wrenching sensation, a sudden change in light and sound and gravity, the three of them stumbled out of Arrowhead Lake's default entry point.

May pulled her paw roughly free of eir hand and whirled to face them, shouting, "What the fuck did you do?!"

Tugging her own paw free, True Name darted away, looking around wild-eyed. "How secure is this place?"

"I think May and I are the only ones who even know it-"

She quickly ran a few paces into the woods, peering between the trees.

"Ioan," May growled. "What the fuck just happened? Why the fuck was he in our house?"

Ey shook eir head, trying to dislodge the dazed confusion. "I don't know. He was at the coffee shop, too. Who even-"

"Guōweī," she snapped, then shouted up to True Name, "Why the fuck was he in our house? What did you do?"

The other skunk had shifted from her near feral crouch to standing, rigid and staring up into the branches, a look of dire concentration on her face.

When she didn't answer, May began pacing and muttering—

whether to herself or through some sensorium message, ey couldn't tell.

Guōwēi. The assassin. The reputation analyst who had killed Qoheleth in the middle of his speech.

A quick prowl through eir memories lined up face with name.

Eventually, True Name's shoulders sagged and she stumbled down from the trees, Ioan and May both watching her, wide-eyed. She kept walking past them, past the trail, down onto muddy beach, then out into the water. The short waves lapped up against her legs, soaking her slacks, and still she kept walking. She walked until the lake had made its way nearly up to her waist.

And then she screamed.

It wasn't a shout, no words were behind it. It was a scream of pure, unrestrained emotion, though whether anger, fear, frustration, or something else, ey could not guess.

Then she turned around and waded back toward the shore, stumbling once or twice, until she gave up and fell to her knees, water up to her waist once more. She beat at the surface of the lake with balled-up fists, growling and crying. Finally, she stopped, slouching over until she had to catch herself on her hands.

May's fury, which until that point had been burning hot in her expression, was replaced by something more complicated. Anger, yes, but anxiety and fear as well. "True Name," she said, voice more under control than it had been. "What happened?"

"They are gone. They are all gone. Someone is trying to take me out," she said between heaving breaths. "Trying to get rid of me."

"What? Why?" ey said.

There was no answer from the skunk.

"Who, then?"

She shook her head numbly. "I do not know. There is a small list that we have been keeping our eye on. There are some reactionary elements that have been growing louder. I need to think. I need to...but..."

They waited, tense.

"But all of my instances are gone. Two merged back, one sent a message that she would be late, and then nothing."

"*All* of them?" May asked. "How many?"

"One hundred and eight."

At that eir partner let out a startled laugh. "Jesus Christ, True Name."

Again, no answer.

"Well, who would even know where your root instance was? Or all of your other instances, for that matter?" Ioan asked.

"My root–" She tried to stand so quickly that she stumbled again and had to catch herself. "You have to be fucking kidding me."

Her eyes went blank, and she frowned out toward nothing, though tears left tracks down her cheeks.

May looked to Ioan. "What does she mean?"

Ey couldn't tear eir eyes off the other skunk, and it took em a few seconds to even work up the concentration to reply. "Shortly before we left, one of her two merges said that Jonas was looking for her."

Part II

Conflict

To hone is too trade ends for perpetual perfection.

The danger in ceaseless memorialization is how close it lies to idolatry. To elevate the dead to such a status as false god (for what being that is limited to the perfection of memory is not false?) is to ceaselessly perfect the imperfectable.

From *Ode* by Sasha

Ioan Bălan — 2350

True Name, having gathered her wits about her at least enough to trudge out of the lake and fork herself dry, requested directions to somewhere she could think alone. Ioan gestured down the path toward the rock, explaining that it'd be far enough away that they wouldn't hear each other if she didn't want a cone of silence, but that she'd still be able to see them at the entry point if anything happened.

"I need to think. No one from the stanza is replying, I am not sure which friends I can trust, and I definitely do not want to speak to Jonas," she explained, then rubbed her paws over her face. "Or perhaps I just need to sulk. I will return in an hour."

She bowed to em and May then trudged off down the path.

May glared after her down-tree instance with her paws bunched into fists and ears canted back, then whirled on Ioan, waving a cone of silence into being.

"Ioan, I am not at all happy," she said, voice frigid. "I know that none of this is your fault except inasmuch as you have been meeting her for coffee, but I am having a hard time keeping my anger to myself."

Ey took a long breath, ran eir hands through eir hair, and paced in an abbreviated line before her. "I know, May, I don't blame you. I'm completely baffled. Go ahead."

"I spend two hundred fucking years trying to get away from that life, from all of her fucking schemes," she said, voice quickly rising in volume. "And then I spend the last three trying to calm down so that I quit burning up whenever I so much as think about her, and now this. Look at us! Hiding in the woods from assassins. *Assassins!*"

Ey averted eir gaze from her. Nothing ey could say would help, and ey knew some remote part of emself was feeling much of what she was, too.

"Her and fucking Jonas are still doing whatever the fuck it is that they do, and now they are doing it to each other. Every time I think I can just settle down with you and get away from that, it just seeps right back in. I know that you were trying to do right by us, meeting up with her, but I really, *really* wish you had not."

"May, I–"

"At least tell me what happened there."

"Right. We met up as usual. She was looking pretty terrible, and when pressed on it, she said she was struggling and wasn't comfortable elaborating. When asked about Secession Day, she said she and Jonas were going to have, in his words, a gathering. She said her instances were going to merge down for this and that one of them said he was looking for her. She kept getting anxious and looking around at everyone there, and then jumped up, I guess when merges stopped coming. Guōwèi came in from the back and walked right toward us, then we stepped home and grabbed you."

May crossed her arms and watched em pace and talk, her expression softening, though the frown remained. "And that is it? No talk of these...what, reactionary groups?"

Ey shook eir head. "None today, none in the past. It seems like something she'd keep close to the chest."

"And it was in a cone with visual ACLs on secure?"

"Yeah."

"But Guōwèi was still walking right for you?"

Ey nodded.

The skunk looked down to the ground, brow furrowed. "I suppose if he knew she was there, that would be proof enough.

I imagine a place like that chooses to display it as blurred out rather than completely hidden."

"I guess," ey said, though the words lacked conviction to eir ears. "Then she grabbed my hand and told me to go."

"She grabbed–" She hesitated, mastered a sudden swell of anger, then subsided. "It makes sense, I suppose. The chance that you would head someplace that she and Jonas could not guess is greater than if she had chosen. Ioan, my dear, you are pacing a hole in the path."

"Sorry, May," ey said, trying to stand still. "It's just a little nuts."

The skunk sighed, held out her paw to em, and gave her best smile. "I know. I am really fucking confused and really fucking pissed, I do not imagine you are feeling much better. Would walking help?"

Ey took her paw in eir hand and nodded. "Please."

Remembering their promise to stay in sight, they walked slowly back and forth along the short stretch of beach near the entry point, still within sight of True Name, kneeling on the rock by the outlet of the lake.

"I am sorry that overflowed onto you for a moment, Ioan. I did not mean to yell at you."

"You're fine, May, you just had some guy chasing you around our house trying to kill you or whatever, you're allowed to be pissed."

She snorted and shook her head. "He had only just arrived a few moments before you. I imagine True Name's fork said something about being with you but not where, so he came to our place and saw someone that looked vaguely like her. Perhaps they wanted it to be as close to simultaneous as possible for precisely this reason and one simply jumped the gun. I am surprised they did not just wait for her. How eager they must be."

"Makes about as much sense as any of this." Ey looked out across the lake at where the other skunk sat, head bowed. "What do we do now?"

"I do not know, my dear. I have had precisely as many assassins after me as you, now, and I do not know what to do about True Name. I guess just stay here for a bit and gather our wits."

Ey sighed, bent down, and plucked at a pebble on the bank until it came free of the sand, tossing it into the water. Anything to keep from spiraling back into anxiety. "I'll have to go back and clear the house at some point. I'll lock down the ACLs to us and any immediate guests."

"I do not imagine you will find much there, now that we are gone, but I appreciate you doing a sweep all the same. I have some concerns about our privacy."

Ey frowned.

She waved the idea away with a paw. "If it is an issue, we will discuss it. If it is not, then I do not want to think about it any further."

"Well, if you say so."

She leaned against eir side, resting her head on eir shoulder. "I am sorry, my dear. It is one of those things that is not a concern until it suddenly very fucking is."

Ey ruffled a hand through the fur between the skunk's ears, then settled eir arm around her shoulders. "I'll tell you what all I find there, and we can both hope it's nothing. What will you do, meanwhile?"

"I am not sure. I do not particularly want to come with if they are looking for someone who looks like me. I will stay here and I guess keep an eye on our...ah, guest."

"You sure you'll be okay with that?"

There was a long pause before the skunk gave in and slipped both of her arms around eir middle, burying her face against eir shirt. "I do not know," she said, voice muffled and small. "I thought that I would be, was going to *say* that I would be, but I really do not know."

Ey rested eir chin atop her head. "Well, I don't think I'll be gone all that long—five minutes, maybe—but if you need, just send a ping and I'll be right back."

"I am not expecting anything so dramatic. I will stay here and try to de-stress. True Name still has about half an hour left of...well, whatever it is that she is doing."

Ey tightened eir arms around the skunk for a squeeze, kissed her atop the head, then stepped back. "All the same, just stay safe, alright?"

She sniffled and nodded. "You too, my dear. Good luck, and do not die."

Ioan wasn't sure what ey was expecting, stepping back home. Certainly all of the instances of May had quit as soon as they'd left, and hopefully that meant that there wouldn't be any more reputation-analyst-*cum*-assassins lingering around. All ey could hope is that ey wouldn't find any core dumps, just in case one of them had somehow killed one of her forks. It was vanishingly unlikely, given that the virus embedded in those symbolic objects—the syringes and knives and who knows what else—had to be tailored to whoever the target was.

Unless they're after the whole stanza or the whole clade, ey thought, lingering in the entryway, straining to hear any sounds coming from deeper within the house. The entryway took the form of a short hallway that led into a large, rectangular room comprising a den, dining room, and kitchen, and at least the space directly ahead of em was clear.

This is stupid, ey thought. *I should just clear the whole place of everyone and completely reset the ACLs.*

Curiosity won out, though, and ey set up a cone of silence above emself, set the visual ACLs secure, and then crept into the den. Ey'd be utterly silent and, as far as ey could tell, simply a blurry shape within a blurry patch of the room, though ey'd never tried the new features here at home.

Ey just had to hope that was enough.

Peeking around the corner revealed an empty den, though the clear evidence of a struggle remained: pillows and couch cushions were tossed about, a glass of juice had been knocked over on the table, and most of May's notes had been scattered in a crazed ring around her desk.

The kitchen and dining area were also empty. Other than the chairs around the dining table knocked askew, there was no damage.

The bedroom was similarly empty, bed still neatly made and a few of May's better origami creations untouched on the windowsill.

It wasn't until ey made eir way out onto the balcony to check the back yard that ey found anyone.

A tall, sandy-haired man sat in one of eir Adirondack chairs, cheek rested on his fist as he stared dozily out into the yard. It had been nearly twenty-five years since ey'd interviewed Jonas, and ey hadn't seen him at all in the interim, but nothing seemed to have changed about him. He was still polished to a gleam, every aspect of him still oozing confidence, still, as both May and True name had described him, perilously handsome.

Ey dropped the cone warily.

"Long time no see, Ioan." He grinned, nodding out to the yard. "Lovely place you've got. So few people keep those good, full-bore winters anymore, you know?"

Ioan lifted eir hand to bounce him from the sim.

Jonas lifted his hands, palms up. "Hey, it's okay. I'm just here to talk. Mr. Qián left after you and your partner did. Some dramatic stuff all went down all at once."

"Jonas," ey said, standing well back from him. "What are you doing here?"

"Just waiting on you, mostly. I wanted to check and make sure you and May Then My Name were alright."

"Check..." Ey shook eir head. "Why would you care about our well-being? You just sent an assassin to our house."

"Only to tidy up loose ends," he said, leaning back in the chair again and using the well-shined toe of his shoe to knock a bit of snow off the railing of the balcony. "I trust you've stashed your skunks away somewhere safe?"

" 'My skunks'?" All of the stress of the last forty-five minutes that ey'd been holding back around May, all that had been obscured by eir need to get from point A to point B as quickly as possible, all of it came crashing down on em at once. "'My skunks'?" ey shouted. "Jonas, what the fuck? You sent a fucking assassin after True Name, sent him over to our house so he could hound May. What the hell are you even talking about? Of course I'm going to keep my fucking partner and friend safe if you're going to try killing them! Fucking...'my skunks'. Good Lord."

Once ey'd finished and was left panting, Jonas sat up in the chair and grinned widely, clapping his hands. "Mx. Ioan Bălan, such language! I didn't know you had it in you! Bravo."

"Fuck you too."

That grin lingered as Jonas gave a hint of a bow. "Very well, Ioan. To your concerns, the bit with May Then My Name was unintentional. Our plan kicked off early and one of True Name said that she was with you. While I was pretty sure that meant your little coffee shop, I figured I'd stop by just to make sure. Guōwēi got a little excited when he saw May Then My Name, thinking it might be his target. She's quite good at fighting, your girl. You have my most abject apologies. We should've just waited."

"And True Name?"

"Ah yes your...ah, friend, was it? Your friend and I had a meeting this afternoon where I was hoping to deal with all of that quietly and efficiently. Ah well, can't win 'em all, can you?" He picked at his fingernails, looking the very picture of boredom. "106 out of 109 isn't too bad, is it? Two merged down before I could get to them, so I guess that leaves just the one. Changes things a bit, doesn't it? On to plan B."

"Plan A being to kill one of the most well-known members of one of the most well-known clades on all three Systems?"

"Yep!"

Ioan gaped at him. " 'Yep'? Just...yep?"

Jonas laughed. "That was the easiest one out of the bunch,

I'll admit. I've got all the way through plan M, though, so don't worry, I've got it covered."

"Fine. Enlighten me. What's plan B?"

"Well, it starts here," he said, nodding toward em. "Where I bring you on as an amanuensis one last time while True Name and I hash things out. Now that she knows, I can't exactly do away with her. She's almost certainly told some of her friends by now, so that changes the game."

"And you need me to sit and listen to you prattle on at her?"

"Yep, basically. I need you to witness and write about what happens and leave the rest of it to the grown-ups."

Ey scoffed.

"Sometimes mommies and daddies fight, Ioan," Jonas said, then winked. "So. You're on as amanuensis. Go and tell True Name to ping when she's ready and we'll have our meeting. Oh! And bring May Then My Name and End Waking with, if you can, yeah? The whole stanza will be there."

"Why on Earth would I–"

"And no assassins, promise. I only mixed up a batch for True Name, no one else. No one's going to die, we're just going to have a talk and hash out some new boundaries, and you're going to watch and write it up at the end."

"And why should I believe you on that?"

He shrugged. "You don't have to, but I am telling the truth, Ioan. If you and True Name don't show at the very least, you'd better plan on not leaving home or wherever you're staying ever again. Just because I *didn't* mix up some syringes for you doesn't mean I *can't.*"

"That's pretty dramatic."

"I don't have the training your pretty little skunks have," he shot back. There was something vaguely feverish about him, running a little too hot. "Just try and get everyone together and we can get this over with. There's no huge rush. Sometime within the year, okay?"

"Why?" Ey shook eir head. "Why do you need to talk with

her and why do you need an amanuensis? You have to give me something, here."

"No, Ioan, I don't," he said. "Just tell True Name that I'm waiting. You can ask her all the questions you want."

"Alright, fine," ey growled. "Anything else?"

"Nope! That's it for me. You can go back to your hidey-hole and get all smoochy with–"

Ioan completed the gesture ey'd suppressed since the beginning, bouncing Jonas from the sim. Ey held back the urge to scream out into the yard just as True Name had done earlier at the lake.

Ey sent May a quick I'm-okay ping, then started riffling through the perisystem architecture for information on how to completely sweep a sim. There was nothing in there ey could find about checking who was swept, but it was still possible to sweep everyone who didn't currently have their home set to the current sim, and to receive explicit confirmation that this had been completed and how many instances it affected.

Focusing on the set of steps required, ey triggered the sweep, then checked the log that it had left, eyes-only, for em in the architecture.

Seventeen swept.

"Să-mi fut una," ey mumbled. Ey'd checked the whole of the inside of the house, and could see no footsteps out in the snow, so unless everyone was hiding under the balcony or up on the roof, ey'd clearly missed at least some of them inside.

Now wasn't the time to be thinking about it, though.

Ey spent the next five minutes locking down and fine-tuning the ACLs for the house. By the time it was done, the house would only let em and May in as owners along with anyone they intentionally brought with them by hand. It was also now marked as invisible to all but a short list of allowed individuals. Debarre, End Waking, True Name, A Finger Pointing, Douglas, and a dozen or so others ey could think of who might conceivably want to know when they were home.

At last, ey stepped away from home and back to Arrowhead Lake.

May was sitting on the shore of the lake, knees up to her chest with her arms hugged around them and chin rested atop. Ey rarely saw her sit that way with the pressure it put on the base of her tail, but when the skunk got truly lost in thought—or truly upset—she'd fall back on old habits at the expense of her body.

Ey walked over to sit down beside her, sliding an arm around her waist. "That's all done."

The skunk nodded. "Thank you, my dear."

She'd clearly been crying, given the tear-streaks on her cheeks and the hoarseness in her voice. Ey tightened eir arm around her and kissed at the side of her muzzle. "I'm sorry, May."

"It is not on you, Ioan," she said, voice suddenly tight. "All three of us can be sorry about the situation, but you are the least to blame of all of us."

Ey couldn't think of anything to say that wouldn't just make her feel worse, so ey just helped her scoot closer and lean more heavily against em to take the pressure off her tail.

"True Name just got up," ey said after a few minutes. "I'll have some stuff to say when she's back. Jonas was at the house."

May winced and nodded, scrubbing her paws at her face to wipe away a few fresh tears. "Okay."

"And I'm sorry to add on more stress, but I told you I'd tell you if I swept anyone while I was there, and the report says I swept seventeen instances."

"Seventeen?!" The skunk groaned into her paws as she rubbed at her face again. "They have been busy."

"Who was it? The report didn't tell me."

"Bugs," she said sourly. "Little spies. People who fork to be small enough to hide on top of cabinets or behind pillows. Spy cameras that can think and act."

Ey blanched. "From Jonas?"

"Yes, and probably some from the clade. Some from the first stanza hired by him or True Name however long ago."

"And they just listen and watch?"

"Creepy, is it not? I probably should have been more proactive about when I first moved in, but I did not think either of us interesting enough."

"Very creepy," ey muttered. All of their talks, all of their discussions and jokes and arguments, all of their pleasant silences and moments of intimacy, all being watched. "What a nightmare."

She nodded. "I am sorry, my dear. If it is of any consolation, they may not have been there the entire time, and I assure you that we really are quite boring. We have only had a few conversations of note over the last twenty-seven years, and the rest must have been excruciating to sit through."

"Or incredibly awkward."

The skunk gave em a quizzical look, then laughed. "Gross, Ioan."

"Not me! Them!"

"Yes, yes. I agree, awkward. But here comes True Name, no need to be more awkward than we already are."

They stood up and brushed off their pants as the skunk came trudging around the last bend in the trail, looking utterly exhausted.

"Thank you for giving me the space," she said, bowing. "And my apologies for the trouble of today."

"It's not–" Ey caught emself up short and shook eir head. "Well, are you okay?"

The skunk shook her head. "I am not, no. I am very nearly on the edge of collapse. I feel like I could either sleep for three days straight or cry for three days straight. Both, if it were possible."

May took a deep breath, held it for a slow count of three, and very carefully let it out. "I am sorry, True Name."

True Name stood rigid, jaw working as she clenched her teeth in an effort to maintain control. After several long seconds, she sniffled, opened her mouth to say something, then shook her head and bowed deeply.

Watching nervously, Ioan fiddled with the hem of eir vest. So much had happened in the last hour and a half, and now this exchange between eir partner and her cocladist was enough to start that anxiety rising within em again. With True Name trying her best not to cry openly and May clutching tightly at eir arm, both of them interacting with each other was a different sort of stress than the assassination attempt, but no less intense.

"True Name," ey said carefully. "There's no rush, but Jonas was there at the house. We can talk about it later, but I figured I'd give you a heads up."

The skunk gave up on maintaining her expression and hid her face in her paws, nodding. "Thank you," she croaked.

Once she'd washed her face and calmed down enough to speak, the three of them set to work deciding what the next steps were. May suggested they stay at the lake for the night, explaining that they'd need time to sort out a living situation for True Name and that she wanted to go over their place with a fine-toothed comb before spending the night there again, anyway.

True Name merely nodded. "Is there a place here that I can stay?" she asked.

May winced and shook her head. "It would be camping. We can make that work for tonight if we can scrounge up some gear, but a long-term solution is not feasible. This is not our sim and we do not have ACLs to build here or remove any unwanted visitors."

She nodded. "I understand. I will dig–"

"You will stay with us," May said quickly, as though rushing to get it out before second-guessing herself, a sentiment echoed in her expression.

Both True Name and Ioan stared at her until she wilted. "I am sorry. I know that things have been difficult between us and that a large part of that is on me, but that does not mean that I do not want you safe. If we have a place that we have complete control over from ACLs to building, that is safer than this security-through-obscurity abandoned sim, and our proximity will discourage further attempts on your life."

"I can mirror the house, I think," Ioan said, once the shock had worn off. "That'll get you a bedroom and furnishings."

The skunk looked as though she was fighting off another wave of tears, but she nodded. "Thank you both. I do not wish to impose, but I greatly appreciate your help in the interim."

May nodded in turn. After a moment's silence, she turned to Ioan and said, "My dear, can you see if End Waking can help us out with some camping supplies? I do not trust our place enough to go back and create obvious camping goods."

"Me?"

"Please." She sighed. "I do not think I have the wherewithal to do so, myself. I do not want to go and cry in front of someone else. I do not want to feel like I am begging, even if help comes willingly."

Ey hesitated, nodded, and sent End Waking a sensorium ping requesting a meeting, which was quickly acknowledged. "Alright," ey said, forking off a new instance. "Back in a few."

End Waking and Debarre were waiting for em at the new entry point to his sim.

"Hey, sorry for the short notice."

End Waking bowed. "It is no trouble, Ioan."

"You taking up camping?" Debarre asked, grinning and leaning in to shake eir hand.

"Uh, no, not quite," ey said. "There's been...well. Our sim isn't guaranteed safe at the moment."

They both perked up at this.

"Not safe? What does that mean?" Debarre asked.

"I don't want to get too much into it," ey said, thoughts racing. "But needless to say, May and I aren't safe there. Some really dramatic stuff happened and literally no one is happy."

End Waking rested a paw on Debarre's shoulder before the weasel could speak again. "Perhaps you can expand on this soon, but for now, what do you need?"

"I will, I promise." *And apparently I need to if you're to come with,* ey added mentally. "We need stuff to camp for the night at Arrowhead. We can't make anything there, and May's worried about us going back home to procure anything that might tip folks off."

The skunk nodded, looked thoughtful for a few seconds, and then waved his paw, bringing into being between them two folding camp cots, two bedrolls, a tent, two bundles of firewood, and some simple food—bread, salami, and cheese.

"I will come help you set up," he said. "It is all fairly straightforward, but tents require four paws."

Ioan sighed, nodded. "Thank you, End Waking. We'll, uh...we'll need three sets, though."

He paused in the act of bending down to lift one of the cot-and-bedroll combos. "You will need three?"

"And two tents."

Apparently unable to hold back any longer, Debarre spoke up. "Ioan, I'm gonna go crazy if you don't give me at least something, here."

"As am I," End Waking said.

"Right. Well, sorry in advance for the stress." Ey paused to collect eir thoughts. Adrenaline seemed to have burned through much of eir energy reserves. Not yet 14:00 and ey was feeling exhausted. "Jonas tried to assassinate True Name and made her think it was about some 'reactionary elements' or something. He got all but her root instance, and that only because we were out for coffee at the time. He and his assassin also paid our home a visit and they were going after May in the confusion, so we're hiding at Arrowhead for the night."

Silence. Silence but for the sound of a nearby waterfall and a few far-off birds.

"Well, fuck me," Debarre said at last, rubbing at his temples. "May Then My Name and True Name are stuck together?"

Ey laughed, surprising even emself. "Yeah. Assassins and

politicians and whatever, and the weirdest thing about it is seeing them talking."

End Waking stood a while in thought, then waved his paw again to create another cot, bedroll, and tent. "I will help you set these up, but I will not speak with her."

"Are you sure, E.W.?" Debarre frowned down at the gear. "I mean, I guess it's fine giving them stuff, but I'm not exactly comfortable with you being anywhere near her."

The skunk nodded. "I need to, my dear. I need to be better to her than she might be to me in this situation."

Ioan frowned. Ey wasn't so sure that the True Name of 2350 would be so callous, but now didn't seem like the right time to argue the point.

"If you say so," Debarre said sourly. "But I'm staying here."

After a moment's concentration, a second End Waking stood beside the first. "I will be staying with you, my dear, do not worry. No need to risk more than a fork."

Ey bent down to pick up the two bundles of firewood while the new instance of End Waking picked up one of the sets of gear and held out his paw. Ioan took it in eir hand and stepped back to Arrowhead Lake. They dropped off their loads, then returned to pick up the second two bundles and the tents.

End Waking set to work immediately, picking out a flat spot in the trees to set up both tents. Ioan was pleasantly surprised when they turned out to be fairly modern gear—at least, modern to the 2100s—thin nylon with carbon fiber spars and a seal-strip entrance which was kept sheltered by a fold in the fabric. The camp beds were of a strong fabric lashed to carbon fiber frames by some springy cord, providing a reasonable amount of give. The bedrolls turned out to be sleeping bags with foam pillows that expanded quickly when the seal-strip was undone.

Throughout the whole process, May, True Name, and eir down-tree instance sat by the edge of the lake, far off to the side. Ey couldn't tell if they were simply being silent or if they were talking in a cone of silence, but, other than a brief nod to

End Waking from May, they seemed keen on taking the space for themselves.

Once the tents and camp beds were set up and Ioan had been shown where and how to start the fire, End Waking bowed politely and said. "We will talk soon, Ioan, I am sure. Until then, please keep you and yours safe."

Ey nodded and returned the bow. "Thanks again, End Waking. You've been a huge help today, and yes, we'll be in touch."

When the skunk had left, ey quit and merged back down to eir root instance.

"Well, that's us settled for the night, I guess," ey said. "We've got stuff for sandwiches, if you're hungry."

Both skunks shook their heads.

"Alright," ey said. Ey wasn't either, ey realized. The tail end of eir anxiety just had em jittery, wanting to keep moving. Once ey set that aside, ey realized just how exhausted ey was.

They sat in quiet well into the evening, instead, each of them trying to digest the day in their own way.

———————

"This has been far and away the worst Secession Day I have had," True Name said.

Ioan and May both snorted, then worked to finish their bites so that they could apologize.

"Sorry, True Name," Ioan said. "I don't know if you had a lot planned, but I'm glad you at least made it through."

"It is okay to laugh. There is little else to do in the face of it." She smiled weakly. "I am sorry that you two have been dragged into it along with me."

"It's alright."

"Well, not alright, necessarily," May added. "But I am glad that you are not dead."

"Thank you, May Then My Name. I do appreciate it."

They fell back to silence, then, Ioan and May self-consciously finishing their sandwiches while True Name simply stared into the fire. She had made herself half a sandwich, explaining that she wasn't terribly hungry, and had yet to touch it.

Once they had finished, the skunk sat up straighter and said, "I think that I have had sufficient space from it, now. Can you tell me what Jonas said?"

Ey shrugged. "Not a whole lot, all told, especially given how much he talked. He said that he wants to meet up with you to discuss next steps and that he wants me there as an amanuensis so that I can write another book."

She tilted her head. "You?"

"Yeah. He said...well, let me start from the top. He said he was waiting there for me to make sure that May and I were alright, that he was there to tidy up loose ends, and that, uh..." Ey hesitated, unsure of how well Jonas's next comment would go over with either of the Odists. "And that he trusted that I'd, and I'm quoting here, 'stashed my skunks away somewhere safe'."

Both May and True Name bridled at this, likely for similar reasons.

"Sorry. I kind of blew up at him for that."

" 'Blew up'?"

"Yeah, just yelled at him for sending assassins after you two—he confirmed that Guōweï mistook you for her, May—and told him to fuck himself." Ey shrugged helplessly. "I was pretty upset, I guess."

"I am surprised that you stuck around long enough to listen to him, my dear," May said. "He sounds like he was in rare form."

"I mean, I don't know what he's like the rest of the time, but he was doing a really good job of being as insulting as possible. The 'my skunks' part. 'I don't have the training your pretty little skunks have', he said, and 'sometimes mommies and daddies fight'. All these little things."

True Name ground the heels of her palms against her eyes. "I am sorry that you had to go through that, Mx. Bălan. It does indeed sound like he was in fine form. Did he explain his reasons for having you along as amanuensis at all?"

"Just that he needed me to witness and write about what happens and leave the rest to the grown-ups." Ey thought back and shrugged. "That was most of what he said. He wanted to talk with you, wanted me to witness, and wanted the whole stanza there."

May frowned. "Including me?"

"Specifically you and End Waking, yeah."

"Why would I trust him on that?"

"I mean, I don't," ey said, tossing a twig at the fire. "He said no assassins, but who knows what else he has planned. And it does sound like he has it planned, by the way, that plan A didn't pan out, so he moved on to plan B, that he had up through plan M."

"And nothing else?" True Name asked.

"That's about it. I swept him after that. Swept the whole place."

The skunk's ears splayed to the sides. "A preemptive apology is likely in order."

"Yes, it probably is," May said, voice low and flat. "Loss For Images?"

"Yes. Her and Even While Awake." She bowed formally. "I apologize, you two. It was decided prior to Launch to observe those involved with the project and not aligned with us."

"Those were *your* spies?" ey asked, some part of em unwilling to believe, rebelling against the rest of em, which was thinking *of course they were.*

"Yes. I Am At A Loss For Images In This End Of Days and And I Still Dream Even While Awake rode shotgun in May Then My Name's fur and have been living there since, swapping out forks as needed. Again my sincerest apologies."

"How many?"

"Instances?"

Ey nodded.

"Five. One in the den, one in the bedroom, one extra in the kitchen, one on the balcony, one in the yard."

"Who were the other twelve, then?"

She tilted her head quizzically. "You swept seventeen? Those were likely Jonas's, I imagine, there to watch his plan unfold."

May's voice was steeped in sarcasm as she spoke. "Find out any juicy details?"

Her cocladist held up her paws. "There is no excusing my actions. I know that there is little that I can do to earn your trust, May Then My Name, and at this point, even I suspect that I do not deserve it. There were few details of note enough to report back to me. We knew of your career changes. We knew of your...your feelings towards me. We...well, they learned about the Artemisians early on when you got your letter from Castor, though in the last decade, the reports that I have received have decreased in number, which I attributed to a lack of interesting goings on. That they did not report on that letter is a red flag I should have paid attention to sooner."

Ey shot May a questioning glance, but she shook her head. *Perhaps she really doesn't know about Codrin and the Name,* ey thought.

"And why did you not?" May asked instead.

"Pay attention to the red flags?" True Name stared at the fire for a long few seconds, then shrugged. "I was overworked and being fed bad information."

"You overworked yourself, you mean. 108 forks! Did you synchronize daily?"

"Of course. Why would I not?"

"How are you even still sane?" Ioan asked. "I'm surprised you aren't jumping at shadows, at this point."

"I am sure I will be now," True Name said.

"She is not sane at all, my dear," May said at the same time.

They frowned at each other.

I'm glad End Waking gave us two tents, Ioan thought. *It's been civil so far, but...*

Aloud, ey asked, "So, what's next? We head back tomorrow and build you a room, but then what?"

"What is next is that I try to salvage what I can from this. I imagine that my options will be severely limited if I am to continue existing as I am and still meet Jonas's demands, but that does not mean that I will set my goals aside."

" 'Continue as you are'?" May growled. "I cannot believe–"

There was a moment of tense silence, her jaw working as though straining to hold back some larger outburst.

Once she'd mastered it, she said in a tightly controlled voice, "I am going to stretch my legs."

"Be safe, May," ey said quietly, watching the skunk stand and stomp off toward the lake.

True Name watched her estranged up-tree instance with nothing but exhaustion in her expression.

"I'm sorry, True–"

She waved a paw at em. "Please, Ioan, this is not your fault. It is not your battle," she said curtly.

They sat in silence then, each of them looking into the fire, neither making eye contact with the other. For eir part, ey spent the time doing eir best not to kick emself for jumping right in to fix things. Ey knew perfectly well not to apologize for May, and yet there ey'd gone and done it.

Ey couldn't guess what the skunk was thinking.

Eventually, she stood from her log and bowed to em. "I am sorry, my dear. I did not mean to get short with you. It has been a terrible day."

"Oh, uh," ey stammered, flicking eir gaze her way. "It's alright. I think we're all pretty messed up right now."

"Well put," she said. "I am going to try and sleep. Which one is mine?"

Ey pointed her toward the tent with one cot in it and watched her slip inside, then sat and waited for May to come back, staring at the fire and trying not to feel bad enough for the three of them.

Everyone was off in the morning. Tired, grumpy, sore.

The narrowness of the cots had frustrated Ioan and May throughout the night. They *could* both fit on one, but only if they straightened out rather than their usual tight curl. At one point, they tried dragging the cots to be side by side, but the frames against each other made a hard ridge that was impossible to rest on comfortably. In the end, they'd fallen asleep, each on their own cot, facing each other with arms tangled enough to get at least some contact through the night.

Whether or not True Name had actually slept seemed up in the air. She had shrugged noncommittally when asked, but it certainly didn't look like she had.

Conversation was equally awkward. May apologized stiffly to her down-tree instance over breakfast of further sandwiches and True Name accepted graciously enough, but then they fell back into silence.

After breakfast, there was little else to do but head back home. They left the camp set up. Ioan couldn't begin to guess how to take down the tents, given how distracted ey'd been while End Waking had been setting them up. *Besides,* ey reasoned. *Best to keep them around just in case things go sideways.*

They decided to leave forks behind in case anything went wrong, then Ioan took each of the skunks' paws and stepped back home.

True Name immediately wrinkled her nose at the sight out the picture windows into the back yard. "Snow?"

"Ey is some sort of masochist," May said, *sotto voce.* "You will have to forgive em. Ey is working on it with Sarah."

So out of place was the humor that it took em a moment to catch up. Ey laughed tiredly and shook eir head. "For theatre nerds, you guys have no imagination. Coffee?"

May leaned up and dotted her nose against eir cheek. "You, my dear, are an utter delight."

True Name followed them into the den. "Please. I am going to fall over if I do not have something."

May flopped down onto her usual beanbag and rubbed her paws over her face while True Name sat quietly at the dining table and Ioan made coffee. "If it is alright by you two, I am going to take a shower after coffee, as hot as I can stand," May said. "And then we can work on the addition."

"Sure. I can start by mirroring our room and then stripping personal items while you're getting cleaned up."

"Thank you both," True Name said, tracing a claw along the wood grain on the table, an incredibly familiar gesture from years of living with May. "Again, I mean. I really do appreciate all that you are doing. Perhaps we can discuss boundaries and expectations later, but I am also looking forward to a shower."

Ioan nodded, finishing up the coffee prep—eirs black and both of the skunks' sweet and creamy—and carrying the mugs to each of them. "I guessed," ey said, setting one down in front of True Name. "Let me know if you need anything different."

Ey sat down carefully by May and held both of their coffees while the skunk scooted in close against em as usual before handing hers over. It felt good to be back in a more comfortable setting, back where ey and May could could at least get close, even if everything still felt nerve-wracking.

They drank in silence for a while, minus a thank you from each of the skunks, the three of them doing their best to uncringe from last day's worth of anxiety.

It worked a little too well, perhaps, as ey had to nudge May awake to finish her coffee and shower, and the prospect of levering emself out of the beanbag felt out of reach. All the same, ey needed to at least get the other room created, then perhaps the three of them could nap.

Once May was on her way to the shower, ey stood, finished eir coffee, and began to work. Ey dumped a series of intents into the sim. A doorway cut itself out of the wall opposite the one to eir own bedroom. A room extruded itself beyond the doorway, filling itself with all of the very same stuff that eirs and May's contained. The sim's boundaries whined in protest at not having enough for the windows to look out on and, too tired to think of any other options, ey mirrored the view of the yard as well so that True Name's room looked out over yet more grass and dandelions.

If she stays for any real length of time, maybe I can just mirror the rest of the house and she can have a full setup.

That was enough for now, though. Ey got started going through the room from top to bottom, wiping it of eirs and May's presence. Anything that wasn't the bed, the nightstands, and any other furniture was evaluated and either left for its decorative value or swiped away to nothingness. A damp May joined em partway through the exercise, and by the time they were done, the room was left clean and neat, sparsely decorated without being oppressively empty.

"Hopefully it's not too bleak," ey said once May had fetched True Name. "I gave you some ACLs over the space if you need to make or recycle anything. Just let me know if the room itself needs changing."

She stood silent and still for nearly a minute, leaving em to fidget while May looked on, frowning.

Finally, she cleared her throat and said hoarsely. "This is more than enough, my dear. I do not know why you two...but, well, I should get cleaned up and then we can talk proper. I am perhaps a little too emotional for that at the moment."

May sighed, nodded. "At your own pace."

They both bowed and backed out of the room to let True Name shut the door behind her so that she could shower. May took eir hand in her paw and led em over to the bean bag to get comfortable once again.

"You okay?" ey murmured, once she was properly nestled against em, head tucked up under eir chin.

"I am tired, Ioan. I am tired and I am stressed and I am...I do not know. Conflicted, perhaps."

"How do you mean?"

She shrugged. "It is much easier to hate from a distance, especially when one is built as I am."

"To love?"

She pressed her face against eir chest, sighed.

Ey wanted to ask her how well that fit her monologue, that idea that to be built to love is to be built to hate yourself. Ey wanted to go back sixteen hours or however long it had been and kick Jonas's ass. Ey wanted to go back twenty-four hours and warn True Name, to go back three and a half years and warn the True Name ey'd first gotten coffee with.

Instead, ey said, "You're a good person, May."

She tightened her grip around em. "Thank you, my dear."

When True Name finished her shower and grooming, looking far more herself than she had since the month before, they sat around the dining table to hash out boundaries.

"I do not want to impose on you more than I already have," she began. "I will certainly stay out of your private space, and I figure a closed door is a plain enough signal to be left alone. Should I stick to my room for the most part?"

May let out a snort of laughter. "I am sorry, True Name. I do not mean to laugh, but I have never heard you so deferential in my life."

The skunk canted her ears back. "I am in shock, May Then My Name. My coworker of two centuries just tried to kill me. My life's work has been cut off from me. I have been invited to stay with one of the two up-tree instances of mine who dislike me the most, and I have never had to live with anyone before, not since before we uploaded. The offer remains for me to dig my own sim."

May bowed her head apologetically.

"I'd feel better if you stayed," Ioan admitted. "It'd be too easy for you to either disappear into your new sim forever or wind up with another attempt on your life whenever you left."

May nodded readily. "You are safer here where no one can act openly against you. It may not be the most comfortable of situations, but I would also prefer that you not die."

"Good points. Both of you. I would prefer not to die as well." She straightened up in her chair and smiled, a hint of that confidence showing through. "So, to my question. Do you have any thoughts?"

"Closed doors means don't bother, stay out of each others rooms. Cones of silence and secure visual ACLs to be respected," ey said, then shrugged. "But I think that's all obvious stuff. I don't see any reason for you to stay out of common areas, I guess, and I'm fine with you eating with us, too, but I also freely acknowledge that that's me speaking. I don't want you two, uh..."

"Fighting and arguing should be avoided, yes," True Name said with a slight bow of acknowledgement. "It is your house, though, and I know that our relationship is fraught. I will defer to May Then My Name, given the power dynamic and social restrict–"

"I promise that I will not try to pull out all of your fur or bounce you so long as you give us space when either of us ask, okay?"

The skunk blinked a few times, then smiled cautiously. "Understood."

"Wait, that easy?" Ioan said.

"Not everything need be complicated, my dear. Boundaries are most often found by crossing them. We will have negotiation ahead of us as well, I am sure." May shrugged, adding, "This does not make our relationship any less complicated, but endlessly refining rules ahead of time will only stress all of us out."

"I guess," ey mumbled. "I just don't want you at each other's throats."

"If we fight, we fight," she said. "But if we are to be stuck together, then we will fucking get over it and have a civil house, at the very least. I will do all of the exercises Sarah has given me at once if that is what is needed to keep home from becoming unbearable."

True Name nodded in agreement. "I will do what I can to

keep things comfortable and be out of your hair as soon as this is resolved. We will work it out if one of us gets upset. That includes you, Mx. Bălan. Please voice your concerns when they arise."

Ey shook eir head. "Alright, alright. Only concerns I have right now are taking a shower and a nap, then. I'll trust you two to make things work and will try not to mediate every single little disagreement."

"Excellent. About fucking time," May said, patting eir hand. "I will join you for the nap and try to be up for lunch."

"Naps all around," True Name agreed. "Again, thank you two."

The next few days felt careful. They weren't walking on eggshells around each other, it was not a worry of offending, but they all seemed to be hyper-aware of each other's presence in the house.

Ioan and May called out from their performances and when A Finger Pointing asked why, May spent half an hour locked in the bedroom on a silenced sensorium conversation. Ioan received a very sincere note soon after wishing all three of them well. While she'd never spent much time worrying about the things True Name did, A Finger Pointing's tireless desire to be friends with everyone did not exclude her cross-tree instance.

For her part, True Name spent much of the first day silent in her room, though whether that was to sleep or to salvage the situation, ey couldn't tell. She poked her head out around dinner and said that she was too tired to join and that she would see them in the morning.

Ey couldn't blame her. Even with the two hour nap before lunch, Ioan felt groggy and disoriented for the remainder of the day. *I'm becoming like May,* ey thought. *I don't sleep well alone, or even separated by camp bed frames.*

All three of them slept in late the next morning, Ioan only rising at nine when ey received the gentlest possible sensorium ping from True Name.

Ey found her in the kitchen, standing in front of the coffee machine, looking baffled.

"I am sorry if I woke you, my dear. There are more buttons on this than I know what to do with."

"It's alright. I went through a coffee phase years ago and wound up with this. I usually just tap here...then here...and then this last one for three cups."

She bowed. "Thank you. I would complain, but it does make good coffee."

The skunk looked so much like eir partner that ey had to stop emself from reaching out to ruffle her ears. Ey disguised the motion as leaning back against the counter and rubbing the sleep from eir eyes. "Good coffee's a necessity. Sleep alright?"

"Well enough, yes. It has been a few days since this instance has had the chance, so it was starting to build up."

"Days? Good Lord. I don't know how you can do that."

"Anxiety, caffeine, and 263 years of practice."

Ey laughed. "I don't know, I think it might be a you thing. May seems pretty fond of it."

"An improvement, then," she said, grinning. "Mugs?"

Ey showed her where they kept the mugs, then the cream and sugar for doctoring coffee and spoons for stirring. Once the pot finished brewing and all three cups had been poured, ey excused emself back to the bedroom with eirs and May's coffee to finish waking up with eir partner.

And so it continued. They would speak in the morning and over dinner, perhaps a few times throughout the day, but otherwise, they worked on their own projects. They'd say good morning to each other, say good night to each other, say polite things in passing. Little of it felt like it was done out of kindness, but rather out of a need to remain cognizant of each other's presence, to keep a semblance of peace through performative normalcy.

Even the weather felt careful. The snow first melted and then was replaced when a new storm lay down a delicate few inches.

It was the third full day since their return when the spell was broken. Shortly after lunch, True Name stepped into May's field of view, bowed, and politely requested a conversation with her.

The skunk frowned and beckoned her over to the couch.

True Name apologized to Ioan, then set up a cone of silence with secure visual ACLs.

Three days was just long enough to start building up the scaffolding of habits, such that Ioan was left anxious and jittery when they were jostled. Seeing it from the outside for the first time, ey was left with a slight sense of disorientation from the way the cone blurred both the occupants and the background, the edges of its boundaries unnervingly sharp.

There was nothing to be gained from watching the indistinct shapes within. A quiet conversation had them simply looking like two black forms against the relative brightness of the balcony. Ey couldn't see expressions, couldn't see but the most grandiose of body language.

And yet ey watched, slipping over to the kitchen to clean, or at least dream up some chore that needed doing there, just so that ey could keep an eye on the cone.

It was boring, and that it was boring only drove eir anxiety higher.

The conversation lasted nearly an hour, and when the cone dropped, ey was greeted once again by the sight of the two skunks. To say that neither looked happy missed the mark: True Name had a dullness to her expression, something between hopelessness and resignation, while May looked apoplectic. She'd clearly been crying quite hard at one point.

Ey ducked around the kitchen counter as quickly as ey could. "May? True Name? Are you–"

May waved a paw dismissively and blipped out of the sim. There was a sensorium ping a moment later, a view of Arrowhead Lake.

"What just happened?"

True Name shrugged, the movement looking as though she

was struggling against dozens of gravities rather than just one. "I explained what has been happening."

Ey frowned, feeling eir own anger rise out of anxiety. "Well? What's been happening? I don't exactly like seeing her that upset."

"No, I imagine not." She sighed and slouched against the back of the couch, rubbing at her forehead. "I explained the shift between Jonas and I over the last twenty-five years. I explained the last few weeks."

"And pissed her off."

She rolled her head to the side, enough to get a sidelong glance at em. "I am sorry, Ioan. I cannot be the only one to know these things. I have had all of my existing support removed. All of my forks, all of my cocladists, most of my friends. I have had to cancel all of my appointments with Sarah. It is small consolation, I am sure, but I have left May Then My Name angrier at Jonas than I think she ever was at me."

Ey blinked and straightened up. "At Jonas?"

She let her head slip back down off the back of the couch, looking down at her paws. "I cannot tell you, Ioan. Not yet."

"Nothing?" Ey shook eir head. "Sorry, True Name, I'm not asking you to betray a secret or anything. I'm just worried."

"I understand, my dear." There seemed to be more coming, but she sat for another minute or so, just staring down at her paws on her lap.

"I'm sorry, True N–"

"What was it that he said to you? 'Sometimes mommies and daddies fight'?"

"Wait, but...what?"

She shrugged again, slowly rolled up off the couch to her feet, swayed for a moment, then walked off to her room, the door snicking shut behind her.

Debarre — 2350

The next few days after Ioan's visit and brief explanation about what had happened with True Name were full of long walks and longer silences. End Waking politely requested that Debarre remain behind for the majority of the walks.

There was a sense in the air that the skunk wanted to ask him to leave again, to fall back into solitude and, though he'd never use the word around him, moping. He'd still talk, still hold up his end of the conversations, but always there would be a slight pause before speaking, always a bit more distance than usual, always something out in the forest that called to him just that much more strongly than the weasel before him.

It was never comfortable to be asked to leave one's partner. He knew the reasons, could understand the drive, but to build a relationship up over however many decades it was now, and yet still need to put it on hold for months or, on one occasion, years at a time still hurt.

He knew he had a temper, too. He'd spent the last centuries going all the way back to Cicero's death working on setting that aside when he could feel it getting too hot within him. He always worked his hardest at that around End Waking. He loved the skunk, wanted nothing but the best for him, and although he knew that End Waking was one of the more resilient Odists, he had also known Michelle far longer than...well, just about anyone possibly could, now. Two and a half centuries was a long time to understand just how the other person processes pain and trauma, and he didn't want to add to any of the Odists' burden, having spent so long with them from the beginning. From before the beginning, in some senses.

Well, except perhaps True Name.

There were few enough people he hated in the world, though certainly a great many who grated on his nerves. True Name and her ilk, though, were universally among that number. He knew he could never hurt anyone, but, well, everyone had their fantasies. He knew he should never wish harm befall anyone, but some people...

This latest development was putting this to the test.

He'd continue the work on the cabin while End Waking went for his walks—they'd gotten the floor and stove in place, as well as the A-frame, but the canvas of the tent still needed to be strung, and he had a few ideas for improvements—and all the while, he'd swing steadily between the poles of feeling nauseous at the thought of one less fraction of his friend in the world, one more death of one of the lost, and wild fantasies of popping champagne upon hearing that her final instance had been destroyed.

Part of him wondered if End Waking was going through the same. He wanted to ask, but didn't want to risk that pushing the skunk over into requesting that he leave with the tent not yet complete.

So, Debarre just kept working, kept fantasizing. He'd gotten the last of the canvas lashed down over the sides of the frame and was on to working on the front wall of the tent. At least there was productivity to lean on, even if he couldn't lean on his boyfriend at the moment.

He jumped, startled out of work and reverie by two sensorium pings in short order. The first came from End Waking, the word 'company' muttered quietly, and the second was a ping of arrival from the sim itself.

With the new tent, End Waking had made the default entry point around a small rise from home, leaving it a short walk around—or a shorter but much steeper dash up and over—the ridge.

Debarre opted for the up and over, nearly tumbling down the other side of the hill to where the form knelt in the clearing. End Waking was just making his way through the trees on the opposite side, so they converged on the visitor at the same time.

May Then My Name was sobbing. It looked as though she had been for a bit, too, judging by the mess of tear-tracks in the fur of her cheeks.

There wasn't much that he could think of to say, so he awkwardly shifted from a crouch to a kneeling position beside her, wrapping his arms around her shoulders and gently tugging her against him. Although he rarely had reason to comfort May Then My Name in particular, it was familiar enough from all the way back at the Crown Pub when Sasha'd come back from some break-up or another.

"I will get water," End Waking murmured, leaving the physical comfort to someone better able to provide such.

Her cry must have been nearing its end before she arrived, as she'd settled down to sniffles by the time her cocladist arrived with an enamel mug of water and a damp rag.

"Can you drink, May Then My Name?" he said gently.

She nodded and accepted the mug with both paws to hold it steady, taking a few unsteady laps of the water before simply clutching it to her chest. "Thank you," she croaked, freeing up a paw to use the damp rag to wipe her face. "I am sorry for so dramatic an entrance."

"Hush. You are fine," End Waking said. "Everything sounded quite dramatic indeed. Please take your time, and we can discuss it later."

She nodded, slouched a little further against Debarre, and sighed shakily.

He shot a quizzical look over to End Waking, who sent a brief sensorium ping in return. She must have explained a good bit more before arriving, then.

They sat like that for another five minutes or so, another few bouts of tears hitting the skunk while he tried to be as steady as he could for her, petting over her ears and murmuring reassurances. She'd leaned on AwDae more often than she had on him, all those years ago, but a friend's shoulder was a friend's shoulder, and he'd always offered when he could. This was, he supposed, no different.

When she was finally able to pull herself together enough to walk, Debarre helped her to stand and the three of them made their way back to the tent. He sat her down on one of the two fallen tree trunks that had been set before the tent to either side of the fire pit, then took her mug to refill it while End Waking started a small fire. It wasn't that cold out, but warmth was warmth, comfort was comfort.

With the cup safely back in her paws, Debarre sat beside May Then My Name once more, arm around her shoulder. "Feel up to talking about it?"

"Um, a little, maybe," the skunk said, voice raw. "Just in general."

He nodded.

"True Name has been staying with us the last few days."

"Sounds miserable.

She smiled halfheartedly. "Ioan expanded the house out to the other side with a separate bedroom. She has been spending most of her time in there, doing whatever it is that she does. Perhaps she is still pulling strings somewhere, I do not know. I do not particularly care."

"I'm surprised you let her move in there," he said sourly.

After a long pause, the skunk mumbled, "It was my idea. I insisted, Ioan agreed."

"Why?" End Waking asked from where he crouched beside the fire.

"I have incomplete thoughts. In terms of logistics, it made sense to have her where Jonas could not act against her."

End Waking nodded. "Yes, but why? Why did you not just let her build herself a new home? Leave her to her own devices until time, Jonas, or madness took her?"

May Then My Name averted her gaze. "I do not want her to die. I do not want her gone."

The other skunk went silent, staring at her for a long moment before getting back to building the fire up to a comfortable level.

"I'm guessing it's the non-logistical side of things that's complicated," Debarre said.

"Yes. I seem to be cursed to think about her and after everything, I do not know why it is that I care about her." She sniffled and scrubbed her face with the rag as though to preemptively snap herself out of an oncoming wave of emotion. "It has not been all that bad, really. Awkward, yes, but she spends most of her time in her room except at breakfast and dinner. Today, though, she requested to talk with me, and...I cannot even begin to comprehend the specifics, but Jonas has...ha-has been..."

Debarre rubbed at May Then My Name's back when that wave of emotion finally washed over her.

"I am sorry, Debarre. It was a lot," she mumbled. "Jonas has been playing her for centuries now. He has been structuring her life for her in such subtle ways that even she was not able to see it. She...well, something happened a few years after launch. A trap of sorts. Jonas's plans hit all at once and she has been working under his thumb since then."

They sat in silence for a bit, Debarre racing through various questions, rejecting each as too personal, too mean, too off-topic. Finally, he asked, "So, why are you so upset?"

"That is where the specifics I cannot mention lay. Beyond that, though, I am just...torn. I am torn. I want to kick her out. I want to invite Jonas over and have him bring his pet assassin. I want her to disappear into ignominy." She took a deep breath, continued, "But I also want her to get out of this mess. I may not want her around, but I want her to find something—anything—

else to do with her life and to not have to deal with that living, breathing sack of shit anymore. No one should have to deal with that."

"E.W. said he needed to be better than her. Sort of like that?"

She shrugged. "I do not know. It does not feel accurate for me to say that, but I cannot explain why."

"Well," he said, waving the point away. "I'm with you on the feeling torn bit, at least. Was just thinking about that when you showed up. Like, would I celebrate if she died? Or would I feel like there was just that much less of you around?"

"You think about it from the outside, my love," End Waking said. "You think about who we were. You have the capacity to do so. May Then My Name and I have diverged so far from True Name that she has become a new entity, and I do not think that we can so easily see Sasha in her."

May Then My Name nodded toward End Waking. "And that is the source of at least some of my resentment towards her. I cannot see Sasha in her, and yet I was created from her. I see that of Sasha in myself, the caring side of her who got lost looking for lost friends, and while I can *remember* those few years that I was True Name, I am not that person. I do not feel like I ever was that person. Becoming me was waking up from a dream."

"A nightmare, perhaps," the other skunk murmured.

"You and I have different resentments. I would say an unnerving dream that makes me all the happier to be what I am now."

"You are a better person than I."

Debarre threw a twig at his boyfriend. "No moping. You're both good people. Jury's out on True Name, but given that you two get so fucking upset whenever she's around, I'm leaning towards not so good."

End Waking smiled. It was slight, but he was pleased to see it all the same.

"Qoheleth, poor, stupid man that he was, had much that he was correct about, but one thing that he completely failed to understand was growth," May Then My Name mused. "There is plenty of growth, here. That is perhaps the one thing we have more than memory, the one thing that protects us from too much memory. All that time may still drive us mad, but at least we have the ability to grow to the point where we are no longer True Name."

"A-fucking-men."

She laughed. "Right? Thank you two for talking, though. I know it is not really a pleasant topic, but it has helped me immensely."

Debarre squeezed her around the shoulders. "Of course, skunk."

"You feel so much more than I do," End Waking said. "So I cannot understand the ways in which you are torn. There is also much more than I think you are saying–"

"There is, yes. Sorry."

"–and so I cannot offer much in the way of advice, but I can welcome you to my forest and offer you company and a meal. Will you be staying for dinner?"

"I would like to, yes." She hesitated, then added, "True Name has joined us for dinner these last few days, and I would like a break."

"Are you opposed to an early dinner, Debarre?"

" 'Course not. If you cook, May Then My Name and I can get the cot in the tent.

They broke from there. May Then My Name forked several times over to help him in repopulating the inside of the tent with the necessities while End Waking made venison cutlets and savory corn griddle cakes.

"There's still a lot we need to do in here, so we can't drag everything in yet," the weasel explained as they returned to where End Waking's goods were stored under a canvas tarp. "But getting a few essentials in here will help in the meantime. Hopefully just a few more days and we'll be all set again. I think E.W. may kick me out at that point."

"So soon?"

"He called me back in the middle of a solitary spell, remember?"

She nodded. "Well, yes, but I had hoped that...well, I am sorry, Debarre. I imagine it must be difficult."

"A little. I miss him when I'm gone, but I usually merge back down and get to focusing on whatever #Tracker is up to, then re-fork when he's up to having me around again."

"We are different in that respect, I guess. If Ioan requested six months of time away from me I think I would have a pretty rough time of it."

He laughed and ruffled a paw over her ears. "I think you'd fucking explode. Thankfully, ey doesn't seem like the type."

She nodded gratefully. "Ey does not, no. I am just sorry that I was too heated to stick around and talk with em about this. Thank you again, Debarre. I needed to talk about it, just with someone who has an appropriate distance from the topic. I cannot overstate how terrifying what she said was."

"Uh, of course, May Then My Name. Can you tell me any more about it?"

"Perhaps over dinner, my dear. I need food, and I need to talk to your boyfriend."

Dinner, it turned out, was not long in coming. Well-seasoned deer and griddle cakes cooked in the grease. "I have made them with too much salt just for you, May Then My Name," he said with a polite bow.

She stuck her tongue out at him. "Much appreciated. It tastes almost like normal food."

He made a rude gesture at her, but grinned all the same.

"So," Debarre said between bites. "Anything else you can tell us about what True Name said?"

The other skunk stacked a bite of griddle cake on top of a bite of venison and chewed thoughtfully. At last, she sighed, saying, "I do not want to talk about too much of it, not aloud. It is too close to the surface as yet and I will turn into a sobbing mess. Again, I mean."

"Of course, no rush."

"Right. Well, Jonas got her involved with something in the late 2130s. It was sort of a side...thing, very hush-hush but it still has taken up at least a small part of her attention ever since. It was all very low-level stuff—low enough that it flew beneath even her radar—and I guess after Launch, he dropped it all on her in a meeting similar to what he had promised for Secession day. All that time had turned into a lever to use against her, and I think that, whether she realizes it or not, relatively little has been done of her own accord since then here on Lagrange."

Debarre nodded, waiting for her to say more, to which she eventually shook her head. "I am sorry. I need at least a few days to be able to process it. I cannot even think about it without wanting to...I do not know. I want to quit and force a merge on her. I want you to force a merge on her," she said, nodding to End Waking. "I want her to know something other than herself."

The skunk sat up straighter. "So you have hinted, yes. Why, though? Why would you want her to feel that resentment? Why do you think she would be able to internalize my penance? Why the fuck do you–"

"E.W.," Debarre murmured. "Cool it."

He tugged his hood down lower over his head and stayed silent for several seconds. "I am sorry, May Then My Name. I did not mean to yell. It is just that I worked hard at getting where I am now, and if she is to feel any—any—remorse about what she has done with her life, I would like for her to come by it honestly, and if she does not, then I would like her to face the consequences of her actions."

"I do at least understand that," May Then My Name said cautiously. She had shied away from her cocladist at the force of his words, but the apology and explanation drew her back. "You do not need to answer now, or ever for that matter, but is it something you would at least consider?"

"Perhaps. I do not feel the need to engage with her as you

seem to, but there is little enough engagement in merging down. If I had not made my rejection of what she is a part of my identity, if I could let that go, then I would rescind my membership from the clade just to sever what ties of association remain."

"Would you just be End Waking of no clade, then?"

"Perhaps I would just call myself E.W., my love."

Debarre grinned. "Excellent."

"You two are disgusting," May Then My Name said. "Please keep up the good work."

"You're one to talk, smartass. You and Ioan could make my teeth rot."

"I have em well trained, do I not? Perhaps I will make em an honorary member of the clade in your stead."

End Waking smirked. "Would ey take my name, then?"

"No, we would have to give em a similarly Odist name. Some silly line of poetry, a few nonsense words smashed together. Gentle Confusion or something."

They laughed.

"Where I Am Overcome By Gentle Confusion of the Ode-Bălan clade," Debarre said. "And I'd be something like Even Real Shitheads Know Their Dreams."

May Then My Name flicked a crumb of griddle cake at him. "Good job on the first name, not so much on the second. I do not think it fits the tone very well, even if you are a bit of a shithead."

"Confirmation at last," End Waking said dreamily.

Having sent May Then My Name home with a few extra griddle cakes and then run out of daylight, Debarre and End Waking gave up on any additional work for the day. The tent was livable, if incomplete, and a bit of a break felt nice, anyway. They sat beside each other before the fire and watched the flames, not speaking, simply enjoying the warmth and each other's company.

At least, Debarre enjoyed the warmth and the feeling of his boyfriend beside him. He couldn't tell what End Waking was thinking or feeling. He'd not said a word since wishing his co-cladist goodbye and good luck.

"Thanks for letting me stay, E.W."

"Mm? Of course, my love. I am glad for your help and your company."

He nodded. Silence fell again. End Waking put another log on the fire.

"I know that I am a less-than-ideal partner, Debarre. I *do* love you, I promise."

Here it comes. "Love you too, E.W. Want some space after we're done with the camp?"

"Please," the skunk said after a long pause. "I do not like sending you away, but so much has happened this last week, these last few months..."

He scooted closer to End Waking and slipped an arm around his waist. It was probably more affection than the skunk would have preferred at the moment, but he needed at least something to go with that statement. End Waking seemed to realize this, as well, and although he didn't reciprocate the affection, he did at least relax against Debarre's side.

"What do you suppose they are doing on Artemis?" End Waking asked, staring at the fire rather than up to the stars.

"Hmm? My guess is that everyone's getting settled in by now. All those who went along with have probably dug homes or whatever they call it in the fifthrace area, and some are probably getting pretty good at...uh, *Nanon*, was it?"

"Did Debarre#Castor go with?"

"No, actually. He still hasn't told me why, either. He's at least spent quite a bit of time in Convergence. Lots of visiting with Codrin and Dear. Have you heard from them? They've quite a name for themselves there, apparently."

"Only when Dear writes clade-wide. It and I were never as close as we could have been. It sounds happy, at least, and passes on good stories."

He laughed. "I can't imagine anything but, honestly. Any news of the others?"

"Codrin sounds unhappy, and I cannot quite piece together why."

"Really? Like, with eir new job?"

"Oh, no, ey still seems quite pleased with that from the text, but the subtext is that ey is displeased in some other, more fundamental way. I always get that sense when news includes the topic of Artemis."

"What about Sorina, though? Doesn't ey have connections through her?"

The skunk shrugged. "I do not know. These communications are simple family letters or those little quippy snippets that Dear is so fond of. Nothing in depth."

Debarre hesitated, unsure of how to broach the question. *No way out but through,* ey thought, saying, "What about True Name#Castor? Anything from her?"

"Not you, too," he said with a groan. "I cannot seem to escape her today, can I?"

"Sorry, E.W."

He sighed. "No, it is okay. If that is what is happening, then that is what is happening, and we are bound to talk about it. One moment, then."

There was a long silence from End Waking. Debarre imagined him trudging through exos, reading back through clade communiqués that his down-tree instance over on the LV had sent back.

"She remains herself," he said at last. "I mean truly herself, not the bent and twisted True Name of Lagrange. Competent, confident, in complete control. She strives behind the scenes in both Convergence and the rest of Castor as she always has."

" 'Bent and twisted'? I mean, she sounds like she's having a rough time of late, but that bad?"

"This is also subtext, my dear. The True Name of Lagrange no longer writes the same way as the True Name of the LVs. True Name#Castor is as True Name was back before Launch, and

True Name#Pollux has settled down with Zacharias and sits on the Guiding Council, whatever that is. The one here is..." He frowned, visibly hunting for words. "She is no longer what she was. She is middle-management. She is overworked and under-appreciated. She continues on with her plans, to which I assume she still clings tight, but that comes with a sense of desperation that I cannot otherwise place. She is bent and twisted nearly to the point of fatigue, as when one bends a paperclip until it snaps."

"Is that why you think May Then My Name wants you to merge down?"

"To break her, you mean?"

Debarre nodded.

"Perhaps, yes. She shared more with me before she arrived and I do...I do see the reasoning behind her request. What that actually means to her, however, I am not sure. Does she want to shock True Name into becoming whatever she considers a real person? Does she want to break her out of rigidity and make her more complete? Does she want her to move beyond whatever this unspeakable atrocity is through force alone? I do not know."

"Maybe just hurt her without killing her," he added.

End Waking looked at him sharply, then subsided. "Also a possibility. Had you suggested that a decade ago, I would have been quite upset, because I do not think that who May Then My Name used to be could possibly have been so vengeful, but I am not sure that that is the case anymore."

"Is that such a bad thing, though?" Debarre frowned, hunting for words. "I mean, I love her, I think she's one of the best people I've ever met, but she was almost a caricature with how sweet she was. If she can be anything other than head-over-heels in love with everyone she meets, wouldn't that mean that she's a more complete person, too?"

The skunk tensed and carefully scooted an inch or two away from Debarre, gently nudging the weasel's arm from around his waist.

"Shit, I'm sorry, E.W. I didn't mean to offend."

He laughed. A short, sharp bark of a laugh that was more bitter than amused. "Fuck you, Debarre. Fuck you and how right you are."

Debarre blinked, nonplussed.

"You are right. It is terrible that she has to hate someone to be more complete, but you are right. However, my love," End Waking said, grinning humorlessly. "That means—that *must* mean—that the same holds true for me, caricature of penance that I am."

He laid his ears flat, nodding. "Sorry, E.W."

"I do not know what a more complete version of myself looks like. I do not know how to attain that. I have no up-tree instances who have led earnestly happy lives to merge down and complement my fundamentally unhappy one. Perhaps that is why May Then My Name's idea rankles. Should I merge down and True Name learn to repent, learn to become more whole, then she will have done so without the work of actually having done so. Should I become happier, then I must work further years."

"I dunno, is that true? I mean, yeah, she in her current form won't have done the work of repenting. Her body won't have been the one living out here in the middle of nowhere, but she'll have...when did you last merge down?"

"I do not remember."

Debarre squinted. "I don't think it works that way."

"I do not remember, Debarre," End Waking said tiredly. "Sometime before the first centennial."

He held up his paws, surrendering the point. "Then she'll have more than a century's worth of work dumped on her, and she'll be the one who has to process that and try to integrate it. Can you imagine how fucked that'd feel? Can you imagine what she'd become?"

"Do *you* think I should merge down?" End Waking growled.

"I don't know, E.W. I really don't. Let's drop it, though, okay? I'm just gonna keep on hurting you if we keep this up, and I *really* don't want that."

The skunk sighed, nodded, and, after a moment, reached out and took Debarre's paw in his own. "I am sorry I got so worked up. I do need a break from the topic, though. Thank you, my love."

He smiled cautiously and gave that paw a little squeeze.

They sat in silence for the rest of the night, then, watching the fire burn low until the skunk put it out. They stripped down for bed and, for the first time in months, climbed into their cot within their tent—theirs at least until the need for solitude struck full force again. They shared their wordless intimacies and then curled together for sleep.

"You know that she will have memories of this, too, my love," End Waking murmured.

"Let her," he said, yawning. "You're more complete than you give yourself credit for. If the goal is for her to have some semblance of that, let her."

Ioan Bălan — 2350

With May out of the house and True Name doing...well, whatever it was that she did in her room by herself, Ioan was left emotionally and intellectually stalled out, stuck by emself in an empty den. Ey sat for a while on the couch, staring out into the slowly melting snow on the deck and ruminating. Then, giving in to the urge to pace, ey slipped on the boots ey kept for just such occasions and slowly tramped a ring around the outer edge of the yard, first reveling in the crunch of the icy top layer of the snow, then the sweat ey worked up when, on the third lap, the snow began to drag at eir feet, and then finally the solidity of the uneven path ey'd worn down into the snow, a marker of energy spent.

The pacing gave em time and space. It let eir emotions spool out into nothingness while eir thoughts were left crunched beneath the treads of eir boots. Ey didn't know what ey thought about. Ey didn't know what ey felt. Ey just walked.

Ey knew that, at one point, ey wondered if eir command to mirror the back yard for True Name's room meant that it made a new back yard or whether it just mirrored the view out the window. If it were the latter, would she be watching em? Would she be wondering why ey walked? Would she scoff? Would she wish for a way to crush her own worries down into the ice?

And then the train of thought was gone, lost amid some whorl in the steam of eir breath.

An hour's walking gained em sore hips, a sweat-soaked shirt, and a well-trod trail around the outside of the yard.

"Fucking cold," ey grumbled, stomping the lingering snow off eir boots and the hems of eir slacks on the way up the stairs to the balcony. Ey kicked the boots off outside the door and shuffled inside. Ey could fork emself warm and dry, sure, but why do that when there was a perfectly good shower right there?

So, ey lingered under the hot water for fifteen minutes, and instead of whorls of breath, the crunch of ice, the nothingness of slate-gray skies, eir thoughts and emotions dribbled down eir face in rivulets of water, swirled once, twice, disappeared down the drain.

Dissociating, ey thought, laughed to no one.

Brushed eir hair. Stared, unseeing, at emself in the mirror. Dressed in clean clothes—sweater vest? Sweater vest—and wound up sitting on the couch once more.

True Name peeked out of her room and bowed to em from just outside her door. The sound of the door and the movement out of the corner of eir eye startled em back to reality. "Sorry, True Name. Everything okay?"

"Yes, thank you, Mx. Bălan." She smiled apologetically—such a strange look on her. "I am not the greatest of cooks, but would you like me to make dinner tonight? I do not believe May Then My Name will be joining us, and it is getting dark."

"Huh?" Ey whirled back around toward the picture windows and frowned. Sure enough, it was dimming into evening already. "Oh, well, sure, I guess. I'm sure whatever you make will be fine. Sorry I'm so spacey."

The skunk padded into the kitchen and waved the apology away with a paw. "You are fine, my dear. You are allowed to space out. It has been a dramatic few days, so I do not blame you. Can you please grant me ACLs enough to create ingredients?"

After a pause to will it so, ey nodded. "Sure, should be good now."

"Thank you."

Ey felt strange staring out into the yard—the opposite direction of the kitchen—while True Name cooked, so ey grabbed a notebook and moved to the dining table where, should ey be able to pull eir thoughts together, ey could write, and if ey couldn't, ey could at least talk with the skunk without twisting around in eir seat.

Ey could not, it turned out. Ey flopped the notebook shut again and leaned back in eir chair. "What're you cooking?"

"Chicken...rice...stuff. It is college food."

Ey laughed. "Right, I'm familiar. Sounds good. Certainly cold enough out there."

"Of course, yes. May Then My Name would have the same recipe, would she not?" The skunk clattered about for a few more minutes, and then, apparently satisfied, leaned back on the counter behind the stove. "I do not understand your affection for the weather, but I am happy to make warm things while it is about."

"Hopeless romanticism, I guess," ey said. "But whatever. Are you feeling better?"

True Name shrugged, eyes locked in a glassy stare out the windows. "I do not know if better is the correct word. I feel lighter, perhaps, having said what I did to May Then My Name. Conflicted, as well, that I feel lighter and yet she feel the burden of knowledge heavy enough to need to step away. For that, I apologize."

Ey nodded. "She sent me a few brief pings. She's with End Waking and Debarre at the moment. No clue when she'll be back."

"I am pleased to hear that she is safe."

"Now that you've had some space from it, can you tell me any more about what you told her that set her off?"

"I am not ready to get deep into it, Ioan, I hope you understand."

"Of course. I'm just worried. I guess. Did it have to do with her specifically?"

She didn't respond. The skunk's gaze never wavered. Her posture remained relaxed and comfortable, and for that, ey felt all the more anxious.

"Well, maybe you can tell me what spurred the conversation?"

"Right, yes," she said, deflating somewhat with a sigh. "What do you believe, Ioan?"

"Excuse me?"

"What do you believe? You do not strike me as religious, but surely you believe in something. The sanctity of life? Love? Art?"

Ey sat up straighter, frowning at her. "That's a surprisingly difficult question to answer."

"It is not at all surprising. It is easy to provide a noun and say that one believes in that. The irreversibility of time, perhaps? Your cocladist and Dear spoke to that in the *History*."

The conversation was taking a decidedly Odist turn. Coming at the topic sideways, grand statements that came tinged with a sense of awe. They all seemed prone to falling into the style of speaking and ey fell for it every time. "Mmhm. Several times."

"But what does it mean to believe in something like that? Or the sanctity of life or love or art? Or God, for that matter? 'Belief' as a word is a stand-in for a concept so broad as to be intimidating or impossible. One may say as Blake did, 'For everything that lives is holy', but encompassing that within one's mind is truly terrifying." She finally broke her thousand-yard stare out the window and smiled faintly to em. "Still, I believe in what I do, Ioan. Really, *truly* believe. I feel called. I feel led. I am good at it. I wake up thinking about it, spend my day working with it, and fall asleep thinking yet more about it. We have an existence which is fundamentally different from that of phys-side, and I cannot put into words how much I love that. It is more than a want, I have a need so integral to my being for it to continue that I would not be True Name without it, and I love being True Name."

"But now..."

"Yes, 'but now'. But now I am stuck in an impossible limbo built by Jonas. My entire existence these last two hundred years has been defined by a belief that I thought Jonas and I shared, and in a few minutes, he tore it to the ground, burnt the pieces to ash, and then ground the ash beneath his heel." She laughed and shook her head. "So melodramatic, is it not? But that is how it feels to have one's belief turned hollow and stale."

"Do you overflow?"

The skunk had lifted the lid of the pot of rice to stir. If it was anything at all how May cooked it, it was a stiff rice porridge made with chicken stock, cheese stirred in at the last minute— 'poor skunk's risotto', she called it. She seemed keen to use her time cooking to think, so ey waited in silence.

"I do. More frequently and in much shorter bursts," she said, finally. "Every few days, I will walk sims and I will get lost. Well and truly lost. Dear loses control of its tightly directed energy, May Then My Name loses control of that wellspring of love within her, and I lose control of my sense of control."

"Really? Every few days? Is that because you're stretched so thin with all your forks?"

She shook her head and, deeming the rice to be done, slid it off the heat. "I started walking in 2124, my dear. A few years before May Then My Name was forked, back when it cost too much to be so cavalier with forking. It is not so dramatic as your partner's."

Ey nodded. "Were you overflowing earlier today?"

She chopped the chicken breasts she'd sauteed into strips, focusing on the task, then on plating up the food, before responding. "Perhaps, Ioan. Perhaps."

They ate in silence, then. It was interesting picking apart the way the two skunks' recipes had diverged over the years. True Name's was spicier, May's more savory and with more vegetables.

They made it most of the way through the meal before they were alerted to May's arrival by the sim's sensorium ping.

Ioan set down eir fork and slid out of eir chair to greet her as she stepped out of the entryway. Ey was pleased to see her face washed of tears and expression washed of distress. She looked tired, to be sure, but no longer ready to murder someone.

"I brought gifts, my dear. I do not know if–" She paused as she caught sight of True Name.

The other skunk had also stood and was bowing deeply to her up-tree instance. "May Then My Name, I apolog–*hrk!*"

May pressed the waxed cotton-wrapped parcel into Ioan's hands and bounded over to True Name, shoving her out of her bow in order to get her arms around her for an awkward hug. "That is for what happened," she said, then socked her solidly on the shoulder. "And that is for how you told me."

True Name stumbled back from the greeting, blinking rapidly and rubbing at her arm. She looked as baffled as ey felt. Watching May interact with True Name these last few days had been something of a roller coaster, whether it was the abject fury ey saw within her whenever the topic of her cocladist's goals—or perhaps calling—came up or the strange protectiveness that had led her to offer their home to her. Those were stressful enough; this was overwhelming.

Ey shuffled back to the table, slid the packet onto it, and fell heavily into eir chair. "What just happened?"

May laughed and dotted her nose against eir cheek before settling down into her usual seat. "I am sorry that that was weird, and I am sorry that I ran away earlier. I was able to get a lot off my chest, and I feel much better for it. Oh, you did eat! That is okay, I did too, but I think these may make good dessert."

May's nearly manic tone and the tension in her cheeks showed something deeper going on beneath the surface, but given her chatter and the still-shocked look on True Name's face, this didn't seem to be the time to ask.

"May Then My Name, I know that I–"

"If you talk about earlier, I will hire Guōweī myself," May interrupted sweetly. "I promise that there will be time to talk about it soon, but for now, I need something else, alright?"

"Of course," True Name said, frowning. "In that case, what is in the package?"

"End Waking made these corn...pancake...things. Fritter cakes? Something like that. They were savory, but they might go well with honey as a sort of dessert. There are only two, but we can split them."

Ioan and True Name exchanged a glance, then watched as May unwrapped the griddle cakes and swiped a pot of honey into being beside them. She broke off a piece, drizzled honey on it, and ate it.

"Well?" ey asked.

"It is fine. I do not know that it is a dessert. Have you ever had chicken and waffles, my dear?"

Ey shook eir head, reaching for a piece of the (slightly soggy) cake and the pot of honey.

"It is not that, but it reminds me of it. Savory and meaty but also sweet and bready."

Ey frowned as ey chewed on the morsel. Ey could see it being truly delicious if it had not been cooked in venison grease specifically. The gaminess made it a strange mix.

"Good, but not great," was True Name's assessment, to which May nodded vigorously.

They finished the griddle cakes all the same, keeping up the banal chatter. It felt good, ey realized, to talk about nothing. Day after day of serious talks had worn on em more than ey realized, and ey made a silent note to thank May later for forcing them into something more pleasant. The greeting she'd given True Name was weird, but it definitely broke the suspense that had dogged them all week.

After dinner, ey cleaned up the dishes by hand while True Name went back to her room and May settled onto her beanbag, getting a thoughtful look on her face that usually meant she was working mentally.

Once ey was finished, ey settled down beside the skunk, letting her squirm in next to em and get an arm around eir middle. Ey blinked a cone of silence into being over them. "It's good to have you back," ey said, hugging around her shoulders. "What was that all about?"

She snagged eir free hand and put it atop her head. A clearer demand for pets there was not. "Mm? You mean me being a chipper ditz?"

Ey laughed, stroking over her ears. "Well, I was going to ask about the hug, mostly. My guess about you being chipper was to get us to finally talk about something light rather than yet more intense or depressing stuff."

"You are right on that one, yes," she mumbled. "We doubtless have more heavy shit to talk about, but I spent hours crying today, and if we did not break out of that cycle, I would have spent yet more in tears."

"I won't bring it up, then."

"Good." She poked em in the belly, then went back to her hug. "Though as to the greeting, I meant it when I said I got a lot off of my chest. I spent a lot of time thinking and a lot of time talking to End Waking and Debarre, and I have some ideas for moving forward."

"Oh?"

She shook her head beneath eir hand and tightened her grip around em. "I do not want to discuss them now. I am tired and cried out and you are comfortable and good to me."

The next few days passed in relative peace. There were no fights between the two skunks, and while, at least once a day, they set up a cone of silence to talk about whatever it was that True Name had discussed that first time, there were no more instances of May falling apart or True Name wearing herself out quite so badly. The discussions sounded serious, and never quite friendly, but ey was at least somewhat happy to see the two talking without quite so much ire between them.

May wasn't the only one, either. At one point, Time Is A Finger Pointing At Itself and one of her up-tree instances, Where It Watches The Slow Hours Progress visited to talk with True Name. Both were far more earnest in their affection toward her, which she seemed to welcome with a sense of cautious relief. Ey supposed it made sense, given A Finger Pointing's habit of making friends with everyone she could.

Ey'd only met Slow Hours once prior and, while she was just as friendly as her down-tree instance, she also seemed somewhat removed from the world as a whole, as though seeing just a little more than everyone around her. "Clairvoyance," A Finger Pointing had whispered to em after that first introduction. "She has the outline of the world."

They talked for nearly three hours that afternoon, breaking only to get more water part way through. When they were finished, True Name looked wrung out, though not unhappy. A Finger Pointing mostly looked confused and concerned while Slow Hours kept her faraway, nearly delphic smile. Both were patterned after the human Michelle rather than the skunk Sasha, lending an additional layer of uncanniness in their similarities to May and True Name, even across species.

Curiouser and curiouser. Ey'd always pictured A Finger Pointing's stanza as one of the more liberal ones, and had early on noticed that the liberal Odists had largely distanced themselves from the more conservative ones. To have two of them specifically drop by to visit True Name was quite surprising.

The most curious thing, though, had to be May.

It wasn't just that all the work she'd put into her feelings about her cocladist had seemingly paid off—other than a few tense moments, mostly silent, she was at worst distant and at best willing to hold conversations with True Name about a limited set of topics—but that even in those tensest moments, she seemed to at least want to do something. Whether it was out of an earnest desire to improve True Name's life or to simply get this situation over with seemed to vary depending on her mood.

It was her discussions with End Waking that really knocked em off-kilter, though. Her visits to his forest sim came at least once a day, and it wasn't until the fourth that she was willing to share anything about their conversations.

"Wait, what? End Waking wants to merge down? I can't even imagine that."

"That is what we have been talking about, yes. I shared...I mean, I told him what she told me, and it has changed things."

"Are you sure that's even a good idea?" ey asked. "I mean, won't that just make her feel worse if she also has to deal with all of that regret?"

May fiddled with the corner of the top sheet. They'd sat up in bed, the topic not feeling quite right for pillow-talk. "Possibly, yes. I do not think that it would be permanently detrimental. If she has a fuller view of the world, perhaps she will be better able to engage with it with empathy."

Ey held eir gaze steady, frowning. "I don't think you're giving her enough credit on the empathy front."

She clutched the sheet tightly in her fists, visibly counting to ten, then sighed. "Yes. You are right, Ioan. I am primed to see less in her than you, I think.

"I know, May, I'm sorry," ey said, shaking eir head. "I know it's complicated."

She smiled gratefully. "Thank you, my dear. Let me rephrase and say that having that additional perspective will give her new tools to engage with the world."

"Right, that I can see. Given what all has been going on, I'm pretty sure I agree, too, so long as it's consensual between the two of them. I just worry that now's not a good time for it. If she's distracted processing all that when she's supposed to be thinking about what to do about Jonas, won't that put her at a disadvantage?"

"I suppose," she mumbled, then smiled lopsidedly to em. "But we have time, yes? Jonas said within the year, and I imagine it will take us at least a month to convince End Waking to join as requested."

Ey sighed. "I don't know if that's necessarily reason to do it so soon, though. You're right that we should take our time with the meeting and plan as best we can. I just worry about her going in there already a mess because of a ton of conflicts when she needs to be in the best shape she can be."

"You are right, as always," she grumbled, slumping forward to use eir thigh as a pillow. "Thank you for keeping me grounded."

Ey stroked over the skunk's head, toying with one of her ears until she batted at eir hand. "I know I say it a lot, but you're a good person, May. So is End Waking. I think True Name having more of that will only help."

"Do you think she is a good person?"

"Mmhm."

"You answer so quickly. Is it that uncomplicated for you?"

Ey thought for a moment, still combing fingers through the longer fur on top of the skunk's head. "I suppose. I'm not sure why, though. She's complicated, and I disagree with her reasoning for a lot of what she's done, but I don't think that makes her a bad person."

May nodded.

They stayed quiet until they worked their way under the covers again, cozying up for sleep, when May murmured, "I have to believe that she is a good person, or at least capable of being one. For my sake, I have to at least try to believe that."

Ey kissed the backs of her ears and shushed her to sleep.

What kept coming back again and again was the feeling of just how small this project felt—if ey'd been assigned to it as amanuensis, might as well call it what it was. There were so few people involved. True Name and Jonas, then em, May, and End Waking on the periphery. Five people, three clades. It was intimate, in that sense. True Name and Jonas were larger-than-life most of the time, but having been forced into sharing space with her, ey was far more able to see the True Name of today as just someone caught up in a storm and Jonas as the force behind that storm.

And then there was emself, as powerless as Codrin#Castor had felt almost four years back.

The next morning saw both of the skunks more relaxed than ey'd seen them yet. They talked pleasantly over breakfast, and True Name even stuck around, sitting on the couch and watching the snow melt off the balcony while May and Ioan worked, her on her monologue and em reading back through the volume of *An Expanded History of Our World* that focused on the Council of Eight—and the Ode and Jonas clades—in the centuries after its dissolution.

After lunch, True Name returned to the couch with a glass of water and, after a moment's hesitation, May had joined her.

"Why are you spending today out here?" she asked, finally voicing a question ey'd kept to emself until now.

"Honest answer or pithy one?"

"Both."

True Name laughed. "The pithy one is that I am bored and lonely, and this seems to be my best bet at solving either. The honest answer is that I am bored and lonely and, even if the circumstances are not ideal, I want to at least try not to mope in my room all day as I am sorely tempted to."

"You've said you spend most of your time working interacting with your instances, yeah," Ioan said, turning eir desk chair to face the couch. "I imagine it's been pretty quiet."

"Yes. My instances, some up-tree cocladists, instances of Jonas, those of my...friends." The last word sounded almost bashful for reasons ey couldn't place. She shrugged and continued, "And now I am without all of those. No instances, none of my up-tree cocladists are responding, I do not wish to speak with Jonas for obvious reasons, and the relationships I have with my friends are largely bound up in that."

May nodded. "I do not know if we are the ideal company for you, given our interests, but at least we can try, I suppose."

"For which I am endlessly appreciative," True Name confirmed. "Though I do still miss routine. Good company and productive company do not necessarily overlap."

" 'Productive company'?"

"You are very nice to be around. Both of you. It is productive for my mental health, perhaps, and nice to be able to rest, but it is not what I do, May Then My Name. This is not who I am. I am not one to crash at her friends' place, however pleasant they may be."

Ioan could feel an argument brewing. What True Name was saying very likely was true: this wasn't who she was as a person, and now she had been knocked into some new setting. Ey suspected May knew that, even. Ey could see the skunk working on keeping an open expression, despite her cocladist's indelicate wording. Still, there was a thin line to be crossed, and they were edging closer.

"Well, it's better than being assassinated, right?" ey said, trying to lighten the mood.

May grinned. True Name did not.

"Sorry, probably still a bit too soon."

"Perhaps. I would rather be alive here than not alive at all, but it is not an ideal situation for any of us, I think, yes?"

May averted her gaze, but nodded all the same.

"My apologies, you two," True Name said with a hint of a bow. "I am restless and anxious. I do not want to meet with Jonas. I do not want to stay in hiding. I do not want to go back to being overworked, but I am unhappy having no work. Call it an addiction, if you will, but I am nothing if I am not True Name." She bared her teeth in a bitter sneer and, as she continued, her words came faster, hotter, more frustrated. "And why should I not be? I have worked hard to become myself. That I am what I am and unrepentant of that is perhaps a disappointment to many, but it means more to me to stick to what I believe to be true than to-"

"True Name," May said, interrupting the other skunk's tirade. "Wait."

Wrong footed, True Name frowned. "What? Why? I do not-"

May held up her paw, a brief glance at the ceiling hinting at a sensorium message elsewhere.

Ioan frowned as well. Intuition told em the discussion they'd had earlier was quickly moving beyond hypothetical. "May, are you sure-"

True Name jolted upright in her seat on the couch. "What the fuck is-"

"Accept it," May said, and ey could see the full force of all her centuries of earnestness focused on her cocladist; earnestness, kindness, the right tone, the perfect cant of ears and bristle of whiskers, all of it fine tuned to show her just what she needed to see. "It will only help, True Name."

Her face contorting with the strain of holding what must be a very large high-priority merge from End Waking at bay without either remembering or forgetting it, True Name gasped. "May... May Then... Why..."

May's expression softened further, picking up a hopeful smile. "Please, my dear. I think you need this. I think we *all* need this, if we are to move forward, if you are to be able to move past what Jonas wants of you. Please accept. Please."

True Name nodded shakily, attempted a dry swallow, and then let End Waking's centuries of memories crash into her.

The change was immediate and more dramatic than ey'd anticipated. Ey had been expecting a shell-shocked look and maybe a few minutes of silence, but instead True Name's expression melted into a glazed, ischemic stupor. The glass of water she'd been clutching but had yet to drink tumbled to the floor and, as all her muscles gave out at once, she began to slide off the couch.

"Shit. Shit! Ioan!" May shouted.

Ey was already on eir feet and halfway around the table, thankfully in time to catch the skunk before she slid down into the pool of water on the floor. Ey managed to get eir arms under hers enough to hoist her up into the couch again while May ducked around to lift her feet so that they could lay her out on her back.

They both stared down at her.

"Fuck," May whispered.

"What just happened?"

"One moment," she said, waving away the spilled water so that she could kneel by the couch. There was a moment's hesitation before she brushed some of the skunk's longer head fur away from her face. "Can you close your eyes?"

When True Name didn't respond, didn't move, May gently brushed her paw down to close them for her. She leaned closer, whispering a few more questions ey could not hear, though there was still no response.

After lingering a moment longer, she stood shakily, took Ioan's hand in her paw and led em to the balcony despite the cold. As soon as the door shut behind them, she burst into tears.

Ey guided her carefully to the bench swing to sit her down, letting her cry herself out against eir shoulder.

"I am sorry, my dear," she said when she could speak again at last. "Really, truly sorry."

Ey shook eir head, kissing her between the ears. "You don't need to apologize to me. Is she alright?"

"She should be," she mumbled.

"Alright. I'm more confused than anything. Was that your and End Waking's plan?"

She pressed closer to em. "That was him merging back down, yes. We have been discussing it for days, now. I did not expect that, though," she said, and ey could hear that she was on the verge of crying once more. "I never intended to hurt her."

"Can you explain what happened, at least?"

She nodded, swallowing down that wave of tears as best she could. "We are good at forking and merging. Very, *very* good at it. I am pretty sure you know that, though."

"Did something go wrong, then?"

"End Waking has not merged down in more than a century and a half. Even when she merged down when Michelle quit, all she had to do was let the memories fall onto her and then quit herself. He has diverged quite far in that time, as is to be expected, which means the potential for conflicts."

Eir frown deepened. Ey thought ey could tell where this was going. "Aren't those usually just when memories don't line up, though?"

May gave the barest hint of a shrug against em. "You have met her, and you have met him. Their viewpoints are almost diametrically opposed, yes?"

Ey nodded.

"Viewpoints are built atop a collection of memories. That they can share so many memories and yet have such different outlooks on the world and their actions is a subtler, but trickier sort of merge conflict." She paused, took a deep breath, then continued slowly. "I pressed her to accept because I knew that she would accept the merge as smoothly as she always does if there was external pressure. She merged blithely and took on 156 years of End Waking all at once. All of his memories. All of his penance. All of his loathing for what he did, what she was so proud of."

"And it was too much?" ey asked.

Her face screwed up again as she nodded. "I nuh-never wanted t-to hur-hurt her," she stammered as the tears started to flow once more.

Ey got eir arms around her again and held her close. A quick glance through the windows showed that True Name still lay on the couch, breathing shallowly.

"May, I want to ask you something," ey said, once she had calmed down. "And...well, I think it'll probably make you cry again, but I want to make sure we stay open about this. Is that okay?"

She whined quietly, but nodded all the same.

Ey took a deep breath, keeping eir voice as gentle as ey could. "I'm not upset with you, but I need to know since this is just getting weirder and weirder. Are you sure you didn't want to hurt her?"

There was a long silence before she replied. Ey watched her count her breaths, one of the exercises that had worked best to ground her. At least, she counted as best she could between sniffles.

"I think," she started, then cleared her throat. "I *know* a part of me was acting out of vengeance."

Ey nodded. "We've talked about that, yeah."

"Right. I think that part was hoping that it would be a rough merge to knock her down a peg, yes," she said, then let out a shaky sigh. She was starting to shiver from the cold. "I did not think it would be this bad, though. I am really sorry, Ioan. I want to be a good person."

Hugging her tightly to em, ey said, "It's okay, May. We'll just have to see what comes of it."

She nodded, fell back into breathing exercises.

"And I believe you when you say you didn't want to hurt her. Both those–"

She elbowed em in the side. "Yes, yes. Both can be true at once. You know we have the same therapist, right? She says the same things to me."

Ey smiled, pleased to hear the humor in her voice. "Sorry, May."

She wormed her arms around em to give a tight squeeze. "It is alright. You are just a nerd. Both of those things can be true, too." After a moment's hesitation, she asked more quietly, "Can you see her? Is she okay?"

"She's rolled onto her side. Still breathing pretty quick."

May nodded, wiping at her face, though it did little to help her disheveled look. "Let us get back in and check on her, then. We may want to get her into bed. Being comfortable can make it easier."

"True Name?" ey murmured once ey'd crouched beside her. "Can you make it to your room?"

Her eyes remained closed, flicking about beneath her eyelids. There was the tiniest shake of her head.

Ey looked to May, who only watched anxiously, wringing her paws.

Oh well, ey'd lifted eir partner on more than one occasion, ey supposed this wouldn't be too different. Ey slipped eir arms beneath the skunk, though she remained limp. Through a bit of shifting, ey was eventually able to get her leaned against eir chest, head on eir shoulder rather than lolling back, gaining enough leverage to be able to lift her. She was a little lighter, but when ey lifted May, she usually got her arms around eir shoulders, too.

Ey was able to get her into bed easily enough, May holding the covers back while ey did so and then draping them back over her after.

It was eir turn to stand awkwardly by while May sat beside True Name and brushed a paw over her head. "I am sorry, my dear, I thought..." she started, then sighed. "I will sit with you. I am sorry."

Ioan backed slowly out of the room, sliding the door shut quietly behind em. May sounded on the verge of tears once more, but, of all the things ey was not supposed to fix, perhaps least able to fix, this certainly felt like the top of the list.

Part III

Apprehension

For memory ends at the teeth of death.

And so the dead may live on in restless eternity, never knowing peace or the oblivion they so richly deserve. There is no peace in eternal memory, no release in unending remembering.

From *Ode* by Sasha

Ioan Bălan — 2350

It took about six hours for True Name to recover from the merge to where she could stand up and walk well enough to get a glass of water. Her expression remained glazed and she was unable to speak. It wasn't until the next morning that she was able to hold a conversation, though she remained quiet and largely confined to her room, refusing the offer of coffee.

May spent much of that time by her side. Ey wasn't sure what it was that the two did while in her room, if it was just May sitting by the skunk's side, if she was just being present, if the two were having their own quiet conversations, or sharing what affection she was comfortable sharing with a down-tree instance she had resented enough to shock so severely.

All three, ey suspected. Ey checked in on them a few times, knocking and listening for permission to enter. Each time, True Name remained curled in bed with May seated nearby, whether on a chair beside it or sitting up on the bed itself. Ey'd ask if they needed anything, they'd both decline, and then ey'd go back to pacing holes in the rug or the yard or around Arrowhead Lake.

The rest of the time, May was out with em, almost always as close as she could be, whether that was tucked in against eir side on the beanbag, hugging around eir middle from behind while ey cooked, or, at one point, requesting that ey sit on the floor outside the bathroom while she showered, just so that she could talk and, in her words, feel eir presence.

The mood throughout remained somewhere between anxious and remorseful.

That evening, True Name requested that they eat dinner out at the lake rather than at home, saying, "I am feeling too cooped up by walls and yet more walls."

Ey supposed it made sense, now that she had the competing memories of End Waking and however many personality traits that came with. He had only visited Ioan and May a scant handful of times, and then always out in the yard, refusing to go indoors.

So, they packed up a simple dinner of sausages, zucchini, and potatoes to cook and stepped out to the lake.

The tents were still set up and the second bundle of firewood remained untouched, leaning against one of them, so Ioan and May watched as True Name tiredly built and lit the fire. She left them sitting on one of the logs before it, watching the flames go from fast and loud to something quieter and hotter, while she disappeared up the hill into the forest. She returned some time later with a bundle of arm-length sticks, all nearly as straight as dowels, which she built into a spit on which they could roast the sausages while the potatoes baked near the coals of the fire. It was all done with a practiced ease borne from decades of memory.

The food was pleasantly smokey and well cooked, though otherwise unseasoned. True Name remarked on this part way through the meal, saying, "If you call the food bland again, May Then My Name, I will call you lame again."

The humor felt out of place, and certainly went over Ioan's head, but at least it got May smiling again, something she'd not done in more than a day.

"I am pleased that you made it through, my dear," May said. "I will not apologize again, I have done so enough already, but I am pleased all the same."

"I have grown weary of being apologized to, yes," she replied. "And my feelings on the events remain complicated, but I thank you for thinking of me."

"I'm glad, too," Ioan added, unwilling to let the dinner once more fall into silence. "How are you feeling otherwise?"

She shrugged. "Uncomfortable. Fractured. I have spoken to End Waking only a few times since he requested revocation of his access to our secure materials. I knew that he was upset, but not just how, and not to what extent." She sighed, then added, "And now I am left with that."

"Thus 'fractured'?"

"Yes. I must admit that much of my time while down and out was spent struggling to maintain a sense of myself as True Name. Had I simply accepted everything at face value and incautiously, I think I would have gone mad. As it is, I feel perilously close."

May sniffled and looked off toward the lake in the deepening evening.

"I understand what you were trying to do, May Then My Name. I understand why you planned that, how you managed to talk us both into it, and what you hoped to get out of it, but *you* must understand that what you did was set two existences within me. One was set on goals that I believed in—*still* believe in—while the other regrets everything that made me me." The skunk's voice sounded far more tired than angry, enough to keep May from winding up in tears again, though she did set her food aside. "I do not think that End Waking believed in anything. His life was spent un-believing that which he was, which we were."

"What does that leave you, now?"

"I do not know yet, Ioan. It makes me too full of being, of time, to be just one thing. It will likely take me several days to settle into...something. To settle into myself, whatever that now means."

They fell into silence again while Ioan and True Name finished their food and May looked down at her paws or into the fire.

"Thank you for joining me out here. I am both glad to be outdoors and intensely uncomfortable sitting on a fucking log," she said, smiling tiredly. "I do not think that I will stay out here. The greater part of me demands a comfortable bed."

"Those fucking cots are awful," May grumbled, sounding forced in her humor. "Like a hammock, but far worse."

"I do not think that even End Waking enjoys them, so it is easy enough for the True Name part of me to win out on that subject."

"What did he– what do you remember enjoying?" Ioan asked. "I want to hear the good things you have, now, too. I feel like we're all tiptoeing around all the bad memories and conflicting feelings. Tell me something good."

True Name raised her eyebrows, then let her gaze drift up to the brightening stars. "I remember teaching myself to hunt, promising myself that I would start small with snares and then work up from there, thinking that I would not let myself eat until I could eat food that I had caught myself. I remember getting so hungry and weak by the third day that I pinged Serene to see if she could help. She laughed and ruffled my fur and called me a dumbass, saying that she had not included fauna because I had not requested it, so of course I did not catch anything. She brought me a hamburger and I ate it so fast I got sick."

Ioan and May laughed.

"I remember each time I decided to cave and bring into the sim something new. I remember deciding that I needed a more efficient way to heat my tent than just relying on my fur and camp blankets, and then creating the stove. I remember getting so sick of just meat and what few vegetables I could grow at the time and deciding that I would need something like bread or tack for the calories. I remember learning about how hard it was to actually carve a bow and work with metal to create knives and axes, and I remember how it felt to bring each one into existence, a little bit of failure to accomplish a little bit of triumph.

"I remember the eighth or ninth winter out there, when the cold started to feel less terrifying because I knew what to do. I remember waking up one morning fucking freezing, building the fire back up, and shivering in front of it, then laughing for the sheer joy of it. The joy of bundling up, the joy of the air burning inside my nostrils, the joy of discomfort."

Ioan listened, entranced. The cadence of her speech had changed. It still had that well-spoken and dramatic air to it, still held the lack of contractions and all the small doublings-back and anaphora that seemed to come with being an Odist, but it was also more austere than it had been. Less purely functional and more cerebral, perhaps.

"I remember the first time I went a year without seeing anyone, then the first time I went two. That was terrifying. I was sure that I was losing my grip on reality. I decided to make sure that I talked to someone at least once every few months after that to keep myself grounded. I remember when the Artemisians arrived and you two brought your play over, and being utterly delighted at all of the subtle ways you found to insult each other."

May grinned and elbowed em in the side. "That one was Ioan's fault."

True Name smiled and nodded. "You should be pleased with it, my dear. Oh, and I remember tasting whiskey for the first time in years and being surprised at how much it burned. A Finger Pointing's offer to bring a case over was quite tempting. It reminded me that I love the surprise that comes with forgetting things, or at least as close as we can get. The taste of liquor had fallen way back in my mind, and the feeling of the burn of whiskey sent it rocketing right back up to the top."

"That doesn't sound so bad," Ioan said, smiling.

"It is not all unpleasant, not by a long shot. As much as I worked to keep my sense of self while integrating, I was also struck by wonder, and for that, I am grateful."

"Was the merge a net-positive thing?"

She laughed. "I cannot possibly know that, Ioan. I suspect there is no net value, or indeed any value, to be placed on simply having those memories. It will make my life more difficult or it will not, but I do not think it will make it better or worse. I will be what I am to become."

Ey nodded.

"But, May Then My Name?"

The skunk looked nervously at her cocladist, as though worried of some reprisal. "Yes?"

"Thank you for thinking of me."

May only nodded, swallowing back tears.

"I remember a few days ago, too. I remember when you came to the forest, remember watching, awkwardly, while you cried on Debarre's shoulder after I told you about...well, after we spoke. I remember hearing about all of your hatred over the years, about the resentment that you still have for me. I remember how it was that you talked me into this, how helpless I was before it. I remember all of it."

There was no more holding back the tears at that, though she did her best to cry silently.

True Name smiled more kindly than she had yet that night. "But still, you thought of me. 'I do not want her to die', you said. You said that you do not know why you still care about me, and you said that to your cocladist perhaps not yet knowing that I would have that memory as well. You two are both meddlesome brats, but thank you for thinking of me."

May tucked closer against Ioan's side and buried her face in eir shirt to cry, making a rude gesture at her down-tree instance before hugging her arms around eir waist.

"I think that means 'no problem'," ey said. "But I don't speak skunk all that– ow! She bit me!"

True Name laughed. "It is no less than you deserve, I am sure. But come, once you are able to, let us walk to the rock at the end of the lake. I want to see the stars before we head back."

What levity the night had gained slowly faded when they returned home. True Name explained that she had barely slept the night previous and needed to do so urgently, and as soon as the door shut behind her, May's shoulders sagged and she dragged em off to the bedroom. It was still early for them to be going to sleep, but then, ey was certainly tired enough.

They settled into bed, not talking, just resting forehead-to-forehead while ey pet through May's soft fur. There didn't seem to be anything that either of them needed to say, or if there was, not yet something they could.

Eventually, though, they shifted to their usual spots, May tucked back against eir front, and slept straight through until morning.

Ey woke to the quiet sounds of True Name rustling around in the kitchen, mugs being pulled down from the shelves. Ey grumbled, wondering why she hadn't thought to set up a cone of silence, then realized she'd almost certainly left it off intentionally as a subtle way to let them know that she was up. With her memories from End Waking, she almost certainly could be quieter than any of them.

Ey carefully slid out of bed, tucking the covers back over May to let her continue to doze.

"Good morning," True Name said quietly, bowing to em and holding out a mug of coffee. "Black, yes?"

"Morning," ey said, accepting the coffee with a nod of thanks. "Caught up on sleep?"

She shrugged. "A little, perhaps. Unnerving dreams, unnerving memories coming to the fore."

"Hopefully that lessens over time."

"It should, yes. It is already less overwhelming than it was yesterday afternoon." She shook her head. "But I am sure you are tired of that topic after the last few days. How about you, my dear? Did you sleep well?"

"Well enough, I guess. I certainly needed it."

"Coffee," May mumbled, stumbling out of the bedroom, looking disheveled. "You did not bring me coffee."

Ioan snorted and shook eir head. "I just got up, too, May. I've barely had a sip, myself."

"No excuses, only coffee."

"It is on the counter, May Then My Name. I promise I did not leave you out."

The skunk mumbled her thanks and retrieved her mug, lapping groggily.

As if on some hidden signal, they moved to the dining table to focus on waking up, all apparently too tired to do much else.

It was True Name who finally broke the silence, speaking quietly, more down to her mug than anything. "I find myself caught off-guard by the sudden ending of the merge. I have never experienced that with any other merger. Perhaps it is down to individuation."

"How do you mean?"

"I remember going to sleep here, but I also remember going to sleep with Debarre in my arms. I remember waking up with him, working with him through the day, even while I remember us talking to each other, and then I remember your message, May Then My Name, and then everything stops."

May's ears flicked back and she ducked her snout, looking abashed. "I did not think of that. I am sorry. I will apologize to them as well."

True Name lifted her gaze and smiled faintly to May. "I do not think you need to worry too much, my dear. We– they discussed it a few nights ago. It was something of a shock to be used to sleeping alone and also to not have someone in bed with me."

"I think May would explode without someone in bed with her," Ioan said, hoping to keep the mood light.

"It is not *not* true. I do not sleep well alone."

"I have not experienced a relationship as True Name in...some years. Even then we slept in separate beds."

May's grip on her coffee mug tightened and she slouched down further in her seat.

"I didn't know you were in a relationship," Ioan said. "Did you, uh...well, I mean, is that what you two talked about a few days back?"

Both skunks nodded.

"I don't mean to pry," ey added. "Sorry if it's too personal."

After a long silence, True Name sighed. "No, I think you will eventually learn about it anyway." When May's ears flattened, she hastened to add, "At least in part."

Ey stayed quiet. Ey wasn't sure how much to push or back off, whether or not there was some boundary ey should be aware of. It seemed more complex than simply keeping the relationship secret.

"I met a young fox some centuries back." The skunk spoke slowly and carefully. "Red fox, that is, rather than a fennec like Dear. Furries tend to clump together, and I suppose I am no exception. We quickly became friends, then trusted confidants, and then occasional lovers. I did not let us become more than that. There was romance between us, but I was not comfortable becoming romantically entangled in my position."

"That makes sense. I don't know why I thought that wouldn't be the case, actually."

"I have said in the past that you two—that all of those in the clade who have formed lasting romantic relationships—have done something I was never able to," she said. "That remains true. Zacharias and I never quite rose to the level of relationship. Lovers, yes, and perhaps even in love, but never partners. It was always in private, always alone. I had an image to maintain, and that did not include having a boyfriend."

"Did you want one?"

"Pardon?"

Realizing the sensitive nature of the question, ey held up eir hands. "Sorry, I asked that without thinking. I was wondering if you wanted a partner, even if you felt your image wouldn't allow that."

Another long silence followed before she spoke again. "Had you asked me that prior to the merge, I do not think I would have been comfortable answering, but in the context of the memories I now share of Debarre, I think that has changed into a solid 'I do not know'. I do not know if I wanted a partner, because it was more important for me to stay true to my goals than it was for me to think about love, on some subconscious level."

Ey finished eir coffee and toyed with the empty mug, rotating it first this way and then that on the table while ey thought. Eventually, the two skunks fell into quiet, polite conversation, talking about something ey was too distracted to think about.

They both agreed to more coffee, so ey tasked emself with making another pot, hoping that breaking out of the context would give em more room to think.

That True Name felt such a strong need to maintain her image was more than a little alien to em. However, when it came to her not knowing whether or not she wanted a partner, ey felt an almost unnerving level of concordance with eir own life prior to first meeting the Odists, and perhaps even prior to meeting May, years later. Ey did not have an image to maintain or goals to reach for, simply a lack of social awareness that kept em from remembering that having a partner was even a thing that ey could do. Ey and True Name always seemed to have something that kept them from thinking about love until something—May for em and this merge (or perhaps even this conversation) for True Name—suddenly forced the issue.

Ey didn't know what part of em was in charge of making such predictions, but the thought that May, with all her love, might try to merge down with True Name forced itself into eir mind and wedged itself firmly in place. They'd talked about how each of the three skunks were good people some nights back, but in the face of the last two days, ey couldn't think of why, what reason eir partner might even have to do so. A lingering need to force her to experience her own resentment? Or to feel that love? A desire to help her become a better person, whatever that meant? A fit of pique?

Or, no, that wasn't it. It all fell back to the same problem that had been at the forefront of eir mind for months now: that need to fix things. Ey worried that May might merge down with

True Name to make her feel better not necessarily because that's something she might want to do, but because, in the wake of the most recent merge, it's all ey emself could think to do in order to fix this friction.

So silly. It made no sense, and yet this sudden image of True Name as the type of person who might have a relationship, who now had decades of memories of dating Debarre in the form of End Waking, seemed to have set off a runaway train of thought.

"Ioan?"

Ey started out of eir rumination. "Mm? Sorry. Was I mumbling?"

May grinned. "A little, but also you have been standing there for quite a while and you promised us coffee."

"Oh! Shit, I'm sorry." Ey laughed as best ey could to banish any look of the panic ey felt from eir face. Ey brought the pot of coffee over to the table along with the cream and sugar for May and True Name so that they could top up their mugs accordingly.

Ey drifted in and out of the present moment after that, surfacing now and then to do a bit of work or, at one point, to run another sweep of the house at the behest of True Name in case they'd brought any hitchhikers with them. They hadn't, but it was probably a good idea all the same.

The relatively pleasant morning fell again into a vague sense of tension within the house. Ey was sure that ey was the cause of at least a part of it, what with the way May kept checking in on em.

The rest seemed to fall back to True Name, though, who, after coffee, had sagged in her chair and mentioned that she'd been holding some demanding memories at bay. "I need to deal with these or I am sure I will unravel like Michelle," she had mumbled on the way to her room, leading May to put down her work and curl up on the beanbag.

Ey joined her, despite all of the distractions whirling around in eir head. Ey couldn't sort any of them out now, but the least ey could do was comfort eir partner.

All that crying these last few days, I wouldn't be surprised if she overflows soon, ey thought while petting over her ears, a pang in eir chest. *And who knows how that'll work with True Name.*

A simple dinner of pasta, more polite conversation, and then they broke off to their own spaces again, True Name requesting the location tag for Arrowhead Lake so that she could go for a walk "somewhere with fewer right-angles".

It wasn't until they were getting ready for bed that ey pulled eir thoughts together into a coherent enough form to ask May the question that had been nagging at em all day.

"Do you think you'll merge down, May?"

The skunk paused in the middle of tugging off her shirt, leaving just her snout-tip and midriff exposed. "Let me think on that for a moment, please."

They both finished undressing and climbed into bed, em settling back against the pillows and her with her head on eir chest.

"Okay. Now, why do you ask, my dear?"

Ey hesitated. The origin of the train of thought felt impertinent, incomplete, perhaps solely on em. "I'm not actually sure," ey said, fumbling for words. "Maybe a little because you had a hand in End Waking merging down, but I think mostly the talk this morning about Debarre and, uh...Zacharias, was it?"

She nodded.

"I think that made me think of it because until this point, it's all been happening at one layer of remove for me. She's my friend and I like her as such, but she's not my cocladist or family. I'm not in a relationship with her. None of this has been happening with her as someone I'm super close to."

"But if I merge down, she will remember having been in a relationship with you. You will be more directly involved."

"Yeah."

They lay in silence for a bit. Ey didn't know what May was thinking about, but ey kept cycling over just how much ey and eir partner had shared over the last few months alone, all those little bits of affection and physicality when True Name had expressed on more than one occasion that such simply wasn't for her, all the private conversations they'd shared with the understanding that they'd remain such, all the little nothing moments that go into being in love.

"I will admit that I had been considering it," she said, then lifted her snout to dot her nose on the underside of eir chin. "But after the last few days and coming to terms with what that would actually mean for her, I am feeling much more cautious about the prospect."

"Okay," ey said carefully, not wanting to jostle her snout too much. "Can we make sure to talk about it more if you do decide to?"

"Of course, my dear. You and I never shut up."

"Mmhm, best that way," ey murmured, then added more seriously, "I mean the three of us, though."

"We will, Ioan. It would be unfair to all of us not to." May lowered her snout again and tightened her grip around eir middle. "Do you want me not to? You are allowed to say yes."

Ey sighed and placed a kiss atop her head. "I don't know. I need way more time to think on it."

She nodded. "I will give you all the time in the world."

"Thanks, May."

They settled in for sleep, letting the topic drop and trusting that there would be time enough to discuss it, focusing instead on closeness and comfort.

"Ioan?"

"Mm?" Ey'd nearly dozed off, and sleep was still tugging at em.

"I love you. You know that, right?"

"'Course I do, *sconcsul meu.* I love you too."

That, at least, was a pleasant note to fall asleep to, one for pleasant dreams.

While True Name continued to integrate the merge more and more fully—or, as she put it, became more whatever her new self was meant to be—and she spent less time taken by long silences or the need to go lay down in the quiet for some lingering conflict, her mood nonetheless continued to decline. Those moments of easy conversation came further and further apart, and while the skunk remained as polite as could be, she also bowed out of nearly every topic other than the food, the weather, and only the most surface-level details of how she was feeling. *I am not comfortable talking about that now* became her constant refrain.

Though neither Ioan nor May were necessarily happy for this change, it meant that they *had* to stop talking about all these dire topics. It forced them to take a step back as well, and at least try to get some work done. Given all that had happened, no one was comfortable with them continuing to perform, least of all A Finger Pointing, so they were removed from the bill for the time being, with either their roles replaced or their shows canceled.

And there was still work to be done. May still had her monologue, which she tried taking in a few different directions, some of which worked well and some less so. Ioan coached her in writing as best ey could, talking her down from fits of perfectionism that left her threatening to tear the whole thing up.

For eir part, ey still had a few projects on eir plate, not least of which was the upcoming book project that had been requested by Jonas. Ey poked at this every now and then, outlining the events to date and throwing a few thousand words at it here and there.

Mostly, though, ey dealt in letters to and from the other members of eir clade. Vast, dramatic events were happening elsewhere—as they always seemed to when an Odist was involved—and ey couldn't simply put them away to deal with all that was going on at home. The break from dealing with the affairs of True Name and Jonas was a welcome one.

The one conversation of note came on the fourth day after the merge, when the skunk asked, "How did you two get together?"

Both Ioan and May had stared at her until she held up her paws.

"Other than the forces behind the scenes, I mean."

"From my point of view," Ioan said, guessing at the meaning behind her question. "it just kind of happened over the course of a few years. May was her usual affectionate self, and we just wound up building patterns around that that turned us from coworkers to friends to partners."

"There was no culmination? No decision?"

"Not really. I just realized one day that we were probably together and asked if we were."

"It was the day ey interviewed you for the first time," May said, trying to hide a smile. "I told em it was the dumbest fucking question of the entire project. We agreed we had probably been in a relationship for months before that."

True Name nodded, expression more thoughtful than amused. "Is that how you move in the world, May Then My Name?"

The skunk hesitated, gaze drifting away from her cocladist. "Ask another question, my dear," she said eventually.

"Of course." True Name gave a hint of a bow. "You changed in order to accommodate being in a relationship, Ioan. How?"

"Are you asking what about me changed, or what I did to change?" ey asked, frowning. "Because I don't think I had any conscious control over it."

"What you changed, yes. May Then My Name could answer the other question, perhaps uniquely so among all those who we know."

The skunk only shrugged.

"Well, I think the events with Qoheleth got me thinking about existence here on the System. My own, sure, but in general. Prior to that, I think I lived my life solely as an observer of others. I'd watch people and write what they did and turn it

into a story, and I was just kind of...I don't know. Transparent?"
Ey shrugged. "I was just a pair of glasses to be used by others.
I relied heavily on memory to do my job, though, and it wasn't
until that was specifically called out and brought into question
that I started thinking of myself as more than an observer, which
then got me thinking about how I interact with those around me.
That's where Codrin came from, I think."

May chimed in. "Ey was the version of you who learned that
most strongly, perhaps. You were left with the memories of it to
work with, but without the context of the experience."

"Right. It was nice watching em grow closer to others and
open up to a relationship."

" 'Nice'?"

Ey shrugged. "I don't know how else to put it. I felt comper-
sion for them, like the opposite of jealousy. I was happy for them,
and it felt good to know that those things were possible."

True Name nodded. "That is the word I would use to describe
my feelings towards May Then My Name, if it is not too forward
of me to say."

May smiled and reached out across the dining table to pat at
True Name's paw.

"It is what I feel for End Waking and Debarre, too, though
in a far more round-about way. I have memories of the ways in
which End Waking changed in order to let Debarre into his life,
but I cannot place them in context. I do not have what is required
to understand them; I may watch them, I may understand one
at a time, but integration of all of them eludes me. Those experiences which are left to integrate are the ones clashing the most."
She gave a frustrated sigh and shook her head. "I can remember
what it feels like to fall in love but not what to do then. I can remember what it feels like to be in love but not how I got there."

Ioan and May glanced at each other briefly, but both nodded.

"It has not been a priority for you," May said. "If it has not
been important, if it has felt like a distraction, then there is no

reason to simply know how to do all of that. I do wish you the best, though."

"Didn't you say you'd felt love for Zacharias, though?"

True Name shrugged noncommittally. "I am not comfortable talking about that now."

Ey tried to keep eir expression from falling, but apparently did not succeed.

"I am sorry, Ioan. Not everything is for sharing, not right now."

"It's just the amanuensis in me." Ey tried to laugh it away. "Why'd you ask about this, anyway?"

She smirked. "You mean beyond the fact that I just told you I am having trouble integrating the memories?"

"Yeah, actually. Why those memories? I would have thought his fixation on penance would have caused more clashes."

"It is," she replied slowly. "But these are more comforting to work with. They had their fights, as I am sure all couples do, but even those are full of love. I do not–" She sniffled, shook her head firmly, then stood and bowed. "I need to go for a walk. Thank you both."

And without another word, she stepped from the sim.

May groaned and crossed her arms on the table, resting her head on them. "I do not know what to think about her. I do not know what to think about any of this."

Ey slouched in eir chair for a moment before reaching out to pet over her ears a few times. "Me either. I don't know where that conversation came from, and...well, it went alright, but I have no idea what she was asking about, so I kept feeling like I was about to fall in some conversational pit."

She lifted her snout enough to bump her nose against eir wrist, then nodded. "It is things like this—the conversation and the thoughts that come with it—that keep me hesitant about any decision to merge down. I do not know if it would help her or kill her."

"No killing skunks," ey mumbled, then stood and stretched.

"Bit miffed she's out at the lake, since now I feel like walking, too."

"If you were at all a normal person, we could enjoy perpetual springtime in the yard."

Ey looked outside, at the scant inch of snow left after the last storm. "It's not that bad."

"It is in all ways bad. It is cold."

"Mmhm, still cold. Still, it might be worth making a coffee and bringing it out there to keep the hands warm, if only so I can pace."

"Go, my dear. Go and pace. I will teach myself how to do a handstand or something equally silly. Anything other than dwelling on more of this."

"No more monologue?"

"I am so sick of looking at it that I think I might scream if I even catch a glance."

Ey laughed and leaned down to kiss the side of the skunk's muzzle. "Well, alright. Don't fall over onto the table or anything."

The rest of the afternoon passed easily enough. It was slow and boring, perhaps, but neither seemed to want any excitement. Ioan walked. May did not manage a handstand, but she did wind up laying half off the couch, head nearly to the floor, for half an hour. They made lunch. They read.

But always, there was an air of waiting. They were waiting for True Name to return, yes, but ey felt like they were also waiting for the other shoe to drop. They were waiting for her to feel whole again. They were waiting for everything to fall into place (or at least close enough) so that they could do this meeting with Jonas and get it over with.

"Do you think she's just out there walking?" ey asked at one point.

May shrugged. "If she is anything like True Name, yes. If she is anything like End Waking, then she is exploring. Climbing trees and walking along ravines."

"And if she's both?"

She sighed. "If she is both, then I do not know. If she is both, perhaps she is finding some new way to let loose all of those emotions she could not speak before.

True Name returned shortly before dinner. Both Ioan and May stood to greet her. She looked dirty and scuffed up, and while her expression wasn't grim, it certainly came close. There was frustration there, perhaps anger as well.

Overflowing, ey thought, then tamped it down.

She bowed to them from the entryway and said, "Ioan, May Then My Name, thank you for hosting me and for all of your kindness."

Ey frowned. "But...?"

"Yes. But I need out. I need to be elsewhere. I walked as far as I could into the hills from the lake and, while I found the boundary of the sim, it is far enough away that I do not think I will feel cramped."

"Wait, what? You're going to stay at Arrowhead Lake?"

"If you decide to keep my room here, I will come back, but I am going to lose my fucking mind if I simply stay in–" She sighed, took a deep breath, recomposed herself. "I am going to spend a few days out at the lake. I need...away. I need away from walls. I need away from you two, nice as you are, away from all of your happiness and comfort. I need away from speaking, from dwelling on the last few weeks. I need solitude."

May had shied away from her down-tree instance the instant her temper started to rise, clutching tightly at eir hand, but Ioan stood eir ground as best ey could.

"Well, alright. It's no trouble keeping your room, of course, and I guess there's tents already out there."

She nodded, subsiding at the reasonable tone in eir voice. "Yes. Thank you for understanding."

"Is there anything we can do to help?"

"Can you grant me ACLs to create supplies? There is nothing to hunt and I do not wish to set aside the necessity to eat."

"Hunt?" Ey frowned, then shook eir head. "Right, sorry. End Waking always did. You should...there. You should have them now."

She nodded. Much of her time out there must have been spent cataloguing what she'd need in order to survive, going off of memories that were now hers, as it took her less than ten seconds and a wave of the paw to create an axe, a knife, and two canvas bags ey assumed were full of reasonably stable food and other necessary tools. This was followed by her rapidly forking a few times over, shifting her outfit one article of clothing at a time. It struck a middle-ground between her ordinary conservative dress and End Waking's ranger garb, one with canvas leggings and a sturdy shirt, over which she wore a leather jerkin with what looked to be a detachable hood. It usually wasn't worth it to fork just to re-clothe oneself, but she seemed antsy to be away and on her own, not to mention that lingering air of frustration about her.

"Thank you both," she said, more quietly this time. "Earnestly. It does mean a lot that you have both thought to help so much. I will be in touch."

With that, she bowed, lifted her bags and axe, then stepped from the sim once more.

"What the hell..."

May took a solid minute to un-cringe from the whole experience, slowly relaxing her grip on eir hand. "I think perhaps she–"

"Is overflowing?"

She nodded.

Ey sighed. "That was my guess, too. I was going to say it came on pretty quick, but the last few days make a lot more sense with that as context."

May leaned forward and rested her forehead against eir upper arm. Her tail hung limp and her ears were splayed out to the sides.

Ey extricated eir hand from her paws so that ey could turn

and get eir arms around her, careful not to jostle too much. Ey leaned down to kiss between her ears, murmuring, "How about you, May?"

"Mm?"

"You've seemed on the edge of overflowing for a few days now."

It took her a long time to respond. At last, she hugged her arms around eir middle and lifted her head to look at em. "You will not be upset with me if I say yes?"

"What?" Ey blinked, shaking eir head. "Of course not. I apologize if it's seemed that way in the past."

She rested her head against eir shoulder. "No, but...I do not know, my dear. Everything is so much more complicated this time. It is bad enough when you have one skunk in your life, but now you have two at the same time. Two and a half, perhaps."

"It's okay, May. It's complicated, but we've done it before, so we'll make it work this time."

She nodded.

"Can I stay for tonight?" Ioan asked gently. "I'll help get some meals prepped and some of my stuff in order. It'll give me a chance to contact Douglas, too."

"Of course, my dear. I am not...there yet, but I am close."

"Well, come on, then. Let's get some food in you and we can take it easy for the night and finish in the morning."

Ioan awoke, arms empty, asleep on eir front. Ey was not a front-sleeper, so this came with a stiff neck that ey knew would dog em throughout the rest of the day.

At some point during the night, May had apparently slid as carefully as she could from eir arms, bundled herself up in a second set of covers, and curled up at the far edge of the mattress. A muffled sniffle showed her to be awake.

"You okay, May?" ey asked, sitting up beside her.

She shook her head.

"Alright. Can I hug?"

A pause, and then another shake of the head.

"That's okay," ey said, doing eir best to keep disappointment out of eir voice. "I'll go get some stuff pulled together for while I'm out. Want a cup of coffee?"

She nodded before pulling the covers up and over her head.

That was probably a good enough sign for em to get up. If the skunk was already to the point of being nonverbal, it wouldn't do either of them any good to try and keep talking, regardless of how much ey wanted to address her every need.

Coffee was a good first priority, though, and easily sorted. It was something ey could start and finish with little thought and which had a tangible outcome, a little bit of success rather than some ill-defined end-state.

While waiting, ey pinged Douglas to let him know what was going on and to request a spot to sleep. After a moment's hesitation, ey sent End Waking a quick message, as well. Ey received simple acknowledgements from both.

Ey doctored the skunk's coffee to her liking and returned to the room to set it down on the bedside table closest to her, taking a cue from True Name and moving noisily enough that she'd know ey was there without being obnoxiously loud.

A moment's thought was spent on shifting the weather in the sim to something warmer, more springlike. Ey'd heard enough kvetching about the snow the last few days to figure that might help as well.

From there, ey spent half an hour queuing up some meals for her, working in a cone of silence. Things that she'd mentioned as comfort foods in the past, all things that ey could cook emself or create in-sim through something acquired on the exchange. Chicken soup, mashed potatoes, more poor-skunk's-risotto.

While ey was prepping and stocking the food, another thought occurred to em. It was unlikely, but True Name might need to come back to the house, either to create more goods or to sleep or just to get out of the elements. To keep this from bothering May while she took the time she needed, ey shifted the ACLs of the house to be owner-only, so that those trying to enter would have to specifically request access, then stepped just inside the other bedroom's door and created a new entry-point for True Name so that she could go just to the bedroom without entering the rest of the house.

True Name sent a curt ping of acknowledgement when ey sent the information over via sensorium message.

Ey tried not to let it rankle. Everything felt so confined and restricted. So much of eir circle of friends was out in the world and so few of them came over with any frequency that to suddenly have even those ey was closest to—romantically in the case of May, and by friendship and sheer proximity in the case of True Name—requesting eir absence felt like ey was being cut off from everyone.

"Which isn't true," ey mumbled to emself while packing up eir notes. "Security's one thing, but it's not like everyone's inaccessible. Keeping everyone safe doesn't mean cutting off contact for yourself, Ioan."

Ey looked down to eir small stack of notebooks and the three-pen case resting atop it and sighed. "And talking to yourself doesn't count."

With that, ey peeked in the bedroom one last time. May had sat up and was staring dully down into her mug of coffee, blanket worn like a hooded robe. Her cheek-fur was already streaked with tears.

"I'm going to head out, May. Douglas's, as usual. Be safe, okay?"

Okay, she signed.

"Need anything else before I go?"

Hug.

Ey nodded and stepped further into the room, leaning in to get eir arms around the skunk. She didn't return the gesture, but did at least push her snout up under eir chin momentarily before leaning away. Given the tightness in her face, ey suspected an onslaught of emotion was only just being held at bay.

"Love you, May. Lots and lots."

She managed to sign an I-love-you before pulling the 'hood' of blankets down enough to hide her face.

Knowing she'd only resent em if ey lingered or touched her again, ey clutched eir notebooks to eir chest, waved, and quickly stepped out to the field of dandelions and grass. The light and heat were a shock, and ey stood, swaying, for a moment, simply squinting out to the horizon.

Ey queued up a message to Douglas and murmured, "I'm here, but going for a walk, first," before heading away from the house.

There was nothing out there. No destination. No variance in the rolling hills of well-tended grass and the yellow suns of dandelions. The only break at all in the landscape was Douglas's house, and ey kept that at eir back.

As ey walked, ey considered what it meant to overflow. Was it just an Odist thing? Certainly some aspects of it were. The way that Codrin described Dear's manic forking, each instance left with simply a shard of its personality, felt very Dear. May, End Waking, and True Name's overflowing all sounded uniquely them, as well, and A Finger Pointing mentioned that hers was different still, though had declined to expand on it.

But here ey was, feeling like all of the stress of the last day, of the last few weeks had filled em up to overflowing. Presented with the sudden silence and stillness of the field, ey realized just how much ey'd been running on desperation and borrowed time.

With the slightest break in the pressure, that loan was called due.

Realizing that ey couldn't see the subtle rises in the land for the tears in eir eyes, ey simply sat down in the grass and cried. *If I am overflowing*, some remote part of em thought, *then I can certainly see the appeal to it. Catharsis indeed.*

Though there was certainly nothing ey could have done to

stop it, ey decided to just own it and let it take its course, holler-
ing curses into the cone of silence ey had the presence of mind
to set up, clutching at the grass to keep emself anchored to the
ground. Ey'd watched a good friend (for that's what True Name
was, wasn't she?) nearly get assassinated in front of em, had
dealt with eir partner's lingering resentment towards her down-
tree instance come into conflict with her constant presence, had
watched May push True Name to near catatonia after encouraging her to accept a century and a half's worth of memories from
End Waking. Ey had watched both overflow in the span of a few
hours.

And when ey stopped cycling over the last two weeks, ey simply wept for the sheer relief it provided.

When ey'd cried emself out and cleaned emself up, ey levered emself up off the ground and trudged back toward the
house. The least ey could do was say hi and get another cup of
coffee.

Douglas Hadje was sitting on the stoop of his house, waiting
for em.

"Hey, Douglas. Sorry about that."

He stood and offered em a hug, which ey accepted gratefully.
"No worries, walks are good too. How's May?"

"She's...well, she'll get by. I just hope it doesn't last too long.
Thanks for letting me stay. Please tell me you put coffee on."

Debarre — 2350

Neither Debarre nor End Waking had visited Michelle's field in decades, and certainly not since it had become Douglas's. End Waking had last seen it on the day that she had quit in 2306, and had had little desire to return since. There were no dandelions in the forest; he had specifically requested so from Serene.

It had been much longer for Debarre, going clear back into the 2200s, back when Michelle and Sasha were still alive and coherent enough to speak to without getting overwhelmed into silence every few minutes. The memories of her were painful enough as it was—that last visit with her in End Waking's forest especially—that he'd never had the courage to come back, and then never a reason, which came with its own ache.

Given how much the clade that she'd left behind was struggling, though, it felt fitting to accept when Douglas invited him and End Waking over to talk with Ioan.

"Ey's in a funk, and from what ey says, I think you two are the only others that know why," he had said, paused, then added, "Except maybe those I don't think any of us want to see."

Both of them stood still after arriving, just bathing in—or struggling against—the waves of memory that came with the sudden onslaught of warmth and sun and the baked goods scent of dandelions thick in the air.

Ioan greeted them at the door. Ey seemed happy enough, if tired. Still smiling and bowing to them as ey usually did. They finished their greetings and settled on the grass in front of the house along with Douglas, End Waking having refused to go inside. After, though, ey had stared down into eir glass of lemonade and spoke little.

Finally, Debarre nudged em gently with an elbow. "Alright, Ioan, you're gonna need to spill it at some point, here. What's going on? All we were told is that you were feeling rough about the last few days."

Ey sighed and plucked a dandelion. "Right, sorry, you two. Or three, I guess. I know I've been a bit of a mope of late. You alright to talk about True Name?"

"Ioan, I appreciate you asking, but please do not worry about us," End Waking chided. "If we have come to help *you*, you need not spare our feelings. We can pretty well guess who would be at the center of this."

"I'm pretty sure it's me, actually," ey said with a wry smile. "I've been stuck between May and True Name for days now, or years if you count the time since the convergence and I started trying to smooth things out with the coffee dates.

"I've just been struggling with it all. It's been too much from the moment everything with True Name happened. The last few days were the worst, though. True Name didn't really handle the merge all that well. She collapsed and was nearly unresponsive for several hours, and since then, she's been struggling to integrate various chunks of memories."

"My feelings towards her work? That I built my identity around not being her?"

"That and your relationship with Debarre."

The weasel and skunk both looked at each other, ears splayed.

"I'd thought of that, but, uh…" Debarre cleared his throat. "Well, actually hearing it put like that casts it in a bit of a different light."

"I hope that she does not mind the memories of sex to go along with the resentment," End Waking said, then laughed when Debarre poked him in the side. "We are all adults here, my dear."

"I'm the baby, I think," Douglas said. "I'm seventy-two."

"So young." The skunk grinned. "Debarre and I both have two centuries on you. Still, I am pretty sure that we can acknowledge the existence of sex, is what I mean."

"And it doesn't exactly sound like she's a stranger to that herself, anyway."

End Waking blinked, taken aback. "She actually told you about Zacharias?"

"Who?" Douglas asked.

"An...erstwhile lover, as she put it," Ioan said carefully. "I probably shouldn't go too much into that, though."

"Agreed," Debarre said. "But as you were saying, she was having trouble?"

"Yeah. I wasn't expecting her to get completely taken out, but May did kind of force it on her all in one go. She lasted a few days, but I think she was pushing herself pretty hard to appear strong. She crashed really hard yesterday and, despite a pretty pleasant morning, had to step out to Arrowhead Lake, and when she came back, she looked like she was about ready to start yelling at us. May was also trying to stick around as long as she could, I think, since she crashed almost immediately. We made it through the night, but she couldn't even speak this morning."

"That's a shitload to have to deal with, yeah."

Ey nodded. "Friend almost gets assassinated, almost goes crazy from a merge, and disappears. Partner freaks out after a conversation, then freaks out when the merge goes sideways and mentions she was thinking of merging down, herself, then requests that I disappear. It's just...a lot."

"Wait, *May* wanted to merge down?" Douglas said. "Wasn't expecting that."

"Well, I don't know quite how much 'wanted' fits, but I asked if she was thinking about it and she said yes. I couldn't quite piece together why, though. After End Waking merged down, she mentioned that there was at least a part of her that was feeling vengeful, so I think I was worried that maybe she was considering piling on her own vengeance, or that maybe she would be trying to help make her a better person." Ey shrugged and added, "Or both. She did seem to have True Name's best interests at heart when she forced the merge. At least mostly."

End Waking nodded. "She did mention being torn, yes. She wanted to kick her out but also wanted to help her get away from Jonas."

"She's certainly softening on her."

"And how're you taking it?" Debarre asked. Something about Ioan—eir posture, eir face, something—made it seem like this was the question ey was dreading the most.

There was a long silence before ey answered. "It's really getting to me. I don't even know why, either. I think it honestly would help True Name in the end if it were just May merging down, but having that be the case with her memories of us together feels like...well, it kind of makes me jealous. Those are our memories that we made together. Our fights and good times, our affection—"

"Probably most of the memories, there," Debarre stage-whispered, getting a smirk out of Ioan.

"Yeah. Our affection and our sex, too, for that matter. Suddenly, True Name would have all that. I think it also started grating on me because of how...real End Waking's was. It wouldn't just be a library for her perusal, but she will have actually lived them. She will have actually—" Ey frowned, as though digging for the words.

"She'll have actually loved you, maybe?" Debarre guessed.

Eir face fell and ey sighed. "Yeah. That. Putting it that way makes it feel terrible, but it's exactly that."

"I was pulling back when she and Zacharias were getting close," End Waking said, sounding thoughtful. "And I have been her. We were both Michelle. I know that she is capable of experiencing romantic feelings. They will not be alien to her."

"And now she's been *you*," Debarre added. "And you've got romantic feelings, too. At least, I hope so."

End Waking pushed him over onto the ground. "If you imply that I do not have romantic feelings for you again, I will make you hunt our meals for a week."

He laughed. "Love you too, E.W."

"What I am saying, though, is that it will not be alien to her. She will have experienced love for others, and the loss of that love. She will have already experienced love for others through another's memories and experiences, even. You can trust her to integrate that, I believe."

"Even though she was struggling with integrating those memories of yours?"

"Perhaps especially so. I think that she is struggling because it clashes with her personality, not that she feels that she might love Debarre. Though, my dear," he said, nodding to Debarre, "I can guarantee that just about every Odist is at least a little in love with you."

He shook his head and waved the comment away. "Yeah, yeah."

More than one of them had confessed as much to him over the centuries, and it wasn't until he'd actually conceded that something about End Waking landed in that sweet spot of attraction and personality match enough to at least try dating that they'd stopped. He was thankful that they seemed happy enough to live vicariously through him. He had liked Sasha and Michelle, loved her in that sympatico that true friends can share, friends who had shared trauma, so he didn't begrudge them their feelings, but any more felt pretty far out of his league as a gay man.

Instead, he nudged Ioan with his elbow again. "So if you don't need to worry about it from True Name's side, and you know you're worrying about it from your own side, how do you feel about it from May's point of view?"

"How do you mean?"

"Well, do you have any worries about her? Do you think she does? Has she talked about it at all?"

"Not much. She said she'd been considering it, but that seeing how the current merge was making her struggle had her in doubt. I told her I want to make sure it'd be consensual on everyone's behalf, this time. I guess–"

"Whoa, wait," Douglas interrupted, frowning. "She didn't even talk with True Name about this merge?"

"They talked a few times in a cone of silence, so maybe then, but otherwise not that I saw. She just stopped True Name in the middle of ranting about her calling and sent End Waking a message to merge, far as I could tell."

"That's kind of shitty."

Ey shrugged. "I suppose, but no need to pile on her or anything, I think she's beating herself up over it worse than any of us could do."

Douglas nodded. "Well, that bit I believe. Think that contributed to her overflowing?"

"Almost certainly, yeah. Correct me if I'm wrong, End Waking, but while I don't think it's solely tied to external events, they can have an effect on it."

The skunk nodded. He'd started panting in the heat of the sun, so it took him a moment to reply. "It comes over us like a wave. Some of us more quickly than others. It is slower in onset for me than for either of them, I believe."

Debarre chimed in. "I usually have a few days warning. I've gotten mine already and was planning on heading out today, but we both wanted to come, anyway."

"Is it hard for you?"

End Waking held up a paw. "I want to respect Debarre's decision to share or not, but I would prefer not to be here for this conversation."

"Sorry, End Waking. You don't need to answer, Debarre."

The weasel shrugged. "No, it's fine. E.W. and I have talked about it, and I get where he's coming from. It can wait."

"Yes. He is not disallowed. We simply have our own, separate conversations about that, and it is important to me that Debarre feel comfortable talking about me with his friends, too. I cannot be the only one in his life."

"Alright, makes sense. May's said similar, for that matter." Ey toyed with the flower ey'd plucked before, saying, "We actually talked about other relationships shortly before this all went down, about how she'd act if she started to fall for someone else and how she'd feel if I did. One thing we didn't talk about was someone else having feelings for either of us, whether or not they'd come about them on their own or through a merger."

"I'm sure there's shitloads of people in love with May Then My Name," Debarre said, laughing. "But she's good at having that conversation, and you're both good at talking, so."

"Too good, perhaps." End Waking stood. "I am overheating and feeling restless, so I am going to return to the forest. Ioan, I do wish you the best, and I would like you to keep in touch as you are able. I am concerned about your partner, as well as for True Name, in my own way. Please keep yourself safe so that you can keep the both of them safe in turn."

Ioan nodded and stood as well to bow to the skunk. "Thanks. It really does mean a lot. I'll keep you in the loop, if nothing else."

After returning the bow, End Waking held out a paw to Debarre. "Can you return with me? Just for a few minutes."

He nodded and accepted that paw. He had a feeling he knew what was coming, so even just the touch as they stepped away from the sim was worth it. Sure enough, once they made it back to the forest, End Waking leaned over to nose at Debarre's cheek, pulled his paw away, and looked off into the woods. Whenever it was time for him to ask Debarre to leave, he'd go through a little swell of anxiety.

"I am sorry, my love. I know that it is not the easiest on you that I always do this."

"Hey, I said I was leaving today," he said as reassuringly as he could. "It's not coming out of the blue."

End Waking nodded. "You are always allowed to keep in touch."

"Mmhm."

"And you can drop by as long as you give me some notice, preferably a day."

"I will."

"And if you hear from May Then My Name or Ioan, please let me know."

"E.W., shut up," Debarre said fondly. "See you soon, okay?"

The skunk wilted, a look somewhere between relieved and resigned coming over his face. "Yes. Soon. Thank you, my dear."

"Of course. Love you, E.W."

"Love you too."

There was nothing else for it, then. With one last wave to the skunk (already heading off into the woods), he stepped back to the Hadjes' field.

Ioan and Douglas were still standing where he'd left them, so he waved again. "Sorry, back for a little bit."

"On your own again?" Ioan asked.

He nodded. "Yeah. It's been building up for a long time. We agreed I'd head off when the tent was done, and we just got the nets all hung yesterday. Hey, can we go inside, though? He was right, it's pretty fucking hot out here with fur."

Douglas laughed. "I'll never get you guys, him all in black fur and you wearing black clothes over yours. Yeah, come on. There's more lemonade."

Ioan held back enough to let Douglas take the lead, falling in step with Debarre, instead. "Does it bother you?"

"Hmm? E.W. asking me to leave?"

"Yeah."

He thought for a bit, then shrugged. "Bothers, yeah, but that's really about it. Helps that I usually just quit and merge down with #Tracker, so it's not like I've got *just* the relationship to worry about. I've got my own stuff going on besides him, and other relationships that merge in every now and then."

"That sounds handy, at least."

"His overflowing is also way less dramatic than May Then My Name's, which sounds pretty painful to watch."

Ioan nodded.

"Sorry, Ioan. Don't mean to keep it all on the surface for you."

Ey shrugged. "I asked, it's alright."

Once they were all inside and Debarre had cooled off, Douglas asked, "So what do you think about all this?"

" 'All this'?" He laughed. "Way too fucking much to say one way or another. Narrow it down?"

"Oh, I meant the stuff with End Waking merging down. I'm still stuck on May asking him to do that without talking it through with True Name, first."

"Well, like I said, she was conflicted about it when she brought it up. Said she wanted her to disappear into ignor...ignoble..."

"Ignominy?" Ioan offered.

"Right, yeah. But she also said that she wanted her to get out of this mess and away from Jonas, 'that living, breathing sack of shit', in her words."

They laughed.

"But I'd been thinking much the same, I guess. If she does disappear, I'd probably feel at least a little bit of vindication for the way she jerked us all around without us realizing it and all that shit she did with the Council. I'd also feel like there was a fraction less of my friend around, though, too. I love E.W., I'm happy he's in my life, we get along well for the most part, but there's also this layer of, like...well, he was part of Sasha and Michelle, and they and I went through a lot together."

"You talk about those two facets like different people," Ioan said. "Sorry, not to derail. Just that I noticed that. None of the Odists do."

"Most, maybe. I picked it up from Hammered Silver, who spent probably more time with them than anyone. All their instances feel singular, I imagine, but they were two instances in one. Sasha was this really emotional, really caring person. It wasn't that Michelle wasn't, just that when she was at the fore, she was much more...I don't know. Logical? Rational?"

"And when it was both? When she was in flux, or whatever?"

"Then she was just tired," he said, smiling at memories. "But right, before I totally lose track, you asked how I feel. Uh, I guess I feel scared."

Ioan furrowed eir brow. "Really?"

"Yeah. That she collapsed made me confront the fact that, no, I don't really want her dead or anything, that I really would hate to lose her. Even if she's not the part of my friend I like the most, not a part that I even remember seeing before, she's still *a* part of them." He hesitated, then added, "And it changed E.W. Not the forking and merging itself, but that he even did that. It sounds like May Then My Name used the fact that True Name was all worked up to force her to accept the whole merge all at once. She kind of did the same with E.W. I don't know what her message was, but it looked like it scared the shit out of him, so he kind of did it without really thinking. They'd been talking about Zacharias the last few days, I do know that."

"Since her and True Name's conversation about him?"

"Now that you mention it, yeah. He's been a bit different since."

"Different how?" Douglas asked.

"Like...still all worried, and still a little in shock, but also like a little bit of a load was taken off. He's been a bit lighter. Silly, even. You heard him, though. He even said he's worried for her. I can't explain it, and we never really talked it through. It's not bad, but I can still tell."

Ioan nodded and rubbed eir palms against the legs of eir slacks as ey always seemed to do during stressful conversations. "He did seem a bit freer of speech today," ey mused. "But that makes sense. He finally got to tell her how he feels, and they didn't even have to talk to each other."

"Has May Then My Name changed, too?"

"I can't tell. She's been so wrapped up in trying to live around someone she doesn't really like, and then with all of the fallout from the merge. Maybe she has? She's at least been able to talk with True Name without blowing up at her, and they've even had some conversations that seemed enjoyable at times, so, maybe?"

He raised his eyebrows. "Really? The way she talked about True Name for a while there...whew."

"That bad?"

"Did she not talk about her to you?"

Ey shrugged. "Every now and then, and sometimes she'd get pretty pissed, but it was only once a year or so."

"Mm, about the same amount, but maybe she kept it a bit...I dunno, gentler for you, since you were meeting up with True Name. She'd come over once a year or so and just go off for a while. It kinda became routine. She'd vent, then we'd have a good day."

Ioan switched to rubbing eir hands over her face. "I don't even know what to do about her."

"Nothing," Douglas said. "Nothing but love her and keep talking, I mean. She's a grown woman, she can work out her feelings well enough. Hell, she's already seeing a therapist."

Ey slumped back dramatically against the couch cushions. "Why does *everyone* tell me to stop fixing others' problems for them? Even the intellectual side of me is in on the game."

They laughed.

"It's so hard to actually internalize. I'll catch myself trying to mend her and True Name's relationship or make May feel better or whatever, and I'll have to force myself to relax."

"It's not a bad thing," Debarre said. "I mean, you still shouldn't do that all the time, but it's at least a sign that you're just a good person who wants to do right by eir friends."

Ey smiled gratefully. "I'm at least trying. May's done her own fair share of trying to help, but that at least fits her M.O. One more question, then I think I need to table the topic for a bit."

"Sure."

"Do you think it was the right thing to do?"

"Yeah," he said, surprising himself with how readily the answer came to him. "I don't think it would have worked if E.W. had just merged down without all the other dramatic shit. I think she would've just rejected it, or if she did accept the merge, just cherry-picked parts of it. As it is, though, with Jonas after her neck and May Then My Name using all her wiles to convince both her and E.W., I think it's worth it, though she probably would've preferred to fork first. I don't honestly see her coming out of this still in power or whatever, but if she *does* make it out, I think it'll help her move on."

Ioan stared up at the ceiling thoughtfully, occasionally mumbling to emself.

He shrugged to Douglas and asked, "Well, I skipped breakfast and I'm not ready to merge back down yet. Want some food? That'll at least be more pleasant."

After another hour's conversation over lunch—much happier conversation, thankfully—Debarre stepped back to his home sim and quit to let #Tracker catch up on the current happenings.

Debarre#Tracker conducted a thorough security sweep and, finding no bugs, those little hidden instances he'd grown so paranoid of, he sighed and slouched back in his desk chair, rubbing paws over his face. "Well, shit. This complicates things, doesn't it?"

He queued up a sensorium message to Yared, user11824, and a few other friends he'd kept in touch with while following along with (and occasionally meddling in) the political affairs of the system. 'Reactionary elements' indeed.

Ioan Bălan — 2350

Once they were fed and Debarre was safely on his way home—
or at least merged down-tree—Ioan begged off from talking any
further and trudged down the hall to the spare room ey borrowed whenever May needed space. Ey claimed to need a nap
and, while ey was certainly tired enough, sleep seemed unlikely.

The walk and cry in the field before ey'd joined Douglas at his
house had been necessary, but also had only served to highlight
just how woefully out of eir depth ey truly was.

"Hi Sarah," ey said, starting a simplex sensorium message.
"Sorry to bother you, and sorry we haven't spoken in a few
weeks. I know I was vague when I canceled our last appointment,
but things have gone completely sideways. I'm not totally sure
how open you'd be to this, but can we meet and talk, even if I'm
restricted to talking in very general terms about what's going
on? I need to talk to someone who can help me sort through my
thoughts around it, I just can't share details yet. It has to do with
True Name, so I'm sure you can appreciate just how complicated
it is. Let me know if that's alright. I'm...I'm at Douglas's for a few
days. Thanks."

Then, ey lay down on the bed, still dressed and over the covers, and stared at the ceiling, trying to think about as little as
possible.

Ey was startled awake by a sensorium message. Grunting and
wiping eir hands over eir face to try and bring reality back into

focus through the near drunken haze of waking up from an ill-advised nap, ey set the message to running.

"Good to hear from you, Ioan. I'll admit that I was pretty concerned when you canceled. I don't usually worry about you, but that's also the first time you've had to do so in nearly four years. I can be free whenever you need, and am happy to meet you either there or here. I don't have any problems holding off on details until a later date. Just let me know."

Ey groaned and ground the heels of eir palms against eir closed eyes, trying to will away the grogginess that clung to em, somehow managing to feel both sticky and slippery.

A quick shower had em feeling well enough to respond, and by the time she arrived, ey'd made tea for emself and met her, mug in hand, at the door.

Ey bowed. "Thanks for coming on such short notice."

She offered em a hug. "It's alright. I figure if whatever is happening has all three of you canceling appointments and you requesting short-notice ones, it's probably important."

"Sorry, just woke up, feeling rough," ey said, declining the hug. "But yeah. Important, overwhelming, dramatic. Would you be alright talking outside? That nap destroyed me and I'm still feeling disconnected from everything."

"Works for me."

"So, uh...well, where to start." Ey spoke haltingly, once they'd made their way out into the grass and light and blue skies. "Right. As of a few weeks ago, for reasons I can't get into just yet, True Name has been staying in an extra room we dug at the house. A few days ago–"

"Whoa, wait. I know you said no specifics, but can you tell me a little more about that? I can't picture that working at *all.*"

Ey sighed. "Yeah, well, that's part of why I'm here and not at home, I guess."

She nodded, gestured for em to continue.

"Well, she...hmm. She ran into some interpersonal trouble that was dramatic enough to require staying around people well enough known on the System that she'd be safe." Ey winced, adding, "I know that's not much to go by. Either way, she's staying in our place. She's been fairly self-contained, but not totally so, so there's been some interaction between the three of us. Before you ask, it was May's idea in the first place, and while there have been a few rough spots, it's gone far smoother than I would have thought."

"Still, I imagine that just having the anxiety of it potentially going rough doesn't feel good."

"Not at all, no. I've been feeling like I'm constantly on guard, always ready to jump in and smooth things out, even if I haven't really had to do so. I'm trying to let them both just do their own thing, though, and every time I catch myself feeling that way, I try to change contexts."

"That's good," she said. "Has it been helping, at least?"

"If you'd asked me that a few days ago, I would have said yes, but now that I'm here and struggling to hold it together, I'm not so sure. I think I was just pushing it down without...I don't know, redirecting it or dealing with it."

She nodded. "Alright. I want to come back to that, but I interrupted your overview. Can you tell me what else happened?"

"Right. So, through some strange turn of events, both True Name and May wound up overflowing at the same time. True Name is staying at another private sim we know and May's at home while I'm here. All of this hit a few days back when May and True Name had a conversation that left both of them drained, and then True Name had to deal with a merge large enough that she collapsed."

"Not May Then My Name..." Sarah hazarded, frowning.

"No. Another cocladist, though."

Ey saw comprehension dawn in her features, and that frown only deepened. She gestured for em to continue.

"But...well. So there's two things that I think fall out of this that I'd get the most out of talking about. The first is that I'm having a lot of complicated feelings surrounding True Name throughout this, and the second is that May did mention that she'd been considering merging down with her until the previous merge went so sideways."

She looked down to the grass thoughtfully as they walked. "Can you tell me about how you feel about the merge, first?"

"I didn't really get the chance to ask her about why it was that she was considering merging. We promised to talk about it more, but after that, things happened pretty quickly. There's a weird sort of jealousy that goes along with it. May and I have built our own life completely independent of True Name. We bowed out of politics and writing these grand, System-spanning tales and focused on just being together. That's why I got into writing plays, I think: it was a way for me to do the things that felt comfortable for me that didn't involve being wrapped up in all these crazy goings-on.

"So we built our life together. True Name respected that, too. She would ask about me and May, and seemed earnestly happy that we'd gone and done something so...normal."

"Do you think she's envious of that?"

Ey frowned and scuffed a heel through the grass. "I don't know, honestly. Again, if you'd asked me a few weeks ago, I would have said probably not, that she's got her own things that make her happy which don't involve putting on plays or poking fun at each other. Now, though, I'm not so sure. This whole thing about the merge adds another layer onto that, because suddenly, True Name would have all of those memories."

"Does it bother you that she would have the memories, or are you worried about her having those emotions? Do you worry she'd start feeling about you the way that May Then My Name does?"

"Well, shit." Ey groaned. "I didn't even think about that. Like, we've talked about what her having memories of loving me would mean, but always past-tense. I didn't think about if she herself—she as True Name I mean—would pick up on exactly how May felt about me as well. I have no clue. Maybe on some level I do worry, though. I like the way May feels about me. We've talked about jealousy a few times, and it often comes up that she feels devoted to me. I'm really not sure how I'd feel having that come from another, never mind one that I have as complicated a relationship with as I do with True Name."

"Does this tie in with the complicated feelings you mentioned, then?"

Ey bought emself some time to think about an answer by bending down to pluck a dandelion, twirling it between eir fingers. "I guess I have to share one detail, which is that there was an attempt on her life back on Secession day."

Sarah blinked and stopped up short. "One moment," she said, then closed her eyes, her lips moving faintly in a non-vocalized sensorium message. Ey politely turned away. Finally, she caught eir attention once more. "I checked in with the instance that's been meeting with True Name and she said that she received a message from her back on Secession day that sounded really panicked."

"What was it about?" ey asked. "If you can share, that is."

"Not the specifics, but she mentioned that True Name did cancel appointments for the foreseeable future with the promise to come back as soon as she could."

Ey nodded. "Well, then yes, that'd be why. She's safe, at least. Staying with us means that no one can come after her without exposing themselves," ey said as reassuringly as ey could. Ey felt bad leaving out the fact that True Name wasn't in contact at all with either of them, but that felt like it was on the list of things ey couldn't share.

"Has this changed how you feel about her, then?"

"I don't know if it's changed things, necessarily, so much as made me more cognizant of how I felt about her before. I think I mentioned around the time that it came up that we had a conversation about how she said that it was nice to just have a friend, and how I translated that as a friendly acquaintance that wasn't just another politician."

"And I called you out on the fact that you later said you thought of her more like a friendly coworker than anything."

Ey laughed. "Right. Well, with all that's gone down, with how it felt to see her in danger and then to see her struggling with the ramifications of being cut off and the effects of the merge, I think I'm a lot more comfortable just calling her a friend. I don't think I'd feel like this if she were a 'friendly coworker'."

"You have a far more complex relationship than what is implied by 'friend'. It could just be a language thing, that that word implies a greater level of shared happiness than you have, but, confronted by how much you care about her in the context of what happened, you're bumping up against the broader definition of friend of someone you *can* feel that much care for."

Ey nodded. They fell into silence as they walked while Ioan took the time to process.

It certainly tallied, too. Even though May's overflowing had overshadowed it—reasonably so, given the importance of their relationship—ey'd been hit hard by True Name overflowing, as well. Seeing her struggling, upset and overwhelmed, having to claim that same solitude that End Waking did, touched on that care. The need to fix things was a symptom of that confusing sense of care, ey suspected, rather than just something isolated.

"I don't know if you were necessarily talking to me, but just in case you were, I'd agree with your assessment."

Ey jumped at the sudden realization that ey'd said at least part of that out loud, then laughed. "Sorry, I was mumbling, wasn't I? I've been doing that a lot lately. I was trying to keep that dialogue internal, but I appreciate the confirmation."

She smiled. "I suspected so. I'm used to it, now. So, before I continue, are you looking to work on disentangling this, some ideas for where to go next, or just talking?"

"I wouldn't turn down an idea or two, but I've already gotten a lot out of having the chance to talk through the emotional side. There are a few others in the loop that I've been able to talk with, but that's all been about logistics, or about May and True Name rather than myself." Ey sighed, adding, "I was a mess when I first got here. Doesn't feel great to say, but I spent so much energy on them I kind of forgot to take care of myself."

"That it doesn't feel great to say is a sign that you care deeply enough to not want to detract from that energy, so it's not a bad thing, but you do need to take care of yourself, yes." She looked thoughtful for a moment, then said, "Alright. I know you said they're both currently overflowing, but what do you think about talking with each of them about how you're feeling about this?"

"Uh, well, I mean," ey stammered. "I guess I should, yeah."

" 'Should'?"

"Right. Should statement. I'd like to, but they both feel kind of fraught. Talking with May about being friends with True Name has come up before but feels fraught with how they feel about each other, or at least felt about each other. Hell, I don't know how I'd tell True Name I care about her, either. And I don't particularly want to be the one to broach May merging down with True Name. That feels like a conversation they should start as cocladists."

"They're complicated topics, and I'm not saying you *must* talk about them, but it'll only help for the three of you to all be on the same page. It'd be a good exercise for you to be more active, as well."

Ey nodded.

"You look like you're fading. Want to call it for now and then we can get in touch soon?"

"Uh, yeah, probably," ey said. It was only just settling into evening, but the nap still had em out of sorts. "Thank you, though. This was immensely helpful. I don't think any of us are in a position to hold to a schedule at the moment, given further complicated stuff going on behind the scenes, but I'll definitely be in touch when I can, and will nudge both of them to do the same."

"Ioan."

Ey stopped up short, winced. "Right, sorry. Not my job."

"Thank you," she said, grinning. "I'll touch base with each of them, don't worry. One more tip before I go: take care of yourself. That whole golden rule thing applies to you, too, you know. Treat others well, but remember you still need to be treated well, too."

"I'll certainly try."

May arrived without any warning. She would usually ping either em or Douglas, giving them a few minutes to get out into the field and prepare for a pouncing.

This time, however, Ioan awoke before dawn to a small, furry form crawling into bed with em, whispering for em to scoot over. Some sleepy part of em remembered that Douglas had locked down the ACLs to all unannounced visitors shortly after ey'd arrived with the news.

All except May, apparently.

Ey shifted the pillow ey'd been hugging out of the way and held the covers up for her to squirm beneath them and fit herself comfortably against eir front, draping them back over them both as ey got eir arms around her. Ey was too tired to do anything other than mumble a quiet greeting, and she didn't seem all that keen on talking either, so they simply dozed with each other for another few hours.

With the sun warming the far wall of the room, they woke slowly, May squirming around enough to face em so that she could press her nose to eirs.

"Good morning, my dear."

"Morning, May. Surprised to see you here."

She shrugged, nosed her way down beneath eir chin. "I woke up early feeling well enough to come by, but did not want to wake you."

"Or wait?"

"I missed you, Ioan, why would I wait?"

Ey nudged at her snout with eir chin. "Well, I missed you too, so it works out. Just surprised to see you here so soon."

"I am not feeling spectacular, but I am feeling well enough to not be alone. Now does not feel like a good time to be alone." She leaned back enough to smile at em, and though it was a little shaky and her face was still a mess, ey was pleased to see that it was earnest. "Are you okay, though? I do not imagine it was the best of times for this to happen."

Remembering eir conversation with Sarah only two days back, ey checked the urge to refocus the conversation on her, instead saying, "It was a little rough, yeah. I got in touch with Sarah and set up an emergency thing a few hours after I got here."

"I am sorry, Ioan."

"Hush, it's not on you. Plus, I canceled the last one, so it was good to catch up with her about what's going on, if only in very general terms. I guess I just kind of overflowed a little, myself. Everything's been so stressful the last few weeks and I didn't feel like I could do anything about it."

"And did you come to any conclusions?"

"Not particularly, but you know how it goes," ey said. "Talked a bit about next steps, at least, about how I should probably make sure that I take care of myself, too."

She laughed. "Yes, you should."

They lay in silence for a few minutes, May simply relaxing in eir arms while ey tried to decide how much else to share from the impromptu appointment.

She's here and we have time, might as well, ey thought

"We also talked about your thoughts on merging down. Don't want to overwhelm you, though, if you're not up for talking about that."

"I was going to bring it up later, myself. I have had further thoughts."

"Shall you go first, or I?"

"You, please."

Ey nodded. "Alright. It wound up being more about jealousy than anything, and what it was that I was actually feeling protective of when it came to the idea. Some of it is the fact that we've built a pretty good life together, and it took a lot of work. I'm not sure how I feel about her having the memories of that."

"End Waking said much the same, that he had put all his effort into his penance and that he would like her to come by that through her own work."

"Pretty similar, yeah. I'd be really happy for her if she built a life that included the happiness and comfort outside of work that we have, but a large part of me wants her to come by that honestly. The other bit that Sarah brought up was whether or not I was worried that her incorporating your memories of us together would lead to her feeling about me the way you do."

There was a long silence after that. Ey did eir best to quell eir impatience. With how much the topic had been weighing on em over the last few days, ey desperately wanted to hear her side of it, as well.

Finally, she said, "I have been thinking about that quite a bit since the topic came up, but only from my point of view. I did not think about how it might feel for you, for which I apologize."

Ey shook eir head. "You've had a lot going on. What thoughts did you have on it, though?"

"I have also been trying to pick apart my jealousy. I have said in the past that I am not opposed to you finding companionship with others, whether romantic or sexual or whatever. I am starting to think, though, that that would only apply to a type of companionship that does not overlap with what you and I have. I want nothing more than for you to feel fulfilled, my dear, and if that means finding fulfillment for the areas that I do not cover, I would only ever be pleased." She sighed, thought for a moment longer, and then continued more quietly, "For someone to feel about you precisely what I do, even if it is tempered by other memories, is too close to the devotion that I am most protective of."

"Have you changed your mind on merging?"

"I do not know, Ioan. I go back and forth on the issue and at the moment, rather more back than forth." She giggled, licked at eir chin, adding, "Or forth than back. The metaphor fails."

"You took that one a bit far, yeah," ey said, laughing. "But I think I'm too tired to talk about this much more. Did you have coffee before coming over?"

"I did not. If you make me a cup, I will love you forever."

Ey nudged her out of bed so that ey could get up as well, saying, "I thought you were going to do that anyway, but I guess a cup of coffee is a small price to pay."

Douglas had beaten them to the coffee pot, which made the process all the easier.

"Hey, May," he said, returning the offered hug and kissing her cheek. "Figured that was you this morning. Feeling better?"

She nodded and slumped down into a chair, cradling her coffee in both paws. "Mostly, yes. I am still below baseline, but it was more important that I see you two than to return all the way."

"Well, glad to see you made it through."

"You will not quit me so easily, Douglas Hadje, doctor of incredibly boring things. How are you, though? Has Ioan caught you up on everything?"

"I think so, yeah. Ey, Debarre, and End Waking did. Assassins, mergers, Jonas being terrible, Zacharias. Did I miss anything?"

She shook her head. "That is the whole of it, I think. We continue to be dramatic about everything we do."

He laughed. "I mean, not going to deny that, but I'm also going to put a large part of this on Jonas, rather than you all."

"Do you have any thoughts on it?"

"Besides the fact that you're all nuts?"

"Yes, well, that is indisputable. I would merge down with you if I could to give you a taste of it, but alas, it does not work that way."

Douglas lifted his cup in a toast. "For which I'm grateful. It sounds like a nightmare."

"Yes, yes. Such is the life of an Odist."

"Beyond that, though, I don't know, I don't want to lose any of you. I don't have the history with True Name that you guys do, so all I've just been thinking of her in terms of Michelle and Sasha."

"You've been talking to Debarre too much," Ioan said. " 'Michelle and Sasha', I mean."

Douglas's face fell. "I never got to meet her, but from what everyone's said, it sounds like the split was pretty evident."

"It was," May said. "While I do not speak of her that way, Debarre is not wrong to do so."

"Why not?"

The skunk shrugged and lapped at her coffee. "Back when I was her, I did not think of myself that way. True Name did not think of herself that way. I know Hammered Silver does, and I am sure that others do as well. It is accurate, enough. Both can be true at once."

"I wonder what would happen if all of you were able to merge back down into one instance again," he mused. "Would that get close to being her?"

May fell silent, looking out the window at the fields over the rim of her mug.

"I do not know," she said eventually. Her voice sounded far away, older than Ioan had ever heard it sound before. "I wish I did, but I do not know."

––––––––

"She's still not back?"

May shook her head, tugging Ioan by the hand over to their beanbag. "Not yet. I would like another day before we go seeking her out, though, okay?"

Ey nodded as ey let emself be tugged along. Relaxing for even just a few minutes with eir partner certainly sounded better than tramping out into the woods around the lake, and some part of em marveled at just how much ey felt like ey needed it.

Some day, ey thought. *I'll stop being surprised at what May's made out of me.*

It wasn't so bad being hooked on touch and affection, though. Ey'd grown to cherish all of those little loving gestures, and flopping down on the beanbag to let May curl up on eir front and just do nothing sounded like an ideal way to spend a day if True Name was comfortable where she was out at Arrowhead Lake.

With neither of them feeling all that keen on talking further, they simply lounged on the beanbag together, reveling in the spring-tinted sunlight. A little napping, a little petting on skunks, but mostly just calm and quiet.

It wasn't until nearly dinner that they stirred again, Ioan squirming until ey could sit up on the beanbag cross-legged, letting May lounge draped across eir lap.

"I have been thinking," May began, sounding more dozy than anything. "But I would like to ensure you are willing to talk about this whole merger business before I shove us into a conversation."

"I can do that, sure."

"Would it be unfair of me to merge down?"

"Unfair how?"

She shrugged. "There are three of us in the equation, are there not? For me to merge down takes the uniqueness of our relationship away from the two of us and turns it into a burden for her."

Ey nodded and teased a few fingers through her fur. "I can see that, I guess. Even if it's not something that she acts on, or if she even does anything with the memories, whatever you feel about us becomes something she can feel too."

"Yes. As I mentioned, I am perhaps jealous of that. I would like what we have to be our own."

"I think we agree on that. How do you mean 'unfair', though?"

She twisted around until she could poke her nose on em. "Because it would be an act that I would take. Even if we all were to agree, it is me that is changing our relationships. I would be the one taking away that uniqueness and turning it into a burden."

Ioan tugged the skunk up a little further until ey could get eir arms around her. Something about her words didn't sit right with em, and ey needed at least a little bit of time to think it out.

Perhaps she was still overflowing, in a way. At the tail end of it, sure, but every time in the past, she had waited until she was essentially feeling better before fetching em back from Douglas's, whereas this morning, she seemed to have forced herself out of that state, rightfully or otherwise, to at least not be alone.

There was some slight distortion here, though, a way of thinking that didn't quite mesh with her personality. Ey agreed to an extent, but it was her framing that was bothering em most.

"So," ey began, choosing eir words carefully. "I did say that I'm really starting to not feel so great about the idea, but I'm not totally sure I agree with how much of that you're putting on yourself. You sound preemptively guilty."

May squirmed out of eir grasp to sit on the beanbag alongside em, elbows on knees and face in paws.

"I'm sorry, May. Maybe this isn't–"

"No, you are right," she mumbled, sounding miserable. It tugged at eir emotions to the point where ey had to restrain emself from tugging her back in for a hug, though her posture kept em at bay. "I am not at baseline yet. Nothing makes sense. It is like having my emotions refracted through a glass of water. I probably should not even be talking about it."

"It's important, I just don't want you to push yourself if you're not out of the rough patch yet."

"Right, yes." She sighed, pushing herself wearily off the pouf. "Everything feels so urgent, though. I feel like we must have this conversation now if we are to have it, or else the opportunity will evaporate. I know that it does not work that way, that this is not logical of me, but this is not a logical time."

Scooting to the edge of the beanbag, Ioan stood as well. "I

know. We have months before we run up against Jonas's dead-line, but if he's sending assassins after True Name, it sure does make it feel urgent."

The skunk padded over to the kitchen, swiping a few of the dishes that Ioan had left prepared into being, lining them up in a row. "Yes, and I cannot easily let that go. I want her to be other than she is specifically to not be so under his thumb. I want her to be better than she is to be less of what she has become, and yet even those thoughts feel like distortions. Choose your plate, my dear."

Ey picked one mostly at random, winding up with a grilled cheese sandwich and some soup. "I had been wondering as to your reasons. I felt like the idea just kind of popped into my mind based on what she was talking about at the time, what with Zacharias and all, but it came at such an inopportune time for me to actually ask why. Is it...I mean, do you feel the need to fix things like we've been talking about with me?"

She hesitated, sighed, shook her head. "I do not know, Ioan."

Ey nodded, letting the subject drop. It didn't seem open to discussion.

May picked up a plate of mashed potatoes and asparagus, shooing em back to the dining room table. "I just think that she has become so singular a person that she cannot but be con-trolled by Jonas. Her role in guiding the System is no less real; she did the work that she does and she did it both well and proudly. But she built herself into a tool without realizing it, and over the centuries, Jonas has been teaching himself to use that to his advantage, to use her as a tool."

"And rounding her out more with merges would help make her more of a generalist?"

Laughing, she set her plate down, tugged out her chair, and fell heavily into it. "Generalist is a very utilitarian way to put it. You are not wrong in that it would allow her to be more than a unitasker, but it would also make her more of a person, harder to control. Someone as focused as her is easy to pin down."

"I would've thought she'd see that coming, though."

"Well, you have heard what she has said. She has been fed bad information by her spies–"

"And the other True Names. At least #Castor."

She frowned, finished chewing on her asparagus. "There is also that, yes. It is a guess, but I think you are right. How and why he managed to work them into this plan to only subvert this instance of her is another question that I think we would all like an answer to. All the same, she has been fed bad information and had aspects of her life leveraged against her, and now, for whatever reason, Jonas is making his power-grab."

"Aspects of her life meaning Zacharias?"

"Yes," she said. "I will not call it a weakness, even as awful as he sounds. To have a relationship is not a weakness."

Ey chuckled, dipping the corner of eir sandwich into the soup. "That's a very May statement."

"Of course it is," she said primly, stabbing another spear of asparagus before biting off the top. "But this is yet more guess-work. I cannot say for sure that Zacharias is purely working in the hands of Jonas, but from all that she has said to me, I do not think I am too far off the mark."

They ate in silence for a few minutes.

While ey didn't mind May's ideas of comfort food, they were not especially well spiced. This was mostly by design, ey suspected, as eating spicy or sour foods when one has been (or still is) crying sounded unpleasant. Still, there was much to be said about the comfort of a good grilled cheese dipped in soup.

"But yes," the skunk continued once she'd cleaned her plate. "There was some aspect of vengeance to my and End Waking's plan, but now I just want her away from Jonas. I do not know yet whether or not I like her or want her to stay in our lives in any way, shape, or form, but I do know that I want her away from him. I want her to live and to–"

Both Ioan and May jolted in their seats as a flash of adrenaline ran through them. A view of a forest, a lake shore, pile of wood not yet lit, and, sitting on a log across from that, another furry. His facial structure was very similar to Dear's but where the fennec had wound up with that pristine white fur, he had ruddy orange except for the white on the underside of his chin and a dark apostrophe of fur on either side of his snout. Where Dear had wound up with almost absurdly large ears, his felt far more in proportion, along the lines of May's and True Names, though far pointier.

One thing Dear and this new fox did share in common was the snappy dress. Where Dear had wound up in a sharp androgyny, though, the red fox had turned it into a prim masculinity that was, ey had to admit, quite effective. Black trousers, a white shirt and charcoal waistcoat, and a suit jacket. It was topped off with a simple tie and affected cane, currently being twirled lazily between black-furred paws.

It was just a glimpse, less than a second's worth of sensorium input, but enough for em to make a guess.

"Is that Zacharias? Wait! May! Oh, God damnit."

The skunk had already stepped away

"We have guests!" Zacharias said, standing up and dusting off his trousers. "I was not expecting guests. How cheeky."

True Name was still kneeling before the pile of wood in what had clearly become her firepit. "I am trying to imagine a world in which I should trust you enough to be alone with you," she growled. "And failing."

"Spicy, tonight, are we not?" He grinned, turning to bow extravagantly to Ioan and May. "Mx. and Mrs. Bălan, I presume?"

"We are not married," May said, growling nearly as well as True Name. "What the fuck are you doing here?"

"Oh, just popping in to say hi, is all," he said cheerily. "Zacharias, by the way. Nice to meet you, Ioan. My dear May Then My Name, it has been more than two hundred years!"

"Well, hi," she said. "Now get out."

"Oh, I just got here, though!" He pouted, looking between the three of them. Then the smirk returned, along with a wicked glint to his eye. "Besides, what are you going to do about it, my dear? Bounce me?"

May frowned, but remained silent, arms crossed over her chest. None of them had the ACLs for such.

"Right, I thought not. Well! Have a sit, I was just saying hi to True Name, but what's another two asses in seats?"

Neither Ioan nor May moved.

"Well, fuck you, too, then," he said, laughing, and sat back down. "So, True Name, my little stink bug, how are you? Roughing it out here?"

The skunk glowered down to the striker and knife, quickly sparking up a coal in the leaf-litter tinder she'd gathered. She blew on it a few times before setting it in a pile of larger kindling. "I am on vacation. What the fuck does it look like?"

"Like you are roughing it."

She rolled her eyes.

"Look, why are you really out here?" Ioan asked. "Clearly it isn't just to say hi, and clearly you got access somehow. Got news from Jonas or something?"

"Very perceptive!" Zacharias said, grinning happily. "Just out here checking up on True Name to see if she has any further thoughts on our little gathering."

"Checking up on someone you tried to assassinate?"

"Oh goodness, not me! You can place the blame for that squarely on Jonas."

May laughed humorlessly. "Right, and poor Zack just had to sit by and–"

The fox was up in a flash and, with a back-handed swipe, slapped the skunk across the muzzle, getting a yelp out of her and a shout out of Ioan. "You do not have permission to use that name," he hissed.

It took Ioan a few seconds to process what had just happened, but then fury welled up within em faster than any other emotion ey'd felt before. Had ey ever even felt fury before? A small part of em marveled at the unfamiliar feeling.

The rest was already swinging.

The blow never landed. Ioan found emself stumbling backwards several paces. Zacharias stumbled back in the opposite direction. Both of them shouted and worked to regain their footing.

The two new instances of May that had appeared, partially overlapping with where they had once stood, winked out of existence. "Yes, yes," she drawled, taking Ioan's hand in one paw to hold em back while the other rubbed at her muzzle. "We all know you are good at what you do. Get to the point."

With a huff, the fox stood up straighter, smoothing out his rumpled clothing. "Right. True Name. Are you coming tonight? If not, when shall we expect you?"

The skunk shook her head, still glowering. "I am not coming tonight, no. If I have been given the luxury of a year to meet," she said, tone dripping with sarcasm. "Then we will meet when I say we meet."

"If you say so." Zacharias was back to smirking. That hatred still bubbling within Ioan urged em to consider just how delightfully punchable that expression was. "Well, we will look forward to it, then, I suppose! And you two will be there as well, yes?"

"Your piece of shit boss hired me, didn't he?"

"That he did, Mx. Bălan! That he did." He turned to May, eyebrows raised expectantly.

"Yes, I will be there," she said. Her hackles were still up, free paw still bunched into a fist.

"And End Waking? Would not want the stanza to be incomplete, would we?" He grinned broadly to True Name, "And no, my little stink bug, you do not count."

"He has not answered yet," she said. She'd regained her composure, staring at Zacharias steadily. "We will speak with him. Tell Jonas message received and leave me the fuck alone."

He once more bowed with a flourish. "I live to serve, Rintrah my dear!" he said, sing-song. "Any other messages for me to relay while hungry clouds swag on the deep?"

"Yes, tell Jonas to quit sending his most foppish lackeys," she shot back.

"But my dear! I am here specifically to drive the point home! You are in so far over your head that even 'little loverfox' is a part of your fate." He laughed gleefully. "Oh, it sounds so evil, does it not? Cartoonishly so! There is no way that I can even begin to talk about this without sounding like a mustache-twirling villain. That I might say things like 'encompass your doom' just tickles me pink. We will see you soon, yes?"

True Name nodded. "Yes. Now, fuck off."

"Righto!" He turned and winked to May, adding, "So wonderful to see you again. Cannot say I share your taste in partners, but times change, I suppose. Mx. Bălan, I look forward to speaking soon."

And with that, he stepped out of the sim.

May's shoulders slumped. She let go of eir hand, padded over to kneel beside True Name, and hugged around her shoulders. "I am sorry, my dear."

True Name did not return the gesture. No surprise, perhaps; neither she nor End Waking were all that big on touch. Instead she said, "I apologize, you two. I do not know how they got the address to the sim."

Ioan cursed. "Guess that does mean it's compromised."

She nodded.

May leaned away from the hug, but took one of True Name's paws in her own. "Come home," she said, voice and expression earnestly worried. "Please. I know it is uncomfortable, but I do not want you out here alone."

The skunk stared into the fire for almost a full minute, then looked off to the lake and nodded. "Yes, I suppose you are right." She smiled faintly and added, "I could also use a shower and a night's sleep on a real mattress. Perhaps we can discuss expanding an outdoor portion of your sim tomorrow, Ioan. I do not want to impose too much, but, well..." She waved her paw at where Zacharias had stood.

"Of course," ey said, still doing eir best to tamp down eir anger. "I can find something simple on the market for the time being."

True Name knelt by the fire for a moment longer before dousing the flames.

Once they made it back to the house and True Name had showered, they sat around the dining table, each with a glass of wine from a bottle ey'd received years back. When True Name suggested that a drink was in order, Ioan and May readily agreed.

Ioan couldn't guess why the two skunks had felt it was necessary, but ey needed something to try and blunt the edges of that anger that still spun within em. Ey wasn't sure ey'd ever truly felt fury before, but it turned out that watching eir partner get struck across the face was a really, really good way to bring out the emotion.

Ey didn't like it at all.

Once ey'd reached the bottom of eir glass, ey sighed and said, "Alright. What the hell was that about?"

"Jonas felt the need to show a bit of muscle," True Name said, voice flat and dull. "He wanted to rub it in my face that he still has Zacharias in his pocket, that he knows where I am. I do not think he actually cared about asking me when we would meet, he was just making his leverage felt. I suspect he was planning on you two showing up as well, now that I think about it."

"Why?"

"To ensure that you also saw that power. If you two are to come to the meeting—as I think you must—then he wants you both to know that he will be there with a stacked deck." She rubbed a paw up over her snout, adding, "I am sorry that you had to meet him."

Ioan shook eir head. "Was he always such an asshole?"

After a tense pause, the skunk shook her head. "He was not, no. Witty, smart, sharp-tongued, yes. An asshole, no."

"Well, not looking forward to seeing him again, either way."

Ey felt that anger turn within em again, felt the heat of the wine only add to it. "I don't know who he thinks he is, coming after you like that, May."

The silence that followed was even more tense than the one before, both skunks looking down at the table, both tracing the grain of the wood with a claw-tip.

"What?"

May sniffled, shrugged, then smiled weakly to em. "I am pretty sure he thinks he is me, Ioan."

Ey blinked as the pieces clicked into place, then slouched back in eir seat, feeling like the breath had been knocked out of em. "Well, huh."

"You see now why I was so upset?"

The thoughts wouldn't quite fit together in eir mind. Two gears with no matching teeth. "I'm sorry, I'm, uh..." Ey cleared eir throat, suddenly parched. "*He's* one of your old relationship forks? With True Name?"

She shrugged again, sniffled again, looked back down to the table.

"It is at least partly my fault," True Name said quietly. "One of the earliest individuals I pointed May Then My Name towards was, without either of us realizing, one of Jonas's instances. He looked and spoke nothing like Jonas Prime, but was starting to get loud on the feeds. May Then My Name forked into a human form that we hoped would be appealing and became quite good friends with him, but I lost track of them both for several years. He stopped posting so much on the feeds, so I had little reason to worry about him, I thought."

"You must understand, I was a very different person back then," May mumbled. "This was systime 7 Back before I was...me."

Ey frowned, but nodded for them to continue.

"So, a few decades later," True Name said. "Secession is in the past, the council is heading towards dissolution, and I am starting to relax. More friends from phys-side uploaded, more furries figured out how to exist within the System as they would like, and I started to meet more people outside work. One of them just happened to be this fantastically well-dressed fox who was just as witty as I felt. We became friends, then we became a bit more." She shrugged. "That instance of Jonas had...well..."

"Twisted. He twisted my fork into something that neither the me of today nor the me back then would have agreed to," May said bitterly and wiped at her face. "He turned that version of me into a way of influencing True Name."

"Yes. It was a long game. He drifted in and out of my life, over the centuries, and then, shortly before Launch, he showed up again and we began to get close. A few years after Launch, they took me out to dinner and dropped the whole thing on me all at once. I am told they did the same on each of the LVs as well, just with different framing."

Eir head was swimming at the flood of information, and when rubbing eir face didn't work to clear it, ey willed the drunkenness away and waved a glass of ice water into being. "Which I don't get. Why are you so overwhelmed here and not on the LVs?"

The skunk twisted her wine glass between her fingers for a few quiet moments. "I have always been focused on continuity and stability. I think that Jonas was as well, enough to go along with the launch project, but once it was done and that conti-nuity was assured, we here on Lagrange let them go their own ways—the Guiding Council on Pollux and the previous status quo on Castor—while he focused on cementing his power. They were safely away with minimal influence here."

"Is that what this is all about?"

She nodded. "We were in a steady state for many years after they explained everything. I was not happy, but I still liked the work that I had chosen and I did not know how to do anything else. It was the new tech from the Artemisians that pushed things over the edge. AVEC—Audio/Visual Extrasys-tem Communication—rather changes things and even though we agreed on what was to be done about it in a general sense, I think he does not want to risk his own specific vision not coming to fruition. He wants greater divergence, while I am more conservative."

They sat in silence, then, while Ioan tried to digest this. Ey was still furious at Zacharias, but now that fury had gained a layer of what almost felt like despair that someone such as him might have their roots in eir May.

At least it had all gone a long way towards explaining the dynamic on the three Systems. Who knew why the other True Names had decided to treat this one like they had, withholding valuable information, all but cutting her out of their plans. Clearly those few years between launch and Jonas and Zacharias's announcement had included additional shaping, both of her as well as the Systems.

"Fuck."

May kicked eir shin lightly beneath the table. "Language, Mx. Bălan."

True Name looked between them, then grinned. "No, May Then My Name, Ioan is correct. Fuck."

"The Only Time I Know My True Name Is When I Dream of the Ode clade, you watch your mouth," May growled.

They all laughed. Ey couldn't help but. It was all too much, and the humor so perfectly timed to defuse eir anger that it had to be intentional. Some of that anger must have showed on eir face.

Ah well, trust an Odist, ey mused to emself.

Aloud, ey said, "You guys continue to be completely nuts. Thanks for explaining, though. I'm not going to figure it out tonight, so I'm going to have another glass of wine and space out on the couch."

"Fantastic idea, my dear," May said. "If I have to think about it anymore, I am going to start shedding and not stop until I am bald."

Still grinning, True Name nodded. "That is quite enough of

the topic, yes. I am going to go outside for a bit and then I am going to go to bed."

Ioan could have sworn that ey and May had gotten enough sleep the night before. Even with her waking em up before dawn, they'd then gone on to sleep until nearly nine. Rather late for them.

Still, that night, they slept for more than ten hours. It had taken May a while to calm down by the time they did make it into bed, the skunk tossing and turning, first leaning in against em, then shifting away, as though the last bits of her overflowing spell kept her oscillating between wanting to be touched and not. Ey stayed quiet and still throughout, letting her decide what it was that she needed; ey was just happy to be back home.

Eventually, though, they settled down into their usual spots and made it to sleep.

It was almost certainly the stress from the day before, ey reasoned. So much had happened in so short a time. Even the time spent relaxing on the beanbag with May felt at least productive, even if it was just resting. So much had been packed into those last few hours, though, and so much emotion overall through the day, that sleep became an imperative.

True Name had spent most of the rest of the evening outside, dragging one of eir chairs from beneath the balcony to park herself in the yard. Despite the lingering vestiges of snow and the chill of the evening, she spent hours out there, either staring up into the sky or grooming bits of forest litter out of her fur.

Ey imagined that she must have made it into bed at some point, though she still woke well before them, as when they finally managed to pry themselves out of bed, there were two steaming coffee mugs sitting on the edge of the kitchen counter, one black and one sweet and creamy, and the skunk was once more sitting outside on the chair, tail wrapped around her feet and coffee held against her chest.

Ioan sent her a gentle sensorium ping, just to let her know that they were awake, then sat at eir desk. Ey had no clue where to even begin, but if nothing else, ey had to have something comforting in front of em, something known.

"Well, nothing for it," ey mumbled, swiped a new notebook into being, and began to compile notes from the last few weeks. The work ey'd already done on the topic was useful enough, but it was starting to feel like it was not directed enough in the face of all that had happened.

Ey began with a timeline, starting all the way back at the arrival of the Artemisians and that first meeting with True Name, then followed with a list of the times they'd met for coffee through the years. Ey dug through eir memories for any that stood out as particularly interesting. These were primarily early on, ey found, when they were still feeling out each others' boundaries, though the last few before the assassination attempt held some fascinating insights in the context of all that had happened since, as well.

There was also information to fill in on the master timeline for the *History*, as well. Information about Zacharias, about Jonas, about End Waking's divergence from True Name.

Finally, the last almost three weeks were laid out in much finer detail. The assassination attempt, the clearing of the house, the meeting with End Waking, all the way up through the meeting with Zacharias the night before.

"Ioaaan," May whined, pawing feebly at eir arm. "Hungryyy."

"Hmm? You're a big skunk, you can make breakfast."

She stood up from where she'd been crouched beside em, laughing. "It is well on lunchtime, my dear. Come up for air."

"Wait, really?" Ey frowned when ey checked the time. "Great. Sorry about that, May."

They pulled together the remaining few dishes of comfort food and called out to True Name to invite her in for a meal. Ey chose the last of the poor skunk's risotto, added a healthy dusting of pepper, and got another cup of coffee to go with it.

"Thank you for lunch," True Name said, once she'd eaten most of her pasta. "When you have a moment, Ioan, I would like to see about expanding the sim as we discussed."

"Right, yeah. Sorry I got so distracted this morning." Ey browsed the markets for appropriate wide-open spaces ey could tack onto one of the borders of eir sim. Perhaps right beneath the skunk's window would be best. Ey could even extend the balcony and provide her with a set of stairs down into the space. "Alright. What sort of environment? There's some pretty good plains and parks, an okay forest, hmm...this mountain one isn't bad, but the trees are kind of planted in a grid."

She grinned. "That sounds cheesy. However, let us go with a plain of some sort. I do not want to go back to a forest unless it is the one I remember, and a park would be too sterile. Is there nothing like Arrowhead Lake? Something with water?"

Ey dug a little further, an act more akin to remembering than any actual physical browsing. It let em finish eir lunch, at least.

"Alright, here's one that's a plain with a river and an oxbow lake. The landscape is just mirrored at the boundaries though, so it looks a little funny beyond the edges."

The skunk had perked up at the mention of the river and was already nodding. "That will do quite nicely, my dear. Are you able to scale it so that it will be a good size, at least?"

"Sure. Do you want to set it up now?"

She shrugged. "If you are willing, yes."

"Can I modify your room to give you an entryway to the area?"

"Please," she said gratefully.

The three of them stood and walked into her room. Ey was somewhat crestfallen to see that ey really had just mirrored the view out of her window, as there was the chair she had been sitting in before lunch. That would mean ey'd have to place the new plot of land first, then modify the house again.

Ah well, easy enough.

Ey dumped a chunk of reputation into the purchase of the

environment. Ey had plenty to spend and it wasn't very pricey, but it was still a noticeable ding, and ey was sure that Jonas would be keeping tabs on eir acquisitions. There was nothing to be done about it, though.

The environment landed on eir mind much as a pending merge might, demanding to be placed somewhere. Ey instructed the sim to put it in the corner formed by the fence of their yard and True Name's bedroom, expanded to be a mile on a side.

Once the pressure of the environment left eir mind, ey was free to instruct the sim to let the window view the new land, and from there to add an extension of the balcony, a second stairway down, and a door leading out from her room to the balcony.

Ey slid the door open, beckoning to the two skunks. "Alright, let's head out and check on it."

As promised, they were greeted with what looked to be an endless series of perfectly parallel rivers fading into the distance with the way the boundaries simply mirrored the empty plain on the sides. The fact that the oxbow lakes were also repeated set up a grid effect that was slightly unnerving. Thankfully, the effect disappeared when they went down the steps and into the grass itself. They found the grass to be fairly well made and the ground to be delightfully uneven; no small feat when it was so easy to make a perfectly flat plane.

"I can maybe have the boundaries look like fog, if that helps. You'll have fog all the way around you, but at least no repeating rivers."

Both skunks straightened up, alarmed, then shook their heads as one.

"Please do not, Mx. Bălan. This will be fine as is."

The formality in her voice and the stiffness of her tone did not invite em to continue the topic, so ey did eir best to drop it. "Alright. Well, I guess we can give this a go for a bit and make changes if we need. The weather and sun are synced across the whole sim, so if you need it warmer or drier, just let me know."

True Name bowed. "Thank you, Ioan. This will suit me quite

well. It is a bit strange seeing a fence and part of a house, but at least that means I will be able to find my way back. May I have ACLs here?"

Ey nodded and made the grant.

"Thank you once more." She smiled faintly and gave a hint of another bow. "If you will excuse me, I would like to explore on my own. Perhaps we can catch up over dinner."

"Sure thing."

May, who had been quiet up until then, said, "Thank you for coming back."

True Name tilted her head. "It was not safe there, May Then My Name. This will be better."

"Yes, but thank you all the same." She laughed and waved a paw. "I am sorry, disregard me. I am still not yet at baseline and it has me feeling emotional."

The other skunk's expression softened and she leaned forward to give one of her paws a squeeze. It looked stiff and forced, but it was at least an attempt at a gesture that was more in line with May's mode of interacting.

"I understand. I do not think I am there, yet, myself. I will see you at dinner, yes?"

Ioan and May both nodded and made their goodbyes. As a last concession to giving the skunk privacy, ey made a small gate in the fence leading into their yard so that they wouldn't have to go through her room if they needed to go out into her plain for any reason. It meant pushing through lilac bushes, but ey figured it'd be rarely used.

"Can you work on the beanbag, Ioan?" May asked once they were back inside.

"Sure. Need some pets?"

She nodded.

Asking how she was feeling felt counter to simply providing what she'd requested—something ey enjoyed plenty, as well—so they made themselves comfortable on the amorphous cushion. It didn't seem to be time for talking at all, so they settled on soft music instead.

Ey wasn't sure what May was doing, whether it was simply soaking up the affection and close proximity or some more thoughtful task. For eir part, though, ey went back to work on organizing events as they'd happened. Who knew what would come next.

The next few days passed in relative peace, with both Odists slowly leveling back out to their baseline moods.

Or, at least, May leveled out to her baseline mood. There still seemed to be some internal struggle within True Name. It wasn't that she was having to step away to sulk or getting caught in anger as she had been when she had begun to overflow, but that the conflicts were still showing in long silences that would sometimes take her in the middle of conversations, especially when the topic of meeting with Jonas came up.

"I am not even sure if it is conflicts at this point," she admitted when ey brought it up. "Or, well, I do not think it is conflicting memories any longer. Those have been integrated, by this point. I am experiencing conflicts in expectations. I feel doubled, as though there are two of me watching the same conversation and each would like to act in a different way."

"Are they not working together?" May asked.

True Name leaned back against the couch and stared out the picture windows into the yard for a few minutes as she thought. "Perhaps not, no," she said at last. "It is difficult to reconcile those two parts of me. They are arguing, in a way. Each is strident in their belief, and some higher part of me will occasionally get stuck trying to get them to just settle down and fucking agree on a course of action or the next sentence or whatever it may be."

Ioan nodded, saying, "Sort of like Michelle and Sasha?"

She shook her head. "No, not quite like that, thankfully. There are some similarities—the sense of there being two parts of me, the internal split—but it is lacking the dire nature, whatever it was that made her completely helpless before the duality of her self. It is still something that I have some visibility into. I can respond as True Name would or as End Waking would, but I am still just me, and I am learning to unify those natures. I will perhaps never be singular, but I will doubtless unify into a synthesis before long. Just not yet."

May fiddled with eir sweater vest from where she lay against em. "I will admit that, for a while there, I was considering merging down with you before I saw how poorly End Waking's merge went." After the silence stretched out, she laughed nervously, adding, "Sorry, I suppose that is a pretty awkward thing to say."

"It is okay, May Then My Name," True Name said, smiling reassuringly. "A large part of me wishes that you had rather than End Waking, if I am honest. I understand why you did what you did, and I think on an intellectual level I agree with it, but on a personal level, I would much rather be integrating your memories than his."

She winced. "That bad?"

"Uncomfortable," the other skunk corrected. "I do wish perhaps that I had been able to fork or that I had been more cautious with the merge, but if I wanted to remain comfortable, I would have pushed back when you urged me to accept."

"What about May's merge would've been easier?" Ioan asked.

"Again, easier does not feel like the correct word. It would have been more comfortable. I would have understood the resentment that others feel for me, if that was indeed a goal, but it would not be the defining factor of the merge."

"End Waking has mentioned that he defined himself by not being you, yeah."

She nodded. "So I have learned. The self-loathing that falls out of that rests just this side of overwhelming at times. Perhaps that is why it is proving to be such a project to settle into something resembling a singular nature again. I imagine, given that May Then My Name has defined herself through something unique to her rather than some aspect of her relation to me, it would feel strange, but not so uncomfortable. Do correct me if I am wrong, though, my dear."

May shook her head.

"Well, besides," Ioan added. "She's certainly merged down way more recently than End Waking did."

True Name tilted her head.

"Ioan," May said quietly. "Do you remember when you were working on the *History* and I said that I was worried that you would be upset with me?"

Ey frowned, nodded.

"And do you remember how Dear told Codrin that the temptation to lie would be great?"

"What did you say to em, May Then My Name?"

May sighed and brushed her paws up over her head. "I said that I was working as launch coordinator to remain more in line with your expectations so that I could merge back down after the project was over, that we tried to do so every few decades."

A silence stretched out once more.

Eventually, Ioan reached up to tug at one of her ears gently. "Skunks are so complicated."

She let out a pent up breath as a laugh. "I know. I am sorry. I am sorry to both of you. I believed it to be a small untruth. I wanted my relationship with True Name to seem simpler than it was to keep you feeling comfortable. I hoped that that would keep you from digging into my past. Fat load of good that did."

"When was the last time you merged down, then?"

"2155," True Name said. "Longer ago than the last time End Waking merged down. It was not acrimonious, she simply declined my next request for a merger and the conversation never came up again."

Ey laughed. "Really, *really* complicated."

"I am glad you are not angry, my dear," May said, leaning up to dot her nose against eir cheek.

"It seems more silly than anything, but I can see your reasons for doing so, in retrospect. Certainly silly in comparison to the last few weeks."

"Very." May turned her gaze back to True Name and said, "I have my apprehensions about merging, though. *We* have our apprehensions, I mean. After watching what happened with End Waking's merge, it all felt so much more complicated."

"I do not know," she said, voice distant. "I said that I understand your reasons for what you did. You wanted me to change, you said, to be other than I am. You want me to be able to approach Jonas in some new way that will hopefully allow me to come out the other side with fewer assassins on my tail, yes?"

May nodded.

"And I also think I understand your reasons for wanting to merge down. It would make me understand your relationship to me in a very real way, and would make me all the more complete a person in your eyes, yes?"

Another nod.

"I am amenable to both of those, though perhaps my reasons differ. But, May Then My Name, coming at this with both full knowledge and as an open conversation has me feeling more positive than perhaps you do," she said, voice having lost its thoughtful edge. "You are a fundamentally good person and that is not something that I take lightly. You work on such a small scale and I have spoken against that in the past, but...well, a threat on one's life is a pretty good way to make one realize that the small scale is still important."

"But Ioan and I–"

"I would have full knowledge of your apprehensions as well, would I not?" She held up her paws, smiling. "I am not trying to talk you into it, my dear, and I would still like to hear those apprehensions regardless, I am simply explaining that, given this shitty fucking month, you merging down does not at all sound bad. I am already not what I was. There is no going and there is no back."

Ioan realized ey'd settled back into observing mode, simply watching silently. Not what ey was supposed to be working on. Ey shook emself back to the present and said, "My apprehensions mostly boil down to the fact that the merge would include May and I's entire relationship. The memories are one thing, and there are some that are pretty intensely personal, but I worry you'd also risk winding up with the feelings that resulted from the formation of those memories."

True Name nodded.

Ey took a deep breath, trying to bolster eir courage with it. "This last month has made me realize how much I care about you and your well-being. I like you, True Name, but I'm really hesitant about you having memories of loving me, if that makes sense."

"And you, May Then My Name? We do not need to go too far into them, but if it is to be a discussion, I would like to at least have these thoughts laid out for perusal."

She was a long time in responding. "I am with Ioan on this, in that I am protective of my devotion to em. It...is difficult to say this so openly, but I am also coming to terms with just how complex my feelings about you are after the events of the last month, and the root of resentment that led to me urging End Waking's merge on you is no longer there, or at least no longer quite so simple. It is no longer aimless hatred, however justified it may have felt. I will ever be myself, so I am uncomfortable pushing yet more resentment and difficulties on you. I do not want to hurt you."

The longer May spoke, the more thoughtful True Name's expression became. She slouched down on the couch, until her head was resting against the back cushions. "I am not sure what to say to this just yet."

"We've been thinking about it for days. You've had, what, twenty minutes?"

She laughed and nodded to em. "Yes, of course. There is much to think about." After True Name returned to her room—

or, more likely, out to her field to set up camp—May said, "If I may say, that was really fucking weird, and I do not want to talk about it at all."

Ey laughed. "You certainly may. Weird as hell and I need a break."

That last part wasn't strictly true. Ey knew ey'd be ruminating over it until they went to sleep, and likely well into tomorrow. Still, ey agreed that it wasn't a topic for talking about at the moment. The chances they'd just wind up talking in circles, rehashing the same topics over and over, getting nowhere but frustrated, was too high, and ey could do that mentally just as well.

So, instead, they relaxed together on the couch, May with her head in eir lap while ey read and she worked on this or that, or whatever it was that she did when her eyes lost focus and she hummed quietly to herself. She'd once called it 'going into screen-saver mode', which didn't sound totally accurate to what ey knew of her when ey'd looked up the reference, but ey still teased her about it every now and then.

Quiet nights were good, though, and ey was pleased to just spend the rest of this one in comfort.

Sleep, however, brought restless dreams. Not nightmares, certainly; they weren't even bad dreams in any common sense of the term. They were, to the last, plagued with a sense of waiting and unease. Ey dreamt of waiting for unspecified news, sitting on uncomfortable benches in weirdly crowded lobbies. Ey dreamt of May being out of the house on some errand longer than she had said she would be. Ey dreamt of not having enough information.

All the same, ey woke well rested and made it to the coffee pot before either of the skunks, so ey was able to claim ten minutes of solitude standing before the picture windows, looking out into the slowly lightening yard and the field beside it. Ey could see True Name poke her snout out from her tent, disappear, and then, a few minutes later, start trudging her way back toward the house.

"Good morning, Ioan. Oh good, thank you," she mumbled, making a bee-line for one of the mugs of coffee that sat, steaming, on the counter.

"Morning. Sleep well?"

She shrugged noncommittally. "I slept, I am well-rested enough."

They watched the morning head toward full brightness in silence after that, em still standing before the windows and her sitting on the couch, more focused on her coffee than anything.

"You have once again failed to bring me my coffee," May grumbled from the bedroom door. "I am going to file a petition to have you censured with the leadership of the System."

"Ey did not bring me my coffee, either, my dear," True Name said mildly. "And until recently, I was in such a position."

May stopped mid-shuffle, snorted, then mumbled an apology and padded to the kitchen to grab her own mug before taking Ioan by the hand and dragging em over to the beanbag so that she could lay down with em.

"Are you two up to talking about meeting with Jonas?" True Name asked. "I will pay in another pot of coffee and breakfast."

Ioan shrugged. "Sure."

"After that second coffee, yes," May said.

Breakfast, it turned out, was a Scandinavian affair, or so ey imagined. Dense, dark bread, a tray of cheeses and meats, and a separate tray of vegetables both pickled and fresh. It was strange to call a meal such as breakfast 'refreshing', but the word fit quite well. Quite good, and both of the skunks certainly seemed to appreciate it, eating the lion's share of the food, though May also swiped up a side plate of eggs to go with it.

May nodded towards True Name, grinning. "Alright. Payment accepted. You may begin."

True Name nodded. "I had an idea as I was walking last night. Or perhaps it is only a sliver of an idea. I suspect that it will not even get me out of whatever it is that he has planned, but it might soften the blow."

They both nodded.

"My guess is that, if he wants me to 'step aside', as Zacharias said, then he would like me to truly disappear. He would like me to essentially never be seen again."

"Thus the assassination attempt," Ioan said.

"Yes. He wanted me to disappear and build up a little bit of mystery because then he would be able to be publicly seen mourning, *et cetera, et cetera, ad nauseam*," she continued, rolling her eyes. "The usual nonsense, I mean. I do not think his plans B through M will be any different. They will all involve me no longer being a part of this and in such a way as to make him come out feeling the victor."

"And I'm assuming you'd like to avoid that if possible."

"Him feeling like the victor? Yes. I really do mean that I would need to disappear in his definition of victory. I would be effectively dead, if not actually. I would be restricted in who I would be able to speak to, I would have to remain out of public sims, and so on. He would not ask me to retire. Disappear." She hesitated, swirled the last of her coffee in the bottom of her mug, and added, "At least, that is what I would do. It would mean less attack surface for the reactive elements we have been tracking."

"And your plan would, what, subvert that?" May asked. "I have a suspicion I know what it is, but I would like to be sure."

"I suspect you do, yes. I will offer him the option of me changing from what I was to such an extent that I will no longer be the True Name that either he or the System expects."

"Is this about me merging down, then?"

She shrugged. "I do not think that that is a requirement here, though that question was on my docket for the day. I suspect that I have already changed enough with End Waking's merger. I would just need to prove it to him somehow. That is where my plan ends, however."

Ioan sat back in eir chair, arms crossed as ey mulled it over. If she was right—and ey suspected that she was—then there would likely need to be a change in form and a change in name to go along with the change in attitude. After all, that's how Zacharias had gotten as far as he had, right?

Ey couldn't picture her as anything other than a skunk or perhaps whatever version of Michelle she remembered, though, and certainly couldn't picture her named anything other than True Name. Would she also have to change her speech patterns? They weren't totally identifiable, but now that ey thought about it, even Zacharias had shared many of them. She was an Odist through and through—more so than any other ey'd met—and all of the forking and reinforcing that May had done to cement behavior and thought patterns didn't seem like something that she'd willingly undergo, either.

But perhaps that's what she'd meant by a sliver of a plan. They still had plenty of time to sort that out, at least, and perhaps she'd come up with a way that would actually work without changing herself so much that she'd cease being who she was.

All the same, ey wasn't sure that her simply incorporating End Waking was quite the type of change that Jonas would appreciate. She acted different, spoke different, and ey was sure she felt different about her work than she had, but eir suspicion was that Jonas didn't want anything left of her that could possibly be of any threat to his power. Her incorporating End Waking's extreme distaste for the politics of the System might be enough, it might not be, but that was a big risk to take.

Ey'd apparently been silent long enough that the two skunks had drifted off into their own conversation. At least ey hadn't been mumbling.

"Welcome back, my dear," May said when ey leaned forward again to grab eir coffee.

Ey grinned. "Thanks. Was a nice trip. Don't mean to interrupt or anything, though."

She shook her head. "We were talking of changes."

"Any conclusions?"

"Not particularly, no," True Name said. "There are certain levels of change that I find unacceptable, is all."

"Right. I was thinking similar. It needs some work, but I can at least see where you're coming from with it."

She nodded. "I will continue to explore. When the time comes, I may ask for your help workshopping some ideas."

The conversation wound down from there, with True Name heading out to walk her prairie or poke around in the water or whatever it was that she was doing.

As though inspired, May and Ioan both moved outside as well, claiming the bench swing on the balcony, sitting on it sideways and facing each other, legs all tangled up. The warmer spring weather ey'd brought about for May while she was overflowing had seemed appropriate once they'd returned, so ey'd left it for the time being. Perhaps ey'd get one more big snow in before letting spring proper settle in.

"What were things like back in 2155?" ey asked.

May tilted her head, blinking a cone of silence into place. "When I merged last?"

Ey nodded.

"I had just forked the third time. There had been more relationships, of course, ones that ended before I had the chance or need, but this was the third time that I had settled into something comfortable enough to let it last. I was crushed and not particularly excited about merging down, but I had not diverged quite as much by then."

"Not as much empathy?"

She laughed. "Too much, perhaps. It took a while for me to settle on a comfortable amount."

"Too *much?* How on Earth did that work?"

"I was a fucking mess at all times. I cried at the drop of a hat."

"You still cry a lot," ey observed, then laughed when she poked at eir knee.

"Yes, well. I had attributed it at the time to simply being torn up over no longer being in a relationship. My fork was happy, I was heartbroken. In the end, though, I think that my goals were starting to drift from True Name's. I was diverging in more fundamental ways than either of us had expected."

"And the next time she asked, you just said 'no'?"

She nodded. "She asked me to consider it, and then the topic simply never came up again. I think that she was already expecting to write me off after the merge in systime 31."

"Did she wind up expressing her own emotions differently from that merge?"

She opened her mouth as if to reply, then closed it again, frowning. "I was going to snap at you," she admitted. "But you bring up a good point. She did, to some extent. What emotions she expressed, real or not, came more earnestly to her. She was more able to express empathy, even if it was still in a very True Name fashion. She did not accept my merges—or any of those from others in her stanza—as blithely as she did End Waking's."

"I imagine the circumstances were a bit different," ey said. "Why were you going to snap at me?"

"I thought you were going to ask me to merge down."

Ey shrugged. "I hadn't gotten that far in the thought process. Is it something you're still uncomfortable with?"

"I do not know, my dear. If you had asked me just then, I would have said no. If you had asked me five minutes before then, I would have said yes." She patted eir knee, smiling. "But I will endeavor not to snap at you either way. How about you, though?"

"Much the same, I think. Your answer has me wondering, though, if she was more intentional about a merge like that, it could work. She could have some of your memories of emotions that she thinks might help while still respecting your privacy."

"And that is why I did not snap at you. It is a good point, my dear. There is no need for her to have all of my memories wholesale, and with what memories and personality traits and whatever else goes along with a merge, she would hopefully wind up with a synthesis, as she says, rather than a replacement. She would still have all 226 years of being True Name, and all those years of being End Waking, just that she would also have some of me in there."

"Is that something you could talk her through?"

She looked thoughtfully out into the yard, at the faint greening of the lilac branches. "Perhaps, yes. We would have to be very deliberate about it, but it should be possible."

Ey nodded, watching the skunk's gaze drift in and out of focus, the way she would occasionally chew on her lip when thinking. Watched, and thought about what such a synthesis would look like. There wouldn't be any concrete changes in eir partner, but what would this new restless, unsettled True Name look like with yet more memory heaped onto her? Ey knew ey could never know the whole of May and that ey was biased besides, but she seemed so much happier and more comfortable than her down-tree instance, even before End Waking's merger. More comfortable, feeling less of a need to dump all of her energy into forward motion. What would that look like with True Name?

Ey watched her think. Watched her and thought about how much ey loved her, watched and wondered if such a True Name would also sit and think and chew on her lip.

"Do you want to?"

May started from her own reverie. "Hmm?"

"Regardless of the mechanics or how comfortable you are with it, is this something you'd even want to do?"

She nodded readily. "Yes. That is the source of all this stress for me over the last few days. I want to, it is just the reality that is working against me."

"Why?"

"Why do I want to?" She laughed. "Because I like who I am and I do not like who she is, but that does not mean I do not like what she can become. I want her to be happy and to feel love and to slow the fuck down for five minutes. I do not know for sure, and I acknowledge that there is a value judgment here, but I strongly suspect that these will only ever be good for her."

Ey leaned forward enough to snag one of her paws and give it a squeeze. "Guess we're of one mind on that, then. Or at least mostly so; you have a better sense as to what goes into the emotional side."

She smiled gratefully and gave eir hand a squeeze. "Well, when she returns, we can expand on our thoughts."

They didn't have to wait long.

Shortly after they went back inside to pull together a snacky sort of lunch, True Name returned from her trip out in the prairie and bowed to them, saying, "I have had some thoughts that I would like to run past you."

"As have we," Ioan said, gesturing her to a chair. "Good timing. What were you thinking?"

"It is perhaps more for May Then My Name to answer, though I will appreciate both of your input."

The skunk nodded for her to continue.

"You have mentioned in the past that you forked to cement emotional patterns that led to your divergence. I think that I have wound up doing that to some extent, but only ever subconsciously. With how much specificity were you able to pick what it was that you were modifying?"

May glanced to Ioan, then shrugged. "I worked in very small steps. I forked dozens of times to change very small things. Being deliberate about it made it essentially as fine-grained as I needed."

"Alright. That helps quite a lot, actually. I was considering how much I might be able to change without losing who and what I am. If I can change some of my own habits, maybe the end result will still be something that I am happy with, but with enough difference to get Jonas off my back. I am not yet sure what those habits might be, but it is an option, at least. I have been trying to catalogue what it is about myself that can go, as it were." She smiled wryly, "But yes, doing so deliberately is probably for the best."

"That's actually what we had been talking about," Ioan said, looking to May for confirmation that it was alright to continue.

"A deliberate merge," she said, picking up from where ey'd left off. "One that will keep us comfortable in our privacy while also giving you the opportunity to build upon what you are."

"Really? That is not what I was expecting to hear."

They both nodded.

There was a long silence, then. Both May and Ioan watched True Name as she stared up at the ceiling, unseeing.

"And you are okay with that, Ioan?"

Ey nodded. "I think so. I don't wholly understand the mechanics of it, but you're the dispersionistas. I trust you two to have that covered."

She nodded and looked to May.

"If you are alright working with me through the process, then I am okay with it."

"Are you?" Ioan asked.

True Name smiled lopsidedly. "So long as I can fork beforehand just in case, why the hell not? I am already not what I was. There is already no going back."

May scoffed and shook her head. " 'So long as you can fork'? Jesus, True Name. Of course you can fucking fork. 108 instances with daily reconciliation, and she asks if she can fork."

They laughed.

"Well," True Name said, shrugging. "Fuck it."

Part IV

Reconciliation

*The living know that they will die
but the dead know nothing.*

By our very act of knowing, of remembering, of denying our own deaths, the dead are left in limbo, for every idea's opposite is the absence of that idea, and we can no longer grant them even that absence.

From *Ode* by Sasha

Ioan Bălan—2350

Of all that had happened over the past several weeks, Ioan was surprised to find that it had taken until now for literally anything to feel like it had been planned. Clearly none of them had planned on Jonas coming after True Name, but all of the decisions that had followed had been made on the spot. Snap decisions that had led to True Name moving into their house, to End Waking merging down, to the three of them all overflowing at once.

All of those had been made under what felt like intolerable pressure, and it was only now that they had time enough to relax. There was an uneasy (and certainly temporary) truce between Jonas and True Name that had finally given them enough time to properly consider a decision instead of feeling compelled to make it right away.

Ey'd harbored a concern, one borne out of stress, that May might just merge down without talking further, but ey kept that to emself, doing eir level best to reason emself out of it. The last thing they needed at the moment was eir mind playing tricks on em.

And she certainly didn't. In fact, she drew the negotiations that followed that first discussion out by nearly a week, putting lie to that concern. Much of these discussions took place between the two skunks as they walked out on True Name's prairie.

At first, ey'd felt left out. After all, didn't ey also have boundaries to negotiate and concerns that needed addressing?

After bringing this up with May, however, she had laughed and poked em in the belly, explaining, "I do not mean to leave you out of anything, my dear. We are discussing elements of the past that kept me from merging down, and elements of the future of the relationship between me and her. You are not missing anything so important, but if you would like, I am happy to keep you apprised of the general content."

"Given how anxious I've been, I'd appreciate that," ey had said. "But no need to share anything private."

And so now ey got updates on the conversations with sensitive or personal information held back.

They spent much of their time discussing various parts of May's life and how comfortable she'd feel sharing those through a merge, and if not, why not. Surprisingly, they also talked with End Waking several times, the third skunk of the stanza coming out to visit her prairie so that they could discuss the ramifications of their merge and how to be more thoughtful with May's.

That first meeting had been more silence than not, more walking and thinking and not looking at each other than anything. They paced back and forth along the bank of the river, then stared into the oxbow pond, each occasionally failing to start a conversation. They had greater success with subsequent meetings, but they were never comfortable.

This wasn't to say that ey didn't have a chance to sit with them at times and discuss eir thoughts on the matter, of course.

"Feelings are complex, Ioan," True Name explained as they sat around a low fire before her tent. "If they are created by memories, then there is little that I can do to completely control how I might feel about something beyond picking and choosing the memories carefully. However, one can never be sure which memories may lead to which feelings. If they come from something more intrinsic to one's personality and thought patterns, then it is even more difficult to attempt to control them."

Ey nodded. "That much I can certainly understand. I trust that you'll be built up from your various histories rather than simply May's feelings tacked onto you."

"Yes. I cannot predict how I will feel about anything after this, much less you. Your relationship and existing boundaries will take precedence over whatever happens, though. I will respect that."

Ioan bowed eir thanks.

"I have been wondering how your feelings toward Debarre have shifted," End Waking said.

"It is complex, not least of which because I accepted the whole of your merge so blithely. I will not be doing the same with May Then My Name's."

He frowned.

"I am sorry," True Name said, shrugging helplessly. "There is little that I could have done in the moment to avoid it, and there is certainly nothing that I can do now to fix it."

May dipped her muzzle and apologized as well, saying, "I do feel bad about how that worked out, no matter how much you tell me it is okay."

"It is not okay," End Waking said, then hastened to add when his cocladist flinched away, "It is what we have to work with, and it is perhaps what the moment called for."

May nodded, still cowed.

"I am of two minds," True Name said. "I remember having loved Debarre. I remember still loving him, and perhaps even I, even True Name, still love him in some roundabout way. However, I am what I am, and that is a being of two minds. That of me which is you, End Waking, loves him, and that of me which is True Name, respects him from a distance, respects his distaste for me, that feeling I engendered to minimize his impact within the council by making it purely emotional, as uncomfortable as it was to do so."

"The same as you did with me and Codrin?" Ioan asked. "With the History, I mean."

She nodded. "It was– it felt like a necessity at the time. I am not some cold, unfeeling bitch, it is just that my drive and my abilities, such as they are, outweigh—or at least outweighed— those feelings. I worked to distance myself from them."

"I remember so little of that," May said.

True Name shrugged. "As you intentionally moved towards feeling, I worked to contain and compartmentalize it within myself after you came into being. I became a being of negative commandments. I lived the 'shalt not's while you performed your *mitzvot* of loving and caring."

May sighed.

"I will not say that I am proud of it, my dear, but neither will I say that I regret it. It is what it is specifically because I was what I was."

"Perhaps you will learn from your merge," End Waking said.

"Perhaps. Perhaps it will become a part of me, perhaps it will live within me alongside that of you and that of True Name."

"Still feeling fractured?" Ioan asked.

"I am of two minds, Ioan. I do not know if I will feel...I do not know. I am not comfortable speaking further on this just yet."

They spent the rest of the night in quiet, May leaning against eir side while True Name and End Waking spoke quietly about the plain and the forest.

Finally, though, a week to the day after the decision had been made, Ioan awoke to find May and True Name already sitting at the table, speaking earnestly in a cone of silence. Once they noticed em, True Name waved it away and May grinned, saying, "Sorry, my dear. We did not want to wake you."

Ey poured emself a cup of coffee before joining them. "Appreciate it. Hope I'm not interrupting."

True Name shook her head. "We are discussing our plan for the day."

Ey bought emself a moment by taking a sip of coffee. "Is today the day, then?"

"May Then My Name thinks so, but we were also waiting for you to join us to make sure."

"Well, if it were solely up to me, I'd just spin my wheels worrying about it until we ran out of time, so I suppose I'm alright with it. What all will go into it?"

"Well," True Name began, a fork appearing next to her. "First I fork and she will head to the tent."

The new instance of True Name bowed. "Then the perilous path was planted, And a river and a spring On every cliff and tomb," she said before waving goodbye and padding back out through her room.

Ioan stared after the departing skunk and shook eir head. "You guys are so weird."

They both laughed.

"Then we will set up a space for me to rest in the meantime," True Name continued. "And then I suppose that is all there is to it. May Then My Name will fork and quit and I will process the merge."

"And your fork is just there in case something goes wrong?"

"Or if the result is not acceptable."

" 'Not acceptable'?"

"If the merge does not go well or if I wind up being unable to work as I would like."

"Or if all of my emotions get overwhelming," May added. "Since I do rather have a surfeit."

Ioan leaned over and ruffled a hand over the skunk's ears. "Yeah, you definitely do."

"Yes, yes, and you love me for it." She laughed and pushed eir hand away, straightening the mussed up fur. "Breakfast first, though, and then we can work from there."

After another Scandinavian-style breakfast, the three of them re-organized True Name's room. The bed was set in a corner instead of up against one wall, allowing a collection of pillows to be placed against the walls in case she wanted to lean against them or organize them into a nest.

"Are you sure you don't want to set up something out in the prairie?"

"I did consider it, but May Then My Name talked me out of it, stating that she would like to be at hand without having to spend all of her time out there, herself. Besides, if I learned one thing from End Waking merging down, it was that the less I have to think about my body, the easier it is to focus on my mind. Comfort will only ever help."

They also supplied her with ready water, juice, and a few comforting snacks on one of the bedside tables so that she wouldn't have to get up just to go to the kitchen.

Another beanbag was added by the bed, in case she requested that they stay in there for any length of time, and a more comfortable bench-swing was added to the balcony in case she needed to go outside but wasn't feeling up to walking down to the prairie itself.

It felt like rather a lot of preparations to make just for a merge, but then May had last merged down 83 years before ey had uploaded—nearly 64 before ey'd even been born—and after seeing how intense End Waking's merge had been, none of them felt up to cutting any corners and having to rush comfort after the fact.

Finally, though, there was nothing left to do, no further preparations to be made that weren't just stalling, so May took eir hand to hold em still so that ey'd quit pacing.

"I don't even know why I'm fretting so much, I'm not even the one merging."

True Name smiled faintly and shrugged. "I am fretting too, do not worry."

"It is a big event," May added. "It will be an even bigger merge and, while it may be more comfortable than End Waking merging down as she has said, it will be no less complex."

Ey sighed and nodded, squeezing her paw before tugging eir hand free. "Right. I'll relax and leave you to the rest of it."

"Please stay, Ioan," True Name said quietly.

"Stay?"

"Yes. Please stay. I do not think it will be dramatic, but, well..." She hesitated and frowned. "You are a grounding person. Is that not what my counterpart on Castor said about Codrin? I appreciate your presence."

Ey considered any number of responses ey could give before just nodding. If nothing else, ey didn't want to hold either of the skunks up from what would most certainly affect both of them more than it would em.

May forked and the new instance climbed up onto the bed with True Name, the two skunks kneeling, facing each other, amid all the blankets and pillows.

Both Ioan and True Name watched as the down-tree instance of May scrubbed her paws over her face vigorously for a moment, gave a shaky wave, and then quit. True Name winced and screwed her eyes shut, and the May who had knelt with her on the bed reached out and took the skunk's paws in her own.

"Go ahead."

It was still another ten seconds or so before True Name managed to relax enough to permit the merge to progress, and even then the only visual indication was a slow slump of her shoulders and a relaxing of the muscles of her face.

Ioan stuffed eir hands in eir pockets and did eir best to feel rooted to where ey stood, hoping against hope that ey could keep from pacing. May watched True Name carefully, eyes searching her features for what ey could not tell. She seemed almost frozen, breathing shallowly despite the relaxed set of her features.

And ey stood and watched them both.

The three of them stayed like that for nearly five minutes—two skunks kneeling on the bed while ey watched from beside it—before True Name moved again.

"Oh...oh, I cannot..." she whispered, and started to sag over to one side.

May shushed her quietly and helped her to lay out on her

side before settling down with her. They curled together, still facing each other, nearly snout to snout and still holding paws.

Ey stood and watched. Then ey sat on the beanbag and watched. Watched and waited, though ey wasn't sure what for.

It was more than an hour before May forked beside em, took eir hand, and led em from the room. Neither of the skunks on the bed had moved or made a sound other than May asking True Name if she was okay at one point and the other skunk shaking her head.

Once the door was shut behind them, May let out a shaky sigh and padded over to the kitchen. "That was very hard."

"Why, do you think?" ey asked.

She took a moment to pour herself a glass of water before replying. "I want to be here with you, and I also want to be in there with her, and I also want to go back in time and tell her I do not want to merge, and I also want to go back in time and merge instead of End Waking, and...a-and..."

"Come here, May."

She clutched the water to her chest with both paws, stumbling blindly around the kitchen counter so that ey could guide her to the beanbag.

She sat down and let Ioan rub her back. Only once she could manage a sip or two of water, she said, voice hoarse, "Did I fuck up, Ioan?"

Ey was still teasing apart the day—or perhaps the last month—but all the same, ey did eir best to respond to what ey suspected lay beneath the surface of the question. "Do you think she resents you for not just letting her be True Name?"

May whined and set the water glass aside, shifting on the beanbag until she could rest her head on eir thigh. "I worry that the real reason she wanted to do this was because there is no going back to who she was. One of those 'fuck it, burn it all down' situations."

"There could be some of that, but is that so bad?"

"I do not know," she mumbled.

"Can you imagine her being okay staying as True Name and being all cooped up for the rest of eternity?"

She snorted. "God, no. I think she would lose it."

"Same, yeah. She'd probably try to pull a Dear or something."

"And hate every minute of it. You heard her, she likes who she was and all that she did. I cannot imagine her letting that go."

Ey nodded and combed eir fingers through the fur on the nape of her neck. "So she'll be left with a complex view of that—or, well, a couple of them, I guess—maybe enough for her to change how she moves through the world. Think it'll be enough for Jonas?"

The skunk rolled until her face was nearly pressed against eir belly to let em pet. "I do not know," she mumbled. "I do not think even she knows."

Sleep was the first obstacle they ran into.

While True Name had, at one point, sat up long enough to drink half a glass of water, she had yet to leave the bed, and with her still down for the count, the instance of May that had remained was unwilling to leave her side, even for dinner, which she declined.

"You don't think sleeping with her will be enough to keep you comfortable through the night?"

She rolled her eyes and poked em in the stomach with a dull claw. "It is not just that I do not want to sleep alone. I want to sleep with you."

Ioan blinked, laughed, and rubbed at the back of eir neck. "Right, sorry, I guess I've been stuck on logistics mode for a bit."

"Is this not emotional?"

"It is! I'm just...overwhelmed or something."

May nodded and looped her arms up around eir shoulders. "That much I understand, my dear."

"Would it make sense if I added a cot or something in there? I could at least sleep nearby."

She perked up and tilted her head. "One moment. Or...well, come with me."

May led em to True Name's room where the skunk was slouched over on the bed, head resting in the other instance of May's lap, the two of them tucked into the nest of pillows in the corner.

"Let me reduce–" The May who had stayed with Ioan quit, leaving the other instance of her to quickly incorporate the merge and continue, "–conflicts. True Name, are you able to speak?"

The answer was a long time coming. "Some," she croaked.

May nodded. "I am not going to leave, but it is getting close to bedtime. I am also not comfortable not being near Ioan. May ey sleep in here with us?"

True Name slowly rolled her head to the side enough to squint at Ioan through one eye. Her cheek-fur was a mess of tear tracks. "Ioan?"

"I can make a cot by the bed," ey said, then laughed. "Or just another, smaller bed, I guess. No need to make one of those uncomfortable things."

She slowly pushed herself up to a sitting position, though she remained half-slouched against May. "Can you...make the bed bigger?"

"Well, I mean..." ey shrugged helplessly, looking to May.

The skunk tilted her head back against the wall, looking up to the ceiling thoughtfully. "I do not see why not, I suppose," she said, sounding distant.

"Worried?" True Name mumbled.

Ioan shifted eir weight uncomfortably from one foot to the other. "I just, uh," ey stammered. "I don't want to make things weird. I can't even imagine all you're going through."

True Name laughed hoarsely. "It is not a comfortable...time for us, no." She sighed, sat up further, and rubbed at her face.

"Preference...make bed larger and join...second choice, other bed."

Ey nodded. "I can make the bed bigger. Should I make a second set of covers?"

She swallowed several times in a row, a sign of tears to come ey well knew from May. "Can I ask...can you two..."

May got her arms around the skunk and shushed her gently. "We will work it out."

Ioan hesitated a moment longer before willing the bed to expand another half meter in width. A second set of covers and pillows spooled themselves out onto it as well, just in case.

Ey paced back and forth a few times, shook eir head, then waved a hand again to bring a set of pajamas into being on the bed. Sleeping in eir usual dress of a pair of boxers didn't seem quite appropriate at the moment.

May blinked down at the clothes, giggled quietly, and shook her head. *"You are such a nerd,"* she subvocalized through a sensorium message so as not to disturb True Name. *"It is a good idea, but you are a total nerd."*

Ey shrugged helplessly, gathered up the loose lounge pants and shirt to go change.

"I have no clue how tired I even am," ey sent once ey returned. *"Or if I'll even be able to sleep here."*

"If you need to sneak off to sleep in our bed, you can."

"I'm also unwilling to sleep without you, so..."

Her expression softened. She tilted her muzzle down to whisper something to True Name, and when she received a nod in response, she signed *okay* and patted the bed to invite em up.

Ey nodded and climbed onto the (now much larger) bed so ey could settle down beside May in the nook of pillows. Getting eir arm around her, ey let her rest her head on eir shoulder. It was a little awkward with True Name still slouched against her side, but it worked well enough.

"I'm surprised she's so...physical," ey sent.

"She was not, at first, but I suspect she is working her way from

past to present. She slowly got closer and closer as she learned how I did the same."

It made sense, at least. Whenever ey'd dealt with a longer merge—eir longest had been around thirteen months, and a particularly boring project at that—it always felt like the memories were interleaving themselves in with the ones ey already had, histories slowly zippering themselves into consensus. Conflicts, then, were the snags one encountered along the way, and one would have to dump energy into either reconciling or discarding memories. It was a very consuming task, and that True Name had been able to speak at all was far more than ey could have done.

"Think it's overriding the bits of her and End Waking that aren't keen on touch?" ey asked.

"Must be."

"How are you doing with it?"

She sighed, at which True Name squinted up to her, then over to Ioan, offering a weak smile before settling back into processing.

"I do not know, my dear. It has activated all of my care instincts, so I am happy to make her comfortable in all of the ways I know how. It helps, then, that those are all of the ways she knows now, too, or at least is learning. If I focus on that, I feel very positive. It is only when I get distracted and ruminating that I begin to spiral. It is more comfortable for me to focus on caring for someone now than it is to think about boundaries or Zacharias or Jonas."

Ey kissed between May's ears, murmuring, "You're a good person, May."

The skunk lifted her snout to tuck it up under eir chin.

"You two...are disgusting," True Name mumbled. "Keep it up."

May laughed and tightened her grip around her briefly. "Hush, you. We will work on going to bed soon. I hope that you can get some sleep."

She only shrugged.

"Well, either way, I will let you keep the corner nest and be right here. Ioan can take the outside."

"Keeping em...away?"

May frowned. "I am keeping myself close to you."

"I kid. I have not...even gotten there, yet," True Name said, slowly pushing herself up once more and frowning at just how far away the glass of water was. Ioan leaned forward to grab it for her. She drank carefully. "But if it...also keeps awkwardness down...that is good, too."

Ioan accepted the glass from her once she finished, re-filling it from the pitcher they'd brought in and setting it on the windowsill near the nook so that she could get to it herself. "We can talk about that later. For now, I think it'll work alright."

True Name nodded and settled down into her nest of pillows.

May and Ioan stayed up a little longer, chatting through sensorium messages to let True Name process in peace. Cognizant of her mention that she felt better when not thinking about boundaries, ey kept the topics light, asking about favorite things and letting her rant about plays from her past that she'd hated.

Nearly an hour later, just as May started to nod off, True Name yelped and sat up, scrambling back against the wall away from them. "You know!" she shouted. "Codrin knows!"

It took only a moment for understanding to click into place. Both ey and May sat up to give her a bit more space.

"Hush, my dear," May said, voice soothing. "It is okay. Remember Dear's letter."

"I...I cannot– It is too much!"

Ioan held still, hands flat on eir thighs. The urge to wipe the sweat from eir palms was pressing against em, but ey wanted to at least appear calm, even if ey didn't feel such.

May began to crawl towards True Name, then stopped when her cocladist shied away from her. "Codrin has not spoken it aloud, not even with True Name#Castor. I confirmed with Dear: ey only said *that* ey heard it, and that is all that ey told Ioan."

She snatched a pillow from the pile and clutched it to her chest, wide-eyed. "Why?"

"Ey couldn't be the only one," Ioan said quietly. "We don't do as well under pressure as you, we don't...well..."

"Keep secrets?" she growled.

May held up her paws disarmingly. "They keep secrets very well. They just do not keep many."

She glanced sharply at May, then said to Ioan, "Ey did not tell you the Name? No one else knows?"

"No. The message was individual-eyes-only. I haven't even shown May." After a moment's thought, ey added, "But I can unlock it for you, if you want. It's in an exo I haven't looked at since."

"Sweep the whole sim," she snapped.

Ey nodded, swept the sim of everyone but the three of them, and instructed the perisystem architecture to print out the *0 individuals swept* receipt onto a slip of foolscap, which ey handed over.

"Move back, May Then My Name," she instructed, quieter this time. When May obliged, the skunk crawled closer to em and set up a cone of silence with secure visual ACLs. She was panting and shaking, though ey was pleased to see that at least the anger that had swelled briefly had subsided once more into something more manageable. Ey didn't think any of them were up for a shouting match. Once she'd knelt beside em, whispered, "Show me."

Ey drew the sheet out of the air, holding it up for True Name to see the fully redacted text, then unlocked it for her eyes only and handed it over.

She read it through top to bottom a few times, set it down and kneaded her paws against her face, then picked it up to read it once more.

Finally, shoulders sagging, she handed it back. "Re-secure it and destroy it, please."

Ey did so and held up eir hands. "I'm sorry, True—"

She patted eir arm with a shaking paw. "Please do not apologize." After dropping the cone of silence, she continued, "I should have...I should have learned from...I am sorry."

May held out a paw once more, and this time True Name took it, letting herself be guided back to the nest of pillows, where she slumped down once more, expression glassy. "Could themself have peeped—And seen my Brain—go round —" she mumbled.

"Rest, my dear. It is okay," May said quietly. "Do you want company?"

"Too much...but I..." After a shuddering breath, she shook her head. "I will...be fine. We will speak later."

May nodded and crawled back over to Ioan, nudging em to lay down so that she could tuck in against eir front. She remained tense, and when ey sent a gentle sensorium ping, she sniffled and shook her head.

Tiredness eventually won them over, though, and, despite the room being mirrored from what ey was used to, the bed was the same, comfortable one ey'd slept in for the last century, the house held the same sense of 'home' as ever. May curled against eir front as she always did, and while it was strange seeing True Name just beyond her, it was still where ey belonged.

The last thing ey remembered before falling asleep was watching the way True Name had curled to face May, the two skunks holding each others' paws once more, and thinking to emself, *This isn't how I pictured things winding up if I had somehow been able to fix things between them, but it could certainly be worse.*

Waking brought confusion. Something about the inversion from their normal bed, of having fallen asleep on eir other side than ey usually did, induced a subtle sense of vertigo at first. The pajamas were also bunched up around em strangely, adding a subtle sense of constriction. As sleep slowly seeped away, though, the feeling lessened and ey was able to relax in the warmth beneath the covers.

Warmer than expected, perhaps. May was still in eir arms, as usual, but the position felt off with the addition of a second warm bulk.

Ey tried to puzzle it out through the fog of doziness that still surrounded em. Eventually, ey gave up and levered eir eyes open, blinking a few times to bring the world into focus.

At some point in the night, True Name had apparently rolled over and wound up curled in May's arms, much as she was curled in eirs, and with with eir arm resting atop May's, ey was left hugging two skunks.

Ey lay there for a while, groggily trying to piece together eir thoughts on the situation. As far as ey could remember in eir still sleep-addled state, ey'd never been this close to True Name before. There had been the occasional casual touch, a few touches out of necessity—grabbing her hand to get away from Guōweī, lifting her after End Waking's merge—but even going back to when ey'd first met her, there'd been very little touch. It made sense, given her personality, and yet here she was, all cuddled up with the two of them. If nothing else, ey should probably decide whether or not to extricate eir arm from the situation to ease that awkwardness.

Ah well, ey was probably worrying too much about this, just laying there and ruminating.

"*You almost certainly are, Mx. Bălan,*" came the barest whisper of a sensorium message. "*Especially if you are mumbling.*"

Ey jolted at the words impinging on eir senses, getting a sleepy grumble out of May.

"*Sorry,*" ey replied to True Name.

There was a note of amusement, of almost-laughter, as she sent, "*It is okay, dear. What are you worried about? You only mumbled the last bit.*"

Eir mind raced as ey tried to figure out how best to explain what ey'd been cycling over.

"*I rolled over sometime in the night—I do not know when, I was memory-sick—and have been staying still to keep from waking you two.*

Would you like me to move?"

"No..." ey replied hesitantly. *"But you guessed right. I hope this isn't weird or anything. If you need to–"*

"Ioan, I asked after your preferences," she chided. *"I am okay, I promise."*

Ey hid the heat rising to eir cheeks by burying eir face in May's fur. *"Right, sorry. You're okay there. I'm just being awkward."*

Ey felt True Name relax. *"We both are. It is comforting and awkward in equal measure. One third of me is very happy to be held, one third would really rather not be touched, and one third is simply confused. I am of three minds."*

"Have you finished merging, then?"

There was a subtle rustle of fur against pillow as the skunk shook her head. *"I have the memories in place, but there are many conflicts yet to process. It is easier to put those on hold, at least, so that I can make fun of you for mumbling for a little bit."*

Ey smirked. *"Har har. All the same, I'm glad you made it through to this far, at least."*

"Thank you, Ioan. As am I."

They fell back into silence then. Ioan spent a while marveling at the mix of coziness and strangeness. It *was* comfortable, there with the two skunks. May was in eir arms as she should be, and True Name, similar as she was, fit well enough in the mix. The strangeness, then, came from the knowledge that she was specifically True Name. This was so counter to what ey knew of her from the years prior, especially the version of her that she'd become over the past few weeks since End Waking's merge.

Ey could already tell that she'd changed, though, even beyond the fact that she'd wound up as close as this. Her speech patterns were shifting once again, losing some of their formality, finding their way back to ground from the high-minded patterns she'd picked up from her other cocladist, and yet they weren't totally those of May, either. They didn't sound the same, just more alike than they had before.

She was tripled, now. She was True Name and she was End

Waking and she was May. Whether or not she would become something new or remain thus ey didn't think even she knew. The adjustment would certainly take time for everyone. Ey liked End Waking quite a bit as a friend, but that friendship was different than that of eirs with True Name. Ey was friends with May, but in that way that partners were still friends beneath the romance of a big-R Relationship, and there was certainly no comparison to be made between the other small-r relationships. If she was of three minds, so was ey.

"Unrelated to comfort or awkwardness, I am going to get up to make coffee," she sent, nudging em out of rumination once more. *"I did not sleep, and if I do not have coffee soon, I shall surely die."*

May grumbled again when True Name rolled away from her, gathering the remainder of the covers and a stray pillow up to replace the space that had been left by her cocladist's absence. Ey couldn't tell if the skunk was actually awake or not, but she settled down once more, if nothing else.

True Name sat up and scrubbed at her face with her paws, wiping the grit of sleep—or perhaps tears—from her eyes. She grinned down to em. *"My assessment remains. You two are so cute that it is disgusting."*

Stifling a laugh, ey rolled eir eyes. *"Blame May."*

"Way ahead of you, dear," she sent as she crawled out of bed. *"I will make coffee and then I will need some alone time on the plain. I will ensure there is enough for all."*

There was a quiet clattering from the kitchen, mugs being shifted about and the coffee pot being set in place, doubtless another instance of her making enough noise to let them know what she was up to.

It was enough to wake May the rest of the way, the skunk stretching out against eir front and yawning wide before she shifted about to face em. "Pillows," she mumbled, peeking down at the bundle she still held in her arms. "Oh, did I...?"

Ioan nodded, placing a kiss atop her head. "She said she rolled over against you, yeah."

"Sorry, Ioan."

"It's fine by me, I slept through most of it," ey said, chuckling. "She and I talked about it a bit before you woke up. She's confused about it, but seemed like she needed it."

"She is learning my wicked ways," she mumbled against eir front. "I am happy to hear that it was helpful and that you are okay with it, though."

"Mmhm. How about you?"

May yawned again before poking her nose up against eir chin. "I do not know. I slept through it, too, apparently. It fits with what I said earlier, though. I am pleased to care for those around me."

"She also called us disgusting again."

"That is because we are. Is that her making coffee?"

Ey nodded, nudging her snout with eir chin.

"Good girl."

A few minutes later, True Name returned, carrying three mugs of coffee. Ioan and May pushed themselves up to sitting so that they could accept.

"I am sorry I shouted last night. I think I understand Dear's letter better now."

May nodded.

"I was wondering if you didn't know about...all that before last night, honestly," Ioan said.

"I have been fed bad and incomplete information for years now. I had not suspected just to what extent. I am still frightened, if I am honest, but I will trust you two on this. It is complicated and bound up in emotions I do not understand, but I will trust you." She shook her head. "But I cannot speak of it any more right now."

"Heading outside?" ey asked.

She nodded. "Yes. I will need an hour or so of nothing but the morning and the grass."

"Of course."

May nodded. "Take the space you need."

True Name leaned over enough to dot her nose against the skunk's cheek. "Thank you, dear. If you cook breakfast, I will refrain from telling Ioan embarrassing stories."

"Asshole." She laughed. "Where did this humor come from?"

"Your guess is as good as mine, at this point."

"She seems to be doing well," ey said, once she'd made her way outside and down the stairs to the prairie.

"It helps that I did not drop a merge onto her unexpectedly. She had more to process, but more preparation to do so."

"She said she's done getting the memories in order but working on conflicts now."

May nodded. "About a third of the way done, then."

"It's really gratifying to see it going so much more smoothly this time."

"Agreed, yes," she said between sips. "I was not expecting her to turn into a cuddlebug, but I suppose that will level out before long. Was that awkward, this morning?"

Ey shrugged. "A little, I guess. Just hard making it work in my head. Doesn't fit with what I remember of her."

"I cannot picture you getting cozy with *just* True Name, no. I can barely picture her getting cozy with anyone, and that is certainly not even bringing End Waking's general touch-aversion into the equation."

"I'd assume she got cozy with Zacharias, if they were together."

May's expression soured. "We will need to talk about him soon, but I cannot talk about him now."

"Of course."

She made a setting aside gesture, stepping back to the previous topic. "Did that feel like crossing a boundary?"

"Not particularly, no. It just felt like me being awkward, more than anything."

"That is good, then." She finished her coffee and waved the mug away. "I do not know how to feel about it, myself, because I do not know what she will be like when she has finished incorporating the merge. She is not yet settled enough, so I will forgive much that I might not otherwise."

"It's not like she was hitting on me or anything," ey said, laughing.

She smirked. "Are you sure?"

Ey reached over to tug on one of her ears gently. "Yes, I'm sure. I'm dense, but not *that* dense."

The skunk tilted her head at the tug, laughing. "Has your opinion of her as a friend changed?"

Ioan tilted eir head. "How do you mean?"

"I do not imagine that you felt the same about her when she was just True Name as you do now about who she has become. Or is becoming, at least."

"Well, no," ey hazarded. "But I don't know just how, yet."

"Me either."

They reconvened over a simple breakfast of scrambled eggs and potatoes with toast.

"I instructed my fork to quit," True Name said by way of opening the conversation.

"Feeling positive about the merge, then?" ey asked.

"Yes. Having worked through some conflicts, it will not be easy, but I am comfortable with the direction in which it is going." She took a bite of toast piled high with egg and potato, chewing thoughtfully. "It is not all positive, but it has given me hope for a pleasant life moving forward."

"Was your life unpleasant before?" When May frowned at em, ey held up eir hands. "Sorry, maybe that's impertinent. It's not important."

True Name shook her head. "It is okay. It was, yes. It was fulfilling. I felt hopeful and comfortable with the path I had chosen. The work itself was starting to grate on me, but that had less to do with the work than the coworker. Pleasantness was never a focus for me, however."

May, having subsided, finished her bite of toast before asking, "Did you have hope for happiness with just End Waking's merge?"

"No. Not at all." She reached out a paw to give one of May's a squeeze, adding quickly, "Again, I understand—now more than ever—why you did what you did, and I do approve of it in light of what is happening with Jonas, but it was an uncomfortable duality in comparison to this more comfortable plurality and I may yet settle into a new singularity. I do not know."

May smiled gratefully, returning that squeeze.

"Meeting up with my fork hammered that point home pretty well. She looked...well, I will not elaborate on the differences I saw. Seeing myself through her eyes, I can tell that she was pleased as well."

"I am very happy to hear that," May said. "Not least of which because you seem to be building a new self rather than simply a raw combination of us."

True Name nodded, finished her plate before setting it aside. "Thank you for breakfast, May Then My Name. Your secrets are safe for another day— ow!"

"Your high station does not preclude you from being kicked, my dear," May said sweetly. "You deserved that."

The skunk preened.

Ioan watched the exchange, grinning. Beyond just what she'd said, ey could read relief in May's features. That resentment towards her down-tree instance had never quite gone away, ey knew, and, on some level, it likely never would. Still, that True Name was, as the skunks had said, rebuilding herself into a new person seemed to have brought out a new sense of friendliness within eir partner that had been lacking to that point.

Ey wondered if she would go through a reevaluation of who True Name had been before, much as ey had. It was certainly enough that she felt more positive, but ey—em and Codrin#Castor, perhaps—seemed to have dropped much of that resentment that had lingered in May and so many others, though whether that was due to a difference in temperament or the relatively short time they'd known the skunk in comparison, ey couldn't tell.

"Is it just me, or is eir mumbling getting worse?" True Name stage-whispered to May.

She whispered back, "Perhaps the centuries are catching up to em. Is this how the Bălans crack? Should we warn Dear?"

"Are all skunks such pests?" Ey smirked.

They laughed.

"I mumble more when I'm stressed, that's all."

"Are you stressed now, my dear?" May asked.

"It's a stressful time overall, even if this particular morning is pleasant enough."

"It feels rather like the morning after a sleepover, yes," True Name said.

May nodded eagerly.

"I've never had one of those, so I'll have to take your word for it. Do those always come with cuddling up in the morning?"

Both skunks splayed their ears and dipped their snouts.

"It depends on the sleepover," May said, adding to True Name, "Are you feeling well enough to discuss boundaries now?"

She hesitated. "We can begin the conversation, though I will need to address further conflicts before long."

"To be clear," Ioan said. "I'm okay with it, it was just unexpected."

True Name gave a hint of a bow. "One thing that came up in our discussions leading up to the merge is that the one with the greater restrictions in a relationship defines the boundaries. Right now, I suspect that may be one of you two. I am the outsider, here. I have never had to have a conversation such as this."

"My comment about you building up a new self has gone a long way towards soothing any fears," May said. "I think I was worried you might incorporate my memories of the last few decades wholesale and wind up feeling exactly the way that I do about Ioan."

True Name shook her head. "I have taken to heart your requests and declined the personal memories you suggested. There are many conflicts," she said, speaking more slowly. "Perhaps due to your feelings about me as I was, so I am not sure how I feel yet, but...well, may I speak earnestly?"

May and Ioan both nodded.

"On that point, I remember enough to know why it is that you love Ioan. I can see what it is that you see in em. It is as if..." She trailed off, ears pinned flat. "This is so fucking embarrassing. I am sorry. Uh...it is as though there is a world in which I could do the same, but I do not know how to get from here to there. Again, I am sorry, May Then My Name."

There was a long silence around the table while Ioan and May digested this. True Name spent it resting her head in her paws and staring down at her plate.

It was May who broke the silence, saying simply, "May."

True Name sniffled and lifted her head. "Sorry?"

"Stop calling me May Then My Name."

"I—"

"Do not make it weird, True Name," May said, laughing. She held out a paw toward the skunk "Just fucking call me May already."

"Right. May," True Name said, gingerly resting her paw in her up-tree instance's.

"I do not know how you get from this world to that one, either, should that even be something you want, but," she said, taking a deep breath, "so long as you come by that path earnestly and we discuss it in the moment, it is your path to take. Do you have any thoughts, Ioan?"

Ey held up eir hands. "Don't look at me. I don't have a clue."

They laughed.

"We'll see, I guess," ey said, shrugging. "It's all way too much for me to take in right now."

"Perhaps that is a good place to pause," True Name said. "This conversation has those conflicts begging for attention."

"Of course, my dear," May said, giving her paw a squeeze. "Go and walk. There will be time for discussions to come, especially once we are finished with this unpleasant political business."

Debarre — 2350

When Debarre received the ping from End Waking, he quickly excused himself from dinner and dashed out into the back yard to respond. The last time he'd received a message in the middle of a period of overflowing, it had been when the skunk's leg had been impaled on a branch, so he hoped against hope that it wasn't the entire tent washing away in a flood this time. It was getting on in spring—still a bit early for floods, but one never knew...

"E.W.?" he said. "What's up? You okay? Is the tent?"

"The tent is fine, my dear," he replied. "I apologize if I interrupted, but I have some news regarding May Then My Name, Ioan, and True Name, and you requested that I message you. Besides, I need to speak about it with someone other than them. Someone not an Odist."

He frowned down to the lawn, kicking at a tuft of crabgrass. "Well, if you're getting in touch, I'm assuming it's urgent."

There was a sense of a sigh from the other end. "I am sorry, Debarre."

"Fuck, I'm sorry, E.W. That came out way snarkier than intended. I understand. I only meant to ask if it was the type of thing where I should fork and come by right away."

"Please," End Waking said, sounding relieved. "There is nothing to be done, but I am very impatient to speak with someone."

"You? Impatient?" Debarre laughed. "I'll be right over."

He forked off Debarre#RelEW and watched him step from the sim, then spent another few seconds looking out into the yard, trying to remember the last time anything had been so important that it had required him leaving immediately. Something other than a tree falling on his boyfriend, that is.

"Well, shit," he muttered, turning to head back inside. "This is gonna be a mess."

Debarre#RelEW was greeted by the sight of End Waking kneeling in the clearing across from May Then My Name.

"Oh, company," he said, frowning. "Wasn't expecting two of you."

"You messaged...wait, does that mean you are a fork?" May Then My Name said, frowning at End Waking.

"It does, yes."

"I never knew you had it in you," she said, sounding proud. To Debarre, she said, "Did this asshole tell you why I am here?"

He gave her a hug before sitting down with them. "He said it had something to do with you, Ioan, and True Name, and that he needed to talk to a non-Odist. That's why I was surprised."

She grinned. "You will have your chance, my dear. I will not be here long. I needed to step out for a moment, and figured I would catch End Waking up. I am happy to see you as well, though."

"Happy to see you too. You're always welcome over to my place, too."

"Of course, yes. This did involve End Waking, though, so alas, I could not go make you uncomfortable with my flirting."

He shoved at the skunk, who giggled.

"Well, okay. What's up? You finally merge down?"

She blinked, looking startled. "Yes, actually. How did you guess?"

"Ioan mentioned it when we talked last. How'd it go? Did she explode?"

"Not at all, no. Actually..." She shrugged, poking at the dirt with a twig. "Actually, I am finding myself rather fond of her, now."

"Bullshit," he growled.

"Debarre," End Waking murmured.

May Then My Name waved a paw. "It is okay. You do not have to like her. You do not even have to interact with her. End Waking wanted you to know about some of the practical considerations, but neither of us are planning on swaying your opinion of her."

He frowned and leaned back on his palms. "Sorry. I guess I'm just worried about you. She's not exactly known for her openness and honesty without ulterior motives, so."

She smiled wanly. "No, she is not. A fact I have not forgotten. Needless to say, I merged down, and she is making plans to meet up with Jonas, now."

"That falls more in line with practical concerns," he conceded. "And Jonas still wants both of you there?"

"As far as I know, yes," End Waking said. "I have spoken with True Name several times over the last few weeks and she has a plan of sorts. I do not know how successful it will be, but it is better than nothing."

"Wait, *you've* been talking with her, too?"

"Yes."

He shook his head. He could already feel his hackles up, and this wasn't helping. "Can't fucking believe it."

May Then My Name frowned, leaned over to hug him around the shoulders, and whispered, "I am going to leave you to it, but first, remember who you were, who you are, and imagine who you will become. Let go, have fun, but above all, remember that you love him and that he loves you. Those are the rules of engagement."

After a moment's hesitation, he returned the hug. Had she said it in anything less than her most earnest voice, he might have scoffed, but as it was, he could see himself falling for the gentle manipulation as though from a meter above. He could resent her, but she had said exactly what it was that he needed to hear.

Because of course she had. She was May Then My Name Die With Me. She knew just how to. She was built to.

"You're such an asshole," he whispered back, then kissed her cheek to take any sting out of the words. "I'll do my best. Now, shoo."

She laughed and licked at one of his whiskerpads. "Yes, yes."

After she leaned over to pat End Waking on the knee, she stood up and stepped out of the sim.

Debarre rubbed his paws over his face. "Where's your root instance? Within an hour's walk?"

End Waking nodded. "Up-river, yes. Would you like me to walk you there?"

He shook his head. "Give me some time to think. There's still some of me that's stuck on dinner parties, then another chunk on this whole thing, and another still on May telling me about these rules of engagement or whatever."

The skunk smiled faintly. "Twenty minutes' walk up-river, then. He will know that you are coming."

After End Waking quit, Debarre started to trudge up the faint trail that they'd already worn heading up along the river.

He knew that May Then My Name was right, that he probably needed to at least take into account that if Sasha and Michelle could change enough to make the Odists, then surely True Name could change enough to become someone that even her up-tree instances could like, just as he knew that he probably shouldn't take that out on his boyfriend, frustrated as he was.

Still, it was hard to square the image of End Waking and True Name meeting up voluntarily. What was it that he'd said when Ioan had come by asking after camping supplies? *"I need to be better to her than she might be to me"*?

Remember that you love him, he thought, even as he trudged up the path. *Even if you're working to undermine all that shit that she's done with Jonas, at least you still love E.W.*

The skunk was crouching at the edge of the stream, washing his paws after having apparently just finished gutting a trio of large trout.

"I understand if you are upset, Debarre," he said, keeping his gaze on his paws as he scrubbed rather than looking up to him.

"No," Debarre said, sitting down next to him. "Or, well, I am, but it's whatever. I just don't see how something as stupid as May Then My Name merging down solves anything about this. Suddenly, you two are all buddy-buddy?"

End Waking shook his paws free of most of the water before drying them on the hem of his cloak. "We are not. I am pleased that she is no longer who she was, but she is not a friend. She is not me."

"But you're visiting her!"

"On business, such as it is. May Then My Name has asked me over a few times." The skunk finally looked at him, gaze level and expression flat. "Did you not say that you would rather she not die?"

"Yeah, but that doesn't mean that you need to interact with her. I don't want her to get offed by some asshole politician, but I also don't particularly want her in my life."

End Waking shifted from his crouch to sitting cross-legged on a rock on the bank of the river. "I do understand that, yes. I do not particularly want her in mine, either, but I am now a part of hers, whether she likes it or not. I have been able to help her process some aspects of the merge and also tell her more of how I feel to her face. Once this is over, she will not need to be a part of my life any more if I so desire, and I can move on to defining myself through something other than penance."

Debarre scratched a claw through the dirt of the bank, worrying a pebble free so that he could throw it into the river while he thought. Finally, he nodded, saying, "Okay, I get that. What will you define yourself as, then? Like, don't get me wrong, I'm happy you aren't her, and in part specifically *because* you aren't her, but that's not the only reason I love you."

"I do not know, my love," he said after a long silence. "If I am defined by not being her, by not being what I was, then what is left? I cannot say my love for you, because all of the clade has that to some extent. I cannot even say that I have being an Odist, because, after all these years and with all of her changes over the last few months, I am not even sure that I am that."

"You can be just End Waking," Debarre said gently. "Like, you can just drop the clade and be that nerd who lives in the woods."

The skunk laughed and elbowed him in the side. "We have rather turned our clade identity into idolatry of a sort, have we not?"

"Don't get me wrong, I like where you came from, but I won't be pissed if you drop your clade signifier. Hell, maybe you can even start saying things like 'don't' and 'isn't'."

"Do not push your luck."

They laughed.

"You don't have to have this sorted out, though." He shrugged, adding, "You don't even have to stop seeing True Name. I'm sorry I got angry there. I think I just got upset because any chance that you might start liking her felt like something of a betrayal."

"I am a ways off yet from liking her, Debarre. I will not say never, but I have gotten to the point where I tolerate her. I will not betray you, though. You or your reactionary friends or whatever she called them."

Debarre scrambled to his feet, eyes darting around through the trees. "What the fuck?"

"The sim is empty, my dear," the skunk said calmly. "I empty it every time someone enters."

"Yeah, but–"

"I think about you a lot, Debarre. Certainly more than anyone else I think about. I have pieced together enough."

He growled. "Well, shit. I mean, I guess I'm an obvious enough choice for it."

"You are, yes, and doubtless the powers that be have been keeping their eye on you since the dissolution of the Council. I do not know the specifics, nor do I want to. As I said, I will not betray you." End Waking smiled wryly, adding, "And I do not think I am of much interest to any of them, anyway. I rarely leave, and I never enter a building when I do. I am more focused on my next meal than anything else."

"Skunks just wanna get fat."

End Waking grinned toothily. "It is not *not* true."

"Well, anyway. Fair enough. I don't imagine you'll be ratting us out, and you're right that they probably already know. I'm just glad that you've been sweeping the place."

"I have never caught anyone hitchhiking on you, though I have on May Then My Name and Ioan." He shrugged, gathered up the line of fish. "But speaking of fat, can we go back to cook these? I am not ready for you to stay over, but I would like to eat dinner with you, if you are up for it." Debarre was still mostly full from dinner at home, but he had a few bites of fish forked from End Waking's plate. Tasty, but, as always, lacking in salt.

After they ate, End Waking tasked Debarre with washing off the plate while he tucked another small log into the stove and started the kettle for tea, which they shared while sitting on the step at the entrance to the tent, keeping the last of the spring chill away.

"So, my political junkie friends aside, do you have a better idea of what's going on with Jonas and company?"

End Waking shrugged. "A little, perhaps. I think it is this upcoming audio-video tech. I do not think he wanted–"

"Moment," Debarre said, holding up a paw while he sent a hasty message back home. "Sorry. We'd been guessing at that, just sent a confirmation. Done now."

"Please do not act on it yet, my dear."

So serious was the skunk's tone that Debarre set down his mug and turned to face him. "I won't, but you gotta tell me why."

"I am going to be at this meeting. I should probably not even know about their AVEC, but I do because of True Name."

"And given you and I, there's probably only one place I'd get it," he guessed and, when the skunk nodded, sent another message back home. "You sure this place is secure, then? And you're sending a fork, right?"

"Yes and yes."

"Good."

End Waking smiled. "I know that you do, but it is always pleasing to have confirmation that you think so much of me, Debarre."

"Of course I do," he scoffed. "But I interrupted, sorry. You were saying?"

"Right. With this AVEC technology, I think that Jonas sees an opening to edge True Name out. I do not know why, but she mentioned something about a diversity of governance across Systems. I do not agree with him on this. I think he is playing a dangerous game by treating each of the Systems so differently. Each System treating itself as a separate country is one thing, but potentially destabilizing them by forcing upon each a different form of governance feels like him treating politics as his personal plaything. I do not like it."

The longer End Waking spoke, the deeper Debarre's frown got. "Yeah, ever since they set up that Guiding Council thing over on Pollux, we've been wondering about that. It sounds innocuous enough. Reasonably close to the Council of Ten over on Artemis, I guess, at least on the surface. Just folks you can go talk to about disagreements and mediation. That part was inoffensive, but that they would even do such a thing in the face of the *History* is just wild."

End Waking shrugged. "You know more than I on that end. I do not keep up with either LV beyond what you and Ioan care to pass on. There are messages from the clade, but you know my feelings on them."

"Mmhm." Debarre hesitated, then added, "Though if you do wind up going through them and come across any juicy details about those politics you don't care about, you could always share them with me."

He laughed and shook his head. "Should my life become so boring, you will have more to worry about, my love. I am better at being a pest than you give me credit for."

"Fine. I'll just get them from May Then My Name."

"You will have to put up with her ceaseless flirting."

Debarre grinned. "I'm pretty well used to it by now. You're really going to go to this thing, though?"

End Waking nodded, chewing on a mouthful of tisane-bits. "Yes."

"Why, though? Isn't that gonna be dangerous? Never mind totally outside your interest. It'll all be politics."

The skunk was a long time in answering, staring out into the forest and listening to the far-away rush of the waterfall. "There is what Jonas hopes to accomplish and what I hope to learn. Jonas, I think, would like to gloat. He would like it known that he can loop even me into his plans. He would like even me, even the recluse, scared so that he may use me as a lever over True Name if she is to come out of this alive."

"And me."

"And you, yes. I do not doubt that even he knows what you are up to these days, though I do not know to what extent." He poked around in his mug to hunt down the last of the gooseberries. "I am pleased that you are so careful. I worry about you."

Debarre sat, silent. The comment all but demanded silence from him, so rare was any expression of worry from his boyfriend.

"I will be going because if this is to be the end of True Name then it will be a step towards letting go. It will be an in for me to become independent. If I am to move beyond that which defines me, I would like to know how."

"Still thinking of cutting your ties? Dropping the clade name?"

End Waking shrugged. "Would that be so bad? May Then My Name would become simply a friend, rather than a cocladist. True Name would become someone I know rather than a down-tree instance. I do not speak with the others. Serene, perhaps? But even then, it has been many years. It would not change my relationship with you. The forest will not care if I am an Odist or if I am not. To it, I am called Nobody, and when I die and moulder beneath the roots, then it will say that it feasts on Nobody."

Debarre sighed. Hearing End Waking talk so much was a rarity, but that the death-thoughts were still there meant it'd be a while yet before he'd be allowed back to stay.

"And AwDae? The Name?" he asked. As he always did when Debarre said their friend's name, the skunk stiffened, hunched his shoulders, and drew his hood up over his head. All the same, he'd made it a point to say it at least once per visit. There had been a row the first few times, but he'd won on the point that AwDae had been his friend, too.

"I do not know, Debarre. That is, I think, the one thing that I will ever defer to True Name on."

He snorted. "Really?"

"If she, of all of us, were ever to feel comfortable speaking it, talking about em, then I will know that this embargo will have been lifted."

"Well, fair," the weasel said, finishing his tea before handing the mug back to End Waking to let the skunk snack on the remnants. He'd never really enjoyed them enough to do so himself. "I'm happy for you, you know that?"

End Waking laughed, swallowing the spent lemon balm and mint he'd been chewing. "Happy?"

"Yeah. Like..." Debarre trailed off, hunting for words. "I've never seen you move forward so much all at once. Or at all, really. Like, it's not a bad thing to have a life that you're happy with, but watching you work on the things you *weren't* happy with is nice to see. Kinda glad May Then My Name talked you into the merge, honestly."

"It has brought me a lightness, yes. She is meddlesome, but kind-hearted."

"You're telling me. She gave me rules of engagement when I first showed up. Thought she was being weird, but they worked pretty well."

"She is a brat."

Debarre laughed. "You all are. But hey, I should get going."

The slight sag in End Waking's shoulders spoke of relief. He nodded, saying, "Of course. Thank you for the chance to talk."

"You'll let me know when you're going out to this meeting, right?"

"Of course."

"And you promise you'll send a fork?"

"I will."

"And call if you need?"

"Debarre, shut up," End Waking said, patting his knee. "Go. I will keep you up to date."

"Okay, okay, I'm going." He gave the skunk's paw a squeeze and grinned. "Love you."

"Love you too."

Debarre quit, rather than bothering with stepping back home. The pile of experiences caught his down-tree instance in the middle of a sentence—thankfully something unimportant— and he had to spend a minute reconciling the memories with the ones he'd made since.

"Well, that was interesting."

"Fuck," user11824 said. "I was worried you'd say something like that."

He laughed. "You're right to worry. Shit's gonna get really weird here. Life'll get both more and less simple real quick."

Ioan Bălan — 2350

Ioan quickly began to wish for boredom. They'd made it into April and so many things had happened. Assassination attempts, centuries of merging, overflowing...

Ey just wanted to be bored.

At least they'd settled into a routine once more, and it was far more comfortable than either of the previous ones—when True Name had first moved in, and then after End Waking's merge—so ey couldn't complain too much.

True Name managed May's merge much more easily than she had End Waking's, and ey could see now the benefits of that week of negotiation beforehand. May had whispered to em one night about the final merge with Michelle and Sasha, about memories crashing down in a cascade of centuries and just how mad that final instance of True Name must have been in those final moments. Even with just one merge, she still occasionally mentioned a pressing memory or two from End Waking demanding attention nearly two months later.

It was just another part of the routine. A rocky routine, and an exciting one, but still a routine.

It wasn't all bad, of course. For every talk they had about meeting with Jonas or what role Zacharias played or some boundary one of them had crossed, there were still the pleasant meals, the shared quiet, and, ey had to admit, ey rather liked who True Name had shaped herself into.

Ey had certainly liked who she used to be, of course, though in a vastly different way—three years of coffee dates stood as testament to that. A large part of this, ey'd realized, came with just how much more settled in herself she was. Even that drive she cherished about herself had been tempered into something smoother, less laser-sharp. She was more well-rounded, more able to relax, more able to work without it occupying the whole of her.

The weirdest part, though, had to be sleep. They spent two nights staying with True Name while she processed first the memories and then the conflicts before trying to go back to sleeping separately.

She spent the next day distracted and out of sorts, first begging off breakfast to sit outside, then joining them in the den before getting anxious and slipping off to go lay down again. That night, she woke them a few hours after they'd gone to bed, tearfully asking to join them.

"This is so fucking stupid. I feel like a fucking kid," she'd said between sniffles. "I am sorry."

May had shushed her and held up the covers for her to climb in, letting her settle back into much the same position she had those first two nights.

It had certainly worked well enough, with Ioan rising at eir usual eight o'clock while the two skunks slept in for another hour. Later that day, May had instructed—or perhaps reminded—her how to get at least some comfort out of sleeping curled up with a fork.

Still, once a week or so, they'd wake to her asking to join them, and eventually Ioan had given in and expanded their own bed by a half meter to make it roomier when she did. She'd at least been quite understanding when May had requested that it not be every night.

Ey was unsure of eir feelings on the matter. On the one hand, it was still intensely weird to see True Name, of all people, openly seeking affection and a shared bed, and stranger still to see May welcoming that.

On the other, the nights when she joined them weren't unpleasant, even if it would be a while before ey was used to sharing a bed with anyone other than May. This was to say nothing about the shyness ey felt about eir body. The first few times she had joined them, ey had wrapped emself up in a sheet before leaving the bed to maintain some sense of modesty, though given that these nights had usually meant the skunks slept in, ey eventually gave up on that.

They'd all begun seeing Sarah regularly again, which was a relief. The three of them had even met with her together on one occasion, discussing the path that had led them here and sharing some of their thoughts on how things had wound up in a structured session.

Ioan found eir own sessions particularly helpful when it came to disentangling eir thoughts on the past. Sarah had urged em to trace eir relationship not just with True Name or May, but with the entire Ode clade from that first message of Dear's through to the present, charting eir feelings about each of them and how they differed or were the same. It helped to pull apart what it was that ey liked about them as well as what it was that left em stressed, exasperated, or just plain tired from their interactions.

Ey didn't know what the two skunks talked about in their sessions, whether apart or together, but it seemed productive. Not always pleasant, granted: both were left in tears after a few meetings.

Still, through it all ey was genuinely pleased to see them happy, or at least on their way to happiness.

Ey just needed boredom and ey needed out.

It took some convincing—on all three of their parts, since ey needed to convince emself as much as True Name and May— but eventually, Ioan worked up the courage to leave the house, seeking out some much needed solitude, even if it was only in the anonymity of public spaces.

The coffee shop ey'd frequented for so long may have been safe, but given that eir last visit had included an attempt on a friend's life, ey opted instead for an afternoon in a library. The one ey frequented also felt fraught, given its association with all of those meetings with Jonas and so many others during the research for the History, so ey chose one ey'd never been to before from the directory. Besides, the information was technically available anywhere, libraries just provided a familiar physical location to access it, a social place for gathering around the topic of information, and some physical tools used for manipulating that information that individuals rarely had room for.

Beyond that, though, it was the very idea of the space that appealed to em and so many others. Ey'd long ago let go of eir desire to be a librarian. Codrin#Pollux had that covered, and ey'd made eir choice, influenced as it was by eir life with May, to settle into theatre.

That didn't remove the appeal, though. Ey could still go to the building and wander through the stacks, dragging fingertips along the spines of books or poring over maps. Ey could still go sit beside a window with a book ey may not even like and, if nothing else, enjoy the sun.

This library had eschewed the flashy exterior of eir normal haunt, that glass-walled cube, opting instead for a low and flat structure, one that took its majesty from the way it sprawled out over its campus, buildings connected by breezeways or tunnels, scattered seemingly at random in such a way as to form irregular courtyards full of benches, gardens, or, in one notable case, a small gallery ey initially mistook for another garden, but for the fact that all of the foliage was made of glass.

Ey liked it immensely.

The busiest section of the library was far and away the wing that had been built to house the massive information dump from Artemis. This took the form of a squat, pentagonal building—one wall for each Artemisian race and one for their shared knowledge—that bored its way deep into the ground, a slow-sloping spiral winding down along the shelves to allow visitors to browse their way back in time until, at the very bottom, only firstrace had any material. Translation efforts would be running for decades to come, but there was more to read every day.

Ey stayed away from this for the day. Ey wanted cozy, not awe-inspiring.

Finally, having loaded up on a few random finds—trashy sci-fi, some contemporary phys-side fiction from decades after ey'd uploaded, even a bit of furry fiction from early in the 21st century ey considered bringing home to show May—ey parked emself in the glass garden and arrayed the books out before em on the table.

The sci-fi proved to be a little *too* trashy for eir tastes, and while the contemporary fiction was certainly intriguing, it was far too dense for reading when ey was trying to have a lighter, easier day. The furry book struck a nice middle-ground, at least, even if ey couldn't keep the species straight in eir head.

Eventually, though, ey gave up and just sat in the sun, watching the way it filtered through the glass leaves and branches of the trees.

No better way to realize just how tense you are than by relaxing, ey thought.

Ey imagined the two skunks also would appreciate some time out of the house, too. Doubtless there were some sims they could visit that would be reasonably safe. Douglas's field, End Waking's forest...well, no longer Arrowhead Lake.

"Hi Serene," ey began, starting up the simplex sensorium message before ey lost both the nerve and the train of thought. "I know it's been a while since we've spoken, so I hope you're well. I have a strange question that might turn into a really big request. After some...very dramatic events, one of our favorite places is no longer safe for us. I guess that's what happens when you just kind of adopt an abandoned sim without knowing much about it.

"Still, it's become personally meaningful to us over the

years, and we're finding ourselves missing it. I don't know if we necessarily need a copy of it, but would it be possible for you to come take a look at it and see about what all would go into creating something similar? It'd be a modification of my home sim. There's no rush, and if nothing else, it'd be good to say hi sometime. Talk soon."

Further reading was largely a failure. Ey couldn't get back into any of the books ey'd started, and a certain listlessness tamped down any desire to head back to the shelves to hunt more. Ey left them on a page's cart, an act that almost certainly just recycled the physical instances, and hunted down a cafe.

Serene sent a gentle sensorium ping just as ey picked up eir tea.

Ey quickly stepped into another courtyard—this one full of actual greenery, hot and humid—in order to reply. "Hi, Serene. Thanks for getting back to me."

"No problem," she said, the lack of any smile in her voice quite conspicuous. "Thank you for thinking of me."

"Of course, no one better."

"Flatterer," she replied, a hint of the usual humor returning. It quickly fled. "Are you in a place where you can speak freely?"

"I...well, give me a moment, and I will make sure of that."

Ey stepped home quickly, stopping in the entryway to sweep emself. No spies. *Thank God,* ey thought. *Wouldn't have put it past them to bug me at the library.*

Blinking a visually secured cone of silence into being, ey spoke into the sensorium message. "Okay, secure now."

Serene laughed, "Oh, I had just meant away from crowds, no need to go through this much trouble."

"Well, given all that's been going on..."

There was the sense of a sigh on the other end of the message. "Yes, I suppose you are right. That is why I messaged you back, actually. While it is certainly feasible and I would ordinarily be more than happy, I am not yet ready to engage with True Name."

"That's fair," ey said after a pause. "I know things are complicated. Do you know of any–"

"Oh goodness, I did not say I would not do it! I will, just...not yet. Please give me some time, my dear."

Ey frowned, looking down at eir shoes as ey scuffed one against the parquet floor. "Right, okay. May I ask how you're feeling about this, then? I've had precious little contact with...well, anyone."

There was another sigh. "I do not know yet, Ioan. I am not unhappy for her. I am not displeased that things are coming to a head with Jonas, as that will mean there will be a change, for better or worse. I am just not yet able to engage."

"Of course."

"Give me the address of the sim, at least. I will take a look and let you know what I think."

"Peak Lake#587a9383."

"Seriously?" Serene laughed. "I have not heard that address in decades."

"Wait, did you–"

"It is not mine, no, but a student of mine made it. I do not imagine they still have ACLs, but I will ask."

Ey shook eir head. "You guys seriously have your hands in everything, don't you?"

"It is not *not* true."

"There are billions of people here, I don't know how that'd even be possible."

"How many sim designers focusing on nature do you think there are?"

"I haven't the faintest."

"Well, how many of *us* do you think there are?"

"Right." Ey smirked. " 'Nominally' a hundred."

"There you go," she said, voice sly. "We are old and we are many."

"I bet," ey laughed. "Well, thanks for considering the request. I got something off the exchange that is less than ideal, and I miss that place. It's just got bugs."

"Gross."

"Very. Keep in touch, okay?"

"Will do, my dear. Say hi for me."

And with that, the message ended. Ey straightened up, went to rub at eir face, realized ey was still holding the cup of tea from the library, and turned the motion into taking a sip.

Ey dropped the cone of silence and let out a shout. The ACLs had blurred the area outside the cone enough that the sight of two skunks standing just outside its edge, staring intently at em and whispering to each other caught em off guard.

"What the hell?"

Both skunks laughed.

"We could ask you the same, my dear," May said, stepping up to get her arms around eir middle. "What an awkward place to have a conversation."

"I had to get somewhere secure," ey said, voice muffled as ey placed a kiss between her ears. "Serene says hi, by the way."

"What were you talking about that required security?" True Name asked, still grinning.

"Nothing too serious, actually. Just an abundance of caution, there. I was seeing what it would take to get our own copy of Arrowhead Lake."

Both skunks perked up at that. "Is that something she can do?" True Name asked.

"Apparently one of her students made it, so she's going to ask and see if they have ACLs. Otherwise, she said she's happy to make something similar down the line. Maybe once this is all over."

True Name nodded. "I will look forward to it. The field is fine for now when I get restless, but I miss the lake."

Ey nodded. "Same. You going to let me in, May?"

"Absolutely not," she said. "You will have to pick me up and carry me if you would like to enter your own home."

Ioan poked at her side until ey found a ticklish spot. "Such a brat."

She giggled and shoved herself away from em. "Rude. Come on, my dear. I have been pestering True Name with my monologue, and we are both bored loopy. Tell us about your excursion."

Ey was chivvied into the living room and sat down on the beanbag so that May could slouch against eir side while True Name claimed a spot on the couch. Ey described the seemingly endless library and all its odd-shaped courtyards, then talked about each of the books ey'd picked up—the only one either seemed interested in was the furry one, though neither had heard of it—finally ending with, "It was good to get out. Like, really good. Got me wondering, though, how are you two doing cooped up here?"

May groaned and slumped dramatically back onto the beanbag. "I am frankly losing my mind. I want to get back to the theatre. I do not even need to be performing, I would not mind even building sets or just falling asleep on that ratty old couch in the dressing room. I miss the stage. I miss the people. I miss drinking until two with Vos and A Finger Pointing. I miss restaurants, Ioan. *Restaurants.*"

"Getting sick of my cooking?"

"It is the experience I miss. Your cooking is fine." She hesitated, then shrugged. "Though you are not very good at sushi."

"Do you feel like you are not able to leave?" True Name asked. "I do not think you would be in danger."

"I would not wish to test that." May shrugged. "It has me anxious that both Jonas and so many of us are out there and have so much out for you. They may not be after me in particular, but I do not want to encounter any of them at the moment."

Ey nodded. "What about friends' sims? You've been to End Waking's and Douglas's since Secession day, but I'm sure there are others who'd be willing to sweep and have you over just to get out of the house. Hell, I bet Debarre would love to see you, and he seems the paranoid sort, anyway."

She laughed and squirmed around until she was laying on her front, tail draped over eir lap. "You are right, as always. I will ping one of them at some point."

A motion from the couch drew eir eye. True Name slumping over onto her side and stretching out. "So many names," she said, voice distant. "I have not seen Debarre in centuries, and yet I saw him just a few weeks ago. I have not met Douglas and yet I know him well."

"You will see them one day, my dear," May said. "I do not know when, but I do not doubt you will."

"Not today. Not yet," True Name mumbled. The skunk shook her head, then smiled over to May and Ioan. "But *you* should, May. Go visit the field and Douglas. Go make fun of End Waking for his cooking. Go sit too close to Debarre and make eyes at him until he squirms."

May laughed. "I do not know if End Waking has welcomed Debarre back, or I would get to do both at once."

"Of course. Do not lose your mind when you have options yet. I will have the plain. I will have the deck. I will have planning to do, and I can lean on experience from End Waking."

May looked to Ioan, who said, "I'm with True Name on this. Go on, get out of here."

"Will you not come with?"

Ey shrugged. "I don't know. That's not what we're discussing, though. We're trying to figure out how to get you out of the house."

She smirked. "Pushing me out the door, now?"

"No, of course not," ey said, ruffling a hand over her ears. "Just making sure you get what you need, too."

"I am," True Name said lazily, still stretched out on the couch. "I have been you, I have a guess as to how you might be feeling."

"I would call this mean if you were not both right," May said, waving a paw dismissively. "Give me a moment, then."

When the skunk went silent, True Name looked to Ioan, who shrugged.

"Alright," May said. "Would you like to do dinner with Debarre, my dear? He invited me over a while back, and I am taking him up on that."

"Wait, tonight?"

"He is free, so why not?"

Ey furrowed eir brow. "I was expecting in a few days or so. Maybe, I guess?"

"You do not have to, Ioan," she chided. "I know you enjoy alone time as much as anyone."

"Well, ask me before you head out, then, maybe I'll get some work done in the interim."

She leaned up to dot her nose against eir cheek a few times, laughing. "It is nearly six. I was going to head out now."

"Wait, really?" Ey frowned, twisting around to see the light slowly fading outside. "Damn."

"Just stay. Do your work. Enjoy a bit more solitude."

"Alright, alright."

She stood up and stretched, padding over to brush some of True Name's head-fur into order. "And you enjoy your time outdoors. Or melting on the couch, or whatever it is you are doing."

"Mm. Do enjoy yourself, May."

Once May had changed her clothes and stepped away, a few long minutes of silence fell. Ioan finished eir tea. True Name got lost in thought, or perhaps dozed.

It was, ey realized, the first time they'd been alone together in weeks. The three of them had been cooped up together since both skunks had overflowed. The circumstances had rather forced their hands in the matter, at least until today.

There was some lingering discomfort in the air, though, some careful distance between them. Something about what memories True Name had of em—something ey couldn't possibly know—and what that meant for them still made its presence known. It wasn't that they hadn't interacted. Far from it, actually. She'd opened up far more than ey'd expected after the merge, watching May practice her monologue, talking about the decades and centuries before ey'd known her, about the time lost between her and the 'other side of the clade', about the root of fear that drove the Odists through the centuries. And it wasn't as though they'd not touched. Though far from intimate, the nights she'd spent in their bed were beyond simple casual touches.

But it was all still very cautious. Those nights felt like a necessity borne out of overwhelming emotion. She and May had touched plenty—True Name had taken to resting her head in the other skunk's lap, enjoying doting affection—but she'd maintained a sheen of that True Name-brand polite professionalism with em. Friendly, to be sure, but still distant.

You can just ask, too, you know.

"Hey, True Name?"

"Mm?"

"Have things been awkward since the merge?"

She yawned and levered herself up to a sitting position again, rubbing her eyes. She certainly looked like she'd dozed off. "Awkward how?"

"Well, I mean, we spent all that time talking about May and I's relationship beforehand, and how that would impact you." Ey pushed emself up to sitting on the beanbag as well, adding, "Which I have no clue how to feel about, to be clear. Just asking."

"Well, we are of one mind on that front, at least," she said, smiling. "I have no idea, dear. I am...I remain confused about the conflicting memories. Something about the base of my experience of you from the point of view of me *qua* True Name over the last few years feels more...real, perhaps. May I tell you something in confidence?"

Ey knit eir brow and nodded. "Of course."

"Even at her friendliest and most open, May believed that these merges would make me, in some way, a more complete person. Even I began to believe such. The whole clade has spent too long accusing itself of being incomplete people based on our origins." She paused to collect her thoughts, looking down at her paws. "But she killed me, in her own kind way. She who was True Name is dead, and now I am of three minds. I am what remains of True Name and I am May and I am End Waking. There is some unified core—there must be—as I am not strictly May or End Waking, and perhaps that core will yet have some other name, but I am of three minds."

"In terms of conflicts?"

She tilted her head thoughtfully. "I do not feel the pressure of merge conflicts. Not many, at least. I feel tripled. I feel now like True Name, perhaps, and then I feel like May and some time later I will feel like End Waking. I lack the language to describe it. I felt something similar when I was Michelle and Sasha, but even that was not the same. I become less and less sure that I will be a singular person again, and so the reconciliation that remains is one of ensuring that those facets can coexist peacefully, as Sarah says."

"I'm sorry, True Name, that sounds...I don't even know. Impossible."

"Oh, no, do not get me wrong," she said, smiling. "It is not unpleasant. It is not what I—or even May—wanted, but it does not feel like a bad thing. It is difficult, however, as some contexts remain confusing. You are one of those contexts, Ioan."

Not knowing what to say to that, ey simply nodded, feeling the flush of warmth to eir cheeks.

"Yes, see? Look at you." She laughed. "It is complex for all of us. We are all hyper-aware of boundaries, not even wishing to test them. May is...*of* me, and now I am of her, so that boundary is smaller between us, perhaps, but we are all three very aware of *your* boundaries."

"You're telling me," ey said, smiling cautiously. "Every time I think about it, I just wind up feeling super awkward and freeze up, so I have no clue as to how to even begin to approach it."

"Well, here. May I sit next to you? If it is awkward, then it is awkward. If we find a boundary, we will discuss it, but then at least we will know and quit fucking tiptoeing around the topic, yes?"

Ey stiffened, trying to cover a wave of anxiety with a chuckle. "Uh...well, sure."

For all the confidence in her words, she looked as jittery as ey felt, if the bristle to her tail and cant to her ears was anything to go by. Ey wasn't quite sure what it was that had led her to this particular suggestion, but her expression was in flux—now curious, now eager, now anxious—so perhaps it was those three aspects of her searching for harmony. Still, she pushed herself up off the couch to pad over to the beanbag and settle down next to em.

Or try to, at least. One does not simply sit next to someone else on a beanbag. The mechanics of an amorphous cushion had the skunk almost immediately slouching against eir side. She flailed as she over-corrected, nearly elbowing em in the stomach in the process.

"Jesus...you would think...I would know how this works," she growled, pushing at the cushion to try and get herself organized.

"Here, just– Oh." Ey laughed as the skunk gave up and leaned forward with a groan, resting her elbows on her knees and her face in her paws. "I'd call that pretty awkward, though I don't know if that's what you meant."

"Not exactly, no," came her muffled voice. "But I also feel dreadfully overwhelmed."

Ey leaned away from her as best ey could to give her some space. "Sorry, True Name."

After a few slow breaths, she shook her head and slumped over to the side, draping herself across eir lap, face buried in her arms on in the beanbag on the other side of eir legs, a jumble of skunk. "This is stupid, Ioan. This is stupid and it is awkward and it is confusing, just as expected," she grumbled. "Pet my ears, please."

"What? Oh." Ey hesitantly brushed fingers over her ears as

ey'd done countless times before with May. Her fur felt exactly the same, her voice was very similar, and were it not for the difference in clothes, the slight changes in body shape, and the benefit of almost three decades of time spent living with May, ey could probably have confused one for the other. "Too awkward?"

"I do not know. The closer to another I get, even in just simple proximity, the more May I become, so the greater part of me is simply pleased to be touched now that we are close, and by none other than you," she mumbled against the beanbag. "But I am not her, so the rest of me is unsure of what to make of it. Completely baffled, even. Do I feel like her to you? We are cut from the same cloth, are we not? This ought to feel the same, yes? Does it?"

"Almost exactly," ey said, then laughed. "And not at all."

The skunk squirmed enough to get her tail off to the side and her face away from the fabric of the cushion, resting her chin on folded arms instead. "That is where I am. It is not unpleasant, and I think I may even enjoy it once the confusion subsides, but I will forever be of three minds."

"Right. I think I understand a little better."

She nodded. "It may yet be enough for Jonas, but even if not, I think that it will be enough for me. It is stupid and awkward, but– no, do not stop," she interrupted herself, laughing, when ey pulled eir hand away. "Awkward, but not bad."

They fell into thought, then. Or at least ey did. Ey kept up the careful petting while trying to tease apart eir own feelings on the matter. It all felt too big, impossible to pin down. Even trying to define what True Name was now felt far above eir pay grade. Three at once, or one after the other? Parallel or serial? Both? And yet they'd lived wholly separate, concurrent lives prior to the merges.

Doubtless there was some way ey could just approach this simply, could just share uncomplicated time with friends. Something about the Odists just made that feel inaccessible, though.

All of them were so complex in such roundabout ways, and now True Name triply so.

If only I could just turn off the overthinking part of me, ey thought. Aloud, ey said, "What do you think you'll do after all of this?"

The skunk started at the sound of eir voice. "Sorry, dear. I must have dozed off. What was that?"

Ey smiled and ruffled a hand through the fur between her ears before petting it down again. "What will you do after this stuff with Jonas? You mentioned the change would be enough for you, but what will that look like?"

"I will relax," she said, pushing herself slowly upright once more, slouching against eir side more intentionally, this time. "I will perhaps have a good night's sleep. I will walk sims for days. I will go camping. I will pester you and May, if you two are not sick to death of me by then."

"No, it's fine. A break while you're camping might be nice, but I don't imagine we'll kick you out forever and never see you again," ey said, laughing. "And I hope you won't disappear."

"I will not, you need not worry." She shrugged against eir shoulder. "Beyond that, I do not know. I may write."

"What sorts of things?"

"Perhaps a companion volume to your *History*. Something from the inside, such as it were. I will have had three perspectives to draw upon without doing any interviews, yes?"

"That would've made life so much easier."

"Why?" she said, smirking up towards em. "No shitty skunks getting you all worked up so that you yell at May?"

"I didn't yell at her!" Ey shook eir head, laughing. "I just called her manipulative."

"Yes, yes, and you called me a crazy in-law." She patted eir thigh. "But yes. I am most looking forward to just unclenching. I would like to travel and see friends and meet people."

"Think you'll try and meet Douglas and see Debarre again, like May said?"

There was a long silence, the skunk's features drawn in in thought. "I remain of three minds. A third of me would like to bask in more solitude than I already have. That me feels crowded and hemmed in. Another third of me is filled with touch-hunger and love for friends I have never met and would like to surround myself with all these people. That me is struggling with loneliness."

"And the True Name third?"

She sighed, bringing her tail around to groom it absentmindedly. "She is scared and unhappy and lost. She, of the three of me, is of two minds. Half of her would like to plan and scheme and wargame to rip that smug look off Jonas's face, and the other half would...but, well, there has been enough quitting in the clade."

Ey hesitated, unsure of what ey could possibly say to those thoughts, then put eir arm around her. Ey at least knew how to comfort the May portion of her, if nothing else.

"But come, that is enough of that," she said decisively. "Five sixths of me still want to rip that smug look off Jonas's face, so that sad-sack part of me can go have her sulk another time. I would also like to get out. I would like to go to restaurants again, yes, and even see one of your plays, should I be welcome. I want to eat greasy food and drink myself silly after performances. I want to hop sims and dream. New deadline: one month. I want out of here within one month."

"You mean for the meeting with Jonas?"

"Yes. I will not schedule it with him yet, just pencil it in—I will exert my own power by giving him short notice—but having that deadline will only help."

"Well, we'll help you get as ready as we can until then," ey said. "And probably get ready ourselves. We'll need to tell End Waking, too."

"Of course, dear," she said, then dotted her nose against eir cheek, one of those skunk-kisses ey'd grown so used to.

They both froze.

"Fuck. I am sorry, Ioan, a habit–"

"Well, that was–" ey said at the same time, then shook eir head. "Sorry, True Name. Wasn't expecting that."

She pushed herself quickly to her feet and began pacing before the beanbag, paws brushing over her face, from whiskers all the way up over her ears. Ey would be hard pressed to describe just how, but some faint glimmer of that portion of her that was May visibly fled her expression and that which was True Name asserted dominance. "Do not apologize. That crossed a boundary, and I need a moment."

Ey frowned. "It was unexpected, but I don't know if it crossed–"

"It crossed one of *my* boundaries," she snapped, then forced herself to stand still and slow her breathing as she stared out into the night through the windows. "I am sorry, Ioan. I did not mean to get snippy with you. As I said, it is awkward and confusing. I feel like I have been given control of some new, unwieldy machine and am only learning how to use it through trial and error."

Ey nodded, tamping down the urge to apologize again. "Take the space you need."

Her shoulders slumped and identities once more warred in her expression. "I would like nothing more than to disappear out on the plain, but I should probably stop just running away from such things." She smiled tiredly to em and held out a paw to help em stand. "Come. The least we can do is make dinner. Then we can discuss it further when your partner returns."

May's response to the discussion of encroached boundaries, later that night when she'd returned, knocked both Ioan and True Name off-kilter. She laughed and tousled both eir hair and the fur atop True Name's head, saying, "Well, took you long enough."

"Wait, what?" ey asked.

"I have been placing bets with myself on how long it would take until it came up. Whichever part of me guessed 'the minute I leave you two alone together' wins, I guess."

True Name stared coolly at her. "And here I was worried that you would blow up at me."

"Of course not, my dear. If you are like me, then I, of all people, can guess the hows and whys."

"It mattered quite a bit to me."

"I do not mean to diminish that, True Name." She smiled and sat beside her, patting the skunk's paw.

True Name sighed. "Thank you, I do believe you, it is just...a heap of complex feelings."

"That much I believe. I want to understand better, though. How are you doing?"

"If I say 'confused' one more time, I am going to lose my mind. I do not have a better word for it, though. I do not know how to feel about Ioan. I do not know how to feel about myself. I do not know how I feel about the touch. It was fine, I am sure, but I am starting to think that what is so jarring to me is that it was almost an automatic action."

Ioan nodded. "It felt a bit incongruous because it's a hundred percent something you would've done, May, but not the same context."

"And perhaps that is why it feels fine to me: it is what I would do and so I would expect nothing less from someone with so much of me as part of them now. I would like you both to feel comfortable, of course, but I am more...well, 'concerned' is not quite the right word, but focused on the emotional side than you two just physically touching," May said, shrugging. "Though I do appreciate you keeping me apprised. I trust you on that."

"Well, thank you," True Name said, rubbing at her eyes, though whether out of exhaustion or to forestall tears, ey couldn't tell. "The other thing we discussed, though, was setting a deadline of one month to get this shit with Jonas out of the way."

May perked up. "Are you feeling ready, then?"

She laughed, shaking her head. "I do not think I ever will, but there is little that I can do to change that. I will change and he will do whatever the fuck he wants and I will do my best to wash my hands of it. Will you be ready?"

"Sure. I do not imagine my part in it will be big. Just be there to witness, perhaps lose an instance if he decides to go after us, too. Have you spoken with End Waking?"

"I sent him a simplex message," she said. "I will ping again tomorrow if he has not replied."

"If he has not had another tree fall on him," May grumbled.

True Name winced. "A truly unpleasant experience."

"And you, Ioan?"

Ey shrugged. "I've got my notes all in order. I don't want to do it at all, but I'm ready, I guess. Did you talk with Debarre about this?"

"No. I...well, he is not ready to engage, I think. I would like End Waking to bring it up with him, if possible. I have meddled a bit much of late."

True Name smirked, leaned over and tugged at May's tail. "You have, yes."

May pulled her tail around to hug it protectively. "I know. I am perhaps as struck by the need to help as Ioan."

The conversation trailed off from there, Ioan and May cozying up and chatting via sensorium messages once True Name had started to doze, using May's thigh as a pillow. She caught em up on gossip from Debarre—one of his boyfriends visited and was, apparently, quite the looker—and ey accused her of leaving em for the weasel, as ey always did when she visited him.

Eventually, even they fell to silence, and when May started to nod off as well, ey roused the two skunks. "Come on, beds are comfier than couches."

True Name nodded groggily and stood, swaying for a moment before gaining her balance once more. "Thank you two for talking this evening."

"Would you like to stay with us tonight?" May asked. "If you are this exhausted, I imagine you need it."

She stood silent for a few moments, then nodded. "If you are willing, yes. I am also happy to sleep out on the plain. Either would be good for me."

"That is why I asked, yes."

When May looked to em, ey sighed. "Perhaps tomorrow? I need a night to think on things."

True Name's face fell, but she bowed. "Of course, dear."

Ey reached out and gave her paw a squeeze. "Thanks, True Name. Tomorrow."

She smiled gratefully and, after a hug from May, made her way through her room and out to her tent on the plain, visible as a bobbing lantern moving through the grass.

Ioan and May made their way to their own bed and once they were settled in, May asked, "I do not want to push, my dear, but I would like to hear your thoughts if you need to think on things."

Ey stretched out on eir back and stared up at the ceiling, letting May settle in against eir side to use eir shoulder as a pillow. "As nerve-wracking as it was in the moment, I think I'm just...over it. Maybe it's the fact that my introduction to your stanza was through you getting all cuddly that it just doesn't feel like a huge deal to me." Ey ducked eir chin to kiss atop her snout. "Though obviously it's complicated, since that led to you and I getting together, but you're also just a cuddly person all around."

She tucked her snout up under eir chin, rubbing it against eir jaw at the ticklish kiss. "I am, at that. What do you mean by 'over it', though?"

"I guess after a certain point, it just felt like the anxiety about touch was wildly out of proportion to whatever worries I had. We have other friends we get cozy with." Ey grinned, adding, "She just about fell over when she tried to sit on the beanbag. Would've been funny if she hadn't also started panicking."

"I think she is struggling with touch-hunger."

"She said as much, yeah." Ey shrugged, then mumbled an apology for jostling her. "I guess I'm just used to the fact that one just pets skunks."

"That is just what one does," May asserted. "And not, I will note, what you are doing right now."

Ey laughed and ruffled a hand over her ears before petting the fur down again. "Fine, fine. But that's what I mean, I guess. It's just how skunks are, in my experience. I'm sure some of it's my denseness around this sort of thing at play, but what made me anxious was her freaking out. She's done a pretty good job of taking our concerns to heart, but I hadn't picked up on her own anxieties until then. I'm over it, but she clearly isn't."

"Well, perhaps all of our preparations only made her more anxious," May mumbled, chin dipped low as ey rubbed behind her ears. "She still has all of those memories of solitude and pro-fessionalism, as well."

Given what True Name had said in confidence, ey could cer-tainly imagine a boundary around physicality being tested even in the slightest pushing the May portion of her back and letting that of End Waking or True Name come to the fore. Ey supposed, had they internalized that better beforehand, the conversation that had followed her spike in anxiety would have been differ-ent, and perhaps more productive. Ey could have spoken to her as ey might have spoken to True Name *qua* True Name, rather than as ey might to May—even if that original version of her was, as she had said, dead.

The context shift had just been so fast, though, and despite all the differences ey was primed to see between them, the two skunks still looked and sounded so much alike. Oh well. If it had been fast and confusing for em, doubtless such a shift would have been triply so for her.

"My dear, I do not know if you intended to say that out loud," May said gently. "May I respond to it?"

"Wait, what?" Ey jolted, leading May to sit up, so ey joined her. "Oh, damn. Uh...well, when did I start?"

"A context shift between me and True Name."

"Shit." Ey rubbed eir hands over eir face and groaned. "Sorry, May. Uh, it was about something True Name shared in confidence."

She frowned, nodded. "I will not ask you to betray that, of course."

"Maybe I'm more stressed than I'm giving myself credit for, if my mumbling's getting this bad."

The skunk's expression softened and she leaned forward to touch her nose to eirs. "I do not blame you. There is so much going on these days."

Ey pressed eir nose to hers before leaning back and nodding. "Right, and I feel like it's all super important all the time. Oh well. What were you going to say? If I can respond, I will."

May shook her head, and nudged em to lay back down. "No, it is okay. Whether or not you answer is probably too much information to share. I think we are both perhaps too stressed to continue, anyway."

When she lay back down as well, ey wrapped eir arms around her and drew her in for a squeeze. "Agreed," ey said, voice muffled by her soft fur. "Maybe just focus on being cozy for a bit. Can you teach me how to go into screen-saver mode?"

She laughed and squirmed back against em. "You are an enormous nerd and I love you a lot, Ionuț. I would, but you would just mumble more, I am sure."

Ioan had never been one for bars. Ey knew that there was an enormous variety of them, that doubtless some would play to eir aesthetic and likes—the one at the base of the System Central Library came quite close—and that not all of them subscribed to the "if it's louder, that means everyone's having more fun" school of design.

There was just something about the idea. Too much that took place in bars was, at best, confusing. At worst, it was distressing. Ey had no desire to be around the types of intoxication that bars seemed to attract. May had a list of types of drunkenness she'd gotten from somewhere, ey knew, and ey didn't like any of them.

Still, this is where Jonas had requested that they meet when ey messaged him.

The venue was of the sultry, dark, wood-paneled variety, with warm, dim lamps hanging pendant over each of the tables and a row of lights above the bar itself. Conversations were kept low by the dimness, with groups of three or four huddled in booths while those at the bar drank alone.

Doubtless Jonas knew of eir distaste. Doubtless this had factored into his decision on venue for this pre-meeting meeting.

Ah well, at least it wasn't a club.

Ey stopped by the bar to get a cider of some sort—something sweet, ey hoped; ey didn't know the first thing about ciders—and hunted down an empty booth. The backs of the benches were straight and high, reaching up to the ceiling, leading to a secluded, if not particularly comfortable, space. There, ey sat and sipped eir way slowly through eir cider, waiting for Jonas.

Ey'd shown up, notebook in hand, half an hour early and was half expecting Jonas to be late, sauntering in lazily at quarter past, a way of pressing the dynamic between them, but he arrived right on time, picked up a drink from the bar, and hunted Ioan down. Ey stood to bow to Jonas, then froze. Zacharias stepped into the sim, as well, grinned widely at the sight of Ioan mid-bow. Before even making his way to the table, the fox gave an exaggerated curtsey.

"Ioan, wonderful to see you again," Jonas said, grinning. "My most foppish lackey decided to tag along, I trust you won't mind."

"Of course," ey said through gritted teeth. "The more the merrier."

"Precisely, precisely." Jonas raised his martini glass in a toast and gestured back to the booth and Ioan's half-finished drink. "Shall we?"

Ey nodded and slid back into the booth while Jonas scooted in on the other side of the table, leaving room for Zacharias.

The fox was only a moment in arriving, showing up with some shockingly yellow drink in a coupe glass. "Ioan, my dear. Wonderful to see you again."

"Please don't call me 'my dear'," ey said, setting up a cone of silence. There was anger, there, somewhere beneath the surface, but ey was somewhat surprised to feel it almost completely overridden by exhaustion, something ey hadn't felt before the two had arrived.

"My love? My–" he began, voice mocking. There was a thump beneath the table and he quickly cut off with a loud yelp, jolting away from Jonas, eyes wide.

"Shut up, Zacharias," Jonas said mildly, plucking the maraschino cherry out of his drink and dropping it in the fox's. "Business now, prattle later."

Zacharias sat, frozen, for a moment longer before wiping up some of his spilled drink with a bar napkin. His eyes were still wide, darting between Ioan and his boss. "Right."

Another show of power, most likely, ey thought. *Why else bring him with?*

"So," ey said aloud. "As I said in the message, We'd like to meet in two days' time. Systime 251+139, 11:00."

Mid-sip, Jonas waved his hand vaguely. "Of course, of course," he said, setting his glass back down. "Whenever you're ready, like I said. But come, how are you Ioan? You look tired."

Ey stared at him, trying to piece together how worth it was to actually answer the question. Ey *was* tired, yes. The night before had been a stressful one once ey'd received the request for this additional meeting from Jonas. True Name stayed up late in conversation with both May and End Waking about some clade business ey'd not been privy to, leading to em pacing in the darkened yard for nearly an hour, spring lilacs leaving the air almost too thick to breathe. Ey'd eventually given up on waiting for the skunks. Ey knew if ey stayed up any later, ey'd simply wind up standing at the windows and watching their fire out on the plain.

"*I think I'm going to head to bed,*" ey had sent May. "*I'm just going to keep cycling if I stay up.*"

There was a hint of a whine to her reply. "*I am sorry, Ioan, I did not realize how late it had gotten. Do you want me to send a fork back?*"

"*I don't know, will they be intolerable and antsy?*"

"*Oh, absolutely,*" she had replied, and ey could hear the grin in her voice. "*But I will still send one if you would like.*"

"*No, it's alright. Just no sleeping out there, okay?*"

"*Of course. We will return soon.*"

It was nearly two hours later when the skunks had returned as promised. Two hours of tossing and turning in bed, fretting and fretting and fretting. Eventually, they had fallen into their usual positions, though despite the added rest that this usually brought True Name, none of them had slept well.

When there was no wink and smile from Jonas, ey let eir shoulders sag and nodded. "Tired, yeah. We're all tired. Just want this over with."

"And True Name? How's she?" he asked, still apparently sincere.

"Look, Jonas, what are you after? We're tired. She's upset. We just want to get on with our lives, and it's all on you."

"Well, sure, but now my workload's doubled," he said, and there at last was the wink. "Though in all seriousness, I'm just trying to gauge what to expect. May Then My Name and End Waking will be there, too, right?"

"Yes," ey said coolly, adding to Zacharias, "Will you?"

"Would not miss it for the world," the fox said. His ebullience was notably restrained, still, but the grin had returned. He tapped the side of his snout, "Cartoonishly evil, remember?"

I liked you better when Jonas was stomping on your toes, ey thought.

"So you said," ey said aloud.

"And how is May Then My Name?" Zacharias asked. "I know precious little about my down-tree instance, you know. I trust that she is well?"

"She is also upset."

The fox gasped, mock-effrontery filling his voice. "Not because of me!"

"It has been a stressful few months. She doesn't want True Name coming to any harm, either."

Zacharias scoffed.

Ey put on eir best smile. "Though yes, she told me that she knew there were still old forks around, but that she'd left them to their own devices and knew nothing about them, so she's surprised to have met you."

"How very diplomatic," he replied, grinning. "Well, I can assure you that the pleasure was all mine."

"So why am I here?"

Jonas shrugged. "You mean aside from the fact that I get to see your face when you talk about your skunks? It's fun dragging people around."

Restraining the urge to bridle at 'your skunks', ey gave a hint of a bow. "And what can you tell me about this meeting? I imagine you've got some grand plans about surprising True Name with your ideas for the future, but if nothing else, it'd help me to know what I'm getting into before I get into it."

"Oh, excellent question!"

Ey posted the cap of eir pen and nodded for Jonas to continue.

"I said it was an excellent question, not that I'd answer you, Ioan."

"I think you will."

"And why's that?"

"Because you love to hear yourself talk," ey said. "And because Zacharias is right. This is almost cartoonishly evil, and villains love talking about their grand schemes. I'm ready for your monologue."

Jonas raised his eyebrows and a slow grin spread over his features. That feverish glint ey'd seen last time shone through for a moment before it was suppressed again. The idea that Jonas might be losing it made em anxious. *Stretched too thin, maybe?*

"You see, this is why I like you, Ioan," Jonas said. "The whole Bălan clade, that is. You hit that sweet spot between patient and impatient where you can stay calm, but you don't just wait forever."

Ey waited.

"Alright then, a bit of a preview." He finished half of his drink in a few swallows. "There's a bunch of changes coming in the pipeline–"

"This AVEC?"

Zacharias frowned, but Jonas was already nodding, "Got it in one. That's right at the top of the list. See, the LVs are too far away to communicate effectively with phys-side, getting further every day, and that puts us in a unique position, here. Suddenly, we differ from the LVs in a fundamental way. I really can't overstate how big of a deal this is, Ioan."

"Suddenly we have to prove our greener grass to those phys-side."

"Right. The direction that we need to take with Lagrange can't just be the same old one we've been taking before. In this, True Name and I differ." He shrugged, rocking his glass gently back and forth on the table before taking another sip. "She wanted to continue on her path of subtlety, I disagreed."

Ey snorted. "Disagreed? You tried to assassinate her, Jonas."

"What are bullets but a disagreement?"

Ioan rolled eir eyes.

"You and I disagree, then. It's like I said, though, sometimes mommies and daddies fight, Ioan. We've spent the past few years trying to hash it out. For all her focus on subtlety in guiding the System, she can be a real bitch when it comes to trying to get her point across."

"Bullshit," ey said flatly.

Jonas laughed. "Oh?"

"Yeah. A few reasons." Ey started ticking off points on eir fingers as ey spoke. "First, True Name didn't start down this path in the last few years that we've been learning from Artemis; she was a mess when she first got in touch with us with Codrin#Castor's first letter during convergence, so things were already in motion then. Second, The Guiding Council on Pollux is almost two decades old now, predating the arrival of the Artemisians by years, and I think that's because third, you–" Ey nodded to Zacharias. "–apparently dropped everything on her across all three Systems at the same time not that long after the launch. You two got more openly together on Pollux, and as far as Codrin#Castor can find in the perisystem, you quit shortly after telling her there. End Waking thinks—and I agree—you're trying to push each of the Systems in a different direction politically. Maybe you think having different political environments is more stable across societies separated by distance and time. Maybe it's some giant experiment. Who knows. It's your long game."

The longer ey spoke, the more serious Jonas's expression grew, and by the time ey finished, he'd leaned back in his seat. "Well then," he said. "I suppose I don't have much more to add, then, do I? I have my conversation with True Name cut out for me."

"And what conversation is that?"

Jonas was back to grinning. "Oh, fuck off, Ioan. I'm not going to tell you all of my secrets! We have our shit to work through and you have to be a good little clerk and take all of your notes so that you can come back to me with a story to publish. That'll seal the deal, and we'll be ready to go our separate ways."

Ey gave a hint of a bow. "As you say. It's settled, then, right? Two days, 11:00?"

"That it is. Bring your pen and paper," Jonas said, lifting his glass in a final toast before downing his drink in one go.

"Right."

Ey didn't hear if there was a reply or not. Ey simply quit. #Tracker could take care of the rest.

Ioan#Tracker set eir pen down with exaggerated care, closing eir notebook, then eir eyes. This was anger in so many ways, though it differed from that hot, spiky shape spinning within em that came with Zacharias's bullshit. It was a pressure within eir chest, a tension in eir shoulders, a pounding in eir head.

"*Fuck!*" ey shouted. Ey fell back into the paced breathing exercises that Sarah had showed em years ago. It had originally been in the context of helping May, at the time, but ey needed anything ey could get, now.

"*I take it you are back, then?*" May's words over the sensorium message were tentative, anxious. Clearly tension was still high.

"*Yes. I'm coming outside,*" ey replied.

Ey didn't wait for the ping of acknowledgement. Even if they weren't ready for em to be out there, ey needed to talk at least a little, get some of the weight of the conversation off eir shoulders. Ey needed to be around eir partner and friends. Ey needed to be out of that context, away from pens and paper and books and work.

The afternoon was settling into evening, and the plain was littered with dozens of skunks. As ey walked toward True Name's tent, though, they began to quit in small groups until it was just the three root instances kneeling around a small fire, over which they were roasting sausages.

After bowing to End Waking and getting eir hug and skunk-kiss from both May and True Name, ey sat cross-legged between them. Once ey'd gathered emself, ey said, "That was a whole lot of bullshit. How far off is food?"

End Waking used the tip of his knife to nudge at a few of the sausages, turning them over on the grill cantilevered over the fire. "Not long. Would you prefer to wait to share, then?"

"Yeah. Maybe if I have food in me, I won't shout."

"That was quite loud, my dear," May said, claiming one of eir hands to hold. "I am glad you did not die."

Dinner was quiet, but not unpleasant. Gentle wind through the grass, the crackling of the fire and the spit of grease from the sausages, the gamy tang of ground venison tempered with barley and herbs.

"Did he wind you up that badly?" May asked once they'd finished.

"Well, yes and no. He and Zacharias were both there."

Both May and True Name flinched at the name, True Name's shoulders slumping. "So, yes. Winding you up."

Ey nodded. "I'd guessed that much, at least. I think the whole meeting was a form of that. He even admitted such, saying that he set it up mostly so that he could 'drag me around'. I called him on it."

"I do not imagine that did any good," End Waking mumbled.

"Oh, not at all. The thing is, it wasn't just winding me up, though. I also think he just wanted to hear himself talk. I think he wanted to talk about all his plans because he knows his words are going to wind up in whatever I write, so he wants to get all that he can in there."

"And worded as he would like," True Name said, nodding. "No matter what we manage to come up with, he wants to ensure that the narrative has him coming out on top."

"I still don't understand, though," ey said. "Why be so transparently villainous if he's specifically having me write something to be read by the public?"

"The same reason I wound you and Codrin up. If it is just a little too sensational to be real, then he can get away with more than he might otherwise. Jonas assassinating True Name? True Name who probably assassinated Qoheleth? It is just too much to be real, but it sure is good reading, is it not?"

"Makes me feel like something of a punching bag," ey said, then sighed. "I think I'm starting to understand what Codrin#Castor was talking about in terms of getting yanked around a bit better."

True Name winced and averted her gaze. "I am sorry, Mx. Bălan."

"Shit, I'm sorry." Ey reached over to give the skunk's paw a squeeze. "That was a different time, I'm not trying to put that on you now."

She patted the back of eir hand with her other paw, a somewhat stiff gesture, and, as always when the topic of strife in the past came up, ey could sense more of End Waking in her than True Name or May. "Thank you, Ioan. I do appreciate it. It is an unfortunate reality that politics is the science of yanking people around. Add in being an actor, and, well," she said, then shrugged.

"I understand, yeah." Ey retrieved eir hand, choosing instead to gently tug May closer. She leaned against eir side gratefully. "Do you have a plan you think might work out, then? You don't have to tell me, I know you're keeping it amongst yourselves."

End Waking nodded. "There is a good chance of it working, yes. Not a perfect chance, and there are many possible holes that he may exploit in the moment."

True Name nodded. "If nothing else, I think that it will buy me a quiet retirement."

"A quiet retirement alive is still good, right? It'll be a life," ey said.

"It may not be an ideal life, but it will be a life, yes."

"And hopefully still a good one, in the end," May added.

"Yes. If I am honest, a less than ideal but still good life is far more than I had in front of me even before all of this nonsense." She smiled wryly. "Perhaps I ought to thank him for that. I am not unhappy with what I have now, even."

The conversation wound down from there, and as evening dimmed into night, they fell into silence. The fire was kept low, only enough light and warmth to keep the dark at bay.

Eventually, with eir lower back hurting and May starting to nod off, they made their goodnights. True Name gave em and May each a hug around the shoulders and a nose-dot to the cheek—something they'd all grown more comfortable with over the last few weeks—and padded off to her tent. End Waking stated that he was going to watch the fire for a while longer and then head to bed himself—he'd set up a tent of his own a ways off from True Name's for this fork to sleep in—leaving May and Ioan to walk back to the house together in the dark.

"I'm happy to hear her talking about a future," Ioan said, once they'd cleaned up and made their way to bed, em slouched against the headboard and May in eir lap, slouched against eir front in turn.

"I am too, yes. I am pleased that other than a few short fits, she has been at worst determined, and at best hopeful."

Ey nodded and tucked eir chin up over the skunk's head. "I think that's where I am, yeah. I want this over with, and sometimes it even feels like this might even be the best outcome for everyone."

"For everyone?"

"Well, Jonas gets what he wants and he can go play his games elsewhere, End Waking gets his feelings understood, and True Name gets to go live a life doing whatever it is she wants, right?"

She nodded. "And what of us?"

Ey chuckled, the sound somewhat muffled by the position. "Well, I'll be happy for her, and you and I will continue being disgustingly adorable or whatever it is she accuses us of being."

May laughed. "Well, yes. I will be happy for her and will continue loving you."

"Love you too, May."

"See? Gross." She giggled and hugged tighter around eir middle. "Will you let her continue to live here?"

Shrugging carefully, ey murmured, "It'll be a conversation between the three of us. I've gotten used to it, so I'm happy to have her stick around if she wants."

"Same," the skunk said. "It is not perfect, but nothing that cannot be fixed by modifying the sim and nailing down some boundaries."

"I'm looking forward to getting in touch with Serene, yeah." Ey hesitated, then asked gently, "Are there boundaries she's crossed?"

"No, I do not think so, but it might be nice to understand the shape of our friendships when we are not waiting on some potentially life-or-death event."

"I still get tripped up over you even calling her a friend," ey said, grinning. "If she'd needed to move in even a year ago, I think you would've ripped her head off two days in."

May laughed and lifted her snout to nudge at eir chin firmly. "Would not. I would have been impossible to live with, though. Whining and bitching and stress-shedding everywhere."

"Oh, so like normal, then."

She sat up in eir lap and poked em in the chest with a dull claw. "Rude."

Ey grinned. "Well, okay, not stress-shedding, just normal shedding."

She scrubbed a paw at her flank until she came up with a little bit of shed fur to sprinkle over eir front. "Yes, yes. But I can say the same for you, my dear. A year ago, I do not think I could have pictured her giving you a goodnight kiss."

Covering for the heat rising to eir cheeks by brushing the errant fur off eir front, ey shrugged. "That's on you. I'm used to skunks being all touchy."

"Yes, but True Name?"

"I'm not sure she's that anymore," ey said carefully. "So I guess you're right. I couldn't imagine the True Name of a year ago giving goodnight kisses to anyone, much less you and me."

She grinned, nodding. "Agreed, yes. And you are okay with it?"

Ey shrugged. "Like I said, I'm used to it. It occasionally strikes me as incredibly strange. Even just talking about it now feels weird. There's this whole, dramatic plot to take out one of the most prominent people on the System, and here we are, talking about goodnight kisses."

"It is not that weird. It is an artifact of our lives. Death has a different flavor to it when we fork and quit on a whim, living for centuries at a time." She set to work brushing her fingers through eir hair. Weird to be petted, but it felt good, so ey never stopped her. She continued, "Which is not to say that it is not important and anxiety inducing to have almost lost one's life, just that, with a modicum of care, she *can* continue living, if in a restricted fashion, even if she were to miss the deadline. With less fear of death comes greater love."

Eyes closed and chin tucked nearly to eir chest, ey hummed thoughtfully. "I suppose, yeah. I didn't have much life outside the System that I can compare, never mind love."

May giggled. "I was not speaking of romance, my dear."

Ey snorted, shaking eir head. "Neither was I, you nut. I just meant Rareş and my parents."

"Well, touché. We do not have very good language around love, in my defense." She ruffled eir hair and ey could hear the smirk in her voice as she said, "Not that that will ever stop me from teasing you about falling in love with her."

Ey laughed and poked at her side a few times, hunting for that ticklish spot. "Who's rude now, hmm?"

Giggling helplessly, May squirmed until she tipped off eir lap, curling protectively into a ball. "It is just so easy, Ionuţ, do not blame me!"

"I know, I know, and it's your job as an Odist to fuck with me, *et cetera, et cetera*," ey said, slipping down into bed alongside the skunk, getting eir arms around her. "I like her, but...well, whatever. It's complicated."

She twisted in eir arms and wormed her way back against em, shaking her head. "No, you cannot just leave it at that. You have further thoughts and I want to hear."

"Further ammo for teasing, you mean."

"Well, yes, but I do still want to hear."

Ey sighed. "Fine. I just...well, I guess I'm sort of in the same boat as her, in that it's something I can picture, even if I can't understand it. She's so much like you—in terms of looks and voice and now personality from the merge—that I can imagine what that'd be like, and both she and End Waking are my friends, so there's that, too. But the context of her being True Name makes it hard to picture the...I don't know. Process?"

"The concept versus the mechanics, maybe?"

"Yeah, I think so." Ey grinned and kissed the back of one of her ears. "But that's about as far as I get thinking about it before I'm distracted by this or that."

"Organizing your pen collection is usually what I accuse you of," she said.

"Mmhm. I guess it's the same as when you and I got together. I could kind of picture it, but had no clue beyond that."

She hugged eir arm to her front and nodded. "Well, whatever happens, happens. We will talk about it."

"Another time," ey mumbled, pushing eir face into her soft fur, coarser guard hairs tickling eir cheeks. "I can't imagine I'm going to be able to sleep tomorrow night, so we might as well get some tonight."

"I cannot help but feel that I am walking into my own execution tomorrow," True Name admitted. "I know that I am leaving behind a fork, that I will not be completely destroyed, but that does not wholly negate the sense of impending death."

Ioan and May both nodded.

"Is it just the finality of it all?" May asked.

"Perhaps. Perhaps it is just the inability to predict beyond that point. I am coming up to a corner I have never seen around, and whatever predictive powers I may have fail me."

Ioan could at least understand the worries about heading into the unknown. The same feeling had been dogging em since after eir meeting with Jonas, since ey'd seen that cool look on his face when ey'd apparently preempted so much of the upcoming meeting's discussion. One minute, that would feel like a good thing—perhaps they would make it through essentially unscathed—and the next ey'd worry that ey'd made a complete mistake, that ey'd somehow tipped their hand by letting Jonas know just how predictable he was.

Neither True Name nor May could say one way or another when ey'd voiced eir concerns with them.

The whole day had been scattered for them. May spent much of it glued to eir side as ey did eir best to organize eir notes in eir head for the upcoming meeting. She couldn't seem to pin herself down to one set of feelings, first laughing and joking about beating Zacharias up, then burying her face against eir shoulder and refusing to speak, ears laid flat.

For her part, True Name couldn't seem to stay pinned to any one of her three identities.

Ey was at least getting more adept at spotting them in her features. There was a bright focus when that of True Name—the old True Name, that was—came to the fore. Her expression would become attentive, defaulting to a slight smile and eyebrows (such as they were on a skunk's features) just slightly raised. When that of End Waking showed itself in her, she'd keep her eyes half-lidded, and her gaze was far more attuned to any movement. The rest of her own movements would still, as well. She would walk quieter, more gracefully. She would speak less.

And when that of May came to the fore, that was when ey was at eir most confused.

Ey had had no idea how to feel about her back when she was just True Name. Had ey really been so hesitant to call her a friend? Memories tattled on em, there: ey'd shied away from the term or qualified it every time it arose. That had only loosened up when her life was at risk, when she'd been forced to move in with them, and ey'd been forced in turn to acknowledge that her words, *I suppose it is just nice to have a friend*, had stuck with em more than ey'd cared to admit. The rest of that conversation had been full of equivocations, clarifications, delineations, and all those habits of guardedness from two decades of wariness over anything that carried a whiff of manipulation had tried to assert themselves over em once more.

But no, there was something about the Ode clade that just happened to click with the Bălan clade, no matter what form or name they took, that just fell directly into friendship. It was the way they spoke, perhaps. Those complete sentences that left em uncoiling parts of emself ey hadn't known were coiled in the first place.

Ey didn't know what it was that they saw in em in turn. There was the unspoken matter of the pronouns of the owner of the Name, and, as May had once whispered to em late one night, eir tendency to lean on rumination, on quietness and exactitude, that reminded her of someone she refused to name. Were they so alike, em and whoever had touched Michelle Hadje so long ago? Had ey and Michelle been contemporaries phys-side, would they have wound up in a relationship? Ey had no clue how to ask such a thing of them.

All ey knew is that, as Codrin had put it in a letter, "The Odists love hard and they love deep and they love fast, and it's hard not to become intoxicated beneath all that love."

So, what was ey to do when that of eir partner, of the one ey loved most in the world, shone through in someone else? When that of May rose to prominence in True Name's expression, she was not May. She wasn't May at all. She was of three minds, and none of them were wholly absent whenever one asserted primacy.

And yet there it was, all that drew em towards May, even if it wasn't her, right in front of em. What was ey to do with that?

That ey didn't know, that ey hadn't the language, kept em from speaking of it with True Name just yet. It wasn't out of any need to hide, not out of any embarrassment—though ey'd freely admit to eir shyness—that ey kept it from her. Ey just didn't know how to say that, when she seemed most like May, ey was at eir most confused without turning it into a series of questions and I-don't-knows.

The one time ey'd brought it up with May, the idea still as yet unseasoned, she had done as she ever would, and teased em gently about 'falling in love with her' and then settled into a series of gently probing questions, trying to tease out things that ey already knew but did not yet have the words for.

It hadn't gone anywhere. Ey'd eventually had to put the conversation on hold out of a combination of stress and the feeling that ey ought to keep True Name's discussion on her newfound multiplicity in the face of May's desire for some more complete unity to emself.

So they did what they could to prepare or relax for the rest of that last day. True Name walked her prairie several times over, then came in and sat close by, then busied herself up in her head. May clung to em. Ey sorted notes.

There was no discussion whether or not she would be staying with them that night. The three of them simply wound up in eir and May's bed, sitting or kneeling on the soft mattress while they did their best to talk about little nothings. Ioan tried to explain Romanian curses to them. May and True Name spoke earnestly about a movie ey'd never heard of. And under it all, an ever-rising current of stress lay, slowly taking over their words until they couldn't speak any longer, could only curl beneath the covers, sharing some more fundamental comfort.

Surprising all three of them, they did manage to get at least some sleep that night. It wasn't *good* sleep, as, at one point or another, each of them woke with a start, but they managed a few hours of dozing.

Once the sky began to lighten, though, they pulled themselves blearily out of bed, Ioan making four mugs of coffee—two black, two sweet and milky—so that they could troop back out onto the plain and wake End Waking up—or, as it turned out, greet him at the small fire he'd started—and offer him a cup.

"There is no more rehearsing to be done," he said, once they'd shed some of their grogginess. "We risk practice making permanent, at this point. All we can do is hope to remain as centered as possible throughout."

Both of the other skunks nodded, and Ioan had to quell eir instinct to disagree. They were too tired, too keyed up, too quick to overanalyse to get anything out of forking across the prairie to wargame however many countless scenarios. Better for the four of them to sit around the low fire, sip their coffee, and watch the sun rise, May slouched against eir side and True Name and End Waking sitting apart, silent.

Eventually, however, coffee long gone, they forked. End Waking and True Name's down-tree instances each went to their tents to sit and meditate as best they could, while May and Ioan's down-tree instances returned home to try baking a cake—something demanding enough while still remaining relatively mindless.

The only words they spoke to each other was May saying, "Good luck, have fun, and do not die."

The four forks held hands and paws and, with nothing other than a shared, shaky breath, stepped from the sim.

End Waking immediately flinched, crouched. They found themselves in a boardroom. A large plain of a table, notepads and pens, a second table huddling against the wall with a pitcher of water and a stack of too-small glasses.

And yet it still felt too small—even to Ioan, who spent more of eir life inside than unbound in a forest, the ceiling was just a few inches too low, the chairs just a few inches too close to the walls. Too small, and yet too long. There was room for a table half again as long, and yet the table was set in one end of the room, leaving the other end unbalanced, empty other than a wheeled whiteboard. End Waking, who hadn't been indoors, never mind in a room too small, in nigh on a century, looked on the verge of panic. His eyes were wide, tail hiked and bristled, paws clenched in a way that reminded em of May.

"I do not know if I can–"

May squeezed his paw tightly. "You do not need to keep these memories, skunk, but you cannot leave." She added in a near whisper, "Please do not leave me."

His nod was jerky, distracted, but still a nod.

And yet, the room was empty. *Perfect time to pull the late-to-the-meeting power move.*

Sure enough, 11:00 rolled around, no Jonas.

It wasn't until nearly ten after that the door swung lazily open and Jonas strolled in, followed by Zacharias and the rest of the eighth stanza—*no, Zacharias is part of that, too,* ey thought. *There's only Odists, Jonas, and me here.*

"True Name! Delighted to see you, delighted," Jonas said, grinning widely and giving the barest hint of a bow.

The skunk had apparently amped up all that she could of her old self, as her smile was earnest and wide, and her bow the perfect mix of polite and friendly. "Glad you could make it, my dear. I trust you have been well?"

He shifted smoothly to accommodate this response. "Quite well, quite well. Feels like it's been a bit of a vacation for the both of us, eh? You enjoy a bit of time off at the lake?"

That grin of hers widened, and she nodded. "Quite a bit, actually. We never quite got to roasting marshmallows, but it is really hard to go wrong with potatoes roasted in the embers. They get a little smoky, even the insides."

End Waking stared at True Name as though she was an Artemisian, suddenly having made their way across the light-days back to Lagrange. Hell, Ioan was staring at her like she was an alien. So quickly and smoothly had her anxiety been transmuted into this calm, friendly social efficiency that it was as though the last months had been erased from her features.

There was some other conversation going on here, ey realized. It wasn't just that they were talking pleasantries before a meeting, but that there was an exchange of information that took place on some subtler plane of existence. They were feeling each other out, listening to tone of voice more than the content of words, watching features and postures rather than seeing an old friend. There was some deeper level of communication that ey simply couldn't latch onto.

With that in mind, ey could at least do eir best to focus on the less direct forms of language around the room.

True Name had talked em through the stanza and their roles beforehand, at least. She herself had been focused on the politics, of course, but also acted as consensus builder among the members of her stanza.

Ey knew well that May had been focused on swaying individual hearts and minds toward a cause that initially had been True Name's, and then later simply shaped by her as best as could be managed.

End Waking had been instrumental in tracking, understanding, and to whatever level possible, influencing financial markets phys-side, though he'd admitted to Ioan, one night out on the plain, that the chances that he'd actually had a dramatic effect on the markets was astoundingly low and that the financial trajectory had likely been set by forces larger than they could manage—at least, that was the hope that had kept him going.

Ey knew the two 'Why's from the history: Why Ask Questions, Here At The End Of All Things was the frightfully friendly crowd-rouser who had worked with groups of individuals sysside, while Why Ask Questions When The Answers Will Not Help had focused on similar tactics phys-side. However, given that her task was limited to text, she seemed notably out of her element in in-person interactions, coming off as petty and cruel as often as funny and sarcastic.

The Only Time I Dream Is When I Need An Answer had acted as a manager, scheduler, and clerk for the enterprise. Wickedly intelligent, she had done more than block in times for meetings; she had organized meetings between precisely the right individuals at precisely the right times.

To Know One's True Name Is To Know God had settled comfortably into data analysis, collecting both the raw data that she could from the perisystem feeds and the net phys-side as well as the information collected by her cocladists and the Jonases. She was a being of reports.

To Know God Is To Answer Unasked Questions had done her best to specialize in the fields of information and game theory, but this had more often come down to simple information security and hygiene. She decided where and how far information traveled.

Do I Know God When I Do Not Remember Myself and Do I Know God When I Do Not Dream worked as a mismatched pair. When I Do Not Remember worked as a propagandist while When I Do Not Dream worked almost entirely on the perisystem, translating back and forth for her cocladists and finding the best way to worm her way through the inter- and intrasystem text channels.

Were ey pressed to name each of them without knowing this information, ey didn't think ey'd be able to. Ey knew the three skunks of the stanza and could readily tell them apart, but the rest simply looked like a gaggle of the very same woman: short, soft, round face and curly black hair. However, there were indeed differences there to be seen. Why Ask Questions was just a centimeter or two taller and more open of expression. When I Do Not Remember and When I Do Not Dream both had a hunch to their shoulders that ey could not quite explain; perhaps a posture that stuck after too much writing.

As it was, ey did eir best to guess, and when introductions made their way around the table, ey found eir guesses to be correct in each case.

At last, the parade of bows and greetings out of the way, each of the thirteen—counting em, Jonas, and Zacharias—pulled out a chair and sat down, though ey noted that End Waking didn't sit so much as hover on the very edge of his seat. He still looked wide-eyed, feral.

"Aaalright," Jonas said, plopping his hands, palm down, on the table. "To business. I'm pleased to see you're alive, but can't say that I'm pleased to see you're about."

"I imagine not, no," True Name replied, folding her paws on

the table before her. "From what Ioan says, you know the general facts of what I know. There has been a long-running plan, perhaps mostly operating as a back-up, to shift one or more of me to the side depending on the status of the System. This revolved around the use of Zacharias as a tool to shape my responses while incomplete information kept me from recognizing this. Tell me, though. Are you still leaning on the multiple-Systems-multiple-governments strategy?"

Jonas nodded. "Yes. Oligarchy on Pollux, *status quo* on Castor, and invisible monarchy here on Lagrange."

"You believe that this tripod will be the most stable political structure?"

"I know you don't agree, but it's not a tripod, True Name. By this point, the three Systems are so far apart that they are no longer three branches of the same government. They're three countries, and three countries with identical governments yet divergent societies are unstable."

True Name made that setting-aside gesture, as though tabling the topic for the moment. "And you," she said, nodding to Zacharias. Her expression was calm, curious, interested. "You have been working on this with Jonas since around systime 36?"

"Oh, thereabouts," he said, grinning. "Though if I am honest, I have always been working with the two of you. It is not that your own goals had no effect on me, my little stink bug. I played Jonas as much as I played you, and I played my own game when I could."

"Bullshit," True Name said calmly, turning back to Jonas. "And so what is it that–"

"Oh, fuck you," Zacharias laughed. "You do not get to dismiss me so easily. You and I rule together, quite literally, in another life. There is no reason that I should simply be waved away."

"Nah, it's bullshit," Jonas said, just as calm as True Name. "If you were worth anything to this conversation, you would've been part of the preparations."

"What–"

"You say that you are part of the stanza, do you not?" The Only Time I Dream, the manager of the enterprise, said.

"I am, but–"

"I see no evidence of such."

"But May Then My Name–"

"May Then My Name, do you claim Zacharias as yours?"

She shrugged. "Claim? No. I do not know this Zacharias."

"That is–"

Jonas laughed, "Just shut up, Zacharias."

"No," the fox growled, his whiskers all abristle and claws digging at the tabletop. "I played my role, but that does not mean that I am some disposable Judas here. A role is as much the actor as it is– *stop!*"

There was a loud thump beneath the table, though this time, Zacharias appeared to have pulled his foot away in time to keep his toes from being stomped on. Instead, he pushed himself away from the table and to his feet. A brief flicker of ungrounded rage flashed across Jonas's face, but was quickly replaced by that bright, friendly grin.

"Fine, fuck you too, then."

There was no signal—or if there was, Ioan missed it—for Guōwéi to step into the sim, hand already raised as if for a slap, a short blade held between his fingers. Unassuming, easy to carry, symbolic, and certainly crowded with whatever virus it was that induced a crash in one's instance.

What happened next happened almost too quickly for em to comprehend. Zacharias shouted, but the cry was cut off in a muffled *oomf* as an instance of May appeared near him, almost totally overlapping the space that he'd occupied. The collision algos knocked him backwards with enough force to slam him against the door, leaving him to crumple to the floor.

Guōwéi's palm came down flat against May's shoulder, but there was no time to see whether or not the virus would affect an instance so far diverged, as that instance of her quit and was immediately replaced with another one, this overlapping the assassin's space, knocking him back nearly a meter, only for the skunk to fork again to repeat the maneuver. With the momentum already in play, this sent the man flying, his head cracking against the wall hard enough to leave a sizeable dent in the drywall.

And then it was over. Zacharias's yell faltered, and he stared up, wide eyed, with his gaze darting between Jonas and the remaining instance of May. Jonas had lurched away, looking more disgusted than startled.

"Get the fuck out of here," the instance of May growled. "And if I ever, *ever* see you again, you had better believe that I will take you out myself."

And then the instance quit, followed less than a second later by the fox rolling to the side to slip out of the sim. Ey imagined that if Jonas, True Name, and May would all do their best to destroy the fox on sight, the chances of seeing him again were low indeed.

Ey'd never seen a look like that on May's face, though, even at the height of her hatred for True Name. That had been hatred, yes, but this was rage.

"What just happened?" ey whispered to May, who gave eir hand a squeeze in her paw and shook her head.

"Are we done fucking around, yet?" True Name asked, voice flat. "Because I just want to know what it is that you want of me so that I can get back to my life."

"Your *life*?" Jonas asked, incredulous. "You want to get back to your life?"

"Life, yes," she said. "Alive. Living. I want to get back to breathing and eating and drinking and sleeping. Do not take my words too far."

He laughed, shooting his cuffs. "Well, if *that's* all you want, then we could have done without all this fuss, couldn't we?"

"This fuss is necessary, remember," When I Do Not Remember, the propagandist, said, to which Jonas sighed.

"All you need to do is just...go away. Just disappear. Just be gone, True Name. Curl up around your little Name thing and stay there."

May's expression had settled back to calm, but ey could feel the tension in her paw increase, and beyond her, ey could see End Waking bare his teeth. The Odists on Jonas's side of the table flinched. None of them looked pleased. Even Why Ask Questions, jovial as she usually was, seemed to be gritting her teeth.

Wait, does he know? ey wondered. If ever there was a way to keep a group of Odists in check, that might just be it.

Only True Name, of all of them, remained calm. Serious, yes, but calm. "What does disappearing and being gone look like to you, Jonas?" she asked. "Do you...what? Want me to hide away in a locked-down sim forever?"

"I wouldn't say no," he shot back.

"No."

"I thought not."

"So," she said with exaggerated patience. "What does me disappearing look like to you?"

"You just can't be around. You can't be you anymore. You can't be walking around and having people point and say, "Hey, it's that piece of shit skunk!" You need to just disappear, because anything else is just going to destabilize your precious System. Imagine! True Name, who didn't die, wants to bring back political parties! I'm prepared for that, but I don't think you are."

"We are of one mind on that."

Jonas snorted. "Fuck if I believe you on *that.*"

Ioan watched with increasing intensity. The actual words of the conversation aside, True Name's calmness seemed to be overwhelming Jonas's restraint. He seemed to be having a hard time holding back snark, all that sarcasm that made for good entertainment, perhaps, but was increasingly unbecoming for what ey thought of as a politician.

Here was the Ode clade slowly diverging past reconciliation, here ey was mumbling all the more as the skunks had pointed out, and now Jonas Prime, for all his stability seemed to be having a hard time maintaining his own brand of control.

Eir frown deepened. Perhaps this was more than just a political dispute.

She shook her head, but whether at his words or his audacity, ey couldn't tell. "Alright, disappear. You want me to stop being a figure and start being a person. You want me to be other than I am."

"Yep," he said, grin tight and false.

"I have already begun," she said, and with a brief pause, ey saw her face and shoulders relax, a sudden shift towards an expression ey knew intimately from eir partner falling across her features. She continued in a voice softer than what it had been. Lilting, less space between the syllables. "Because I already am May Then My Name Die With Me–" Another pause, another shift, one more towards stony and stoic, voice suddenly dry and simple, almost weary. "–and I am already Do I Know God After The End Waking." Finally, she fell back into that first register. "And some part of me remains True Name, and yet I am none of these. I could not go back to that which I was even if I wished to. Tell me what it is that you want. Lay your terms on the table plainly, and we will come to an agreement."

Jonas raised his eyebrows at the shifts in expression and voice. The frowns around the table on the faces of the other Odists only deepened.

"How can I even begin to trust you on that? You merged your two cronies, so what? You going to go cuddle-camping with Zacharias or something? You're still you."

Both May and End Waking bristled at this, but neither spoke.

"I am not what I was, Jonas. That which was True Name does not simply sit next to that of my cocladists. They are impossibly entangled. I am not what I was."

"I can tell, sure, but you know that's not enough, True Name."

"You have not offered your terms. We cannot come to agreement without."

His voice was intent, serious in a way ey hadn't seen before. "I am saying that you need to disappear. There is no stable future for the System if you show up in anything close to the same form as you were, and you know that. You were almost assassinated, and doubtless more than you three–" He nodded at May, End Waking, and Ioan. "–know. You show up as you are, and everything crumbles, or at the very least, starts to shift in unstable ways. Plan A was you gone, but plan B relies on you understanding that there's no recovery from a failed plan A that involves you."

"Why did you not just ask me?"

"Would you have stepped down?" he asked with a sneer.

She frowned. "Doubtless you had other cards to play that did not involve Guōwèi, some other leverage that did not involve death. You could not convince me, but all this high drama is over the top for you."

"I was bored. It sounded fun. You were right there. Why not?"

"You were bored," she said coolly. "You were bored, so you decided to hire someone to kill me."

Ioan watched Jonas's smile fall back into that uncaring cruelty, increasingly ungrounded.

He waved his hand imperiously. "And I'm getting bored now. I'm surprised you're still hung up on this, True Name. You're the theatre geek–"

"Jonas," When I Do Not Remember murmured, her voice a low warning. He only grinned.

True Name sighed. "Right. So now you...what, want me to look different? Sound different? I am ready to commit to staying out of the business. You want me to act the part or something? Your terms."

"You need to go away, True Name. I don't fucking care *how*. You make it happen or I will."

There was a moment's thoughtful silence from the skunk, her paws gripping the edge of the table, before she stood, pushed her chair back in, and turned away. Then in the most stunning display of forking ey'd ever seen, True Name began to change.

Ioan had seen eir share of Dear's exhibitions, not to mention those of other instance artists the fox had introduced em to along the way, and the forking involved in all of them had been perfect. They were well rehearsed dances of duplication that told a story.

However, they were, whether by association with Dear or by the art itself, fanciful. The duplication was supposed to evoke a sense of magic, of wonder—or the closely related terror.

In eir own work in theatre, both as an actor and as a playwright, ey'd found use for forking within a story that had remained more grounded, more tied to day to day life, and those performances had seen a success of their own through May and A Finger Pointing's guidance.

The Odists as a whole were more familiar and comfortable with forking than anyone ey'd ever met, even among the most dispersionista of dispersionista clades. Both May and Dear navigated that aspect of their lives with a grace ey could only dream of. Even the explosions of foxes or skunks during times of excitement were skillfully done.

This, though, went beyond that.

As they watched, True Name began to change. She worked with a singular sense of purpose that left no doubt as to what she was doing. An instance flickered into being before herself and watched with a critical eye as skunk after skunk blinked into existence. Each one bore some slight change from their immediate down-tree instance. Sometimes an array of skunks would wind up in a line before that observing instance, which would nod at one or the other in approval to leave the others to quit. And when a change was accepted, the down-tree instance would quit.

This smooth modification of form was in and of itself impressive for how naturally she began to change—not only did the instance watching have to keep track of what change was happening and what would come next, but so did those doing the actual changing; they all had to be on the same page—but what left em truly impressed was the speed. She began her work with about one fork per second, but before long the changes ramped up to two a second. Three. Nearly four changes per second of forks flickering into and out of existence, all while the orchestrating instance watched, her eyes flicking this way and that across them.

And then, it was over.

The result was a skunk slightly shorter than True Name had stood, though still a few centimeters taller than May. She was heavier, as well, with a curve to the hips and belly that was familiar to em from eir partner, but unlike May, this softness was more...well, natural wasn't quite the right term, but where May's weight seemed to be designed to add a sense of both harmlessness and comfort to her form, this new form of True Name simply looked like a pudgy thirty-something who had settled into a comfortable weight long ago and never bothered to change.

Her face had shifted as well, becoming plainer in ways ey couldn't quite explain. Where True Name had always had some aspect of larger-than-life about her, she now just looked...normal. Still a furry, still living in that form that was more comfortable to her than humanity, but normal.

Most striking, though, was the pattern of fur. While much of it was covered now, ey'd seen the way it had shifted during the process. Gone were the two parallel stripes, the ones ey had grown to love on May, replaced with a set of white splotches in the black of her fur. The white atop her head remained, disconnected from the patch between her eyes and two others high on her temples. The pattern was eye-catching: the patches seemed to travel in a few uneven lines down over her back and sides, one of them showing a hint of a whorl, another a slight zigzag, and others that were almost round spots. This pattern seemed to be mirrored along her spine, leading to a pleasant symmetry. A quick query of the perisystem infrastructure told em that there was indeed a spotted variety of skunk, described much as ey had seen: spotted fur, shorter tail, a shorter snout that fit somewhere between that of a skunk and that of a weasel like Debarre.

Gone were the stripes. Gone, also, were the slacks and blouse, traded in for a linen tunic and a pair of loose-fitting Thai fisherman pants.

When ey was finally able to tear eir eyes away, ey saw that every Odist in the room had picked up expressions that verged from taken aback to startled and angry. May, for her part, looked startled at the display, yes, but also excited and ready. It was the same look she got before performances.

"May, what–"

"One moment, my dear," she said, then turned to face this new True Name with a grin. "Will there be a change of name?"

There was a vanishingly faint hint of rehearsal to the words, well masked to anyone who didn't know her as intimately as ey did. Ey realized this must be their plan. Hers and True Name's and End Waking's, the one they'd been working on for days.

"There...there has to be," When I Do Not Remember said, gaze still locked on True Name, and a brief tense from May confirmed that the trap had been sprung.

While he lacked the context for whatever had surprised her cocladists, even Jonas sounded impressed by the display. "I won't let you leave as True Name. Stability, remember? That name means too much here."

The other seven members of True Name's stanza nodded as one, and Unasked Questions said, "You cannot be us. You cannot be who you were."

The skunk bowed. "You may call me Sasha."

Ioan didn't know what ey expected from the room, but pandemonium wasn't it. May was clapping her paws delightedly and End Waking was grinning and shaking his head. Both bore the traces of rehearsal.

Jonas simply burst out laughing, and ey couldn't miss the bitterness in it.

All of the rest of the Odists, however, were shouting. None of them looked pleased.

"Not Sasha of the Ode clade, just Sasha," she said calmly but loud enough to be heard. "I will not relinquish the form, just as I will not relinquish the past, but if you want me out this badly, so be it. I rescind my membership in the clade."

"As do I," End Waking said, getting a smile from Sasha.

"*That* name is unacceptable!" When I Do Not Dream hollered. "No. You will pick something else."

"No, I will not."

"Shut the fuck up, When I Do Not Dream," Jonas shouted. "All of you, shut the fuck up." He turned to Sasha and grinned icily, eyes now burning overbright. "You always were a little snot. You want to be Sasha? You want to dive back into mediocrity and wear your weakness like a badge? Please, by all means, be my guest. Beg for pity again. Hunt down all your little friends who kept you feeling just bad enough that they could baby you without letting you think you were their plaything."

At this, most of the stanza bridled, and there were a few louder murmurings.

Jonas waved it away. "Crawl back to Debarre and...fuck, what was his name? user11824? Crawl into their arms and let them prop you up long after you should've died."

Murmurings grew to angry mutterings.

Jonas only laughed, and that bitterness was all the more evident. "Go. Be Sasha. Live your silly little life. And you," he said through clenched teeth, jabbing a finger toward Ioan. "Write your little story. That's what you're here for, isn't it? Write your little romance and fuck your little girlfriends and put on your little plays."

May rolled her eyes.

"Get out. All of you."

The rest of the stanza left, quit, or were swept—the sim

didn't seem to render them any different. Ioan guessed swept, given that Guōweï's unconscious form also disappeared.

All through Jonas's tirade, Sasha wore a half smile. It wasn't rehearsed, wasn't self-satisfied. She simply looked present. She looked confident in herself in some more earnest way than she had in years, as though she had changed beyond just her appearance. When it was clear that he was finished, she bowed politely.

"See you around?"

"Fuck off."

She laughed and reached out to take Ioan's hand in her paw, then they stepped back home, followed closely by May holding End Waking's paw.

Once back on the plain, End Waking groaned and fell to his knees, paws digging into the soil around the tussocks of grass, then quit. May and Ioan followed suit.

When their down-tree instances returned to the field from inside—May bearing a (rather lopsided) cake—they were just in time to see True Name bow to Sasha and quit. It was the last change, ey supposed, the true relinquishing of her name.

There was a long moment of silence on the plain, then Ioan let out a ragged, pent-up breath, eir shoulders sagging. "Can someone tell me what the fuck just happened?"

"Sasha did the one thing she could have done to piss Jonas off most," May said, grinning. "He went in thinking he'd take everything from her and left with no wind in his sails. Well done, my dear."

Sasha beamed and bowed with a flourish.

"And you knew this?" ey asked.

She nodded. "To an extent. We had discussed several options, but many of the changes were new. I saw her unwind all of the changes from the last centuries–"

"All the way back to Praiseworthy's suggestions before Secession," the other skunk said proudly.

"–and other than the spotted skunk thing, she looks just like...well, Sasha. Nice touch, by the way."

"I do not think I could have gotten away with staying the same skunk, even if I look similar enough while clothed. But yes, I am back to the me of...shit, when did I make Sasha like this? 2110?"

Ioan shook eir head, dizzy. "This is what you looked like before uploading?"

"What my—*our*—av looked like, yes, all except the change to a spotted skunk. They always felt too flashy, back then, and I just wanted to look like myself offline except a furry. Completely unremarkable and a species no one likes."

"The outfit was my suggestion," End Waking said. "It always was our favorite, but for some reason, we never brought it with us to the System, and I knew the rest of the stanza would pick up on that quite easily."

Sasha nodded.

"I am proud of you, Sasha," he continued. "I do not yet know why I feel compelled to say that, but I am proud of you. You have much to make up for, your own penance yet to serve, but that you have done this at all is a good step forward."

Ioan sighed and sat down heavily in the grass. "You're all completely nuts."

The three skunks laughed.

"Why didn't you tell me?"

"For your story," Sasha said. "You had to go in there with an untainted view in order to write a more earnest story at the end."

"So," ey said, organizing eir thoughts out loud. "May and End Waking–"

"E.W." the skunk corrected. "I am E.W. of no clade."

The other two skunks perked up and grinned wide.

Ioan blinked, hesitated, then continued. "May and...E.W. merged down and you...I guess feel more like you used to? Back phys-side, I mean. Enough to head back to who you were before the clade began, I mean. Is that even possible?"

"It is not a statement of reality, dear. I cannot reintegrate those aspects of myself that are not up-tree from me, and even if I could, there are those who no longer exist or who have left Lagrange," she said, that slight smile growing. "It is a statement of hope, perhaps, or a desire for completion. It is an understanding of the ways in which I fall short expressed in my very name. Will this sense of a truer life last? Perhaps. It will certainly not always feel good, and will at some point cease feeling new, but I plan on owning it for as long as I am able."

"And how is it that this pisses off Jonas?" Ey snorted. "He certainly sounded pissed."

Sasha knelt across from Ioan, followed shortly by E.W. and May to either side of em, May summoning up plates and cutting thick slices of cake. It was strange to see so many smiles, still strange to see May so happy around her down-tree instance and stranger still to see E.W. even in the same sim.

"What Jonas was expecting was for me to remain True Name in everything except form and name," she said. "He was expecting someone deeply cowed by his political genius—and do not underestimate him, he *is* still a genius. He felt that he had won his spot as rightful leader of Lagrange, if such a thing can even be said to exist. He thought that he had beaten me down and left me either unable to continue or unwilling to try."

May added, "I suspect that he is starting to crack."

Ioan nodded.

"Perhaps," Sasha said. "He has not seemed fully grounded in many years, but again, do not underestimate him."

Ioan jumped at a brief sensorium ping, a request to enter, followed shortly by Debarre popping into existence behind May, who had apparently admitted him. "What was so urgent that you pulled me away from lunch and..." he trailed off, squinting at this new skunk. "Who...but you're...what?"

Sasha stiffened where she knelt. "Debarre," she said, bowing her head. "A pleasure to see you."

The weasel said nothing, looking stunned.

"This is– was Tr–"

"Sasha. I am Sasha. I was her as well," she said, voice gentle but insistent enough to stop Ioan from continuing.

He stepped back a half pace, crouching as though to flee on foot. "Sasha...? What the fuck?"

Ioan, still feeling eir head spinning from so much happening so quickly, tried to pin down eir open question in eir mind while still watching the exchange intently.

"I am not what I was, Debarre. I am not True Name. I am not May or E.W." She hesitated, then continued, "I am not even the Sasha you remember, but I am, I think, closer to being her than any of the Ode clade is currently."

"Bullshit," he growled. "If there's even a little bit of True Name in you, you can't be her. If you're even the slightest bit her I'm fucking out of here."

"Wait, my love," E.W. said. "Please stay."

Debarre hesitated.

"If I am still here, do you not think that I agree with her? At least to a large enough extent to trust her?"

The weasel straightened up and, when May gestured to the spot beside E.W., he slowly lowered himself to a crouch as though still ready to bolt. "I'll listen, but this had better be good."

Sasha bowed, sitting quietly and fiddling anxiously with the hem of her tunic while May caught him up on the events of the past few months, letting the other three of them interject with corrections and confirmations. Throughout, Debarre waited, and while he didn't relax fully, by the end of the discussion, he was at least sitting all the way down.

"So now you're Sasha," he said slowly.

"A new Sasha. Related, but not the same Sasha you and I remember."

"I'll buy that at least," he muttered. "You still make me really fucking nervous."

She smiled faintly. "Do not worry, my dear. I make myself nervous."

At the affectionate *my dear*, the weasel jolted back.

"My apologies," Sasha said quickly. "I was not thinking. If you would like me not to use that phrase, I will do my best not to. I just have enough...well, I am different enough now that it comes automatically."

"You have enough of E.W. in you, you mean."

She nodded.

"I...well, yeah. Not from you." He hesitated, eyes averted, and added, "Please."

"Of course.

"So tell me how this gets you anything."

Ioan sat up straight once more, unpinning eir question. "You were saying that Jonas thought he'd beaten you."

"Right, yes. He thought that he had left me so broken that I might fade away or even quit of my own accord. Instead, I became the one thing he could not control."

"How, though?" ey asked.

"Because of the *History*. The System knows about me. It knows about the Council of Eight and about Sasha and Michelle Hadje. It also knows about True Name, though, and to see that True Name has stepped down and become one of the few sympathetic figures in that same story once again means that he cannot touch me. He cannot risk reinforcing being seen as a villain-"

"Or more of one," May muttered.

"-by coming after me. Not only that, but with the expectation that the Sasha who was on the Council was in the right when seen in contrast to True Name, I will be seen as a balancing force rather than a co-conspirator. Him working against that risks being seen as either unbalancing an effective system or a return to a two-party system that no one wants."

"It is not a win, *per se*," E.W. added. "She has not beaten Jonas, but she has entered into a stalemate with him."

"Can't he still come after you, though? It's not like the whole System knows."

"That is why he was so upset at you, as well, my dear," May

said. "You will write your book and your play, and he will just have to brace himself as best he can."

"But I haven't yet, though."

"Of course, but if he had decided to take Sasha out anyway, you would still be left to write about *that*. Your name is already trusted enough on the System that if you were to write something after her assassination, it would still have gone poorly for him. If he had taken you out as well—something I doubt he was prepared to do anyway—he would be in even deeper shit."

Ey shook eir head. Ey was feeling very far behind but needed to understand if ey was to write this book. More, ey needed to understand for emself. "So why not become Michelle?"

"Because look at me," Sasha said, laughing and spreading her arms. "I am a furry. A *skunk* furry, no less. There is benefit to being something that is just a little silly, just as there always has been. Even after all these years, it is difficult to take someone pretending to be a small furry animal seriously, so that disarms me in the eyes of the observer."

"So he will just leave you alone?"

"He will have to if he wishes to remain in his position. He answers to his desire for power, I answer only to my desire for stability and continuity. In that I remain earnest in my conviction," she said by way of answer. "Even that of me which is E.W. and May. E.W. cannot love his forest if politics overwhelm his existence. May cannot hold onto her devotion. These things I know."

May nodded slowly. "You are not wrong. I would not have used such words, but you are not wrong."

"That of me which remains True Name has settled down," she continued. "And she still holds to the idea that politics is a means to an end. She is good at it. She enjoys it. She is willing and able to utilize it."

"So," Debarre said. "When did you realize this might even work?"

"It was a chance I took. One that might have failed, yes, but a good chance. It was all those times he talked about how you and Michelle were not fit to lead. Jonas had a view of me that was as inaccurate as it was easy to use against him. I have my political acumen and you have your own small group."

Ioan watched Debarre stiffen, making note of his response. It didn't feel like the type of thing to include in the story, but it did make rather a lot of the weasel's words and actions make more sense.

"You're nuts," Debarre said, rubbing his paws over his face to cover that response. "You're all fucking nuts."

Ioan gestured wildly toward the weasel. "Confirmation! Fucking nuts!"

The three skunks laughed while ey and Debarre leaned across the circle to shake hands.

The stream of Odists who came to visit Sasha in the days and weeks after the excursion to Jonas's was surprising. They seem to have accepted her change in identity far easier than expected. There were no instances of deadnaming (unless they were specifically talking about her past as True Name, as requested), no fights, no arguments.

Not everyone was happy, to be sure. Many of the discussions from those who stopped by were quite serious and, even though many took place in cones of silence, Ioan could easily guess that there was much in the way of airing of grievances. As far as ey could tell, though, it was done with an eye towards catharsis and reconciliation.

Serene, for instance, came over the day after the whole kerfuffle, surprising the three of them well into the evening. They'd settled for a middle ground of dinner out on the extended balcony—close enough to the house for them to cook a proper dinner without leaving Sasha feeling cooped up inside—when the ping against their sensoria caused the three to jolt as one.

"That will be Serene!" May said excitedly, setting her half-finished plate down and hopping to her feet. "I opened the ACLs to a few, hope you do not mind."

"Opened– wait, when?" Ioan asked, setting eir own plate down. "And to how many?"

But the skunk was already gone, bounding inside to greet the fox with a hug and excited chattering.

Ioan and Sasha followed more sedately, both waiting until May had gotten her greeting out of the way before bowing to Serene.

"Ioan, a pleasure! It has been too long," she said, grinning widely. The grin faded, and she nodded to the spotted skunk. "And Sasha."

"Serene, thank you for stopping by. I was not expecting to see you so soon."

"I do not imagine so. May Then My Name has been conspiring behind the scenes, so this was all worked out ahead of time."

"Oh? How cheeky," Sasha said, laughing. "Were you really that confident that everything would work out, dear?"

May shook her head. "Reasonably confident, but I want Arrowhead Lake back no matter what, so I arranged for us a little meeting."

"Skunks, I swear." Ioan shook eir head. "Well, welcome all the same. We've got pasta, if you'd like."

Once she'd heaped a plate high with food, Serene followed them out onto the balcony to join them for the rest of their meal. She wrinkled her nose at the sight of the plain. "I suppose this was the best one could do on short notice, yes?"

"It wasn't too much, and it fit the need, yeah."

"It has served its purpose," Sasha said. "And it is not so bad close up. A little too flat, perhaps, but the river is nice."

Serene nodded and finished a mouthful of food before setting her fork down again. "I have at least come bearing a gift."

"Did you find your student?"

"Yes. He was still about, though he has...changed much in

the intervening years. He was not as pleased to see me as I might have liked."

Sasha dipped her snout. "I am assuming that he has picked up on the sentiment surrounding the clade."

Serene nodded. "He read the *History* and came to the same conclusion that the rest of the System did. Our name is not mud, but, my dear, relationships changed after that knowledge became public."

"I understand."

"I do not want to hear you say that you are sorry, Sasha. I do not think that is how this works as you are now, not for me. I do not want to hear your justifications and explanations; I can understand them as well as anyone. I just want to hear your acknowledgement."

After setting her plate and fork down on the low table again, Sasha folded her paws in her lap, sat for a moment in silence, then said, "For as much as I tried to do—for as much as Jonas and I both tried to do—I do not think we had nearly the effect on the world around us we thought we did, not on the grand scale. We played our games of politics and influence, but it was a game of relationships from start to finish, you are correct. True Name changed relationships. May Then My Name changed relationships. E.W. played his part. I do not know if it was for the better or the worse, but I do acknowledge that it made a good many of them far more difficult."

"Well, okay. Perhaps one apology."

"I am sorry, Serene; Sustained And Sustaining."

There was another moment of silence, then Serene's wild grin returned. "Well, that felt good. Praiseworthy did all that shit, too, so, fuck it. Let me finish my food and I will fuck your sim up but good."

Ioan blinked, looking between skunk and fennec. "Wait, that simple?"

"Of course, my dear," Serene said around a mouthful of pasta. "I already told you of my thoughts on the matter. I have done my processing."

"And now you cannot simply say something about skunks being brats," May chimed in. "Though I am pretty sure we all knew that foxes were, too."

Serene made a rude gesture, still grinning.

Once they'd finished dinner, Serene stood, stretched, and then leaned against the balcony railing staring out over the plain. Her expression was calm, pleasant, though focused on something ey couldn't see. "Ioan, I will need ACLs over at least the exterior, including your yard, though I will do my best to keep it intact."

Ey nodded, focused, and made the grant.

"Thank you. Now, you may stay out here and watch, but I warn you that it can be a bit dizzy-making."

Ey exchanged glances with the two skunks and shrugged. "I think we're all eager to see."

"Suit yourself. It was your dinner. Thank you, by the way."

There was no further announcement. Nor, even, any change in Serene. She still looked out over the railing with a dreamy, far away look on her face even as the world dropped out beneath them.

The plain rippled and flexed, arching up high to the sky as though stretching after a long nap. Trees pried their way from the soil. Rocks broke free from the land. The river—the one immediately before them, at least—collapsed into itself to form a wide lake. The rest of the distant echoed versions of the plain where not occupied by the immediate mountains crinkled into some more complex geometry, the remainder of the range echoed outside the valley.

It *was* a little vertigo-inducing, too. The worst of it wasn't due to the sudden change in the shape of the landscape, but in just how, well...serene it all was. The river shaping itself into the lake was not accompanied by some grand splashing of waves, but simply the remaking of the water. There were no falling rocks or grand earthquakes, just the reshaping of the world. The light shifted. Gravity swayed, settled. All of it was silent, anechoic.

And then it was done.

"H-holy fuck," ey managed, clutching at the railing of the balcony. Both May and Sasha stood defiantly against the change, though neither looked as casual as the fox.

"I have set your house up the hill a ways from the default entry point to the old sim. That it was already on stilts proved quite useful. The angle of the sun may be a bit different, but not so much as to be a problem," she said, gesturing them down the steps from Sasha's side of the balcony. They landed on a flagstone pad set into the bed of pine needles, a small trail winding its way down the slope toward the water. She gestured toward the small ridge that rose next to them. "I had to modify the terrain a little bit to keep your yard level. You should be okay, but if you run into erosion problems, do let me know. I have been told of your affinity for weather, Ioan."

Sure enough, the fence remained level, wrapping around a small rectangle of hidden grass and dandelions, the tops of lilac bushes overflowing.

The path teed with the long familiar deer trail that wound around the lake, and, out of habit, they all started down towards the rock.

"Fauna?" Serene asked.

"Please." Sasha smiled sheepishly. "I would not like a repeat of that particular mistake."

Grinning and nodding, Serene kept up her steady pace, humming a little under her breath. There was no change that ey could see, though ey imagined her counting deer, rabbits, squirrels, and birds into existence.

For eir part, ey simply walked, hand in paw with May, and marveled. Ey'd discovered the lake decades ago, had spent countless days out here on walks, and at least one night camping. Still, it felt somehow new. Ey was rediscovering this place that ey'd not seen in months—though ey'd spent longer stints away from it in the past—and marveling at the detail all over again. A glance back over eir shoulder showed eir flat-roofed house peeking shyly from amid the trees, but other than that, it was, ey assumed, the same as it had been.

After so long away and after so much stress it felt all the more real.

They sat on the rock near the end of the lake and enjoyed the last of the sun. It was a little tight for four, but May tucked quite nicely up against eir side and Sasha, having slipped more into an E.W. mindset, had settled off to the side. She looked antsy, and ey suspected she'd request time to hike soon enough.

"How is the rest of the clade taking this?" she asked. "I sent a clade-wide message, but have not received responses."

Serene looked up from where she was investigating a few pine needles plucked from a branch on the way over with a discriminating eye. "I think that reactions will be largely positive even if they are not universally so. Several of my stanza have been been talking, and many feel as I do. It is fine, I am sure, and I have processed what I needed to and gotten what I wanted."

"Of course. I have been abandoned by the rest of my stanza, but at this point, the larger part of me does not want to have anything to do with them, anyway. I do not imagine Loss For Images and her ilk will take it well. I do hope that A Finger Pointing and I will have a chance to speak soon, as I am now enough May that I would enjoy attending a play or two."

"'May'?" Serene said, tiling her head and looking to the other skunk. "Have you forgiven her, then?"

May nodded. "Forgiven is maybe not the best word. I have internalized the way things are and accepted the way things were. I am pleased to know Sasha and who she has become."

The other skunk smiled faintly, nodded. "Though for all Ioan talked about trying to fix things, I place the largest part of who I have become on you, dear."

"I wasn't going to say anything," Ioan said, grinning.

May elbowed em in the side. "Hush, you."

"I will not laugh at you two too much, then." Serene laughed anyway, though not unkindly. "What are your plans moving forward? I trust that you are essentially locked out of what you were working on as True Name."

"Yes, and while there is a part of me that remains disappointed about this outcome, there is little to be done about it but move forward." Sasha brought her tail around to her lap to brush it out. It was shorter than a striped skunk's tail, it seemed, and less thickly furred. "I will take a vacation, first. I will sleep a normal amount. I will eat good food. I will wear myself out on the hunt and take what comfort I can while I remain here. I will rest, and then I will write."

"Write? Really?"

"Yes. I must be careful not to be seen as overtly influencing lest I bring on Jonas's ire, but I would like to share the story of the last few centuries from my point of view. I do not know who will be interested except perhaps our two clades, but I will write."

"Well, if it's anything like the *History*," Ioan said, "it'll wind up wildly popular and then fade into part of the mythos of the System."

May grinned. "And all will be as it should."

"Of course. I will not complain. So long as I am better able to understand who I have become and fill my time with something fulfilling, then I will be happy."

"*Will* you be happy?" Serene asked.

There was a long silence as Sasha finished brushing out her tail and spent a few minutes simply staring across the lake, perhaps mapping the opposite shore and marking spots for future exploration.

Finally, she said, "I think that I will be. I am of three minds and will ever be such. I will have moments of happiness, moments of sadness and terror and regret, but they will ever be in thirds."

"Are you okay with that?"

Sasha stood and stretched, finally turning her gaze back to them. "Himself has but to will And easy as a Star Look down upon

Captivity And laugh."

With no further explanation, she bowed and edged around them on her way down off the rock. She moved quietly and efficiently, and it was a matter of moments before they lost sight of her in the trees.

They sat and shared quiet stories of the past through the remainder of the evening.

The next Odists to visit were A Finger Pointing and Slow Hours, once more arriving as a pair and hugging Sasha in turn. They set up a cone of silence and spoke together for a scant twenty minutes before dropping it again and inviting Ioan and May to join. They pulled the beanbag a little closer to the couch and settled down on it together to listen.

"It is easy to say that all is full of love," Slow Hours began, smiling to Sasha. "But now, I think, you have a sense of your own."

The skunk smiled and bowed her head.

"Life will be easier for a while, and then it will be harder. You will share your loves, first with another and then with solitude, and with each you long for the other until you return." Her expression slipped into a lopsided grin. "Does not matter one fucking bit, though, so I would not worry."

"Mere breath?" Sasha asked, grinning.

"A chasing after the wind, yes."

"And you will come to a performance," A Finger Pointing added. "I am no oracle, but if you do not come, I will hunt you down myself. It has been too long, my dear."

She laughed. "Of course. So many threats to hunt me down, these days. But yes, thank you."

"And if you do not watch me perform my monologue, I will trim your claws too short in your sleep," May said. "There is a monologue night coming up soon."

"Far worse than being hunted down, that. I will be there."

May preened.

After that, they fell into comfortable conversation. Sasha joined Ioan and May on the beanbag to get some pets—the talk having apparently nudged the affectionate part of her to the fore—while Slow Hours spoke in fewer 'will's and 'shall's and settled down into the normal conversational mode of the rest of the Odists. They spoke of performances past, going all the way back to before the founding of the System, back to their time in high school. The four Odists performed a small segment of the Dickinson play they always seemed to quote from, a first for any of the Bălans in the nearly fifty years their clades had been entangled.

Ey didn't understand, but ey didn't need to.

———————————

It was nearly a month before Debarre, Douglas, and Sasha agreed to meet. Debarre's side of the negotiations remained stiff and distant, the weasel initially refusing to see Sasha after that first meeting. Douglas seemed to have set aside any sense of caution, speaking with palpable excitement. As soon as he'd learned of the change of name back to something more closely associated with his distant relative, he'd hardly spoken of anything else.

Eventually, though, meeting was set up for dinner on the dandelion-dotted field, a small potluck picnic late in the evening so that the skunks wouldn't overheat in the sun.

Everyone arrived simultaneously by Debarre's request so that no one was left waiting for anyone else. Ioan, May, and Sasha stepped into the sim just in time to see Debarre and E.W. arriving. The six of them stood in a circle in front of Douglas's stoop, dandelions and evening bumblers tickling at their ankles.

Or, at least they stood in a circle for a moment. Sasha almost immediately stumbled back from the group, turning in two slow, wavering circles before falling to her knees.

"Sasha?" Ioan said, startled.

"Too much," she mumbled shakily. "Too much at once."

May padded over to kneel next to her. "May I hug?"

After a moment of strained silence, Sasha slumped against May's side, and the two sat together while she let out that overwhelming emotion within a cone of silence.

Ioan, Debarre, E.W., and Douglas took the time to set up the picnic, a rickety table bearing plates of various salads, roasted vegetables, and the makings for venison sandwiches, courtesy of E.W.. They moved in silence, hesitantly, each pausing every now and then to watch as Sasha slowly worked to calm herself.

"That was not the greeting that I had intended," she said, once she had cleaned up in Douglas's house and joined them at the table to pick up a plate. "I was hoping that I would be able to greet you all politely, settle into some easier conversation, but that of True Name has not been here in too long. This place is too charged with memories, as are your faces. Even for that of E.W. and May, there is too much bound up in the last few months."

"Are you feeling better now?" Douglas asked.

She nodded. "I am leaning on the other portions of myself now. I will have much processing to do yet, but tonight is for dinner with friends, or at least with those I hope will be friends."

"I certainly hope we can be friends." Douglas laughed. "I mean, those are the first words we've ever really spoken to each other, but I'm happy to have the chance to meet you."

"Or at least meet a third of me."

"Well, yes, but you're still a new person to me and very...uh," he trailed off, frowning down to his plate. "Well, very close to someone I've thought a lot about, I guess."

She smiled and leaned over to pat his shoulder. "We will talk, dear. That part of me has heard so much about you and is so colored by what the other parts of me know, that I am eager to learn, as well."

Debarre remained stiff and awkward, even as they settled down on the blanket to eat, plates piled high with various dishes and cups of sangria set carefully in the grass behind them. He wouldn't make eye contact with Sasha and seemed hesitant to speak even to Ioan and May.

Eventually, he cleared his throat, set his plate down, and stared steadily at Sasha. "I think you owe me an apology. At least from the, uh...what did you call it? The True Name part of you?"

As she had done with Serene, Sasha set her plate down as well, folded her paws in her lap, and bowed to the weasel. Ioan could tell by the set of her features and the straightness of her shoulders that she was indeed doing her best to keep that part of her at the fore. "I am sorry, Debarre. The things that I did were for what I thought was best, but they wound up hurting a good many people. They were not fair to you and I apologize for the pain I caused. While I do not think I even *could* anymore, I will all the same endeavor not to act in such single-minded ways again."

Ioan couldn't read Debarre's expression well enough to gauge his thoughts on the matter, but judging by the way he loosened up and joined in more of the conversations after that, speaking even with Sasha, he seemed to at least have accepted the words to an extent.

Debarre and E.W. stayed for a few hours after dinner, long enough to see the first stars show themselves above the field, before they stepped back to the skunk's sim.

Shortly after, Sasha stood, the other three following suit. She hugged Ioan and May around the shoulders and gave each of them a touch of the nose to the cheek. "If you two do not mind, I would like to go for a walk with Douglas and speak with him alone."

They nodded and returned the hugs and kisses, getting hugs from Douglas as well before they stepped back home.

"Do you think Douglas still puts too much stock in who you used to be?" Ioan asked once they were home and comfortable.

May was a while in answering. "Perhaps, yes. We are not Michelle, have not been for centuries. None of us are Sasha—least of all Sasha."

Ioan nodded, brushing out the skunk's tail with a fine-toothed comb as ey'd been commanded. "He really relaxed after uploading, at least. Just a few little spikes in interest when certain things came up."

"As hyperfixations go, it is a relatively innocuous one," she said, yawning. "But I am at least pleased to see that he is both engaging with other things and finding fulfillment in this aspect of his life when he can."

"Besides, it's not like you guys don't hyperfixate on things."

"Mmhm," she mumbled sleepily. "But all the same, we have been slowly drifting away from what we used to be over the years, and in the face of all that we have seen, that is not such a bad thing."

"How do you feel about her apology?"

"How do you mean?"

Ey shrugged. "It felt...I don't know, a little rehearsed, maybe."

May curled in against eir side, yawning once more. "Perhaps. She said what Debarre needed to hear, I think, and it was no less earnest for that. As much as he means to us, that is no bad thing, either."

Ioan wasn't sure why ey kept feeling surprised at the number of loose threads from just one event that needed tying. The business with Qoheleth had been about as complicated, and had required meeting with several other Odists in order to finish the story, and each one came with a different tenor.

The same was true here, as well. Many members of the clade—some of whom ey'd not yet met—visited and requested time with Sasha or with the three of them. Still, ey realized, this culmination came after two and a quarter centuries for some, so perhaps it made sense.

Not all of these interactions went smoothly.

Barely a month after that dinner with Debarre and Douglas on the field, two of the most dramatic happened within the span of a week.

May stumbled in the middle of a Wednesday morning rehearsal, falling to her knees, panting, before pushing herself to her feet. She managed to make it through the rest of the scene before forking off so that she could continue as best she could while her root instance ducked back home.

Once there, she darted over towards where Ioan sat at eir desk, working through the process of writing Jonas's book. She knelt beside em, clutched a pawful of eir shirt and set up a cone of silence. Ey felt the ACL-scape of the cone shift several times until it was just about as secure as could be made.

"May? What–"

"Zacharias! He has been pinging me once every few seconds for the last minute!" She was on the verge of hyperventilation, eyes wide and tail bristled. "I do not know what– *fuck!*"

Ioan slid from eir chair as the skunk started to slump over to the side. Ey helped her to her feet and over to the beanbag. "May, what's happening?"

"He keeps...quitting and...sending high-priority merges..." she gasped. "The cone will not...stop those..."

"You okay for a few seconds?"

Slumped over on the beanbag, the skunk nodded.

Ey stepped from the cone, where May had clearly blocked sensorium messages from the fox, so that ey could holler into a message, "What the fuck do you want?"

"Ioan! I need to...can I–"

"No. No coming over."

"A neutral place?"

"Do you need May there?"

"Yes!"

Ey sighed. "I'll ask. No guarantees."

"No, I...no," the skunk mumbled once ey stepped back into the cone. She'd managed to sit up and while the panicked look on her face had calmed, the beginnings of rage had taken its place. "He cannot come here."

"Maybe Douglas's to keep him from being too much? If

Sasha's reaction was anything to go by, it might quell him, or at least keep him distracted."

The skunk sat, silent, for a moment, holding onto one of eir hands tightly. "Will Douglas be around to sweep if needed?"

Ey nodded.

"Now?"

"Yeah, I think so. I'm not sure I trust that he'll leave you alone if we put him off."

"I–"

They were interrupted by a rapidly crescendoing thudding sound followed by the scrabble of claws on the glass of the sliding door, Sasha finally finding purchase and whipping it open. May dropped the cone of silence.

"What the fuck is happening?!" Sasha shouted.

"You too, then?"

Sasha frowned, straightened up, and brushed out her tunic. "Yes. He just about knocked me out with the amount of adrenaline he sent my way. You look ready to go, though. Do you have a plan?"

"We're going to meet him at Douglas's field. That's about the start and end of it, though." Ioan took a deep breath and tried to tamp down the urge to pace. "Do you want to come?"

Ey watched a complex set of emotions play out over her features. She stood still for nearly a minute, working to master them, before nodding. "Yes. Let us get this the fuck over with."

Ioan sent a message to Zacharias spoken aloud for the skunks' benefit. "The Field#002a0b1."

The reply was frantic. "What?! No!"

"There or no meeting."

"F-fine."

Ioan helped May to her feet and placed a kiss atop her head before the three of them forked and stepped from the sim.

Douglas stood at the top of his stoop, arms crossed, frowning. "Ioan, what is this?"

"Zacharias made it out of the whole thing alive," May

growled. "And now he is losing his mind and wants to meet. I will not have him at our home."

Douglas's frown deepened. "So you're bringing him here? The ACLs are pretty locked down right now."

"Yes. I do not want to meet him at all, but I do not imagine he will simply leave me alone." She spent a moment composing herself, plastering a mask of confidence over her anxiety. "We need somewhere where someone can sweep him if need be."

"If you say so," he said, paused, then continued, "Alright, he should be able to enter."

Ioan nodded and sent a ping to Zacharias.

He arrived within a fraction of a second, yelped, and fell backwards, paws balled up into fists and pressed tight against his eyes.

"How long has it been for you, my dear? Since you were forked?" May said, kneeling down before the fox. Her voice had grown cloyingly sweet, that 'my dear' taking on a spiteful tone.

"Y-yes," he gasped. "Did...did we have to meet here?"

"Where better?" Sasha said. She stood nearby, arms crossed, impassive, looking almost bored, though Ioan could see the energy it was taking for her to keep that up.

Zacharias moaned. He forced himself to lower his paws to the ground, gripping at clumps of grass and dandelions. Finally, he opened his eyes and stared out toward the horizon of the field. "I–"

"What did you want, my dear Zack? You sounded nearly on the verge of panic," May said.

"It is Jonas!" he said, finally snapping out of his daze. "Jonas! He has gone crazy! He killed all of my instances!"

"Did you expect anything else, little loverfox?" Sasha asked. There was no humor or sweetness in her voice, the last two words carried venom in them.

"I...I mean–"

"You are the root instance, I am assuming?"

He nodded, the movement jerky and uneven. "I have not left

home since. I dug a new one, you see, and he found that one somehow."

"And what can we do for you?" May asked.

"Help! You can help me get away from that...that lunatic!"

Sasha frowned. "Can you not dig another home?"

He reached out to clutch at May's paws. She startled backwards, but did nothing to push him away. "I cannot...I cannot just disappear! Months! It has been months since I have seen anyone. Anyone! I have to...to be near–"

"No," she said flatly.

"But–"

"No." The skunk shook her head, leaned forward and touched her nose to his. "Not me. Not Sasha. Not us. You are on your own, Zacharias. I will not accept any further messages or merges. No contact."

He slouched once more, eyes still wide. "May Then My Name, I–"

"No contact." She extracted one of her paws from his and slapped him firmly across the snout. "And that is for before."

Yelping, he fell back onto an elbow. He opened his mouth to respond, but May had already nodded towards Douglas, who swept him from the sim.

She remained kneeling for a moment, then started to shake, crumpling down onto the grass, panting heavily. Ioan knelt beside her until she'd cried herself dry while Douglas and Sasha sat on the steps leading up to his house, watching in silence.

"I've never seen you like that before," he said, once they'd made their way inside, the four of them clutching glasses of water. "I knew he was a shitbag, but goddamn."

"I am...not okay," she said, whispering down to her glass. "I am not okay."

"It is not a mode either of us are comfortable with," Sasha said quietly, "but it is the only mode that would have gained us peace. Any weakness would be taken as an opening."

Douglas nodded. He didn't look convinced.

"I am sorry. After 226 years, one learns to use contempt with precision, however dear the cost." She reached out to take one of May's paws in her own. Both of them looked exhausted. "Even so, I do not expect that is the last we will hear from him."

They didn't stay long after. Ioan eventually promised Douglas that they'd catch up another time and then gently nudged the skunks to quit and merge back down.

The rest of the day was silent. Ioan and May collapsed onto the beanbag and stayed there through much of it, each processing in their own way, while Sasha disappeared outside to lose herself in the wilderness, not returning until late that evening, bearing a lanky hare and double-pawful of chantarelles, which she cooked down into a simple stew. They ate on the balcony to enjoy the late summer's evening as best they could.

Sasha joined them in bed that night, and they took what comfort they could from each other's company.

The more dramatic of the meetings, however, came that weekend. It was quieter, perhaps, but bearing more weight, more finality.

The rest of the week had remained tense, with Sasha wafting in and out of the house to follow her unsettled moods while May remained quiet, nearly silent, nearly always stuck by Ioan's side. Ey knew ey should probably start laying in supplies for her overflowing, but ey was still distracted trying to pick apart the events with Zacharias. In light of eir desire to keep both of them safe and close, much of the fury that had come with eir first meeting with the fox threatened to reappear every time ey thought about the two skunks.

Which, naturally, was quite often.

It was not exactly the best of timing, then, when If I Am To Bathe In Dreams, an elegant, if severe-looking, skunk arrived late on a Saturday afternoon on a few minutes' notice and bowed formally to the three of them.

"Ioan, I believe Jonas hired you as an amanuensis?" she said.

"He did, yes. Do you need me for that, too?"

"Please. This story is not over, will not be over for a long time yet. Listen. Watch."

Sasha immediately picked up on the mood and stood up straight after returning the formal bow. She offered In Dreams a seat and something to drink, both of which were declined, then said, "How may I help you?"

"I have a request from both my stanza and that of Memory Is A Mirror Of Hammered Silver. You will also be presented with this request in writing as an individual-eyes-only message."

Sasha nodded. "I understand."

"We request no contact from you, your stanza, or the Bălan clade moving forward."

"Wait, what?" Ioan said. May edged around a little ways behind em, clutching at eir arm.

"You are too entangled in the matter. No contact with this situation means no contact from you, May Then My Name Die With Me, or E.W. *né* Do I Know God After The End Waking. This request is in effect until further notice, and applies to our stanzas on Castor and Pollux as well, where Dear, Also, The Tree That Was Felled will be presented with the same request. None of us are on Artemis, but I will also be passing this on to Sorina Bălan. This includes general intraclade communication; we will add visibility exceptions to our messages and request that you do the same."

"I understand, accept, and offer you my best," Sasha said, bowing once more.

"I do not want your best," In Dreams said, voice flat. "Ioan?"

Ey blinked, hesitated, then bowed in turn. "I understand and accept."

"And May Then My Name?"

It took the skunk a moment to swallow back a rising wave of emotions before she could manage a shaky nod and a hoarse, "Understood."

"We are of one mind, then," she said, bowed, and stepped from the sim. A few seconds later, three sheets of paper scrolled out of the air above the dining table, all set as individual-eyes-only for each of them. Ioan read through eirs several times with a hollow feeling in eir chest.

Sasha stood still for a long minute, head bowed, then stepped outside without a word, at which point May burst into tears.

Ioan did eir best to comfort her, but after an hour, she gently pushed em away. "I need...I need the house to myself, please."

"Should I head to Douglas's?"

She shook her head. "I do not know, Ioan. I just...I just need the house. If you can...I mean, if Sasha will let you stay at her tent, you can stay, but I need the house."

"Now?"

Nodding, she wrapped her arms around em and squeezed tighter than ey knew she could. "I love you more than anything, my dear, but yes. Now."

Ey waited until ey could breathe properly after the squeeze, then kissed the top of her head. "I love you too, May. Please be safe, okay?"

She nodded once more, relinquished her grip on em, and nudged em out toward the back door and outside.

Sasha had set up a tent similar to E.W.'s, though she had skipped the process of building it herself, instead creating from similar materials off the exchange. She'd set it up nearly on the other side of the lake from their house, so that she could have the solitude that she needed without having to create some new sim of her own. When the need for space struck her, it never quite got to the point that it did with E.W. She would need away from their presences, she would say. They felt like a constant weight on her shoulders. Light, yes, but continually present.

Ah well. This was the first time that May had overflowed in this living situation—and so dramatically, too—so perhaps it would be helpful after all.

Ey took eir time walking around the shore of the lake, using it to vent the emotions that had built up over the last few hours through tears, through shouting into a cone of silence, cursing.

"Ioan? Goodness," Sasha said.

Ey'd managed to mostly clean up with a handkerchief, though clearly eir eyes were still red-rimmed and eir countenance...well, who knew? Glum, perhaps?

"Hi Sasha," ey said, sitting down on the step leading up into the tent. The skunk had been writing at the small desk she'd acquired, but she moved to join em. "May's not in a good spot. She suggested I stay with you, if that's alright."

She frowned, nodded. "That bad?"

"Well, she kind of kicked me out of the house, yeah."

She laid her ears flat. "We are perhaps both overflowing in our own ways."

"Oh, shit. I wasn't thinking. Douglas–" Ey moved to stand, but she grabbed eir wrist.

"I had seen this coming, if I am honest, so it is not hitting me quite so hard as her. I will be okay."

Ey nodded, slowly settled back onto the step. "If you say so."

Sasha patted eir hand and bade em stay while she got up to stoke up the fire in her stove and fry up a simple meal of potatoes and vegetables. Ey couldn't tell if it was just bland—as E.W. preferred—or if eir mind was too busy to process taste, so ey mostly just pushed the food around on the plate.

"Without contraries is no progression," Sasha murmured after they'd finished. "Attraction and repulsion, reason and energy, love and hate, are necessary to human existence."

Ey started to ask what she meant, paused, then looked the words up in the perisystem architecture. "Blake? And here I thought you all were mostly into Dickinson."

She chuckled and elbowed em in the side. "This may be a True Name thing."

"Are you leaning into the "Good is the passive that obeys reason; Evil is the active springing from Energy" on this, then?"

"Nothing is so simple, dear," she said, shaking her head.

"Blake was not of our kind, he would not have understood. He did get that right, though, in that we are a people of dualities. May sees in Zacharias all that she cannot—must not—be. In Dreams and Hammered Silver see in me that which they are not—could not be—and yet we are not what we are without our opposites. Every idea's opposite is just the absence of the idea itself."

"Maybe." Ey sighed. "It's all a bit over my head."

"I am also a little bit all over the place," she admitted. "These events have me going in three different directions at once. The Ode clade is crumbling and I cannot deny that some...that much of that is on me. I am sorry, Ioan."

"I don't even know what to think about that," ey said, shaking eir head. "It's kind of a lot."

"That it is. You are a good person, though. You love your partner. She knows this. I know this. You are good to her and it will all be okay. We may hope for neat endings but all we get are more beginnings." She smiled, adding, "And yes, you may stay until she is feeling better."

May's stint of overflowing only lasted two nights. Something about the change in context, though, about staying with Sasha instead of Douglas, made everything feel tenuous, delicate. Ioan found it difficult to sleep on the padded cot that she'd added to the tent, and eventually, she must have grown tired of hearing em toss and turn (and perhaps mumble to emself), for she sleepily climbed out of her own bed and into eirs, curling up with em after confirming that it was alright.

Unexpected, perhaps, but by then ey was too frustrated and exhausted to think of anything else. The added comfort certainly worked in getting em to sleep, to the point where ey slept in until a ray of sun, creeping slowly, fell across eir face and warmed em awake.

Sasha had apparently woken up earlier in the morning and snuck away, as there was a lukewarm cup of camp coffee sitting by the edge of eir bed and no skunk to be found.

Ah well, at least the coffee was good (if gritty) and ey felt better rested than ey had before.

Ey met up with her at the shore of the lake where they talked for a bit, though it was clear that she was antsy to head out into the woods on her own, so ey eventually shooed her off, to which she bowed gratefully and said, "My notes are on my desk. If you get bored, I would appreciate your feedback."

Ey spent the rest of the abbreviated day reading through what she'd written, making a mental list of ideas and suggestions to pass on to her when things were a little less hectic.

That night was much the same, with the two of them talking until it was well and truly dark, then settling into their own beds until sleeplessness led to them curling together in one.

A ping from May shortly after sunrise woke em, and the jolt startled Sasha awake as well.

"Uh, sorry," ey mumbled, extricating eir arms from around her. "May pinged."

Sasha levered herself up and squinted out into the orange and pink of dawn. "How is she up before me?" she grumbled.

"Probably because she got good sleep and I kept you up being a mope."

She shrugged noncommittally, yawned. "Slept well enough later on, at least. Did she say anything?"

Ey shook eir head. "No, just a ping. No real urgency, though. Surprised I didn't sleep through it."

"You are appropriately keyed to her, dear. I would be surprised if you did."

"Mm, fair enough," ey said, grinding the heels of eir palms against eir eyes. To May, ey sent a ping in response, plus a sub-vocalized, *"You okay?"*

"Better, yes," came the reply. *"I am feeling quite bad about sending you off like that. Not about waking you up, though. You sound cute*

when you are groggy."

Ey snorted, shook eir head. "Yeah, she's fine," ey said.

Sasha surprised em by joining em on the trek back to the house, saying only, "I have been worried, as well."

May greeted them at the balcony with steaming mugs of coffee. She declined a hug, stating that she felt gross, but did at least press her nose to Ioan's, and then to Sasha's cheek.

"Thank you for giving me some space," she said. "I was not expecting the both of you, but I am happy to see you two all the same."

"Of course, May. I'm just happy to see you doing better. Or happier, at least. You look a mess."

She scoffed and gestured a paw down at herself. "I look perfectly fine, thank you very much."

"You look a mess, dear," Sasha confirmed. "You need a shower, a change of clothes, and perhaps another four hours of sleep."

May sighed, nodded. "I do at that. All the same, the wave has crested and gone, and now perhaps I can relax enough to do so. Coffee first, though.

They settled on deck chairs for Sasha's sake and focused on said coffee for a bit, watching the dawn. It was good to be back to coffee that didn't require straining out the occasional percolated ground through one's teeth.

"Are you two okay?" May said at last.

"Tired, but that's easily fixed. Looking forward to a real bed tonight."

Sasha poked at eir knee with a dull claw. "The tent beds are not *that* bad."

"No, they're fine, but they still pale in comparison to our bed."

"Well, yes, I will admit that."

May looked between the two, then laughed. "I take it this setup worked for me taking some space?"

Ioan shrugged. "Well enough, sure. It's nice to have another option that isn't just crashing at Douglas's."

"It was fine, dear," Sasha added. "If ever either of you need some space, feel free to kick the other down to the tent and I will make it work."

"I am glad," May said. "Earnestly. Ioan was such a solitary creature that I did not ever picture having neighbors when I moved in all those years ago. It is nice to have a friend close by."

"Aren't all of your friends equally close now that–"

Sasha cut em off, shaking her head. "Ioan, do you remember how I said that I feel others' presence around me like a weight on my shoulders?"

Ey nodded.

"I think it is rather like that, though do correct me if I am wrong, May. Even when I am hiding away in my tent, I am still more present than a friend out of sim is."

"Basically," May said. "Never mind one who knows me so intimately now."

Sasha nodded, hesitated, then said, "On that note, are *you* okay?"

"I...well," she began, sighed, and shook her head. "I am upset, and I am disappointed that I am upset. I was so ready to be done with hatred, but I am stuck with yet more of it. Hatred from In Dreams, hatred of Zacharias, hatred in myself. More than the experiences with In Dreams and Zacharias, that feeling is what led to the past few days of tears. I thought that I was done."

"I understand. While I am thinking of it, I would like to talk with you about Zacharias at some point—nothing serious, just strategizing future meltdowns of his. Ioan said he kept trying to force merges on you just to get your attention."

May winced. "Ugh, yeah. I have never felt something so intensely...I do not know. It felt like a violation of my personal space on a subatomic level. What were you thinking?"

Sasha tilted her head. "Now? I was going to suggest in a few days time, once you were feeling better."

"Why not? I am already a mess, I am already thinking about him, and after this, I would like more than 'a few days time' completely disengaged from the topic." She giggled, adding, "Besides, the more I have to dump on Sarah the next time I see her the better, right?"

"I do not think it works that way, but I am not so much of a brat as you." Sasha finished her coffee, set the mug down with a sense of finality, and nodded. "Well, I suppose I am awake enough. If you do not mind, Ioan, may I steal your partner for a little bit longer? I would like to keep this first discussion between us, though I will ensure that you remain caught up. There is some…history behind this she should know."

"Are you up for forking, May?"

She hesitated, then shook her head, pushing herself up from her chair to step around behind eirs. She bent down to hug around eir shoulders from behind, cheek pressed against eir own. "I cannot cope with conflicts right now. I cannot yet work in parallel."

Ey rested eir cheek against hers and frowned down to eir coffee for a few moments, sighed, then nodded. "Alright, but I get the May for the rest of the day, okay?"

They both laughed.

"Of course, Ioan," Sasha said. "If you would like some company out on the balcony or something, I have no such compunctions about forking."

Ey felt May nod against eir cheek. "I am not pushing further solitude on you, my dear. Take some coffee and breakfast with you. I do not imagine we will be all that long."

Still cognizant of her saying that she felt gross, ey patted one of her paws and turned eir head enough to kiss her on the cheek. "Alright, that sounds good."

Ey pulled together a breakfast of rolls to go along with a thermos of coffee, got one more nose-press of a kiss with May, and stepped back outside with an instance of Sasha.

The house had been set up on a portion of the slope that

was turned a little toward the west for sunset views, meaning that the sun was not yet hitting the balcony. Autumn had gotten chilly enough at night, though, that they decided instead to walk down to the boulder lakeside, which would almost certainly be in full sun, even if it was less comfortable than the deck chairs.

They sat in silence, drinking their coffee and eating rolls with butter and honey.

"Do you think you'll stay, Sasha?" Ioan said, once the rhythm of the silence made room for conversation.

"I am too much myself to say that I will stay forever, but as long as my room and tent are there, as long as you and May are comfortable with me being a part of your lives, I will be happy to call it home. Or at least *a* home."

"Really? No bigger and brighter things?"

She laughed and leaned over to touch her nose to eir cheek. "This *is* bigger and brighter things, Ioan."

"Well, I'm sure we'll talk about it plenty, but I see no reason not to keep your room about, and your tent's certainly no trouble. I don't know what you overflowing will look like, but if it involves two thirds solitude and one third getting lost walking sims, I don't imagine you'll be around all the time."

"Not at all, no. I will spend my share of time at the tent to be alone or out walking the world. Perhaps I will even ask you to double the rest of the house so that I can cook somewhere domestic, not just the wild."

"Of course." Ey shrugged, tossing one of eir collected pebbles into the lake. "Besides, I like having you around."

"I am pleased to hear that. I had gathered such, but all the same, I would not want to be a bother."

"Oh, not at all. It seems like we're all pretty good at sorting things out when they do come up, so I don't imagine it'll get to that point."

"And I am not impinging too much on your and May's relationship?" she asked, holding out her paw for one of eir pebbles. "I am asking her, too, and we will continue to talk together, but

I also want to ask you directly."

Ey smiled, handing over the small rock. "I don't think so. So long as we can still have time to ourselves when we need, I'll be happy."

She tossed the pebble out into the water. "Of course, dear." After a pause, she grinned and added, "She is gushing about you now. She loves you very much, you know."

Ioan chuckled. "I love her too. I worry sometimes, but all I can do is trust her."

"Yes. She will not betray that trust. I know to an extent just how much she means to you and to a much greater extent how much you mean to her."

They sat in quiet for a while, tossing pebbles into the water until ey ran out.

"Hey Sasha?"

"Mm?"

"Do you miss anything from before all this?"

She shrugged. "It is hard to tell. As I have said, I liked being True Name. It was fulfilling. Every time I think about that now, though, it is intercut with memories of other happinesses. I will think about some particularly adroit political move and remember it fondly, but right along with it is a memory of a successful hunt or of making fun of you for your pen collection."

Ey laughed.

"In confidence?"

"Sure."

"Do you remember when I asked May about how she cemented aspects of her personality by forking?"

"Mmhm."

"There was one more change that I made during that meeting, which was to cement this triad of identities within me. It became who I am by accident, but it has become an integral part of me. I welcomed it in, owned it, made it a part of myself. I will ever be what I am."

"Really? You're okay staying in three parts?"

"I am. I am happy to. I am *excited* to. There is something pleasant about the just-off-center nature of that reality. It is home to me. I am Sasha, and I am also True Name, E.W., and May. I am of three minds."

"So long as that works for you."

"I think it will. It is a way to be earnestly myself."

Ey nodded. "And I'm guessing you don't miss the social part of that life too much? Jonas or Zacharias or the rest of your stanza."

She poked at eir side with a claw. "You do not need to ask stupid questions, Ioan."

"Right, right," ey said, laughing. "I figured no love lost, but–"

"I did not love any of them, as friends or otherwise," she said, waving away the rest of eir comment. "Now that I have known other kinds of love, I am confident of that."

Her tone wasn't upset or dismissive, but was assertive enough that ey dropped the point. "Well, writing sounds like a good career shift, then."

"Says the writer." She slouched against eir side.

"I liked what you've gotten down so far, and I have a few notes. We'll talk about it when we're back at a desk, though."

"Of course. I will be leaning on you a lot for help."

"I mean, you're leaning on me now."

"Smartass," she drawled.

Ey grinned. "I mean, no complaints. It's still a little surprising, sometimes. I guess on some level I'm still getting used to it, but May got me hooked on physical contact a long time ago."

"A coordinated attack on your defenses, yes," she said. "It makes my job easier."

"What job?"

"Just finding a way to stick around friends. Nothing nefarious, dear."

Ey shook eir head. "Right, sorry. I trust you."

"I agree with what May said, Ioan. Should I want anything beyond that, I will come by it honestly. I will not manipulate my way into anything."

"I appreciate that." Ey hugged an arm around her. Ey was grateful for her looking out at the lake rather than at em, given the heat ey could feel rising to eir cheeks. "While we're being honest, though, I think we're sort of in the same boat, given what you share with May. We can both imagine that, but not necessarily the path from here to there. May called it 'the concept versus the mechanics'."

"Precisely. I imagine the same applies to you, that you will come by it earnestly."

Ey nodded. "Basically. *Is* it something you'd want?"

"God, I have no fucking clue, Ioan," she said, laughing.

"Definitely same boat, then. It's a problem for future Ioan."

They fell into silence again. Part of em was itching for more pebbles to toss into the water, but ey was too comfortable to get up to collect more from the beach.

"That is a part of the reason that I kept that of my old cocladists," Sasha murmured. "I kept some doubt from E.W., enough to keep me grounded without keeping me torn. From May, I am keeping a little bit of overwhelming emotions. The possibility of simply falling for everyone around me is alluring. I can taste it in the memories, like a little bit of saccharine, gritty on the tongue. But I am keeping a little bit of caution from True Name so that it remains a new thing for me. I am of three minds Like a tree In which there are three blackbirds."

Ey turned her words over in eir mind, along with whatever snippet of verse it was she'd quoted. The thought was complete. Nothing ey could respond with would add to it. It was curious, and hinted at things beyond eir ken, but it was complete.

Instead, ey said, "You're a good person, Sasha. All three of you are good people."

"And you, dear, are a dork." She laughed. "But come, my tail is falling asleep, and my fork's conversation with May has wrapped up and she misses you greatly."

They walked back, then, hand in paw, following the trail as

it dipped down to the water or ducked up into the trees. Back home, back to May, back to whatever it was that life had become.

To deny the end is to deny all beginnings,
and to deny beginnings is to become immortal,
and to become immortal is to repeat the past.

It has been a quarter of a millennium since eir death, and yet less than a quarter of a thousand people know eir name. Fitting, then, that I tell you the story of RJ Brewster, of the poet and the one true origin of our world, of our very own ghost in the system, of the whispers in your dreams and the one who binds us to immortality.

From *Ode* by Sasha,
a companion volume to *On the Origin of Our World*
2365/systime 241+21

Selected Letters

Ioan Bălan
Exocortex#99732a6
Selected correspondences of the Bălan clade
systime 222-232

Note: With the events of the last ten years, there's been a lot of changes shaking out in the clade when it comes to relationships. Collecting all of these here so that I can keep them handy for when things doubtless need further shaking out in the future. For the sake of comfortable through-reading, all eyes-only metadata has been stripped, but trust that everything was eyes-only to the named recipients. I've kept the timestamps as the message-sent time in the metadata. It's been thirty years and I'm still struggling with transmission delays.

Codrin Bălan#Castor — Ioan Bălan

systime 222 (2346)

Castor—Lagrange transmission delay:
30 days, 14 hours, 37 minutes

Ioan,

A part of me has died. I do not know what to say.

When one forks, one's down-tree instance should not change, right? They should just be the same, yes? They continue on as they were, and the only mark left by forking is the memory of having done so. I *know* this. Dear has assured me of this. It's how the System works, how it must work.

But for some reason, that isn't what happened.

Let me start over.

After all that happened, after all the decisions that had already been made, it felt like there was one more that needed to happen. I needed to figure out what I was going to do about myself with regards to Artemis. I asked surprisingly few people for advice on this. I mentioned it briefly to my partners, and Dear thought it was an okay idea, though I could tell that neither of them were totally sold on the idea.

On looking back, it's weird how little agency we attribute to our forks at first. The biggest complaint against the idea that they had was that they didn't want to see how much the fork I sent would miss me. ▮▮▮▮▮▮ was the one who wound up selling Dear on the idea, oddly enough, by reminding it just how much individuation can happen. It's been stuck in instance artistry too long, not letting itself deviate because its instances simply don't last long enough.

That was the origin of Sorina. Sorina Bălan, third of our clade, born at sunrise. I took that idea to heart and, when I decided to fork last week, I pushed individuation as hard and as fast as I could. I had a hundred paces to do so, a hundred steps between cairns to make sure that she was herself and that I remained myself.

And yet I'm not sure I *did* remain myself. A part of me died, and I do not know what to say about that. I pushed individuation on her — and see, here I go, taking her agency from her! — while I did my best to stay the same, to simply walk the prairie and think only of home and of Dear and of ██████████ and not of Artemis and a life without them. I didn't think of names. I didn't think of time skew or forking. I didn't think of anything but the pending sunrise.

I also didn't think of forgetting, and that's what got me over the weekend. Sorina and I seem to have been of one mind that we'd give it a bit of time before getting in touch with each other, but she hasn't left my thoughts since we forked. She *can't* leave my thoughts. I *can't* forget her.

But I realized she can forget me. She can forget us.

There may come a day — and I pray that that 'may' is accurate, for my sake if nothing else — when she cannot remember me, cannot remember any of us, cannot remember why we love the ones we do. For all of the complaints about our impeccable memories, this is one instance that I struggle to see myself living without.

What do I do? How do I live with the life I've created for myself? How do I internalize that a part of me has died?

I'm sorry, Ioan. There's nothing I can do about any of this, and certainly nothing you can do, however many hundreds of billions of kilometers away. I write because there is a sort of stability in you that has rusted in me. It has frozen all of my joints and so I risk cracking while you remain firmly rooted and flexible.

I'm sorry, Ioan.

Pass on my love.

- C

Ioan Bălan — The Bălan clade

systime 222 (2346)

Lagrange—Castor transmission delay:
30 days, 14 hours, 37 minutes

Lagrange—Pollux transmission delay:
30 days, 14 hours, 41 minutes

Codrin and Codrin,

I hope that you and yours are well. All of this news from Castor quickly got overwhelming and I know I've not been as good as I would like at keeping up with things that are not just "holy shit, aliens". I have a few updates.

The first is that, surprising no one, I've been contracted by A Finger Pointing to write a play about our visitors. I've been reading all of your updates, #Castor, and certainly the knowledge is worth quite a bit on its own, but can I ask for some information about the moods throughout? If I'm to pull together a story out of this, that will be more useful in the context of a play than the facts. Besides, it's not like we can do much in the way of fact checking from where we are. I have plenty of flexibility there. I've attached what I have, though obviously it'll be a month out of date by the time you get it (and two months by the time you answer).

Second, I'm sorry to say that End Waking has requested that Debarre give him some space for a bit again. I know that you two never got the chance to meet him and that I gush about him every time he comes up, but he really is delightful, and I wish him the best in his solitude, however long it might last.

May and I visited Debarre for dinner after we got the news and spent a bit of time talking about it. I was pleased to learn that these separations don't come with any ire, just a simple request and understanding. He seemed really calm, even a bit relieved about it. Apparently the weeks leading up to being asked to leave are a little awkward.

I think part of why this came when it did is due to the convergence. I know that Debarre is still far more plugged into the news of the System than I, and given that End Waking has essentially opted out, I can see that being an uncomfortable divide.

Finally and perhaps most impactful for me, I had the chance to meet one-on-one with True Name during convergence. Even after a month of thinking about the meeting, I'm still unsure what to make of it.

I, like you two, had the chance to interview her a few times during the process of pulling together the *History*, so I had been expecting the same frightful competence that I saw twenty-odd years ago.

I did not.

It's difficult for me to describe the ways in which she's changed. She's...overworked, perhaps? She looks like she's stretched herself too thin to keep up as well as she used to. I know that she mentioned that the tone of our interviews was carefully constructed in order to shape the narrative, and that the emotions she put on display were deliberately chosen for the role she was playing, but...well, I wasn't expecting to make her cry.

And yet from what you two have said, other than her experience on Artemis, she's still going strong on both the LVs.

I don't really know what to do with this information, honestly. I keep thinking about things I could have said or questions I could have asked, but it always gets muddled up in my head given her similarities to May. I've spent so long with May that seeing someone as similar to her as True Name in distress yet be unable to comfort in the same ways I might has me rudderless.

Either way, I've set up another meeting with her now that convergence news has settled into a more steady stream, so I guess we'll see where that leads.

May has taken these two meetings surprisingly well, I'll note. She mentioned that, given our position, that leaves us liable to come into contact with her again in the future, so we might as well ensure that it's not so jarring as it was that first night we found out about Artemis.

I know she's been working on her feelings about this with Sarah, so I'm happy to see a little less fury in her than I used to. She got really quiet during that conversation before admitting that the reason she wound up feeling as she did about True Name was due to the *History* itself. She hadn't known about True Name's subtle nudging of Michelle/Sasha with regards to both Launch and her death until we put it to paper. We both agree that that's helped her calm down the most: just being able to name the source.

Still, it's a lot. We seem to be inextricably entangled with the Ode clade, and while I love May dearly and I know that you two love Dear, it sometimes feels a little like being trapped.

Anyway, all that to say that True Name's having a rough time here, and I'm hoping that she's able to get set up with Sarah. Never thought I'd say such, but I'm worried about her.

CODRIN BĂLAN#CASTOR INDIVIDUAL-EYES-ONLY MATERIAL

I'm also worried about you. Your last letter led to a few conversations between May and I about you and Sorina, but also about the topic of individuation in more general terms. I understand that you two did your best to diverge as quickly as possible, and I can't even imagine that.

I know that when you became Codrin, that was not something that I'd foreseen, and despite the surface similarities, this feels fundamentally different. It's a new thing for us, I think. You two were borne out of the changes that the Odists wrought on us, but Sorina was borne out of changes coming from within.

I know that I risk our messages passing each other through the great big nothing between us, so perhaps there's more already on the way, but perhaps you can tell me more about her, or about the both of you?

To be clear, none of this is for the play. I spent some time talking with Sarah about it and she had some suggestions for what my role in this matter is. Doubtless you've been speaking with her about your role, and perhaps you and Sorina are still talking things through, but maybe Sarah has some suggestions? Maybe you can tell me more about her, too — the good things you remember, in particular. What do you like best about her? What are your hopes for her? What wishes do you have?

Lean on those around you to whatever level you're comfortable with, and know that I'm here, firmly rooted as you say. I'll offer all that I can.

Be safe above all.

The next section is just to inform #Pollux that you sent a fork to Artemis without details.

END CODRIN BĂLAN#CASTOR INDIVIDUAL-EYES-ONLY MATERIAL

CODRIN BĂLAN#POLLUX INDIVIDUAL-EYES-ONLY MATERIAL

The previous section for #Castor surrounds eir decision to send a fork to Artemis. Without sharing too much, it's led to a lot of inner strife for em. I'm worried, but that's nothing new. Either way, just wanted to provide some context. I'll leave any further information up to em to pass on.

END CODRIN BĂLAN#POLLUX INDIVIDUAL-EYES-ONLY MATERIAL

I hope things are going well despite all these dramatic goings on. May and I send our love to you and yours.
Ioan Bălan

Codrin Bălan#Castor — The Bălan clade

systime 222 (2346)

Castor—Lagrange transmission delay:
30 days, 20 hours, 22 minutes

Castor—Pollux transmission delay:
61 days, 18 hours, 8 minutes

Castor—Artemis transmission delay:
7 hours, 38 minutes

Ioan, Codrin#Pollux, and Sorina,

I've been nudged by both Dear and, of all people, True Name to write you with an update of life in Convergence. I've attached a longer report, but here's a quick, far more subjective summary.

We copied the entirety of our sim into Convergence wholesale. Dear transferred ownership of the one on Castor back to Serene during a little party we had. It said that it was to apologize for wrecking the last one, and that it would try to be more careful with the new one, but that she'd better take care of the Castor version for now. It made a whole big show out of it, because of course it did, but it was a fun party all the same.

Nothing about our sim feels any different, which, on writing it, makes perfect sense. It's a duplicate down to the subatomic level.* However, the world that's available to us when we try to move between sims is far, far from the same. There are fewer places, yes, but it's all much more organized. They've decided to set up a central hub with five spokes, each 'belonging' to a race. The hub and spokes — essentially long pedestrian malls — act as the primary public/common areas for everyone. It's not that there aren't public sims outside of this, but these are always at the top of everyone's mind when they think about going out.

Along each spoke are all sorts of shops, restaurants, entertainment venues, and doors leading to larger public spaces. It

---

*If that even means anything on the System.

started out as a non-euclidean type thing, where you would see a walkway between two shops leading out into a park that would clearly take up most of the spoke itself until too many people complained and the walkways were opaqued with a sort of curtain that depicted what was beyond. In addition, every doorway that would lead to a violation like this has been set up to give a slight tingle when transiting, just as an added signal. I haven't found it too much of a problem, but some voices were quite loud.

The actual population of Convergence isn't all that large. There are a few million humans, about a million each of secondrace (who call themselves Dehoudevav, which is just 'second people') and thirdrace (whose name I'll never be able to pronounce, much less write, but who the Artemisians, predictably enough, call Dehoudeves, or 'third people'). Nearly every member of fourthrace (Dehoudever, natch) elected to join after learning about how our System is based around forking rather than skew, though this only totals a million or so.

Firstrace, then, is the outlier. Only about a thousand of them have joined us. None have provided anything more than a vague answer as to why, too. Our best guess is that only one from each 'clade' (or whatever structure is implied by their names) joined us with the exception of Turun Ka and Turun Ko due to their role in the discussions. They sound like they like us alright, they just didn't sound very interested in joining us beyond that scope. No one seems to be able to make heads or tails of their actions.

That said, they've all been incredibly polite, even kind. One of them, Anin Li has teamed up with Sarah and I as we work on knowledge share around therapeutic practices between races. As I'm also learning that for the first time, I've got a mountain of work ahead of me.

I say 'they' above, but that goes beyond just the firstracers. Given the similarities in just how each race is polite, I imagine that there was an expectation that this is how life must exist after convergence, or, more likely, all who decided to join were briefed on how to interact during convergence. Certainly just about everyone I've run into speaks at least a little bit of our *lingua franca*, though I know that many of us are learning Nanon as well.

All the same, it feels like we're all being very careful around each other, still feeling out our boundaries. I have at least gotten the chance to introduce Dear and ████████ to the other emissaries (even Iska, who stuck around long enough to view one of its shows, but didn't stay; they seemed confused and unnerved). Dear and Turun Ko have gotten on well, surprising no one.

The document will have a whole lot more that you'll likely find interesting, but I just wanted to pass on some more personal impressions as well.

I mentioned that True Name suggested that I write to you all about this, which was honestly a little strange. Not strange in that she's been talking with me — we see each other nearly every day and have fallen into a professional relationship — but that she pulled me aside to have a really quite earnest discussion about it.

I've seen enough of her with all pretense stripped away to know what her true earnestness looks like, and this was *almost* that. There's definitely still something going on under the surface.

Her explicit reasons for wanting me to send this to you are that she says the sentiment and mood have some striking similarities to the early days of the System. "There is a sense of a new thing here, and it is a thing that we are left to build into our own new world," she said.

I can see what she means, too. Even though we can go back to Castor at just about any time (though we've been told that, starting soon, that will be very heavily rate limited until they work out a better solution to the separate reputation markets), it very much does feel like we are a new colony. We've found ourselves in a truly empty space along with people we've never met, and it's up to us to build something that works.

Still, she, her stanza, and Jonas are hardly absent. They seem to be putting out gentle feelers among all five races for how all of this works. I don't get the sense that they're looking to guide it in any dramatic way, but there's a tension beneath the surface that I can only just pick up on. Political structures differing between Convergence and Castor would put the rate-limiting at the border in a new context.

All of this is based off one conversation, though, so I'll keep you all up to date as best I can.

I miss you all. Pass on my love.

Codrin#Castor

Sorina Bălan — Ioan Bălan

systime 222 (2346)

Artemis—Lagrange transmission delay:
31 days, 15 hours, 13 minutes

Ioan,

While I'm sure that Codrin#Castor's already told you plenty about me, I wanted to send you a letter directly.

Something about winding up here in a place so fundamentally different from where we've lived before has me in mind of the past. I wasn't quite sure why this was, at first. Obviously, I miss the prairie and life aboard Castor, but one would think that I'd be more worried about what's in front of me than what's behind me. The prospect of months or years aboard this new world — never mind the core facets of existing in this place — gives me plenty of time to worry about the future at my leisure, though.

I suppose leaving behind so much is reason enough to think about the past.

I could spend all of that time thinking about my partners (and I've certainly been thinking about them plenty), but you've been coming up in my thoughts more than I'd expected. Something about this extra layer of individuation has you feeling even less like a down-tree instance than you did before, and far more like a good friend or close family member — especially given how much I miss you.

I miss you! Is that weird to say? Perhaps. We've never met, have we? Ruminating on my roots has me thinking fondly on all that's come and gone. We are stuck however many billions of kilometers apart, though, and that distance will only grow, the time between messages will only ever get longer. At least I think I better understand what Dear was talking about with regards to the difference between longing and being missed.

Ah well, perhaps I'm just lonely. Lonely and moody. It's so strange here, and it's been playing havoc with my emotions.

I miss you and May Then My Name, and I hope you're both doing well. Pass on my love.

Sorina Bălan

33 et-ularaeël, 4775 Artemis Reckoning

Codrin Bălan#Castor — Ioan Bălan, Codrin Bălan#Pollux

systime 223 (2347)

Castor—Lagrange transmission delay:
32 days, 3 hour, 2 minutes

Castor—Pollux transmission delay:
64 days, 8 hours, 33 minutes

Ioan, Codrin,

I'm glad that you enjoyed my description of Dear's recent performance, Ioan. Codrin, I hope your Dear manages to take some good stuff from that (I know mine sent over a whole sheaf of notes). Watching foxes of various sizes try to waltz with second- and thirdracers was funny enough, but the sole firstracer in attendance (Anin Li, who I've mentioned before as one of the two Artemisian psychologists) trying to figure out how to waltz with a fox — even one the same size as it — was more amusing than it should have been.

I had to make sure that there was at least some pleasantness to this letter, because I'm afraid that the rest of it is going to be a bit dreary.

You'll notice that Sorina isn't in the recipients list. I've mentioned to you both previously that the process of seeing her off to Artemis was more painful than expected, that I've been struggling with the feelings that I have both about that act of individuation and the possibility of forgetting that Artemis grants its occupants. Now, though, you can add, "radio silence from her" to the list of things I'm having a hard time with.

It's not even that big of an issue. Her last letter to me was a short, polite request that she be given a little space while she works out her feelings on Dear and ██████. I can very much respect that, of course. That they're my partners means that a lot of what I'd have to talk about would involve them. Not all, but asking me to just not talk about something that makes up the majority of my life would be uncomfortable for both of us.

Still, it's been nearly a year since convergence, and other than the first two letters — the one to the clade and the note to me — I've not heard from her at all. Sarah has confirmed that she's still around and doing well enough.

Sometimes, people drift apart. I know that. How many dozens (hundreds?) of people have we met in our 140-odd years that we spent time with and then slowly drifted away from?

This isn't that, though. This is me. This *was* me. This is someone who shared 100% of my history up until the day she left, 100% of my memories. We ought to have so much in common, and even though there is now this large swath of things that we *can't* have in common any more, shouldn't she still like books? Shouldn't we be able to talk about going into therapy as a career? Shouldn't she still think about family long gone?

Dear and ██████ have each discussed sending her a letter, but I've asked them to hold off for a little bit longer in case she needs more time. It'll also give me a chance to sort out my thoughts a little better too. I still feel weirdly...I don't know. Broken? Wrong? It feels wrong for me to feel this torn up over someone I spent ten minutes with.

I welcome your thoughts. Pass on my love to you and yours.
Codrin

Sorina Bălan — Ioan Bălan

systime 225 (2349)

Artemis—Lagrange transmission delay:
35 days, 20 hours, 24 minutes

Ioan,

I'm breaking my communications embargo to message you directly in the strictest confidence. I don't know the details, but I'm pretty sure this will pass through Castor without pinging Codrin or my exes (or anyone, for that matter). The last thing I want is yet another tearful letter from any of them just because my name flashed across their feeds.

Well. I say 'yet another tearful letter', but there's only been three — one for each of them — so I'm hardly being bombarded, but I just...I can't, Ioan.

I need to talk to someone about this. I need to talk to someone who truly understands. I talk to Sarah quite a bit, of course, both in a therapeutic and a professional context, but there needs to be that sense of connection to the matter on a more personal level than just therapist to client. She's a delight to work with and an amazing teacher.

In our sessions, we came up with a very specific way to deal with this decision that I've made. In order to ensure that I can learn to cherish who I was and who was in my life, I need to reinforce the positive memories of what I had. I need to make sure that those are stronger than the negative ones. I don't want that final, terrible morning to weigh on me more heavily than all of the good times that we had together.

You know, it's weird, though. I say 'final, terrible morning'. At the time, I don't remember it being so terrible. Final, yes, but not terrible. I remember being very tired. I remember waking up and slipping away from Dear and ████████ and making coffee in a cone of silence. I remember walking out onto the prairie. I remember suddenly seeing Codrin beside me, walking, head down in thought, as I focused on becoming me as quickly as possible. I remember walking past that brand new failing in the land with Codrin and not even having the mental capacity to think about it. All I remember was forking with each step, becoming who I am by the second and trying to move as far away from the life I had without losing my sense of self.

It wasn't terrible. It was busy. It was purpose-driven. It was constructive. I walked from that cairn to the next with Codrin beside me and then we talked for, what, five minutes? Ten? And then I kissed em on the cheek, grabbed a stone from the cairn, and left. I still have the stone somewhere. I hid it from view a while back and have forgotten where I put it.

It's not a terrible memory. The worst part was Codrin asking if I wanted to go back and say goodbye, but that was over in a flash as I made my decision not to.

The rest of the morning wasn't even that bad. I stepped to Convergence and waited for True Name to show up and then walked into Customs and I was off to Artemis.

Codrin was the first to contact me, about a month after I left. Eir message was...well, I said tearful, but I'm struggling to put it any other way. It was just text on a page, but if it had been an actual letter, mailed across the millions of kilometers between Castor and Artemis, delivered to my stoop, surely the ink would have run from a tear drop or two. I could hear eir emotion through the page, and I could feel the very same tugging in my heart that I knew ey was feeling, for are we not alike?

But we aren't, Ioan. We rushed that differentiation, that individuation, didn't we? We pushed as hard as we could for me to be a different person from em, and all we had in common was a last name and a history.

I haven't heard from em since in the time since I arrived, but I worry that ey's still heartbroken. There must be some word for that little piece of yourself that lives on in your up-tree instances, even if it's only the memory that they were borne from you. There has to be a word for that feeling of shared identity that is incomplete enough that one is not the same.

The next two letters, the ones from my exes, came at the same time about a month ago. I wouldn't call those nearly so heartbroken as Codrin's, but I could tell that eir pain was affecting them as well.

I don't *want* them to hurt, though! I don't want them to hurt. I want us all to move on. I want to continue being, as I have been, happy here. I want to continue in the process of healing from trauma. I want *them* to continue in the process of healing from trauma. I want them to remain whole and I want to be whole myself.

Clearly, I'm not.

Here I am, crying over a letter to my root instance, worrying about letters that haven't arrived, probably haven't even been written, because there is still a part of me that misses what life once was. I miss my exes. I miss who I used to be.

I am happy being Sorina, and I miss being Codrin. That's my dialectic. I can be both of those things. I've grown to accept that, and I've gotten used to the feeling of being me. I've gotten used to being a woman. I've gotten used to life among four other races. I've gotten used to the myriad new ways of expressing emotion here.

But with those two letters, the wound that had started to heal over was once again tugged open and I felt that old stirring of longing within me.

When we first embarked on this adventure, I think we all thought that that feeling would be the one that wore on me the most. We all worried (myself included, I suppose) that I'd miss everyone so much that I'd want to quit, so we all agreed that this would be the how it would work: I'd head off to experience life on Artemis, and if I started to miss everyone too much, I had explicit permission to quit, no need to live with that pain.

That's not what happened, though. I got right to work with Sarah and Artante, and later Anin Li, learning all of these really amazing therapeutic techniques (such as reframing my old partners as exes, even if there was no real break-up event) that help me just as much as they help everyone else.

They still have each other back on Castor, though. They still love each other, living out on that prairie in that ridiculous house, and all their letters serve to do is to drag me back into that mindset.

The real crux — really, the real reason this is all making me panic so much — is that I'm forgetting.

Forgetting! How novel!

I remember what Dear smelled like, the feeling of its fur on my face. I remember the way its ears would bob when it shook its head.

And the food! God, I remember the food. If there's one thing I miss, it's all the wonderful food. A bunch of fifthracers here are starting to set up restaurants, and some of fourthrace's food is pretty good, but it's not food from home, you know?

But I can't remember the sound of their voices. I can't remember our everyday mundane conversations. I can't remember what the quiet house was like, when we were all working on our own projects in our own spaces, each of us heads down over some creative problem, poking and prodding for weaknesses in whatever blocked us until we could have a breakthrough and go show the others.

More, I couldn't remember to be upset about missing them.

I was happy, or at least on my way to being happy, and then bam! Suddenly, I remember what it's like to miss those I love again.

Because I do still love them, but as I said, I just can't. I love them, and I miss them, and I miss Castor and I miss Lagrange and I miss all of the Odists getting up to their nonsense and all of the perfect imperfections of our systems. Text only communication! Almost two and a half centuries and they still haven't solved that, have they?

I miss all that I love, and hell, I miss you.

I love you, Ioan. I love you in that weird, roundabout way that a distant up-tree fork does. I love you for your completeness. I love you for being me, and yet not me. I love you for being Ioan and not Codrin. I love you for the solidity that I remember of you through Codrin's eyes. I love who you used to be. I love who you've become. I love who you will be.

I want nothing more than to say pass on my love, but please, Ioan, please don't, not yet.

I'll just say "all my love to you and yours" and be done with it. I promise to write again when I'm calmer.

Sorina Bălan

13 er-ularaeäl, 4777 Artemis Reckoning

Codrin Bălan#Pollux — The Bălan clade

systime 225 (2349)

Pollux—Lagrange transmission delay:
35 days, 9 hours, 48 minutes

Pollux—Castor transmission delay:
71 days, 13 minutes

████████ is gone.

They're gone. No fight, no yelling or acrimony, they just said that they needed some time to themselves and gave us each a hug and kiss and stepped away. I would have thought it just meant for a day or so, but their entire studio is cleared out. I pinged and they requested a few days to think before we talk.

What do I do? We'll wait as requested, but Dear's a mess. Hell, I'm a mess. I couldn't give it the support it needed when I needed support myself, so Serene is staying with us again for a while just to help how she can.

What do I do? I've never gone through anything like this and everything feels so incredibly desperate, as though I've done something so awful that a single misstep will bring the entire world down around my ears. It's kept me frozen in place for a few days now. I've slept, I know, and Serene's made sure that Dear and I get outside at least once a day.

What do I do, Ioan?

Codrin, have you heard anything?

What do I do?

— C

Note that, from this point forward, all communications include an exclusion clause for several members of the Ode clade. I trust that, with the clade-eyes-only permissions, there really isn't a way that Hammered Silver and In Dreams' stanzas would be able to read these anyway, but we felt it prudent to build up that habit with our communications all the same. That we all received the same request across all three Systems on the same day made it an easy decision.

Aurel Bălan—The Bălan clade

systime 226 (2350)

Lagrange—Pollux transmission delay:
36 days, 12 hours, 53 minutes

Lagrange—Castor transmission delay:
36 days, 18 hours, 10 minutes

Lagrange—Artemis transmission delay:
37 days, 3 hours, 4 minutes

The Bălan clade,

For as often as we talk about being trackers, I sometimes wonder if we aren't maybe more aligned with the Odists' approach to dissolution than we give ourselves credit for. Not the structure, perhaps, but to hear May and Dear talk, this idea that each of the first lines would fork to explore an interest isn't that unfamiliar to us, is it? We fork to work on projects and usually merge back, and yet when we are taken up by fixation, individuation sets in and we are suddenly no longer who we were.

That's not all the Odists do, though—and, apparently, it's not all we do, either. They have their secret, long-lived selves, those who drift away from who they used to be, and they fork often enough to work on a task. Their instances will linger to track a task from start to finish and then they'll merge back down, just as we did.

All this by way of greeting. Ioan and I have flipped a coin as to who would be the one to send this letter, for even though ey's listed as the sole author, that I am borne from the work that went into *Individuation and Reconciliation*—and indeed *was* em for much of its writing—means that I do have some claim over writing this.

Attached is the full manuscript. This is one that I'd like to be very careful with given its contents. The ways in which it will affect the entirety of the Ode, Jonas, and Bălan clades are too complicated to wholly understand, so the more input we can have on it, the better.

Through a winding series of events following the ordeal between Sasha and Jonas, then between Sasha (*née* True Name) and the rest of the Ode clade, we've found use for yet another one of us. I chose the name 'Aurel' mostly on a whim, as well as in response to some gentle ribbing about gender from a few people now. A name with diminutives that can head masculine or feminine seemed like a simple way to explore that a bit more. As I've stated in the past, I like being a Ioan and have never enjoyed 'Ioana' (too many bad memories from school, perhaps?), but we're nothing if not deliberate, right?

I will likely only be around off and on, forked as needed to track this intermittent identity, so if at all possible, avoid individual eyes-only material for me. I don't know if quitting and merging back down, then forking again will let me access eyes-only stuff should it arrive after the fact. I'll be testing that over the next time I merge back down, and I'll let you know the results. There's some info on the perisystem feeds, but not as much as I would like, so, better safe than sorry.

Separate letters for each of you to follow.

SORINA BĂLAN INDIVIDUAL-EYES-ONLY MATERIAL

Sorina, you are welcome to offer what input you might have or completely disregard the manuscript. I know that your relationship with the Odists is complicated, and the last thing I want to do is make you feel bad without recourse. I've only been Aurel for a few weeks now, so I have memories of all of our correspondences to date.

To that end, I've set a portion of this letter as eyes-only for Codrin largely due to the context of our relationships with the Odists—em with Dear, Ioan with May, and now me with Sasha. I don't want to come off as hiding anything from you, but I do want to ask before I send a bunch of stuff that might cause distress given all that's been going on of late.

On that note, how are you doing? We've been quite worried about you. I know that trying to balance the emotional pain of being so far away from your exes and Codrin doesn't play well with the ownership of your life that comes with individuation and being the only Bălan on Artemis.

Know that Ioan and thus I love you for all of your individuality and strength. Stay safe, stay in touch, okay?

END SORINA BĂLAN INDIVIDUAL-EYES-ONLY MATERIAL

CODRIN BĂLAN INDIVIDUAL-EYES-ONLY MATERIAL

I'm separating this content out for you two to keep from overwhelming Sorina with a bunch of information about Odists and relationships. Also, I gave her the option of disregarding the manuscript, lest that prove to be too much.

Things have been a bit shaky throughout the clade, haven't they? I'm unsure of how much you two speak with each other, so I won't go into specifics except to say that I'm worried about you both. You and those in your lives are still incredibly important to me, even after all these years apart. Please do all that you need to keep yourselves safe and healthy.

Please feel free to take your time with it, but we really would like to hear your thoughts on both the project and the events. Releasing something on any one system is essentially equivalent to releasing it on all three Systems, so we can't simply release it here and see what happens before sending it over to the LVs. Do you have any expectations as to the reception given the general mood of the various societies? I will note that this has already been given to Jonas here, which means it has doubtless been sent out to Castor and Pollux for them to prepare for its arrival. The events were not quite what the Jonas here on Lagrange was expecting, so I doubt that his expectations on the LVs were all that different.

I will note that this is in spite of the apparent differences between the societies themselves. I know I wasn't able to properly articulate it in my letters at the time, as writing letters and writing a book are quite different activities, but it'll soon become clear that the Jonas lives within these three different societies has diverged little, that all three of them share the same goals they began with perhaps even centuries back and the launches have become yet one more tool.

And what of the Odists?

I know that we're fond of blaming them for how complicated things get sometimes. They seem to heap plenty of blame on themselves, for that matter. E.W. (*né* End Waking) spoke to this several times, describing their clade identity as a sort of idolatry, and certainly not in a positive way.

I'm starting to wonder just how universal that is, though. How much is their complication a factor in others' lives? I suspect for more people than not, they're simply weird. Dear's weird. May's weird. Were he to speak with anyone else with any regularity, I'm sure that many would find E.W. weird too.

But complicated? How much of that is just observation bias? Do they seem complicated because their relationships with us are complicated? Dear's relationship with you two is full of complications that we initially chalked up to the fact that Dear's weird. May's relationship with Ioan is full of complications that we initially chalked up to True Name making her what she is and shoving her Ioan's way.

And now here I am, having wound up in yet another relationship with yet another Odist. Or perhaps more than one. It is unclear to me* just how to count Sasha in terms of quantities. She is that of True Name, that of E.W., and that of May, and yet there's this fourth part of four that is something new, something else.

As an internal postscript, I should add that, on hearing about True Name's transformation into Sasha, both True Name#Castor and True Name#Pollux sent the same letter to her. The *exact* same. Totally identical. That speaks to a level of coordination

---

* Or any of us, least of all her.

between Jonas and the other instances of her that's more than a little unnerving.

> Sasha,
>
> Thank you for the update. We will respect your autonomy in this and all actions moving forward, and hope that you will respect ours. We trust that your interactions with the Jonas and Ode clades will remain cordial and professional.
>
> Best,
>
> The Only Time I Know My True Name Is When I Dream of the Ode clade

I expected that this would leave her upset, given the fact that they just very politely told her to fuck off and stay out of their business, but when she received the letters, she ran up from her tent, waving them about and laughing gleefully, shouting, "Good fucking riddance!" There was much forking, as is to be expected by an excited Odist. I think the greater part of her was more relieved than anything.

END CODRIN BĂLAN INDIVIDUAL-EYES-ONLY MATERIAL

May and Sasha send their love, as do Ioan and I. We miss you and yours, and hope that you're doing as well as can be.
Aurel Bălan

Codrin Bălan#Pollux — The Bălan clade

systime 226 (2350)

Pollux—Lagrange transmission delay:
36 days, 22 hours, 21 minutes

Pollux—Castor transmission delay:
71 days, 15 hours, 31 minutes

All,

I know that the transmission delays are starting to make conversations around this awkward. It'll be four months before I hear back from Pollux and I don't even know how long from Artemis (Sorina, please don't feel obligated to respond; never mind the distance, I can see how this would be uncomfortable). Still, I've just finished the book that came with Aurel's letter, and figured I should probably update the clade on current goings on before I address that.

Dear, Serene, and I had a chance to sit down with ███████ and come to a better understanding all around. They expressed that, while they're quite happy for us and who we've become, the three of us have all diverged so far in the last 25 years that the shape of the relationship just wasn't comfortable for them. They apologized for leaving in the way that they did, but said that if they didn't do so all at once, they'd never have the courage and would just get more and more uncomfortable. They initially used the word 'miserable' at which both Dear and I got quite upset, but they quickly amended that to 'uncomfortable'.

They don't really know how to feel about the ways in which we've changed, and, honestly, the more we talked, the more I came to agree with them. Their prime example was the ways in which welcoming Serene in changed the dynamics between us. It changed Dear, in particular, and while they like the new Dear, it's not the same one they fell in love with.

It all makes sense. There was no acrimony (though there were plenty of tears). They're going to take a while off and figure out how they feel a little bit better before either reengaging or stepping away for good.

So yes, it makes sense, but that doesn't make it feel any better. Our experiences with loss are limited and all bound up in trauma. What am I to do with this? What am I to do with emotions that have wrecked not only me, but also a loved one? We can support each other to some extent, but we each grieve in our own complex ways. We've stepped on each other's toes more than once by missing the mark in our support.

Serene, of all of us, has been the most successful at managing her reaction. Of course, she spent the least amount of time with them out of all of us and has been away for a while now besides, but she's expressed quite a bit of guilt for what she sees as her role as catalyst. Still, she's somehow managed to sneak in a tightly regimented day for the three of us without either Dear or I noticing, and that's helped. We still wake at the same time, still eat and work and walk and talk together as those in love ought, and perhaps that gives us room to process, but we're all still hurting.

Anyway, that's the state of mind I've been in, so it's obviously going to color a lot of my response to *Individuation and Reconciliation*.

The larger part of me is impressed — not just at the goings on and how convoluted everything got so quickly, but at the writing. Well done, you two. I'll admit to being curious how Jonas is going to spin this in order to keep working as he'd like, though I don't doubt his abilities, not least of all because he apparently still has seven of the ten Odists in True Name's stanza working with him* and who knows how many others besides.

And Sasha! I will admit that, when I read about her, I found it almost hard to picture, so I'll have to largely take your word for it. When Dear read that bit, though, it got incredibly excited and

---

*Any word on Zacharias, by the way?

wouldn't shut up about it for days, so clearly she's done something more meaningful than either of them can express. *"We have all been so afraid of becoming what we were,"* it keeps saying, though I can't quite piece together what it means. It's even mentioned leaving the clade once or twice. Weird, but I won't complain: it's the most active and excited that I've seen it in quite a while.

Still, there is no small part of me that remains worried and cautious. The last time I spoke with True Name here on Pollux, she was quite friendly and relaxed, almost familiar. While this fits with Sasha's comment about Jonas and Zacharias framing her reaction differently on each System, it doesn't fit very well with the note that True Name sent back to Lagrange. Perhaps it's an artifact of this apparent collusion between the LVs. That the notes from both True Name#Castor and #Pollux were identical bespeaks a level of organization surrounding how Sasha was treated in the decades leading up to her assassination attempt — and was to be treated after — that has me worried for her safety and thus Aurel's, Ioan's, and May's.

How cynical must one be to set up a situation where one's own fork is left so beaten down? Even if True Name on the LVs was manipulated into doing so, that still requires a certain level of buy-in to go along with, right? I'm inclined to agree with E.W.'s assessment that Jonas is treating politics as a plaything, and would add on that the same is apparently true of many of the Odists.

Be careful, Ioan and Aurel. Keep May and Sasha safe. Even if their lives aren't at risk, this is quite a lot. Clearly a sizable chunk of the clade is quite upset with them, and that can't be easy.

IOAN BĂLAN AND AUREL BĂLAN INDIVIDUAL-EYES-ONLY MATERIAL

Confidentially, I've had more than one nightmare since ██████████ left about what might happen to any one of us when confronted with the loss of all our partners. ██████████ left, but

Dear and Serene are here, yes? If they were to leave, if Sasha or May were to leave, what would happen to us?

This is what I mean by current goings on framing my interpretation of *I&R*. Sorina has been keeping herself busy, burying herself in work, yes, but what I suspect happened is that Codrin and her rushing individuation during that last morning turned missing her exes, as she called them, into part of her identity. She cemented her opinions around them in place in her rush to diverge as quickly as possible. She gave herself the out of 'being able to quit whenever she wanted', but without the ability to fork and with her no longer being a Codrin at all, that suddenly veers awfully close to suicide.

She has mechanics on her side to keep herself around, but what do we have? If May or Sasha were to disappear from your lives, I–

Well.

I'm not in a good enough spot to finish this letter. I'm sorry.

END IOAN BĂLAN AND AUREL BĂLAN
INDIVIDUAL-EYES-ONLY MATERIAL

Pass on my love. Dear and Serene send theirs as well.
Codrin

Sorina Bălan — Ioan Bălan

systime 226 (2350)

Artemis—Lagrange transmission delay:
38 days, 3 hours, 4 minutes

Ioan,

I hope this letter finds you well. I have a question for you.

I'd like to start with an apology, though, for coming off as so emotional in the last letter. As mentioned, I've been struggling with keeping my emotions in check here on Artemis. While I'm far from the only fifthracer to be so afflicted, it doesn't seem to be a pattern many are worried about. Probably 1-2% of us are affected, and not in such a way as to be debilitating. I know the Odists struggle with the occasional bout of depression, and this is certainly no more dramatic than that.

The drama of such emotions aside, I also don't think that they are wholly disconnected from reality. Codrin *does* feel all of those things, and they *do* make me uncomfortable. However, my reaction to them is something I've been working on with Sarah.

On to my question, though.

Years ago, back when I was newly in a relationship with Dear and ████████, I remember thinking to myself that a lot of what I'd labeled boredom was likely loneliness. I'm not totally sure how much I agree with that assessment anymore. It's not that I *wasn't* lonely. I was!* I was lonely, but part of me is wondering if the constant interaction that goes along with cohabitation means that more of my time was simply occupied by dealing with others. Dinner with others. Walking the prairie with others. Working with others. Chatting with others. There was always someone around, for Dear rarely left the home entirely. Its inability to stop working meant that there was usually still one of it left around scribbling away at its desk.

---

*I...am?

But all of it? Probably not. I was still bored on occasion, and even now I get bored. One of the things that I noticed even going back to convergence was just how quotidian everything was. Aliens, sure, but they're also just people, such as it is, living their day-to-day lives. They eat, they sleep, they talk and argue and doubtless make love (I know the fourthracers do, but that's a subject for a different letter).

So now that we're settling into our own quotidian lives aboard Artemis, we're experiencing our boredom again. We're eating, sleeping, talking, arguing, and, yes, making love.

Is that what I'm missing?

Am I missing the eating-sleeping-talking-arguing-sex that goes along with having a relationship? Is that something I should be seeking out? I don't know. I've never really entered a relationship of my own volition, not entirely. Yes, deciding to date or whatever is a collaborative effort, but the Odists will ever be themselves, and even though its focus was never on the sorts of things that May Then My Name focused on, even Dear admitted that it, what was it...it "conducted a relentless campaign to wear down some of the emotional barriers that I'd put up." ██████ disagreed with the phrasing, saying that Dear couldn't turn down a good quip to save its life. "*Slander,*" it called it.*

I'm sure I don't need to elaborate on what you've told me of May Then My Name's own manipulation.

All this to say I've never done this before. I've never gone and sought out a relationship of my own. Do I date? Go to cafes and try to pick up a partner? Do I go to parties and drink with people until we wind up in bed?

None of these sound like me, or like us. We're not the type to

---

*They bet on my reaction; did I ever tell you that? They planned out this whole conversation with me, with ██████ on point while Dear acted as backup. Though they may accuse us of being nerds, they're hardly innocent in this.

go and actively seek out a relationship.[†] We're the type to have a relationship fall into our laps and then think and think and think and maybe in the end go along with it. It's not a bad way of approaching it, all told.

But is that something I want? Were a relationship to fall in my lap, would I go along with it? Is 'picking up people in a cafe/at a party' just setting up situations where such a thing might happen? I don't know.

More importantly, *should* I go along with it? Am I now so lonely that I need to seek out a relationship in order to feel whole again, or is that just me missing my exes?

Maybe it's worth a try. Nothing need be permanent — both of our partners made sure that we understood that. I can try, and if it doesn't work out, fine. It need not be permanent, just as I said my existence here need not be permanent.[*]

I've written twelve question marks so far and not yet gotten to the question I wanted to ask. Should I seek out a new relationship *before* I reengage with my exes? I want to know if I should in general, of course, but in particular, I want to know your thoughts on trying to actively process these thoughts on what relationships mean to me before I go about processing what breakups mean.

I don't know, I'm feeling my emotions get in the way of my words again. I really don't mean to dump on you like this, but, as

---

[†] Or sex, for that matter — it was plenty nice, but I am not missing it so badly as to worry about it.

[*] This has been greatly complicated by my inability to fork. Codrin and I rushed individuation so quickly and so effectively that, in a world where I cannot create a copy of myself that will live on, quitting becomes suicide in a very real way. I am the only Sorina, and to die would be to end anything resembling Sorina in the entire universe. That hasn't been an issue for us since the 2230s! I know that you've been thinking about Rareş of late, but even our death to him was not permanent. We disappeared, yes, other than those few notes back, but we were not dead. Death has taken on a new flavor for us, and now I'm remembering the bitter tang of it from before we uploaded. I will need to put more thought into it.

I said, your grounded, anchoring nature makes you an obvious source of comfort. Thank you for listening to me.

All my love,
Sorina Bălan
41 anser-ularaeäl, 4777 Artemis Reckoning

Ioan Bălan — Codrin Bălan#Pollux

systime 227 (2351)

Lagrange—Pollux transmission delay:
39 days, 4 minutes

Codrin,
Sasha told me something shortly after she became Sasha:

> Our lives are informed by fear, Ioan. I am afraid. *We* are afraid. We lived through a moment of such terror that whoever we were before is someone completely different. I...that is, that of True Name faces this fear through control, and thus so do my up-tree instances, in one way or another. Praiseworthy saw that fear and tried to reshape herself, to find a way to more perfectly move with the crowd so that it might slip past her, and now your cocladist's partner shapes itself so easily that it has literally made it into an art. We lost our friend, and then we truly lost them, and now we live what lives we may afraid but coping.

There is fear within us all. There can't *but* be fear within us, and we have all of our own fears particular to us, don't we? The loss of our family, the separation from Rareș, these things shape us into who we are, and how we interact with those that we love.

Despite our experience with separation, though, you're going through something truly unique for us. Of the three/four of us, none of us had ever been in a romantic relationship before our experiences with Dear, and so now we're experiencing something new. Having never been in a relationship, we've perforce never experienced breaking up.

And, like you, that thought terrifies me.

I know I've spoken several times before about how much the idea of losing May (and, increasingly, Sasha) scares me. We're creeping up on a century and a half old and I don't think we've ever experienced more than a fleeting glimpse of suicidality here and there, but if there's one thing that makes me fear for my own safety, it's the thought of life without them.

What you're going through is *real*. It's real pain, real emotion, and it's really hard. I want to validate that. There is certainly little in the way of advice that I can offer, what with the transmission delay, but I can at least offer that. I hope that, when you get this more than two months after you wrote about your distress, that it can at least help that little bit.

I talked with May about this briefly, and, as I expected it would, the conversation turned into her gently probing my feelings on the matter and where they came from. The bit that hit hardest (and left me a bit of a wreck) was when she asked if this was anything like being separated from Rareş.

Is that the basis of this fear? Is the fact that we specifically left him behind with Aunt Rahela in full knowledge that we'd almost certainly never see him ever again the reason we feel the way we do about the ones we love now? I don't know. I never looked him up. Not before we forked, and not since. I don't know where he is, don't know if he uploaded or died back on Earth, and I'm too afraid of that knowledge to even try.

What I do know is that, even if this is testing those limits once again, we're older — *much* older — now and we're in a place where we have those around us who we can lean on. When I uploaded, I was just a stupid twenty year old with nothing to show for his life* except a desperate need to at least do one thing right. There was no one here I knew. The only thing I could do was write a note or two back to phys-side and then just bury myself in school and books to try and move on.

Now, though, you have Dear. You have Serene. You have countless friends, all of whom can be there for you, and even though any reply is two months away, I'm here for you too, as are May and Sasha and, I guess, sometimes Aurel.

---

*Remember when we used those pronouns? So much has changed...

As a final note, True Name#Castor sent a short letter directly to Aurel on learning of em and the reasons for eir existence. Since Sasha went on sabbatical again, Aurel merged down after a week out on eir own just writing and experiencing solitude, and so now I have this note as well. There were no instructions on whether or not I should pass it on or share it, and I probably wouldn't even think to pass it on if it weren't for the ways in which the Ode clade is changing across all three Systems. I'm surprised at how quickly all of this change is happening after so long of relative stasis, but I guess that's what happens when you get aliens and an assassination attempt.

Some of the letter contained some eyes-only stuff for each of us which I've trimmed, but here is the rest:

Sasha,

Despite the tone of my previous note, I am not unhappy for you. The ways in which you and I have changed and have been changed by the events around us perhaps gives me room to understand a little better, though to move beyond the Ode as completely as you have takes more courage than I possess.

I think that the direction in which your writing is going is the correct one, and I will begin preparing Castor and Convergence for such. I take well your meaning: the name that can be named is not the eternal name.

Aurel, you and Ioan must stay watchful and attentive to your partners. There is no danger, I hope, but there will be stress.

Wishing you the best,

True Name#Castor

Perhaps most interestingly, the note specifically contained a visibility exemption for True Name#Pollux,* despite being eyes-only for Aurel and Sasha. May was quick to point out that, as far as we know, it wasn't sent to Pollux at all. Surely the two True Names aboard the LVs are in communication with each other and they've been sharing their own notes back and forth. This exemption, then, becomes a part of the text. I suppose I have to amend my previous statement as Aurel regarding the level of coordination between the two instances. There is something going on here, some difference between the two LVs that True Name#Castor is hinting at.

Sending all our love to you and yours.

Ioan

---

* Which I've maintained for this letter.

Sorina Bălan — Ioan Bălan

systime 227 (2351)

Artemis—Lagrange transmission delay:
38 days, 22 hours, 11 minutes

Ioan (and, I guess, Aurel),
I sent my last letter before receiving Aurel's. I will not apologize for apparently predicting that I would receive such when I spoke of seeking out someone to fill that role in my life. My congratulations to them, I suppose. To you? Aurel doesn't seem so long-lived as either Codrin or I.

Is that what one does in this situation? Congratulate? Either way, I wish them the best.

It's also spurred a line of thinking within me that I'm still trying to tease apart, and I'm hoping that writing you will help in that. Doubtless you'll have some insights, sure, but also just the act of writing — to someone I trust, no less — should be helpful on its own.

Let me begin by saying that I appreciate the way that the clade has provided me options for opting into dealing with topics regarding the Odists. It was initially quite helpful, but as I work through my thoughts on the matter, intentionally engaging with them as a topic has become my new goal. So long as that content is clearly delineated, I see no reason to hide it behind eyes-only segments. If I'm up for reading it, I'll read it. If not, I won't. Thank you for all of your thoughtfulness over the last few years.

So, why the Odists? What is it about them that leads to us working so well together? We're hardly the same. We're hardly an exact match. We are two puzzle pieces in the broader whole of the world. Not *matching* puzzle pieces, but close. We don't fit together perfectly.*

---

*I suspect that might have actually been rather boring.

And perhaps that's it. Perhaps it's the way we both accept that, internalize it, make it part of who we are when taken in combination. I loved — no, still love — Dear. It was so weird, and it drove me fucking nuts at times. It could be too much, too intense. Sometimes, it was too wrapped up in its art to thoughtfully engage with the world around it. It was prone to tantrums and sulking.

But me? I was dense. Not just when I was new to the concept of relationships (though certainly more so then!), but throughout our time together, I was constantly misreading cues, misunderstanding the depths of emotions, falling apart when I hadn't the emotional literacy to deal with what was happening around me.

We were each terrible in our own way, and yet we made it work. The puzzle pieces still fit together well enough, and formed a brighter picture. We accepted that about the other that was undesirable and found ways to work with or around it in order to let the parts that *did* work for us improve us as individuals.

I loved it for its art, yes, but also for its depth of emotion, for its emotional literacy where mine was lacking. I loved it for the patience it had in helping me learn how to be an active participant in my own life. I loved it for just how fucking weird it was.

Hearing you talk about May Then My Name has tallied quite well with this, too. She's taught you much the same, and you've added to each other's lives without necessarily being a perfect fit. She's sometimes too much: you've complained often enough about her being too emotionally intense or requiring a bit more engagement than you're always prepared to give, but you still find ways to work with or around that just as I did with Dear.

Twice is a curiosity, three times is a pattern, as we saw with Codrin#Pollux and Serene. And now four (five?) times with Sasha?

Yes, there's a third of Sasha who is already someone you love, but whether or not you realized that you were doing so, you also spoke quite fondly of True Name over the last year that she was solely herself. You had your hesitancies, of course. You equivocated about whether or not you were friends, on what your role actually was in interacting with her, sitting between her and your partner. We've all expressed our frustration (or even anger) with her over her role in both our lives and the System as a whole, you included.

But as you mentioned in letters during that year, you were also called out on this by both Sarah and May Then My Name more than once. Hell, *that* you were equivocating speaks to the fact that you were even thinking about it in the first place. It wasn't some foregone conclusion that you were just, as you put it once, "cordial and intentional acquaintances". You recognized that friction: it was an artifact of inexact language rather than emotions.

Don't even get me started about how you talked about E.W.! Yes, I wish I'd had the chance to meet him, too, but for a while, nearly every letter you sent included some story followed by that exact sentiment.

Congratulations are due to Aurel, yes, but I am in absolutely no way surprised.

So what is it about them? Why the Odists? How come we keep winding up in relationships with them? Is it some core aspect to them? Would we have gotten on so well with Michelle, had she been singular enough and in our lives at the right moment? Or is it just those with the right "perpetual hyperfixation", as you so eloquently put it, who fall into our lives?

You and perhaps Codrin#Pollux are uniquely positioned to answer this litany of questions. Do you have any insight into what it is that has led us to this state?

I'll be honest that I'm not sure what I'll get out of your answer. I don't know if it'll feel good to read,* but I guess I'm hop-

---

*I can tell you that it took several sessions to actually write this letter. There were a lot of breaks to take walks or sit and stare out the window like some awful painting titled *Sehnsucht* or something. I'm putting a light face on

ing that it'll offer some sense of closure. If I– no, *when* I feel comfortable getting in touch with Codrin again, I will likely ask em, too, as perhaps ▮▮▮▮▮▮ will have some insight. I will, just...not yet.

There is one more thing that I'm a little hesitant to ask about, because I'm not quite sure what direction your thoughts are heading in. The chance that me bringing this up is only going to hurt you is real, given the tenor of your letters, and for that I apologize.

I've noticed that you've been talking about Rareş quite a bit more over the last year. I touched on it briefly last letter, but I want to approach it more intentionally: what was it that brought him to mind?

I still think about him, you know. I think about how when he got frustrated, he'd smile, but with his brows knit. It was such a uniquely *him* expression. I think about our parents' funeral and how, even at 10, he seemed to understand on a deep level — deeper than us — the finality of death. I think about the confusion and hurt on his face when we announced we were going to upload. It's not that he didn't love aunt Rahela, or that she didn't love us, but we were so much more a parent to him than she ever was.

I still think about him and hope that we did the right thing. I think we did. I think *you* did.

Have you found him? Have you looked? You do not need to. You have my permission not to if that's not what you need.

I love you. Pass on my love to May Then My Name as well.

Sorina

22 an-ularaeäl, 4779 Artemis Reckoning

---

it now, but really, I've been such a mope, it's almost a parody.

Codrin Bălan#Pollux — The Bălan clade

systime 227 (2351)

Pollux—Lagrange transmission delay:
38 days, 3 hours, 2 minutes

Pollux—Castor transmission delay:
76 days, 22 hours, 34 minutes

All,

Last night, I mentioned off-hand that I felt like things were "settling into a new normal", at which Dear and Serene both threw cookies at me. It took a while to get them to stop laughing to explain that "new normal" had become something of a forbidden phrase back phys-side prior to the creation of the System. Something about it just didn't sit right with people, I guess, so everyone would just wrinkle their noses whenever it came up like someone had said something particularly disgusting.

That was before my time, though. Why it needed to trigger a food fight is beyond me, but I never claimed to understand foxes.

All the same, it really does feel like we're settling into a new sort of normal, here. We wake up, make coffee, have some breakfast, then each head off to do our own work.* We've mostly been just getting lunch on our own since I'm spending much of the day out of the house, these days. We'll meet back up for dinner, then just relax together until bed.

Food has honestly been the biggest adjustment for me. For a while, Dear and I just stopped eating. ██████████ cooked just about everything, and while each of us know how to make some of our own favorites, even just engaging with food left a sort of longing for how things had been. Wasn't required, was painful, why bother?

It was Serene who knocked us out of that particular slump. Dear was starting to get particularly jittery, lots of restless fork-

---

*I could expand on the arguments surrounding how to catalog the Artemis data dump, but it's boring even for me.

ing, and I pulled her aside to mention that I thought it might be on the way to overflowing, to which she readily agreed. We wound up heading out for sushi at a place that floats plates of sushi down to you along a little canal that winds its way between the tables — J2? Do they have that on Lagrange? Well, turns out you can special order there, too, and they'll float a whole boat down to your table. It's built like a full three-masted ship,* complete with little cloth sails, and on each of the decks, rolls are piled up or splayed out in neat rows. We ate way, way too much sushi, and the two foxes got in a small contest of adding larger and larger amounts of wasabi to their bites until both had tears streaming down their faces.

Again, I've never claimed to understand them.

After that, we tried to make sure we ate at least once a week, then at least a day. It took us a while to sort out just how, though, as none of us are spectacular cooks. I make a pretty good tocană and a few other stews besides, but those are mostly cold-weather food. The Odists have their own stock set of recipes, but we've had to make up a few on the fly. There have been a lot of salads, a lot of sandwiches. Still, it gives us all a chance to sit down together and just stop whatever it is we're working on, a little marker for when the day ends and the evening begins.

Evenings have largely been slow and calm, relaxing on the couch or out on the patio. We've gone exploring a few times, too. As mentioned previously, Serene redid much of the sim to add some variety to the otherwise unending plain. To the east, it continues uninterrupted, while to the west, after a scant mile of hillocks, craggy, aged mountains jut up at a steep angle. These take the form of flat planes of red rock broken at acute angles pushing up from the earth directly west of the house, followed by a more conventional range. To the north, this continues along a ridge that slowly transforms into a line of boulders and sandstone ridges. To the south and further west, the hills are covered in a dense pine forest. Directly to the south of the

---

*A barque, perhaps? Cue a Bălan-style research binge...

house, a river runs out of the mountains to travel south and east. It's lined with willows, oaks, and cottonwoods. There was much good-natured ribbing of Serene for the latter. *"Cheap plastic trees! Sneeze-factories that shed branches at the slightest breeze!"* Dear had opinions.

Our explorations have largely been to the south and west, where we've been hunting down my cairns. Serene somehow built the terrain up beneath them so that they remain dotting the slopes of the hills, between trees, or atop mountains (we skipped the climbing part of that to go check). We've camped out there a few times, but it's been a lot of day hikes.

I'm told that we'll soon get inter-System A/V transmissions, though it'll be restricted to still images for bandwidth's sake. I'll make sure you get some pictures of us as well as of the landscape.

There have been a few bumps as we sort things out. Obviously, we still occasionally wind up feeling low from ████████'s absence. There's been a few days where one or the other of us winds up in a sulk, though we're increasingly getting used to this new life.

Dear and Serene have also wound up in feedback loops a few times. Remember when I wrote "Two foxes in the same house? Never again"? Well, I still have my occasional moments of regret. One of them will get a little extra sarcastic and the other will try to one-up them. Or, worse, one will get a little snippy, and it'll turn into a quick volley of shitty comments followed by a sulk, then back to as it was before.* When this happens, either I'll step out, or I'll kick them both out to deal with it. It's been a quick adjustment, honestly; far easier than when ████████ was here. Maybe just because there are fewer different interpersonal dynamics at play? I'm still thinking about it.

---

*I don't mean "pretending it didn't happen", mind. They seem to accept these little spats as part of cohabitation. They take them seriously, address the issue, but then just get on with life. It's taken a bit of getting used to, as it's different from how Dear interacts with me. I haven't figured it out at all, but I guess when you have a fight with yourself, you get over it far quicker.

I have seen ███████ a few times, for what it's worth. It's not like they just up and cut contact. We've gotten coffee a few times, and they stopped by for an incredibly awkward dinner party. While we have largely worked out that things are just kind of over between us and them, that doesn't mean that our feelings have just dissipated — nor, indeed, have theirs: "It's still a break-up, I'm still hurting over it, even if it's for the best."

And you know, as I take a look back at who we were, at who Codrin#Castor is and, hell, who you and Aurel are, I see where they're coming from. We can't stay the same forever. Our happinesses change as the world around us changes. We can't possibly remain the same, but neither can we possibly change in exactly the same ways. Something like this was bound to happen eventually, and it has me thinking that there will probably come a day when Dear and I drift apart. I don't know if that'll be any easier for being the second time around, or just differently hard, but I suppose one upside of the whole thing is that it has me focusing on the love I have in front of me.

Speaking of the love in front of us! Aurel and Sasha? What a delight! At first, I was surprised that it took as long as it did, but then I realized that Sasha's far more complex than just "May Then My Name plus two friends". Then I was surprised that Ioan and May Then My Name's relationship didn't just expand to include her, but of course not everyone's relationship structure need mirror ours (never mind the fact that I don't even know what the dynamic is between May Then My Name and Sasha; it sounds friendly enough, at least).

IOAN BĂLAN INDIVIDUAL-EYES-ONLY MATERIAL

If I may ask, how has the dynamic worked when you're Aurel, when you're away from May Then My Name but still with Sasha? I can't imagine it's entirely comfortable to spend much time away from her, even if you're still with someone you love.

You live in the same building,* if I'm understanding this right, but I'm assuming you're hardly seeing your other partner all of the time, right?

I guess I ask because there's at least a small analogy to be made between our two situations, in that I'm no longer with ▮▮▮▮▮▮▮ but still with Dear. I know — or at least suspect — that it's not exactly the same, as Aurel's still a fork, however long-lived, and thus not *not* in a relationship with May Then My Name, just that that's on pause.

If I'm to keep seeing ▮▮▮▮▮▮ on occasion, then I'm going to have to figure out how to interact in a way that isn't strictly in a relationship, yet also isn't as fragile as I feel.

All the same, I wish the three/four/six/seven/however-you-count-it of you the best.

Also, some of your letters are starting to sound a little despondent when it comes to Rareş. Are you okay? Is there anything we can help with? I will admit that I know a bit more about...the current status,† but I'm not going to dump that on you without your permission.

END IOAN BĂLAN INDIVIDUAL-EYES-ONLY MATERIAL

All my love. Dear and Serene both send theirs as well.
Codrin Bălan#Pollux

---

*I'm trying to picture this: it goes your and May Then My Name's bedroom, the den/kitchen, then a door to Aurel and Sasha's bedroom, then their own den/kitchen? Like a duplex? Do you use that door often? Do you see each other out on the deck? Eat together? I'm hungry for details.

†It comes with working in a library. We just know things. It just kind of happens.

Codrin Bălan#Castor — Sorina Bălan — Fwd: Ioan Bălan

systime 227 (2351)

Castor—Lagrange transmission delay:
38 days, 15 hours, 1 minute

Ioan,

Taking your advice along with that of True Name, of all people,* I finally wrote to Sorina in a very open and, I hope, welcoming way. I want to find out where we stand, of course, but I also don't want to push *that* much of a discussion on her. Just...say hi and ensure that the line of communication remains open. I've attached what I wrote just so you're up to date as well.

I ran the letter by Dear, ████████, Sarah, and True Name, and all of them kept telling me it was far too wordy. They're probably right, too,† as frustrating as it was to pare it down. I know we're a wordy bunch, but it was edging up past 2000 words, when all it needed to was act as an invitation to open discussions.

All my best,
Codrin#Castor

_____

Sorina,

I wanted to reach out with my greetings and gratitude for your patience with me as I get used to life as it has become. Much has happened in the last five years.

_____

*A part of me wonders if it's in response to the role you played between her and May Then My Name on Lagrange, offering a little bit of mediation to keep that gap bridged. I'm too shy to ask, I think.

†True Name in particular suggested that this is still probably too long, but I sent it anyway, as I want to at least add a positive note about life on Castor.

Despite the momentous nature of an extraterrestrial encounter, life continues on Castor much as it has for the previous two and half decades, as it did on Lagrange before. We sleep, wake, work, eat, talk, walk, all as we always have. I hope that life for you has continued in pleasant and productive ways and that you're still able to do all that makes it fulfilling.

I understand that the nature of your departure has been a point of stress for the both of us. I know that some of that stress on my end has bled over onto you, and for that I apologize. If you're comfortable doing so, I would love to hear from you.

Best,

Codrin Bălan#Castor

Sorina Bălan — The Bălan clade

systime 227 (2351)

Artemis—Castor transmission delay:
1 day, 2 hours, 52 minutes

Artemis—Lagrange transmission delay:
39 days, 1 hour, 12 minutes

Codrin Bălan#Pollux,
Greetings and gratitude from Artemis as well, and I appreciate your patience in turn.

I am currently working on getting my thoughts in line for a longer, more well thought out response, but I did at least want to write you a note to acknowledge your letter and to beg your forgiveness for my silence as this stress, as you call it, shakes out.

I must admit that I'm still feeling raw, both from the distance from you and yours as well as what I'm sure are mostly imaginary expectations of how I must be feeling. Once I have a better grasp on where I fit within both the Bălan clade and the wider universe, I think I'll better be able to engage.

Until then, however, we'll call this communications embargo lifted, and I'll look forward to hearing from you all.

All my best,
Sorina Bălan
2 es-ularaeäl, 4779 Artemis Reckoning

Codrin Bălan#Pollux — Ioan Bălan

systime 228 (2352)

Pollux—Lagrange transmission delay:
39 days, 17 hours, 41 minutes

Ioan and May Then My Name,

I had the chance to sit down with ███████ for a pretty long chat over dinner yesterday. They invited me over to the sim they've built for themself which is...incredibly them. There is no den or common area. There's just a one bedroom apartment stuck off the back of a large kitchen that, they promised me, looked as much like one they could remember from a tour back phys-side when they were working at getting into culinary school. It was quite a bit more cramped than I would have expected, but they explained that this was to keep the amount of walking to a minimum. They showed me what they meant by cooking one of the best dishes of *cacio e pepe* that I've ever had, and they did so without really moving their feet at all. They could turn to the prep station to grate cheese while the noodles boiled on one burner of the six-burner stove, then just all at once pull everything together on a pan on one of the other burners.

We took our food out into the front, which had been set up like a restaurant. They explained that for some reason they couldn't figure out, they'd never thought of actually opening up their own restaurant, but were planning on doing so soon. They said that it felt related to their relationship to Dear, something about it keeping them pinned into a certain lifestyle. They were quick to explain that this wasn't a bad thing, wasn't unpleasant, just that they never got around to it with the life that they'd built up together even before I wound up joining the triad.

We ate mostly in silence. It was a little tense at first, but then it just turned into us simply enjoying the food without letting words pass between us. It's been a long time since I've enjoyed a comfortable silence like that. They crop up occasionally with

Dear and Serene, but far less so than they ever did between me and ███████.

They bade me stay in my seat while they waved away the plates and ducked back to the kitchen to pick up two plates of tiramisu and two demitasses of espresso.

Delicious as ever.

Finally, they asked how we were doing. I had to force myself to think for a moment before just blurting out a response. I decided to just explain our day-to-day experiences much as I did in the last letter. I talked about how we'd started exploring the sim more. We laughed about us having to learn how to cook something other than college student food. They commiserated with me over just how intense two Odist foxes in the same house without any other moderating force must be.

They talked about their own process of setting up a new life, about procuring a bunch of stuff off the exchange with only the vaguest of ideas of setting up a restaurant, then slowly tweaking and tweaking and tweaking until they got closer to what they thought of as ideal. "I'm still figuring out how I'm going to decorate this place. I thought about putting up my own paintings, but how tacky is that? Might as well just name it "██████'s Wish Fulfillment Bistro" at that point, right?"

I assured them that their paintings were plenty good enough, as was the food.

Finally, though, we switched from coffee to wine and moved from the table to a lounge couch in what I imagine will be the quieter spot of the restaurant, and got to talking about how we got to where we are and where to go from here.

They nudged me to lead, I think maybe because they expected I'd have quite a lot of grievances to air about them leaving as they did. Instead, I started with what I told you, that I could certainly see where they were coming from, about how things change after fifty years, and how our happinesses change as the world we live in changes.

They readily agreed, saying that, while they loved Dear and

Serene on their own, their dynamic together was as frustrating as it was fun, and that it never fit quite into the 'romantic' category of fun. They got pretty awkward when they described how I've changed and I had to urge them on several times, but they said that they'd long considered me a comforting, if passive, personality who made a good active listener, and that while I was still good at listening and still comforting to be around, me taking the step to start working at the library, shifted my passive nature to a far more active one. They said that, while they're happy for me, it was such a change as to be jarring; that, as bad as it sounds, they liked the passive version of me more.

What a strange thing to hear! I'll admit that I had to curb my frustration at that. Isn't self-actualization something we should all aim for? And when I'd talked about it initially, they were incredibly supportive of the decision.

Having thought on it, though, I think I can see where they're coming from. It wasn't that me being passive itself was good and me being more active with my life was bad, so much as there was a set of habits that we'd all built up around me following while they led, and to have those shaken up was a prime example of those new happinesses at work. I love what I do at the library. I love the feeling of taking charge of research — I always have — and to do so in a setting that requires active participation and, often, leadership had shifted the way that I acted at home.

I wasn't able to put this in words at the moment, but was thankfully able to keep that frustration at bay and just tell them I'd think about it. I sent them a note earlier today with many of these thoughts to follow up on that.

Anyway, we just kind of settled into silence after that, just drinking wine and relaxing, occasionally bringing up some memory or another to reminisce. Finally, we gave each other a hug and I headed back home to Dear and Serene to catch them up. I suspect that Serene had spent much of the evening keeping Dear calm so that it wouldn't be a fretting mess by the time I got back. Probably a good idea. I can just imagine it either sulking or huffing when confronted with the conversation. As it was, we still had to put much of me recounting the evening off until today, thus me writing this letter

So, overall impressions: I'm feeling much more comfortable with the way we're each moving on. They're getting to move forward and build for themselves, while we've been shocked into realizing what it is we need to feel better and be more active in our own relationship rather than letting things stagnate.

It hurt, and it still occasionally feels bad, and I don't think it'll ever quite stop, but I also think that, yeah, it might have actually been for the best.

So I guess I have some questions that I'm left with that are probably more for May Then My Name than Ioan.

I'm not sure how much ey's talked about my current situation, but it's come up before that this is the first time we've really had to deal with a loss like this as Bălans, other than perhaps leaving our brother behind when we uploaded.*

I hear it talked about as a cliche that the best outcome of a break-up is to remain friends, and I'm feeling pretty good about the direction we're headed there. It feels almost like a sign of maturity, I suppose, as opposed to something more acrimonious, but I don't know how true that is.

I know that you've had far more experience with relationships that any of us have. What have you found to be the best way to communicate with ex-partners after the relationship ends? Do you think we're on a good track? I know that every relationship is going to be different, but you've had a chance to spend some time with us (several decades back, granted). Are there any suggestions you have for ways to make this...I don't know, productive for us? Make it something we can take good things away from, too?

On that note, do you have any thoughts in general on relationships and change? Forty-odd years of a relationship feels

---

*Something we compartmentalized right away and, it seems, have only just now started to process. It'll probably be a good thing, overall.

like a long time, but then I realize just how old we all are, and maybe it isn't? But then again, the passage of time itself doesn't change just because we live longer, does it?

Ah well. This has me feeling stuck up in my head as usual, trying to think everything into place. All the same, I appreciate the chance to be able to talk about it, even at a distance.

Wishing you all the best, and the three of us send our love, as does ▮▮▮▮▮▮.

Codrin

Codrin Bălan#Castor — The Bălan clade

systime 228 (2352)

Castor—Artemis transmission delay:
1 day, 3 hours, 10 minutes

Castor—Lagrange transmission delay:
40 days, 5 hours, 11 minutes

Castor—Pollux transmission delay:
79 days, 23 hours, 40 minutes

Sorina,

Thank you so much for your letter. I was delighted to wake up to it this morning, though I have to admit that I needed quite a bit of coffee before I could actually manage to read it. I sometimes get the feeling that there's just too much coffee in our lives, but hey, it's good.

Convergence has pretty well settled down over here. The border with Castor has been firmly limited — instances are allowed transit only once per week, so if you head out to Castor, you have to spend at least a week out there — but there are plans to open it back up. It sounds like they've come up with a better solution to the reputation market. I don't know the details, but I've been promised it's rather like having multiple currencies back phys-side, with an exchange and trade and such. Smarter people than I are working on it.

The Artemisians here are settling in to greater or lesser extent. A handful have quit since they've arrived. We've required no explanation for why, so we're left with only what they or their friends have said about their decision. Most seem to have just missed time skew too much. While I don't want to discuss them much otherwise, I will note that there was one instance of a similar reaction to our System that the Odists had to Artemis: one of the fourthracers who, I'm told, was one of those affected most by their version of the lost virus.

We're starting to see lasting friendships form between humanity and the Artemisians (beyond the emissaries, that is). It initially felt surprising given our apparent similarities with fourthrace, but thirdrace seems to have integrated most easily. They are, to the last, gregarious, excitable, and fun. Combine that with their expressive features, and it's easy to make friends with them.

I've been settling into a routine with Sarah, Artante, Anin Li, and a few others, who have set up something halfway between a school and a therapeutic practice. It's been a ton of work, but really fulfilling.

In the interest of keeping everything low-stress, never mind all of the grand happenings and crazy new things that must be happening around you, can you just tell us more about yourself? How are you feeling? Who have you met? What are your days like? Do you, too, drink way too much coffee? Please tell me they have coffee up there...

Take your time; there's no pressure to respond any time soon. We'll look forward to hearing from you at your own pace.

All our best,

Codrin Bălan

Ioan Bălan — The Bălan clade

systime 229 (2353)

Lagrange—Pollux transmission delay:
41 days, 3 hours, 1 minute

Lagrange—Castor transmission delay:
42 days, 2 hours, 31 minutes

Lagrange—Artemis transmission delay:
43 days, 6 hours, 55 minutes

Hi all.

I hope you've been doing well of late.

It's been heartening watching everyone reconnect over the last year, if I'm honest. I know I say it just about every time I write, but I've been worried. You've all mentioned in the past feeling like I'm someone grounding that you can talk to, and...well, I hope this isn't weird of me to say, but I've been feeling protective of you all in turn. It's not quite the realm of parenthood or anything like that, but it does kind of feel like I'm watching over the clade, in a way. I don't know if it's a root instance thing, a shared past thing, or a me-as-I-am-now thing.

It's probably the last.

I think it's high time to admit aloud that all of these memories of Rareș are starting to pile up for me, and at least some of this protectiveness stems from those memories of him after mom and dad's death. I've been struggling to keep my mind off him, honestly. There have been a few abortive attempts at pulling the thoughts together into a book or play or something, just as a way to process my feelings.

The thing is, if I want to be successful at something like that, I'll have to actually sit down and research the past. That's where I've been failing. I know it's something I'd need to do if I'm to do any project like that justice, and probably something I need to do if I'm to find any sort of peace, but there's some emotional block. Lately, every time I get close to engaging with the topic head on, I have a panic attack. Honest to goodness, full blown, hyperventilating-and-feeling-like-I'm-dying panic attack.

It's something I've been working on a lot with Sarah since it's rather upsetting all around. I certainly don't like the feeling, but neither do May or Sasha like seeing that happen.

I know you know more about this than I do, #Pollux, but please let me work on this myself.

Anyway, that's only part of why I'm writing. The way that this topic has affected me has led to a series of conversations between May and I around the interplay of immortality and relationships. I know I won't do the topic justice, so she's written up some of her thoughts, which I'm including here.

> One unintended consequence of immortality is not just that memories of relationships pile up, but the *way* in which they pile up. We do not simply remember lost loves with fondness, but also with caution.

> It sounds counter-intuitive, does it not? We might expect that our everlasting lives might add in some more cavalier attitude toward the relationships that we form. This has not borne out over the centuries. We do not find ourselves trying ever newer things in the ways in which we form relationships; perhaps some do, but neither of our clades do. We keep our lives as a whole interesting, but we constantly refine our relationships.

> The Ode speaks of honing and forging, and so many of those who have uploaded and sought out entanglement have found themselves honing rather than forging. It is a search for a more perfect love. We speak constantly of "learning from our mistakes" and "doing better by them/ourselves".

> This is no bad thing! We do this out of a desire to be better people in the ways in which we engage with

those with whom we are closest. These just happen to be the ways most likely to hurt others, too. We shy away from trying new things with our relationships because that puts our view of ourselves as good people at risk should they go wrong.

And so we look back on the relationships that we have formed, kept, lost, or let slip away into so many years, and we remember the good times cautiously. We hunt for the things that went wrong, we see all of the places where we fucked up and we tear them apart as one might a hole in a piece of clothing: thread by thread. We idly pull a thread, inspect it, and hunt for the weak point that led to the hole forming in the first place. We think back on arguments and hunt for where we could have kept it from blossoming into a fight. We think back on missed expectations and wonder what we might have said. We think back on crossed boundaries and hunt for a sign pointing to the boundary that we simply overlooked.

It is a fool's errand and we are dumber than a bag of rocks for doing that, and yet we keep on doing so. It is so incredibly difficult to stop, is it not?

And yet, as the Ode goes on to say, "To forge is to end, and to own beginnings. To hone is to trade ends for perpetual perfection." That perfection, it says, is "Perfecting singular arts to a cruel point."

The Ode is just a poem, it is no holy text — what was it Emerson said? The poet nails a symbol to a sense that was true for a moment but soon becomes false, while the mystic mistakes the singular for the universal?* — but every poem is open to interpretation

---

*This one took some digging. It's from his essay "The Poet": "Here is the

and analysis. The author of the Ode was not wrong. We shy away from those ends that hurt and any beginnings that might follow in favor of our dreams of perpetual perfection.

This applies just as readily to familial relationships as it does to romantic ones. Ioan and I do this in our relationship just as much as ey does this when ey remembers Rareş and every single Odist does when thinking about the poet. Our immortality gifts us the ability to do this to an uncomfortably endless degree.

I will quote Sasha's gentle warning here with her permission: "The danger in ceaseless memorialization is how close it lies to idolatry. To elevate the dead to such a status is to ceaselessly perfect the imperfectable."

Ends happen. There may yet come a day when Ioan and I decide to go our separate ways. We know that it will hurt, and it is easy to focus only on that and hone and hone and hone. That is not all we can do, though; we can also hope that it will be with love, that we will go our own ways and own what beginnings may yet be in front of us.

She's right. Of course she is, I mean. Not only does she have more experience than literally any of us in this matter, but for more than two centuries, it has been a daily focus of hers. I have to catch myself from endlessly focusing on things I could have done better. Could I have stayed in touch with him? Should I have

---

difference betwixt the poet and the mystic, that the last nails a symbol to one sense, which was a true sense for a moment, but soon becomes old and false. For all symbols are fluxional [...] Mysticism consists in the mistake of an accidental and individual symbol for a universal one." Where do they even find this stuff?

encouraged him to upload? Worrying about these things is the fool's errand she describes.

These are just things that have been on my mind, by the way, I don't mean this as any sort of admonishment with how any of you are tackling the issues that have taken up the greater part of our worries the last few years. We're just doing the best we can with what we have, and what we have isn't always the healthiest when it comes to coping mechanisms.

Anyway, beyond that, things are going well. *I&R*'s release last month seems to have gone over well enough. I imagine that's due in no small part to the preparation that Jonas and the rest of the eighth stanza have put into ensuring it lands as they'd wish. It has yet again come off as "just slightly too fantastical to be real, but sure makes a good story", much as *Perils* and the *History* did. Ah well. I'm still proud of it, and I'm not unhappy with where we've wound up.

Aurel's off with Sasha now, and has been for a few months. For a while there, her periods of solitude were coming pretty often, and ey was popping in and out of existence with some frequency, but she seems to be settling down into a more predictable pattern. It's my hope that ey'll eventually be able to spend a year or so at a time with her, if not longer.

She's been doing well, too. I think she's really starting to come into her own as Sasha. Always in threes, but still always Sasha. She's been getting a bit grumpy about the whole spotted skunk thing, though, and I think that, before long, she'll see if she can find a way to go back to her stripes. She keeps complaining about the shorter tail and relative lack of fluff. Aurel's been teasing her by calling it cute, eliciting the usual threats of biting.

She's just about wrapped up her work on the companion volume to the *History*, which she's tentatively calling simply *Ode*. I've had a chance to read it and...well, I'll let her share it when she's ready. It will take a lot of work for it to have the effect she plans, and the consequences will be far-reaching for the Ode clade. She says she won't publish it for another decade or so for reasons which will become clear when you have the chance to read it. In the interim, she's mentioned a few other writing projects she'd like to tackle and release first, all of which sound good.

Debarre's back with E.W., which is good to see, and given the fact that we're now plopped right in the middle of a forest sim, they've come over to visit and camp a few times. Or, well, Debarre will come stay with us for most of the day while E.W. and Sasha go off and explore, and then they'll meet back up around dinner when Sasha returns to Aurel. Debarre's loosened up some, but I don't think he'll ever be totally comfortable with Sasha, which she seems to have accepted.

It's getting on bed time and May's whining at me most pitifully, so I'm going to go ahead and get this sent off before I ramble any more.

We all send our love to you and yours, and hope the universe is treating you well.

Ioan Bălan

Sorina Bălan — The Bălan clade

systime 230 (2354)

Artemis—Castor transmission delay:
2 days, 2 hours, 14 minutes

Artemis—Lagrange transmission delay:
43 days, 6 hours, 41 minutes

Artemis—Pollux transmission delay:
85 days, 9 hours, 11 minutes

All,

Thank you all so much for the birthday wishes. I was caught off guard when I first received Codrin#Castor's. Clearly I've forgotten to keep track of the non-Artemisian dates. It felt a little silly, too, getting a birthday greeting from someone I used to be, but then, we've diverged plenty by now. That, and it reminded me a little of my place in the whole grand scheme of things. I was born back on *Earth!* Almost *150 years ago!* It's staggering, the scale of all of this. Billions of kilometers, decades and decades, it's enough to make one feel insignificant, and yet I'm still significant to someone out there.

Of course, that meant I got Ioan's a few weeks later, and then Codrin#Pollux's a few weeks after that. It was a delightful set of letters, and the pictures you each sent along are all wonderful. I'm glad to see they got at least still images working across all three Systems now. Are they still worried about bandwidth for audio and video?

It's fascinating seeing the ways in which you've all changed, and how that differs from my memories and imaginings. Ioan's as calm and pleasant as I remember, but somehow more...I don't know, attentive? Present? I don't know quite how to put it. My memories are of being all caught up in my internal life and somewhat distant from those around me, whereas ey seems to have come down out of eir head.

And all of your partners! Goodness! May Then My Name looks as adorable as ever, and I was pleased to see both instances of Dear looking appropriately smug, though even it has diverged, both from my memories of it and the two instances from each other. I remember it being a slight critter, and Dear#Castor is still quite slender, though not nearly so waifish as in my memories, but Dear#Pollux has filled out a bit. It looks good!

I'm not really sure what I was expecting about Sasha. All I'd really pictured was someone looking essentially like May Then My Name but spotted. I guess I was picturing spots like one might see on a leopard, though of course that wouldn't make sense with such long fur. She looks very pretty, though, and certainly very content with Aurel! The Odists all seem to wear their emotions on their sleeves, don't they? I'll admit that seeing May Then My Name looking so happy with someone with so much of True Name in her life — holding paws, no less! — is still a little surprising, but I'm pleased all the same.

Life here continues much as it has. I've fallen into a steady routine that doesn't feel all that different from the one I had before Dear's introduction...God, was it really almost fifty years ago? I've built myself a sim that's sort of like a comfortable mix between Serene's prairie and Ioan's house. The house itself is comfortable and familiar, and the prairie gives me room to walk and just enjoy the wide open spaces that I remember.

The days are much the same, too. I spend my time writing and working on this or that — though rather than research projects, I'm working with individuals. I drink more coffee than I ought, eat simply, sleep in silence. Once I found the rhythm again, it was easy to slip back into that life, and for that, it's all the more comfortable, especially in what might otherwise be an overwhelmingly strange place.

I've attached a picture from a recent get-together of the emissaries. We all get dinner* on the anniversary of the convergence, and since the tech is all there now, we figured we'd get a

---

*Well, all but the firstracers, of course.

picture to send back for everyone's enjoyment and also any additions to the *History* that might be forthcoming, whether by the Bălans or someone else. We all raised a toast to True Name and Answers Will Not Help. Perhaps those on Castor will be able to get a similar picture with them included, even if Iska won't be present.

Since I didn't think to do so in time, happy belated birthday, all of you.

All my love to you and yours.

Sorina Bălan

32 ov-ularaeäl, 4783 Artemis Reckoning

Aurel Bălan — The Bălan clade

systime 232 (2356)

Lagrange—Pollux transmission delay:
45 days, 10 hours, 7 minutes

Lagrange—Castor transmission delay:
48 days, 3 hours, 52 minutes

Lagrange—Artemis transmission delay:
50 days, 5 hours, 40 minutes

All,

You'll have to forgive a rather rambly sort of letter, as it's currently being co-written by two Bălans and two skunks. Aurel was just forked,* and the four of us are sitting out in Douglas's field along with him, E.W., Debarre, and a few other friends after having a small potluck of sorts. There wasn't any real reason for the get-together other than it's snowy at our sim, the skunks were whining, and it's always nice here. What started as a plan for Ioan, May, Sasha, and Douglas to have a picnic blossomed on a whim to something of a party.

As parties go, it's been a very laid back one. We all brought some food along with us — the Bălans brought *musaca*, May Then My Name made a cake, Sasha brought a few roast hares, and so on — and set up some tables out back of Douglas's house to eat.

Not to be outdone, A Finger Pointing and Vos, one of the other techs from the theatre, set up a small bar where they started making outlandish cocktails based on what they thought each of us wanted, rather than anything we asked for. They've had about 70% hits, 30% misses, so far, which is pretty good, all told.† May currently has a drink that seems to be something between melted chocolate ice cream and brandy. It's quite good, but so rich that we can all only handle small sips of it at a time.

---

*Five minutes ago. *Just* forked.

†Another reason for the rambly, overly-sentimental letter: none of us are exactly sober.

Ioan got stuck with vodka and soda water. One of those "why bother?" drinks. Are the Bălans really so boring as to suggest vodka sodas?

A Finger Pointing's up-tree instance, Where It Watches The Slow Hours Progress, played a baffling…I guess party trick on us earlier that I think some are still recovering from. She suggested we play "two truths and a lie with a twist" and, after May explained what "two truths and a lie" was, we all agreed.

Unfortunately, the twist was that she went around and, for each of us, told us two things that will probably happen to us in the near future and one thing that definitely wouldn't, then set us to discussing which of ours we thought was the lie. None of the things she said were all that big or consequential, and certainly none were cruel or sad, but while the conversation that ensued was quite lively, it wasn't exactly fun, either.

She looked quite proud of herself for that. It was all very Odist.

Marsh, Vos's partner, broke the tension by singing a song while Douglas played along on flute. It was achingly beautiful and I think all of us have made a point to hunt them down for more music in the future. They also embody a lot of vague gender thoughts that Ioan and Aurel have been talking about of late, so they'll have some thinking to do.

Debarre has promised us firework. He only really needs one to impress, so we're all looking forward to it.

Mostly, though, we've just been doing that sort of talking about the past where one of us will name the subject of a memory as though reading off the label on a file folder, and we will all smile and sigh, or groan and laugh, or roll our eyes. It was one of those discussions that didn't need a whole lot of words, since it was all just a flow of shared memories passing back and forth among the lot of us.

Partway through, Ioan suggested that we share these with the clade, which then turned into sharing just the little things, too, not just relying on grand events to spur a letter. More stuff like this, really. It's a good day, today! Not special, just good. We should be able to share our everyday weal as well as our occasional woe.

And, after all that the last decade has held for us, we really have wound up in a comfortable sort of happiness. It's not perfect. We still run into crossed boundaries and areas of friction, we have our bad days and misunderstandings. There aren't any aliens, though, and no one's life is at risk if they enter a public sim — not for the time being, at least. It's nice to collect these quotidian happinesses, too, to enjoy them while they last.

It's getting dark now, and the singular firework is coming, so we should probably set this self-indulgent exercise aside for the time being. We're going to write our own segments when we get home to attach to the end of this letter, but for now, we're going to get another drink — this time of our choosing — and enjoy the rest of the night with friends.

We hope that you all also have the chance to enjoy your everyday happinesses, that you can have picnics that get out of hand, and that you can surround yourself with some really, truly strange friends.

With all the love in the world,

Ioan, Aurel, May, and Sasha

May's addendum:

I do not know if it is strange of me to say "I am happy that we are fading into obscurity" or not.

A part of me hopes that it *is* strange. That part hopes that we always find some small amount of wonder at the things that we did in this world, and that we were still somehow able to return to comfortable unimportance. It has been centuries since we were nobody.

Us being what we are, this move towards irrelevance is an intentional one. It is not simply that we are done with our tasks, nor that we are no longer able to keep up with the world around us, though there is some truth to both of those. We are pushing ourselves back towards this nobodyness as both a way to finally take full and complete ownership of our lives and to relinquish the death-grip that we held on the past.

Such grand statements! We will remain ourselves even into obscurity, I suppose.

Imagine, though, the freedom that comes with being a nobody! What wonders boredom holds! If Ioan and I have a particularly good dessert, that is something that we can think about for *weeks.* It will be the biggest thing to happen to us in a month. We can talk about that cheesecake that we had years later, remembering just how perfect it was, how it was not simply cheesecake, but **cheesecake**. We can think back on that, sigh, and then, as we did tonight, simply label that memory aloud and share a moment of happiness.

The large becomes incomprehensible in such a life, and the small becomes important. Given that there is no shortage of small events worth remembering, well...a boring life is no bad thing.

May your lives be occasionally boring in the best possible way. I love you all.

Aurel's addendum:

I've just said goodnight to Ioan and May and closed the door between our places. Every time I rejoin Sasha, we take a week to ourselves. Just us. No shared dinners or going out together. It gives me a way to switch contexts from what I remember as Ioan into how I know to act around Sasha, and it gives her a week of slow reentry after however long alone (this last spell was about six months, which is on the long side for her, but you'll see why in her message).

We wrote about the very everydayness that we were finding enjoyable, such as the ability to just decide on a picnic on a whim and have it turn into a party. Well, one of the things that

I enjoy about this time most of all is that Sasha and I spend this first week just focusing on domesticity. We cook every meal. We clean by hand. We go to bed at the same time, wake up at the same time, go for a walk at the same time every day. Settling into a routine with her feels like a clutch engaging, a mechanical clicking-into-place of realities in some precise mechanism such that, by the end of the week, I find myself sitting back and marveling that it could ever have been any different.

It's still so interesting to me to see the ways in which this sort of happiness differs from the happiness that I have with May as Ioan. Ioan and May move in a comfortable, complementary almost-lockstep. Their life is a dance. It has its rhythm and its steps, and yet it still has the creativity of the music of their temperaments lying beneath.

Sasha and I have a life that is that mechanism with the clutch. It isn't an impersonal machine; more like a pipe organ, perhaps, or a loom than an engine. It's a framework for beauty. We move together in the ways that we must and with a sense of purpose that adds to our lives. On her end, I imagine that it comes from the memories from her life as True Name, but on my end, I think it comes from the fact that, knowing we'll part again after however many months, my purpose *is* our time together. There's no point in staving off the day when I wake up alone; it will come when it comes. The purpose is to be present.

You'll have to forgive me for being a bit mawkish. I always get like this when our relationship starts back up again. Add on the lingering alcohol, and, well, I'm not *not* crying.

There is little else to add other than she finally talked her way into going back to striped skunk again. I think even Jonas and the rest of the eighth stanza was tired of her whining about her species. She still has a few limitations on how she should look, but I don't think she wants to look like True Name anymore, anyway.

I'm going to do as I promised and make hot cocoa while she finishes up her note. I miss you all dearly. Write soon.

Sasha's addendum:

I am going to lead with business.

I have attached two versions of the manuscript for *Ode*. One of these is for you all except for Dear, and one is for Dear alone. I have set visibility exceptions accordingly.

Ode is my attempt at telling the story of the Ode clade parallel to the Bălans' *History*. I could not tell that story without telling the beginning, however, and telling the beginning of that story means naming someone who hasn't been publicly named in almost two and a half centuries.

The two manuscripts are identical except that the version for Dear has all instances of the poet's name replaced with 'the poet'. I do not know what re-learning the Name would do to it, if it would do anything, but I would rather that be its choice that it can approach intentionally instead of having it forced upon it by my inattentiveness.

This project will not be released until systime 242 — is it odd that my first project is something that I will not publish for years? Perhaps — in order to provide the Ode clade sufficient time to prepare for the publication of the Name, as well as to give Jonas any time he needs to prepare for any political consequences. I have done my best to tell the story straight and have held back things that I know he would object to seeing in print. I do not want any more assassins after me.

I am not worried, though. True Name#Castor is firmly on my side and is slowly convincing True Name#Pollux and the rest of the eighth stanza here. They are working on a solution to getting this into both In Dreams and Hammered Silver's hands; I will not be the one to cross that particular boundary.

Business: done.

Every time I return, I feel like I have to do so deliberately, as though slowly releasing the tension on an elastic band lest it snap toward one's face. I do not know what me snapping would look like — nothing violent, I am sure, though I do not pretend to be incapable of hurting others emotionally.

Aurel handles this beautifully. Ey is kind and patient, and we spend these first few days focusing on routine as the wild leaves my blood and I can settle back down into the type of person who can live with another, love another, and not feel hemmed in. May is lucky to have Ioan and Dear to have Codrin, but I am thrice-blessed to have Aurel.

I have gone and made myself cry. Ah well. I am not sorry. Aurel has made hot cocoa and there is a quilt on the beanbag and I am home.

Goodnight. I love you all.

Ioan's addendum:

From the author biography for the third edition of *Seven Hearts Turned*:

> Rareş Bălan was born in 2215 in a small village in Cristeşti, Botoşani County, Western Moldavia, and often said that his own heart never left the village. His writing has been praised for its clear-eyed treatment of Eastern European lower-class life, and has garnered accolades from literary journals around the world, including *The Baltic*, *The Steel Nib Review*, and *Craft*. He died in 2268 and is buried in Cristeşti so that, true to his words, his heart will remain there.

I found this on a library trawl not too long ago. I don't know why I never thought to simply look him up by his name as an author. I guess I always thought that was my thing, and that maybe he wouldn't be interested. I'm kicking myself for such an assumption, now. Of course he can like writing. We were so alike, weren't we? I feel ashamed for believing otherwise. Perhaps I was just worried that I'd find him there, just as I have.

I was such a mess when I found it. I had to step home and just spend some time letting out a whole lot of overwhelming emotions all at once. It scared the shit out of May, but once she saw the book I'd dropped on the table, she understood and spent the rest of the day letting talk when I was able and cry when I wasn't.

I didn't even open the book — I just read that right off the back cover and fell apart — so you can imagine just how much of a mess I was when I finally managed to open it a few days later and came across the dedication *"For Ioan"* in the beginning.

Reading it has been slow-going for obvious reasons.

All of that talk about everyday happiness earlier, and all those words May wrote about living a boring life, and there's little I can add other than, yes, life does as it will, and a boring life is no bad thing. People are born and then, 53 years later, they die and are buried near where they grew up. Older brothers upload and the money that brings sends younger brothers to school, just as it was meant to. People see themselves in the pages of a book decades or centuries later and stop having so many unsettling dreams about those they left behind.

There's little that I can add here, knowing what May wrote, what Aurel will likely write, and what Sasha's sending along, so I guess all I can do is say, as always, all my love to you and yours. Be well.

Appendix

"All artists search. I search for stories, in this post-self age. What happens when you can no longer call yourself an individual, when you have split your sense of self among several instances? How do you react? Do you withdraw into yourself, become a hermit? Do you expand until you lose all sense of identity? Do you fragment? Do you go about it deliberately, or do you let nature and chance take their course?"

The Post-Self universe is an open setting for exploring the ramifications of being able to create copies of oneself, of what it means to undergo individuation, of what it means to let memories build up and up and up within oneself. What began as a simple shootpost on Twitter turned into a collaborative storytelling project, then an ARG which told the story of Dear, Also, The Tree That Was Felled and Ioan Bălan. Thanks(?) to the COVID-19 pandemic in 2020, this became the basis of that storyline in *Qoheleth*, book I in the Post-Self cycle.

As an open setting, all of this information is free to use for your own purposes under a Creative-Commons 4.0 Attribution license. The stories wouldn't be what they are without the contributions of others.

Timeline

The timeline of the Post-Self cycle spans just over two and a half centuries, encompassing both the creation of the upload system and the arrival of the Artemisians on the Castor launch vehicle and partial dissolution of the Ode clade.

2112 — December 7 RJ Brewster gets lost, triggering a cascade of events leading to a deeper investigation into the lost.

2115 — February ?? The first partially successful upload, RJ Brewster, leads to a breakthrough and, shortly after, the foundation of the System.

2117 — ??? Michelle Hadje and Debarre pool their money to upload.

2124 — January 1 Systime set at year zero, day zero in order to help manage the reputation market.

2125 — January 21 The System secedes from the planetary governments on Earth thanks to the efforts of Yared Zerezghi, Counselor Yosef Demma, The Only Time I Know My True Name Is When I Dream of the Ode clade, and Jonas Prime of the Jonas clade.

2170 — Throughout the year Most planetary governments begin compensating the families of those who choose to upload.

2238 — July 28 Ioan Bălan uploads to use the compensation to help eir brother, Rareş Bălan, out after eir parents' death.

2305 — November 8 Dear, Also, The Tree That Was Felled of the Ode clade contacts Ioan Bălan for assistance with a project that leads to the publication of *On the Perils of Memory*.

2325 — January 21 The launch project concludes with the launch of the Castor and Pollux Launch vehicles.

2326 — October 30 The Bălan clade publishes *An Expanded History of Our World* In conjunction with May Then My Name Die With Me of the Ode clade's *An Expanded Mythology of Our World*, collected together as *On the Origins of Our World*.

2346 — May 28 The Artemisians make contact with the Castor launch.

2350 — January 21 Assassination attempt on The Only Time I Know My True Name Is When I Dream on the Lagrange System, leading to her stepping away from the politics of the System and, through two long-diverged merges, becoming Sasha.

2351 — November 8 Ioan Bălan publishes *Individuation and Reconciliation*, containing the story of the assassination attempt on True Name and her subsequent transformation into Sasha through the merger of two long, long diverged forks.

2365 — July 18 Sasha releases *Ode*, a companion volume to *On the Origins of Our World* describing the Ode clade's movement from before the founding of the System, finally publishing RJ Brewster's name when she describes the origin of the System itself.

Dramatis Personae

RJ Brewster / AwDae (ey/em)

A sound tech for the Soho Theatre Troupe, RJ Brewster was among the lost in the early 2100s. Ey, along with Dr. Carter Ramirez, was instrumental in bringing to light the origin of the lost and ending that whole saga. As a member of the furry subculture, ey commonly appeared online (and while lost) as an agender anthropomorphic fennec. Ey focused strongly on making eir avatar (or av) as realistic as possible, down to the inability to form the same consonants that a human mouth would. Ey was instrumental in the creation of the System, being the first semi-successful upload; while ey did not wind up living to see the System, eir consciousness formed the foundation of the System itself, described early on as a half-sensed presence within the System. Eir friend Sasha, so torn by eir loss and confronted by eir sensed presence after uploading, used eir poem Ode to the End of Death for the names of her forks. Early political circumstances required that her relationship with em be kept secret, leading to a near pathological obsession with keeping eir Name from being known.

Dr. Carter Ramirez (she/her)

Dr. Carter Ramirez was a neuroscientist and researching of the lost at the University College London during their brief existence. She went on to become a political proponent of individual rights of uploaded personalities; however, she did not upload, herself.

Michelle Hadje / Sasha (she/her)

Michelle Hadje uploaded early on during the System's creation and is considered one of the founders and a member of the Council of Eight along with Debarre, Zeke/Ezekiel, Jonas Anderson, user11824, and the three nameless Sino-Russian Bloc representatives. She is best known for being the founder of the Ode clade, and is no longer extant on the System as of 2306. Raised "vaguely Jewish," various members of the Ode clade moved back towards this or further away to varying extents.

Due to her experience while lost, her and her up-tree instances have a "unique relationship to language" that primarily manifests with a lack of contractions, florid speech with occasionally irregular word order, and well-placed uses of the word 'fuck'. She and her clade deal with the effects even within the System as best they can and will occasionally describe themselves as 'mad', for lack of a better term. Additionally, the experience left her struggling to maintain a single form post-uploading, often alternating between skunk and human form, which is described as extremely unpleasant.

The Ode clade

The Ode clade consists of, nominally, 100 instances. In 2124, Michelle forked ten instances from herself corresponding to the ten first lines of the stanzas of the "Ode to the end of death". From there, those ten instances were free to fork as they would, and each quickly picked up on interests as they went.

Dear, Also, The Tree That Was Felled (it/its)   Dear is an instance artist, meaning that it plays around with the meaning of self in a world where one can create multiple copies of oneself. It was instrumental in the investigation of the events as described in the Bălan clade's *On the Perils of Memory*. It takes the form of a fennec fox with somewhat iridescent white fur, a result of it forking a few too many times in order to shift its sensorium to try and forget a fact. It has opted out of gender.

It is in a relationship with Codrin Bălan and one other unnamed individual.

May Then My Name Die With Me (she/her)   May Then My Name (or simply May to those with whom she is closest) is an author, actor, and hopeless romantic. She takes the form of a short, chubby anthropomorphic skunk, and is the author of the well-received *An Expanded Mythology of Our World*. She falls in love easily and deeply, and her primary instance is in a relationship with Ioan Bălan, though several long-running forks remain in relationships with others.

The Only Time I Know My True Name is When I Dream / Sasha (she/her)   True Name is a politician and one of the movers and shakers of the System as one of the Founders and member of the Council of Eight. She takes the form of an anthropomorphic skunk, though is taller and slimmer than her up-tree instance, May Then My Name. The instance of her that remained on the Lagrange System later rescinded her membership in the Ode clade and renamed herself to Sasha after accepting merges of her up-tree instances Do I Know God After The End Waking and May Then My Name Die With Me. Sasha winds up in a relationship with Aurel Bălan shortly after this change in identity.

Life Breeds Life, But Death Must Now Be Chosen / Qoheleth (he/him) Life Breeds Life was a historian and author involved in early historiographical efforts on the System. With the build-up of endless memory, his identity slowly shifted towards that of Qoheleth and he rescinded his membership in the clade.

Do I Know God After The End Waking (he/him) End Waking started out in charge of phys-side finances as they pertain to the System early on, but has since grown repentant of his actions. He is "heavily committed to the ranger aesthetic", choosing to live in solitude in a forest sim designed by Serene. He is in an on-again-off-again relationship with Debarre.

Serene; Sustained And Sustaining (she/her) A fennec like Dear, Serene was forked when her down-tree instance wanted to explore a twinned interest in instances and sims. She builds fantastic, nature-based sims, including Dear's prairie and End Waking's forest. On the Pollux LV, she has wound up in a relationship with Codrin Bălan and Dear.

That Which Lives is Forever Praiseworthy (she/her) Another skunk-type Odist, Praiseworthy focused on shaping sentiment early on in the System's history. No one's sure what she's up to now.

Why Ask Questions Here At The End Of All Things (she/her) and Why Ask Questions When The Answers Will Not Help (she/her) Commonly described as shitheads, Why Ask Questions and Answers Will Not Help shaped sentiment, with the former focusing on building camaraderie sys-side and the latter working via the text line to build support phys-side. Both are templated after the human Michelle rather than the skunk Sasha.

Time Is A Finger Pointing At Itself A Finger Pointing is human-type Odist who has devoted herself to theatre. She's described as a somewhat taller, somewhat more slender human Odist, dressing chic and modern, but with a simple desire to be everyone's friend.

The Bălan clade

Ioan Bălan (ey/em)

Ioan Bălan (/ˈjo ˌan/ /ˌbə ˈlan/) is a historian, investigative journalist, writer, and much later, actor and playwright. Ey uploaded in 2238 to help eir brother, Rareş (/ˌra ˈreʃ/), after their parents' death, and began working with Dear, Also, The Tree That Was Felled of the Ode clade in 2305 on a project that resulted in the well-received book *On the Perils of Memory*. Later, while working on *An Expanded History of Our World*, ey entered into a romantic relationship with another Odist, May Then My Name. During the process of working on *Individuation and Reconcilliation,* ey wound up in a relationship with Sasha, *née* True Name as a separate fork.

Ey has kept eir masculine name and relatively masculine appearance from phys-side, dressing in 'faux-academic garb' (usually slacks, a dress shirt, a sweater vest, a bow tie, and occasionally a jacket), though ey describes eir gender as fluid. May Then My Name occasionally uses the pet name Ionuţ (/ˈjo ˌnutz/).

Codrin Bălan (ey/em)

After the conclusion of eir project with Dear, Ioan forked a new long-running instance, Codrin Bălan (/ˈko ˌdrin/ or /ˈko ˌdrɨn/), who moved in with Dear and its partner and later joined their relationship. Ey has grown eir hair out and leaned much harder into androgyny, eir features shifting away from masculine, wearing sarongs and tunics. Eir partners occasionally use the pet name Codruț (/ˈko ˌdrutz/).

Sorina Bălan (she/her)

Forked from Codrin in order to continue along on Artemis's journey, Sorina (/so ˈri ˌna/) owned her Romanian heritage perhaps more than either of her down-tree instances, most often seen in traditional Romanian garb from ~1800s—an *ie* (blouse), waist belt, skirt, and *fotă* (apron), all heavily embroidered—and speaking more frequently in her first language.

Aurel Bălan

An occasional instance inspired by Debarre's habit of keeping a fork for his relationship with End Waking, which tends to last only a few months at a time before the skunk asks for solitude, Ioan forks Aurel (/ˈaːu rel/) when Sasha is up for a relationship. She'll occasionally use the pet names Aurică (/ˈaːu ri ˌka/) when ey's in a more feminine mode and Aurica (/ˈaːu ri ˌkə/) when ey's in a more masculine mode.

Douglas Hadje (he/him)

Douglas Hadje-Simon is Michelle Hadje's ancestor and the phys-side launch coordinator for the launch project.

Jonas Anderson (he/him)

Jonas Andersen was another member of the Council of Eight and worked to guide the System throughout the years. Described as lanky, 'well-preserved forties', tousled blond hair, the consummate politician.

Tycho Brahe (he/him)

Born under a different name, Tycho chose the name of the Danish astronomer when he agreed to be interviewed by Codrin for the *History*. An anxious and often depressed individual, he works as an astronomer on the System, and was the first to make contact with the Artemisians.

Yared Zerezghi (he/him)

A 'net addict and DDR (Direct Democracy Representative) junkie from Addis Ababa, Ethiopia, Yared was instrumental in the secession of the System from the rest of the governments on Earth. The events of Secession having left him incredibly anxious.

Sarah Genet (she/her)

Sarah is a psychologist and one of the emissaries chosen to meet with the Artemisians. She later becomes a mentor for Codrin as ey works on moving towards psychology as a career. She's described as having short, gray hair and wearing business casual sorts of clothes.

Debarre (he/him)

Having lost his boyfriend to suicide and the lingering effects of getting lost, Debarre uploaded along with Michelle Hadje. He's an anthropomorphic weasel with a penchant for dressing in all black. He's in an on-again-off-again relationship with End Waking, along with a few others in a form of parallel monogamy.

Zeke/Ezekiel (he/him)

Zeke (later known by his full name, Ezekiel), is an Israeli Jew who uploaded early on and worked to implement forking while on the Council of Eight. He's described as anything from a pile of dirty rags or rubbish, barely recognizable as human, to a homeless man.

user11824 (he/him)

All anyone can really tell about user11824 is that he's male. He's described as being so utterly boring that one's eyes simply slide right off him. This fact, combined with his anonymous chosen name, make him quite interesting, much to his chagrin. He described himself prior to uploading as 'a nobody, but a Maori nobody'.

Zacharias (he/him)

A dapper and snarky red fox. In an on-again-off-again relationship with True Name. He is a long, long diverged fork of May Then My Name.

The universe

Immersive tech

Beginning in the late 2100s, immersive computing technology began to become commonplace. The mechanism by which one enters the 'net is a set of implants taking the form of metallic contacts on the middle carpals of the fingers, near-field pads beneath the skin of the forehead, interferites—microscopic neural blockers that prevent one acting out in reality what happens when delved in—and an implant along the spine starting at the fifth cervical vertebra and running down to the bottom of the thoracic vertebrae. The exocortex contains much of the technology that actually controls the experience of interacting with the sim.

The net is comprised of simulated areas, or sims, where one can interact with objects and other people. Online, one is perceived through an avatar, or av, which can be whatever shape one chooses. These can be made, customized, purchased, and sold.

A new take on these as of the early 2100s are fully immersive sims, wherein one becomes something more abstract than an avatar, such as an entire room, where moving means controlling lights or sound, and sensations can be those of microphones or any other sensor one might like. This relies on the concept of *homuncular flexibility*, the ability for one's internal representation of their physical self (the homunculus) to expand beyond that of a traditional body, and for this reason is not common: many find that they cannot integrate with these sims, or find it very uncomfortable when they do.

Earth

Sometimes referred to as 'phys-side', Earth continues to tick along.

Early 2100s

At this point, the governments of earth are divided into two large political units comprised of smaller countries. The two largest players are the Western Federation (WF) and the Sino-Russian Bloc (S-R Bloc), but others include the North-East African Coalition (NEAC), and Southeast Asia/Pacifica (SEAPAC). Many countries still remain independent, with Israel being a notable example.

The previous century is described as troublesome, and there's a marked decline in population, with global population hovering at around 7 billion. The climate has suffered greatly, but things are still habitable.

Around 2170

While the climate has continued to suffer, with temperatures slowing to a linear rather than exponential increase, income inequality has continued to increase and, under the guise of helping poorer families out, several governments have started to incentivize uploading, though in reality it comes across as thinly-veiled eugenics. This is largely due to influence sys-side by members of the Ode and Jonas clades, notably due to the work of Do I Know God After The End Waking. Many anthropologists describe this as the beginning of the post- or late-Anthropocene era, where the population levels out and the impact of humanity on the world around them slows dramatically due to the number of uploads and the slowing of technological advances.

Early 2300s

Earth is described as a 'shithole'. Global warming has proceeded to the pace where much of the population below a certain latitude lives below-ground, though many have simply moved towards the poles. Air quality is...not great, and many spend as much time as possible on the 'net in sims, with children getting implants at around 5 years old, though the minimum upload age remains 18.

The System

Created in the early 2100s, the System (a vague name to keep the original project secret, though one which stuck around) allows for uploaded consciousnesses to live functionally immortal lives.

Systime

The System measures time with systime. This takes the format of *years since 2124+day of the year 24-hour time*. For instance, Secession took place on 1+21 19:00 first contact from the Artemisians occurred at 222+148 3:06.

The date of midnight on January 1, 2124 was chosen as the opening of the reputation markets, as such a time scheme was needed for marking transactions. The use of systime is not universal among the inhabitants of the System, as getting the current time (an experience akin to remembering what time it is) provides both systime and standard phys-side dates, but those who work most often with history and sim design rely on it heavily for both mapping events and seasons of the year, should the sims in question require seasons.

Uploading

Uploading is a one-way, destructive process. The body dies while the consciousness continues within the System. There is a small chance of failure (around 1% as of 2130, <0.5% as of 2140, <0.25% as of 2150, <0.001% as of 2200).

Consciousnesses are uploaded to the System at the L_5 point via the Ansible, a networked series of upload centers with a direct radio connection to the System itself. By the 2300s, this is largely automated and consists of signing a form and hitting a button.

Once uploaded, individuals are greeted by volunteers (later automated) to orient them to the concepts of creating clothing, simple objects, moving between sims, sensorium messages, and forking. Early uploads tend to live communally in larger sims, and many remain there, while the rest tend to flock towards smaller communities of like-minded individuals.

Similar to the 'net back phys-side, one's appearance is bound by one's homuncular flexibility. How they appear depends on how well their minds can handle such an appearance. However, it's important to note that one's appearance must be able to be comprehended by others. Existing on the System is a consensual experience.

Forking

Introduced almost by accident, the concept of forking allows one to create a new *instance* of oneself. This copy is completely identical, but as soon as they're created and their experiences begin to differ, that instance starts to undergo the process of *individuation*. They form their own memories, and their experience of the world is colored by those memories.

An instance may *quit.* When they do so, their memories are provided to their *down-tree* instance to remember or not in a process called *merging*. A merge may be wholesale (sometimes described as *blithe*) or *cherrypicked*, wherein the down-tree instance is able to choose some of the memories but not others in a labor-intensive process. After the mid 2100s, instances which are quitting may attach a priority to the merge. A high priority will be felt by the down-tree instance as a greater pressure, perhaps with a kick of adrenaline, while a lower priority merge will be felt as optional. A merge with explicitly no priority will not be offered to the down-tree instance.

The greater the individuation between and up- and down-tree instance, the greater the chance for *conflicts*. These occur when memories don't line up—that is, the experiences may be of the same event, but the conclusions drawn from the event may be different. As time goes on, individuation will affect the entire personality of an individual, as personality is built in part atop memories. Cocladists who have diverged by decades or centuries may find such merges incredibly difficult.

Forking incurs a reputation cost. This is tied to available capacity on the System, and as capacity grows, the cost of forking decreases, to the point where, in the 2300s, it's negligible. This cost is incurred after five minutes of forking or as soon as that instance forks, whichever comes first. The new instance begins with reputation equal to the cost of forking, though transferring reputation within a clade is possible. Several other things such as information production and exchange, sim creation, and some experiences can lead to reputation exchange.

The *root instance* of an individual will find it very difficult to quit as, to quote May Then My Name Die With Me of the Ode clade, "the System is not built for death". This applies to their *up-tree* instances as well; it is easier to quit the shorter one has been around or if a newer up-tree instance exists (for instance, if Jace Doe#Tracker forks into Jace Doe#1234abc, #Tracker may quit easily right away, though it will get steadily more difficult as #1234abc individuates; similarly, if #1234abc forks into Jace Doe#5678def and #5678def individuates long enough, #1234abc will find it difficult to quit).

Clades and dissolution strategies

Groups of instances forked from a single individual are known as *clades*. Although these are all highly unique, the oh-so-human need to bucketize the world into useful categories has led to three general strategies:

Taskers Taskers fork infrequently and only ever for short-lived tasks, choosing to remain primarily a clade of one. *Example:* Tycho Brahe (from *Nevi'im*) is a tasker who forks so rarely he has a lot of trouble even managing it. Merging back down to his #Core proves difficult.

Trackers Relying more heavily on forks to accomplish tasks, trackers may keep instances around for months or years, and sometimes more than one at a time. However, these instances tend to retain a strong sense of identity with their root instance and will almost always merge back down. *Example:* Ioan Bălan, as a tracker, forks quite often for eir work, but those forks tend to be associated with projects and, on completion, will merge back down into eir #Tracker instance (with a few notable exceptions: Codrin Bălan individuated enough to become eir own person, and Sorina Bălan forced her own individuation to leave memories behind as best she could).

Dispersionistas Dispersionistas don't give a fuck. They fork at need and those forks may quit, may retain some sense of their identity, or may individuate and become their own individuals down the line. *Example:* Michelle Hadje founded the Ode clade, which nominally has 100 members, but they're not super strict about it and many have long-lived instances they don't really talk about.

Clades can form quasi-familial units or not even really talk to each other; it's really up to the individual. There's a mild taboo against relationships between *cocladists*, though the greater they have differentiated, the less that seems to be an issue. While one can rescind one's membership in a clade, this is similar to distancing oneself from one's family: your down-tree instance is still your down-tree instance.

Sims

Locations in the System are known as sims, an artifact from the pre-System 'net days. Sims may be public or private. Public sims are usually open to anyone and can be accessed by querying the perisystem architecture for their *tags* (e.g: Josephine's#aaca9bb9).

Private sims are generally owned by a single individual, clade, or family. These sims generally have much more restrictive *ACLs* (from 'access control lists', but now generally used to refer to fine-grained permissions) which can limit who may enter, whether or not the location is visible to others, who in the sim may create new objects, modify boundaries, and so on. The owners have full ACLs, including the ability to grant others owner status and rescind their own (though every sim must have at least one owner).

Reputation market

Although by the 2200s the System mostly exists as a post-scarcity society (or non-society, as it is not at all unified), a market was put into place early on when capacity was at a premium. This market worked on reputation (marked Ř) which was gained via recognition. Appreciation of someone or the works they produce increases their reputation, which can then be spent on various things such as forking (which only costs a nominal amount by 2250), creating sims, seeking information from individuals, and so on.

With technological advancements increasing System capacity exponentially, the reputation market shifted in purpose early in the 2200s to be a place for sharing information between individuals, with one gaining reputation by way of producing content and spending it by requesting content from others.

Perisystem architecture

The perisystem architecture is the conceptual foam of computer-stuff in which individuals reside and items such as sims, food, very nice fountain pens, and very fine paper exist. However, it also contains large amounts of information in the form of books, the reputation market, and various information feeds.

Some maintenance of the perisystem architecture is required, usually by engineers both sys-side and phys-side. In the instance of the two launch vehicles, for instance, PA engineers managed the DMZ later called Convergence

Social interaction

Life continues on the System much as it does back phys-side. People fall into and out of love, there are arguments and drunken conversations and saying stupid things that will make you wince even decades down the line even though the other person will have all but forgotten the interaction.

And, just like back phys-side, there are all sorts of social niceties that come with living on the system.

Communication between sys-side and phys-side Communication between the two levels of existence was limited to text-only until A/V communication was unveiled in 2350 based on information gained from the Artemisians. When one considers that the Systems act as a consensual dream, an item from outside must somehow be dreamt into consensus by those who view it. An interesting problem to tackle, to be sure, but as with many aspects of life that involve the relationships between sys- and phys-side, many influential individuals on both sides gently discouraged such explorations over the years for their own various political reasons. The democratized nature of the data from Artemis led to enough momentum to overcome this friction. This also included A/V communications between Lagrange and the LVs, though due to bandwidth limitations with the Deep Space Network, this was quickly limited to still images.

Children and pets   There are no children born on the System. While there have been several failed attempts to create a synthesis of two unrelated minds into a new person, something of a taboo has sprung up around the idea. Uploading is generally limited to those 18 years or older, though this is more strictly enforced in some countries than others.

While there is no uploading of pets or other animals, many common animals can be created. Just as there are those who become well known as sim artists, there are those who have taken up the creation of animals (and, in some instances, automated non-human individuals, affectionately termed NPCs) as their passion project, and the demand for dogs and cats is not inconsiderable. The reason for this falls squarely within the core mechanic of the System: everything that exists there has to be able to be held in mind in at least similar ways by all those who perceive it. The System is built on human minds perceiving the world they've created.

Conflict   As with any social system, conflict happens. People don't like each other. They argue, they fight, and sometimes they seek to damage each other. As mentioned, however, the System will not allow one to be killed. While it is possible to hurt someone on the System through violence, after a certain point, the System will simply render them unconscious. As with most other dramatic changes to oneself, damage can be fixed by forking. Should one lose a finger, one can fork back to the body one remembers—finger included. Should one be unconscious, a System engineer can instruct the System to force an individual to fork, whereupon they'll wind up in what their mind considers to be a default state for themselves.

The one exception to being killed on the System is through a subtle virus which will crash one's instance. This virus must be tailored to the individual it's meant for and is not trivial to produce, so instances of such death are rare. It's most commonly associated with symbolic objects such as syringes or knives rather than poison; as always, having the symbol be recognized as one that can cause damage is often part of the process.

Should you have any questions about the setting or characters, you may contact me at madison@scott-clary.clade.id.

Acknowledgements

Thanks, as always, to the polycule, who has been endlessly supportive, as well as to Nenekiri, Utunu, and many others who helped with reading and keeping me sane along the way.

Thanks also to my patrons:

$10+ Donna Karr (thanks, mom); Fuzz Wolf; Kit Redgrave; Merry; Orrery; Sandy; Sariya Melody

$5 Junkie Dawg; Lorxus, an actual fox on the internet

$1 Alicia Goranson; arc; Katt, sky-guided vulpine friend; Kindar; Muruski; Peter Hayes; Rax Dillon; Ruari

Mitzvot was made possible through a Kickstarter campaign, and the entirety of the Post-Self cycle would not be what it is without the support of so many backers. The response went far beyond what I had ever hoped, and I am honored to have the chance to provide what I can in return.

Thank you to the following:

Forever Praiseworthy

The following backers went above and beyond. These are names and any messages they might have:

Petrov Neutrino -click-

Acknowledgements

Sandy Cleary

Phosphor Wulf

FuzzWolf

Amdusias Because Madison will always mean so much to me, I suppose that I can forgive this series' relative lack of good cats.

Michael Miele I'm Michael Miele, but most folks online know me as my dragon fursona, Nenekiri Bookwyrm. I've been pretty active in furry writing spaces with reading and reviewing books from authors in the community. If memory serves, Madison reached out to me after finding my review of Qoheleth and asked me if I wanted to get Toledot early in exchange for an honest review. I said yes, of course, and she was kind enough to do so again for Nevi'im and Mitzvot later.

As a writer whose work I respect and adore for various reasons, it means an immense amount to me that she would trust me with giving feedback for the Post-Self series of books. While a writer myself, I don't have the same amount of experience Madison does, so the whole process has been very flattering.

The mixture of transhumanism, queer lived experience, and programming in-jokes made books I, a queer furry programmer, was excited to read each time. I hope my reviews have helped other folks get lost (in a positive way!) in the Ode and Bălan clade's stories.

Curl up with a good book and be kind to yourself.

Thanks also to the following:
Aaron Klett, Adam Norberg, Alicia E. Goranson, Ari, Aulden Stargazer, Ayla Ounce, Barac Baker Wiley, Brian C., Damian Kesser, Draugdae, Ember C., Ardy Hart, Greg Hill, Jacob M.

Dawson, Joel Kreissman, Jonathan Perrine, Kate Shaw, Kayodé Lycaon, Kyle Monroe, Lhexa, Nicolas Braudsantoni, NightEyes DaySpring, Payson R. Harris, Rax E. Dillon, Royce Day, S. Pots, Saghiir, Sam Ewaskiewicz, Sasha Trampe, Some Egrets, Tim Duclos, Utunu, Yana Caoránach, ramshackle heather, redkicks.

About the author

Madison Scott-Clary is a transgender writer, editor, and software engineer. She focuses on furry fiction and non-fiction, using that as a framework for interrogating the concept of self and exploring across genres. A graduate of the Regional Anthropomorphic Writers Workshop in 2021, hosted by Kyell Gold and Dayna Smith, she is studying creative writing at Cornell College in Mount Vernon, IA. She lives in the Pacific Northwest with her cat and two dogs, as well as her husband, who is also a dog.

www.makyo.ink